Dedalus European Classics
General Editor: Timothy Lane

# Cousin Bazilio

*Eça de Queiroz*

# Cousin Bazilio
## (A Domestic Episode)

Translated and with an Introduction by

Margaret Jull Costa

Dedalus

Supported using public funding by
**ARTS COUNCIL
ENGLAND**

Published in the UK by Dedalus Ltd
24-26, St Judith's Lane, Sawtry, Cambs PE28 5XE
email: info@dedalusbooks.com
www.dedalusbooks.com

ISBN printed book: 978 1 910213 37 7
ISBN ebook: 978 1 907650 35 2

Dedalus is distributed in the USA & Canada by SCB Distributors,
15608 South New Century Drive, Gardena, CA 90248
email: info@scbdistributors.com www.scbdistributors.com

Dedalus is distributed in Australia by Peribo Pty Ltd,
58, Beaumont Road, Mount Kuring-gai, N. S. W. 2080
email: info@peribo.com.au

*Publishing History*
First published in Portugal in 1878
First Dedalus edition in 2003
New Dedalus edition in 2016

*Translation and introduction copyright © Margaret Jull Costa 2003*

The right of Margaret Jull Costa to be identified as the translator of
this work has been asserted by her in accordance with the Copyright,
Designs and Patents Act, 1988.

Printed in Finland by Bookwell
Typeset by RefineCatch Ltd, Bungay, Suffolk

A C. I. P. listing for this book is available on request.

# Books by Eça de Queiroz which are available from Dedalus:

When *The Illustrious House of Ramires* is published by Dedalus in 2017 Dedalus will have made all the major fiction of Eça de Queiroz available in English in new translations by Margaret Jull Costa. Portugal's greatest novelist has been well served by the finest translator of Portuguese into English allowing English readers to enjoy to the full the fiction of Eça de Queiroz.

Titles currently available:

*The Mandarin (and other stories)*
*The Relic*
*The Tragedy of the Street of Flowers*
*The Crime of Father Amaro*
*Cousin Bazilio*
*The Maias*
*The City and the Mountains*
*Alves & Co*
*The Mystery of the Sintra Road*

Forthcoming in 2017:

*The Illustrious House of Ramires*

# The Translator

Margaret Jull Costa has translated the works of many Spanish and Portuguese writers.

She won the Portuguese Translation Prize for *The Book of Disquiet* by Fernando Pessoa in 1992 and for *The Word Tree* by Teolinda Gersão in 2012, and her translations of Eça de Queiroz's novels *The Relic* (1996) and *The City and the Mountains* (2009) were shortlisted for the prize; with Javier Marias, she won the 1997 International IMPAC Dublin Literary Award for *A Heart So White*, and, in 2000, she won the Weidenfeld Translation Prize for José Saramago's *All the Names*. In 2008 she won the Pen Book-of-the-Month Club Translation Prize and the Oxford Weidenfeld Translation Prize for *The Maias* by Eça de Queiroz.

In 2014 Margaret was awarded an OBE for services to literature.

# Introduction

José Maria de Eça de Queiroz was born on 25th November 1845 in the small town of Povoa de Varzim in the north of Portugal. His mother was nineteen and unmarried. Only the name of his father – a magistrate – appears on the birth certificate. Following the birth, his mother returned immediately to her respectable family in Viana do Castelo, and Eça was left with his wetnurse, who looked after him for six years until her death. Although his parents married later – when Eça was four – and had six more children, Eça did not live with them until he was twenty-one, living instead either with his grandparents or at boarding school in Oporto, where he spent the holidays with an aunt. His father only officially acknowledged Eça as his son when the latter was forty. His father did, however, pay for his son's studies at boarding school and at Coimbra University, where Eça studied Law, and was always supportive of his writing ambitions. After working as the editor and sole contributor on a provincial newspaper in Évora, Eça made a trip to the Middle East. Then, in order to launch himself on a diplomatic career, he worked for six months in Leiria as a municipal administrator, before being appointed consul in Havana (1872–74), Newcastle-upon-Tyne (1874–79) and Bristol (1879–88). In 1886, he married Emília de Castro with whom he had four children. His last consular posting was to Paris, where he served until his death in 1900.

He began writing stories and essays as a young man and became involved with a group of intellectuals known as the Generation of '70, who were committed to reforms in society and in the arts. He published five novels during his lifetime: *The Crime of Father Amaro* (3 versions: 1875, 1876, 1880), *Cousin Bazilio* (1878), *The Mandarin* (1880), *The Relic* (1887)

1

and *The Maias* (1888). His other novels were published post-humously: *The City and the Mountains, The Illustrious House of Ramires, To the Capital, Alves & Co., The Letters of Fradique Mendes, The Count of Abranhos* and *The Tragedy of the Street of Flowers*.

★ ★ ★ ★ ★ ★ ★ ★ ★

Leiria, the setting for Eça's first novel, *The Crime of Father Amaro*, may also have provided the inspiration for *Cousin Bazilio*. When the latter was published in 1878, many people were convinced that he had simply transposed to Lisbon the protagonists and events of a scandalous affair that had shaken Leiria in 1870, the year in which Eça took up a post there as an administrator. Whatever the truth of this, according to Eça himself, the book was intended as an attack on the kind of 'Lisbon marriage' which he described as 'an unpleasant meeting of warring egotisms and [which], sooner or later, descends into debauchery', adding that it was also, and perhaps more importantly, an attack on contemporary bourgeois society.

*Cousin Bazilio* is indeed much more than just another tale of adultery. The adultery and its consequences are set, as always with Eça, against an extraordinary gallery of characters: the pompous pillar of society, Councillor Acácio, who writes books no one reads and who sleeps with his housekeeper; wily Tía Vitória who can turn her hand to anything, from finding a young, willing maid for an ageing bachelor to conducting a little light blackmail; Ernestinho, the civil servant who moonlights as a writer of theatrical melodramas; plump Dona Felicidade, who suffers equally acutely from wind and from her unrequited passion for Acácio; the impossibly refined Viscount Reinaldo, the hopelessly romantic and sexually voracious Leopoldina . . . the list goes on.

And parallel to Luiza's downfall runs the brief, ill-fated rise of her maid Juliana. Indeed, it is perhaps the life-or-death struggle between these two women that makes *Cousin Bazilio* such a remarkable work. It is rare for a nineteenth-century novelist to paint such a detailed, even sympathetic picture of the servant's lot. Juliana's dream is to own a shop selling

2

knick-knacks and to have a husband, but she is happy to make do, when she gets the chance, with a carpeted room, drawerfuls of crisp underwear and a few silk dresses – in short, a little bourgeois ease and comfort. The servants in the novel are expected to leave their bed at midnight to make tea for guests, some are dressed in grimy rags and have chilblained fingers, others cannot sleep for the heat or the cold or the bedbugs and must rise before dawn to do the starching and ironing, risking dismissal at the first sign of any serious illness. Eça is just as acute on the pleasures of life in service – the camaraderie, the gossip, the rumbustious sex when the master and mistress are away, the filched dishes of quince jelly and the odd glass of wine.

They and their employers occupy parallel universes, their lives touching only when the servant (female) becomes the confidante or blackmailer of the mistress or where the servant (male or female) becomes the bedfellow of the mistress or master. While Luiza's life is blighted by indolence and that of Juliana by unremitting drudgery, Eça makes it clear that, despite the very real differences in wealth, comfort and status, the options of both mistress and maid are equally limited by social convention and financial dependence.

However, what made the book an instant bestseller in 1878 – the first edition of 3,000 sold out at once and the book was immediately reprinted – was not so much the social realism or even the social satire as the sexual frisson afforded by the story and the scenes of adulterous sex. Cousin Bazilio was the only one of Eça's novels to be translated into several languages during his lifetime. His own father praised the book, but chastised him for one particularly frank scene between Bazilio and Luiza, declaring that this was 'realism at its crudest' and advising his son to avoid, in future, 'any descriptions that ladies cannot read without blushing'. The book made Eça famous, but possibly for the wrong reasons.

Cousin Bazilio was equally successful in Brazil, though it received a mixed critical reception. The Brazilian novelist, Machado de Assis, while admiring certain scenes and episodes and the author's style, accused Eça of being merely a pale

3

imitation of Balzac or Zola. His other criticism of *Cousin Bazilio* seems to have been not only, to use his words, 'the crude sensuality' of some of the descriptions, but that Luiza was too banal a figure to be a heroine, and that Eça had allowed a servant, of all people, to dominate the second half of the novel.

Writing years later, the Portuguese novelist, José Régio, on the other hand, declared *Cousin Bazilio* to be not only Eça's finest novel, but also his most human. Eça may mock the banality of these bourgeois Lisbon lives, but his characters are not mere cardboard cut-outs. Luiza, for example, is undoubtedly emptyheaded; she may, like Emma Bovary, have her imagination overly stuffed with foolish romances and so prove easy game for the likes of Bazilio; yet she does, within her capabilities, learn from her mistakes and make every attempt to redeem herself. She is, ultimately, a deeply affecting figure, as are Juliana, Dona Felicidade, Sebastião and Jorge. Indeed, Eça's description of the latter's sufferings towards the end of the book must be one of literature's most telling accounts of the pain of sexual betrayal.

The book may well have been intended, in part, as an attack on the hypocrisy of bourgeois marriage, and yet all its characters crave domesticity (a state, incidentally, in which Eça himself later found great contentment). Both Jorge and Luiza long to have a child; Dona Felicidade, Sebastião and Julião, all in their very different ways, yearn for conjugal bliss; Councillor Acácio erroneously believes he may have found it . . . The few exceptions – Leopoldina, Bazilio, Viscount Reinaldo – are all deeply corrupt. The title of the novel may be *Cousin Bazilio*, but Bazilio is merely the catalyst, and as if to underline this, when the second edition was published, Eça added a subtitle: 'A domestic episode'. For it is the home that matters, and it is the home that the rootless Bazilio so thoughtlessly destroys.

# I

The cuckoo clock in the dining room had just struck eleven. Jorge, sprawled in the old, dark morocco wing chair, closed the volume of Louis Figuier he had been slowly leafing through, stretched, yawned and said:

'Aren't you going to dress, Luiza?'

'In a minute.'

She was still in her black peignoir, with its braid edging and large mother-of-pearl buttons, and was sitting at the table reading the newspaper; her slightly tousled blonde hair, still dull from the warmth of the pillows, was coiled up on top of her small head with its pretty profile; her skin had the soft, milky whiteness of all fair-haired women; with one elbow propped on the table, she was stroking her ear, and that slow, gentle movement set the tiny scarlet rubies in her two rings sparkling.

They had just had lunch.

The carpeted room with its white-painted wooden ceiling and its pale, green-sprigged wallpaper was light and cheerful. It was July, a Sunday, and very hot; the two windows were closed, but one could sense the sun outside glittering on the glass panes and searing the stone balcony; an absorbed, sleepy, Sunday morning silence reigned, and a vague, languid lassitude brought with it drowsy longings, desires for the cushioned shade of a wood somewhere in the countryside, at the water's edge; the two canaries were asleep in their cages, which hung between the bluish cretonne curtains; a monotonous buzz of flies hovered over the table, settled on the unmelted sugar at the bottom of the coffee cups, and filled the room with a somnolent murmur.

Jorge rolled himself a cigarette and, very relaxed and cool in his cotton shirt, with no waistcoat on and with his blue flannel jacket unbuttoned, he sat staring up at the ceiling, thinking about his trip to the Alentejo. He was a mining engineer, and, the following day, he had to set off first to Beja, then to Évora,

5

and then south again to São Domingos. The idea of that journey, in July, seemed to him an irritating interruption, a flagrant injustice. Fancy having to make such a journey in a blistering summer like this! Spending days and days being shaken about on the back of a hired horse, across those endless, dark, scrub-grown Alentejo plains that sweltered beneath the lustreless sun, to the accompaniment of the constant buzz of horseflies! Having to sleep in oak forests, in rooms that smelled of baked brick, while hearing all around him in the dark, torrid night the grunting of herds of pigs! Feeling the hot breath of the scorched fields waft in through the window! And he would be all alone!

Up until then, he had had a post at the Ministry. It would be the first time that he and Luiza had been apart, and he was already homesick for this room, whose walls he himself had helped to paper before their marriage, and where, after the joys of the night, they would sit on after lunch in this state of sweet indolence!

He stroked his short, fine, very curly beard, while his eyes lingered tenderly on those familiar pieces of furniture, all of which dated from the time when his mother was alive: the old cupboard with its glass doors, the decorative, gleaming silverware; the ancient, much-loved oil painting that he had known since he was a child, in which one could just barely make out, against a cracked background, the coppery tones of a plump saucepan and the faded pinks of a bunch of radishes! On the wall opposite hung the portrait of his father: he was dressed in the fashion of 1830, had a round face, bright eyes and a sensual mouth, and on his buttoned-up tail coat he wore the insignia of Our Lady of the Conception. He had been a most amusing fellow, a Treasury employee and a keen amateur flautist. Jorge had never known him, but his mother said that the portrait was so like his father that all it lacked was the power of speech. He had lived all his life in that same house with his mother, Isaura, a tall, rather anxious woman with a sharp nose, who always used to drink hot water with her meals; but, one day, after attending mass in Graça, she had died suddenly, without so much as a murmur.

Jorge had never resembled her physically. He had a strong, manly build. He had his father's admirable teeth and broad shoulders.

From his mother he had inherited a placid temperament and a gentle nature. As a student at the Politécnica, he used to go to his room at eight o'clock, light the brass oil lamp and open his textbooks. He never went to taverns or spent the night carousing. But twice a week, regular as clockwork, he would go and see a young seamstress, Eufrásia, who lived in Poço do Borratém, and who, on the days when her Brazilian lover was out playing whist at his club, would receive Jorge with a great show of caution and with passionate words; she was an orphan, and there was always a faint whiff of fever about her small, skinny body. Jorge deemed her overly romantic and used to tell her off about this. He had never been the sentimental type: his fellow students, who sighed over Alfred de Musset and wished they could have loved Marguerite Gautier, accused him of being 'prosaic' and 'bourgeois', but Jorge would simply laugh; he was always immaculately turned out, with never a button missing from his shirt; he admired Louis Figuier, Bastiat and Castilho, had a horror of debts, and was perfectly happy.

When his mother died, however, he began to feel very alone: it was winter, and his rather solitary, south-facing room at the back of the house received the full brunt of the gusting wind as it moaned long and sadly about the walls; at night especially, when he was bent over his books, his feet on the footwarmer, he would be filled by a languid melancholy; he would stretch out his arms, his heart filled with but one desire, to embrace a sweet, slender waist and to hear in the house the rustle of a dress. He decided to get married. He met Luiza in the summer, one evening in the Passeio Público, the main park and public promenade. He fell in love with her fair hair, her way of walking and her very large, brown eyes. The following winter, he was given a permanent post, and they were married. Sebastião, good old Sebastião, his closest friend, had said, nodding gravely and slowly rubbing his hands together:

'He got married on a whim, yes, almost on a whim.'

But Luiza – little Luiza – turned out to be an excellent mistress of the house: she was a careful and competent housekeeper; she was very clean and tidy, and happy as a bird, a little bird who enjoyed both her nest and her mate's caresses; and that small, gentle, fair-haired creature brought real charm to the house.

Kindly Sebastião then said, in his deep bass voice:

'She is indeed the worthiest of little angels!'

She and Jorge had been married for three years. And what good years they had been! He felt that he himself had improved; he was more contented, more intelligent even. And as he sat there now with his legs crossed, his soul overflowing, pondering that sweet, easy existence, exhaling the smoke from his cigarette, he felt as comfortable in his life as he was in his flannel jacket!

'Oh!' said Luiza suddenly, staring at something in the newspaper and smiling.

'What is it?'

'Cousin Bazilio is coming to Lisbon.'

And she read out loud:

'Arriving any day now from Bordeaux will be Senhor Bazilio de Brito, a familiar figure in Lisbon society. The gentleman in question – who, as you will know, emigrated to Brazil, where, by dint of honest toil, he has apparently recovered his fortune – has been touring Europe since the beginning of last year. His return to the capital is a cause of great joy to his friends, of whom there are many.'

'Absolutely!' said Luiza with great conviction.

'Well, I certainly hope so, poor chap!' said Jorge, still smoking, and smoothing his beard with the palm of his hand. 'And he's made himself a fortune, has he?'

'So it seems.'

She glanced at the advertisements, took a sip of tea, got up and went over to open one of the shutters.

'Goodness, but it's hot outside, Jorge!' She stood blinking in the harsh, white light.

The room, at the rear of the house, looked out onto an empty lot which was surrounded by a low wooden fence and overgrown with tall plants and random vegetation; here and there, amongst the scorched summer greenery, large stones glittered beneath the perpendicular sun; and an ancient fig tree, alone in the middle of the garden, held out its thick, motionless leaves which, in the white light, seemed tinged with bronze. Beyond were the backs of other houses, all with balconies; there were clothes hung out on canes to dry, the white walls surrounding other people's gardens, spindly trees. A kind of dust dimmed and thickened the luminous air.

'The birds are practically falling out of the sky!' she said, closing the window. 'Imagine what it will be like in the Alentejo!'

She came and stood next to Jorge's chair and slowly stroked his curly black hair. Jorge looked at her, already anticipating the sadness of separation; the top two buttons of her peignoir were undone, showing the beginning of her soft white breasts and the lace on her nightdress: very chastely, Jorge buttoned them up.

'And what about my white waistcoats?' he asked.

'They should be ready by now.'

And to confirm that this was so, she summoned Juliana.

There was a Sunday sound of starched petticoats, and Juliana came in, nervously fiddling with her collar and her brooch. She was getting on for about forty years old and was extremely thin. She had small, pinched features and the dull, yellow complexion of one who suffers with a weak heart. Her large, sunken, bloodshot eyes darted restlessly, curiously, here and there, from beneath red-rimmed eyelids. She wore a large false hairpiece in the form of imitation plaits, which made her head look enormous. Her nostrils twitched nervously. Her dress lay flat over her chest, and the skirt, puffed out by her stiffly starched petticoats, was short enough to reveal small, pretty feet, shod in tight serge bootees with gleaming toecaps.

In her strong Lisbon accent, she reported that the waistcoats were not yet ready, that she had not had time to starch them.

'But I asked you especially, Juliana!' Luiza chided. 'Oh, well, see what you can do, but the waistcoats have to be ready to be packed tonight.'

And as soon as Juliana had left the room, she said:

'I'm beginning to hate that creature, Jorge!'

Juliana had been working in the house for two months, and Luiza simply could not get used to her ugliness, her odd mannerisms and the affected way in which she said 'het' instead of 'hat' and 'scissoars' instead of 'scissors', the way she slightly rolled her 'r's, and the sound of the metal-tipped heels of her shoes; and, on Sundays, in particular, that hairpiece, that pretentious footwear and the fine black leather gloves she wore all grated on Luiza's nerves.

'She's just awful!'

Jorge laughed:

'She's a poor woman with barely a penny to her name, and she does a first-rate job of starching and ironing.' (At the Ministry, his shirt fronts were a constant source of amazement!) 'As Julião so rightly says, I'm not so much starched as enamelled. True, she isn't very nice, but she's clean and she's discreet.'

Getting up, with his hands in the pockets of his loose flannel trousers, he added:

'And the way she looked after Aunt Virgínia when she was ill . . . She was an absolute angel!' He repeated this solemnly: 'Day and night, she was an absolute angel! We're in her debt, my dear.' Looking very serious, he began rolling another cigarette.

Luiza said nothing, but kicked at the hem of her peignoir with the toe of her slipper; then, frowning slightly and staring hard at her nails, she said:

'Well, I don't care. If I get fed up with her, I shall simply send her away.'

Jorge stopped what he was doing, struck a match on the sole of his shoe and said:

'Only if I let you, my sweet. As far as I'm concerned, it's a question of gratitude.'

They both fell silent. The cuckoo clock sang out twelve noon.

'Right, I must be off,' said Jorge. He went over to her, cupped her face in his hands and, gazing tenderly down at her, murmured: 'My little viper!'

10

She laughed and looked up at him with her magnificent brown eyes, luminous with love. Touched, Jorge placed a resounding kiss on each eyelid. Then pouting, he asked her:

'Do you need me to bring anything back for you, my love?'

All she wanted was that he should not be home too late.

He had to deliver a few letters, he would take a carriage, it was only a step away . . .

And he left, singing in his fine baritone voice:

> The Golden Calf is lord of the world,
> La la ra, la ra.

Luiza yawned and stretched. It was such a bore having to get dressed! She would have liked simply to be dozing off in a pink marble bath full of warm, perfumed water! Or else to be rocking gently in a silken hammock, with all the windows closed, listening to music! She shook off one slipper and sat looking fondly at her small, milk-white foot with its tracery of blue veins, thinking about all kinds of things: the silk stockings she wanted to buy, the parcel of food she would make up for Jorge's journey, the three napkins that the laundress had lost . . .

She stretched again. And with one bare foot on tiptoe and the other shod, she went over to the sideboard where, from behind a jam jar, she removed a grubby, much-read book; then she sat down, legs outstretched, in Jorge's wing chair and, resuming that same loving, caressing touch of fingers on ear lobe, she began eagerly reading.

The book was *The Lady of the Camellias*. She read a lot of novels; she had a monthly subscription with a shop in the Baixa. When she was eighteen and still single, she had been mad about Walter Scott and about Scotland; at the time, she had wanted to go and live in one of those Scottish castles which bore the clan's coat of arms over its pointed arches and which was furnished with Gothic chests and displays of weapons and hung with vast tapestries embroidered with heroic legends which the breeze from the loch would stir into life; and she had loved Evandale, Morton and Ivanhoe, all so grave and tender and all wearing an eagle's feather in their cap, pinned in place with a brooch in the form of a Scottish thistle made out of emeralds and diamonds. But now she was captivated by the 'modern': Paris and its furniture and its romantic novels. She sniggered at troubadors and drooled over M. de Camors; and now her ideal men appeared before her wearing a white tie, leaning in the doorway of a ballroom; these men were endowed with a magnetic gaze, were consumed by passion and were always ready with some sublime remark. A week ago, she had discovered Marguerite Gautier, whose unhappy love affair filled her with a kind of misty melancholy; she imagined her as tall and thin, wearing a long cashmere shawl, her dark eyes burning with a mixture of passion and fever; even the names of the characters in the book – Julia Duprat, Armand, Prudence – had for her the poetic flavour of an intensely amorous life; and that whole destiny was played out, like a piece of sad music, against a backdrop of lavish suppers, wild, delirious nights, worries about money, and melancholy days spent sitting in the back of a carriage beneath an elegantly grey sky as the first snows fell upon the avenues of the Bois de Boulogne.

'Bye, Zizi!' called Jorge from the corridor, on his way out.

'Oh, Jorge!'

He came back into the room, doing up his gloves, his walking cane under his arm.

'Don't be too late, all right? And bring me some cakes from Baltreschi's for Dona Felicidade. Oh, and could you drop in at Madame François and ask her to send me that hat. Oh, yes, and . . .'

'Good heavens, what else?'

'No, it's all right, I was going to ask you to go to the bookshop and have them send me some more novels, but they're closed today!'


Tears shone in her eyes as she finished the last page of *The Lady of the Camellias*. And lounging in the chair, pushing back the cuticles on her nails, the book fallen in her lap, she began softly and tenderly singing the final aria from *La Traviata*:

*Addio, del passato . . .*

She suddenly remembered the item in the newspaper announcing the arrival of cousin Bazilio.

A slow smile spread across her full, red lips. Cousin Bazilio had been her first love! She had been eighteen at the time! No one knew about it, not even Jorge or Sebastião.

Besides, it had been a mere childhood romance: she herself would sometimes laugh, remembering certain sweet, sentimental outpourings, certain foolish tears! Cousin Bazilio must have changed a lot. She could picture him so clearly – tall and slim, with a distinguished air, a small, black, upturned moustache, a bold eye, and a habit of putting his hands in his trouser pockets and making his money and his keys jingle! That 'affair' had begun in Sintra, during long, hilarious games of billiards played at Uncle João de Brito's country house in Colares. Bazilio had just arrived back from England and looked terribly English, shocking all Sintra with his white flannel suit and his scarlet cravats, which he wore looped through a golden ring. Those games had taken place in the downstairs salon, which was painted ochre yellow and had about it an ancient, opulent air; a large glass door opened on to the garden, down three stone steps. Growing around the fountain were pomegranate trees from which she used to pick the scarlet flowers. The glossy, dark green leaves of the camellia bushes formed shady pathways; fragments of sunlight sparkled and shivered in the water of the pool; two doves, in a wicker cage, cooed softly; and in the rustic silence of the garden, the sharp click of the billiard balls had an aristocratic tone.

Then came all those episodes so typical of any Lisbon love affair that has its beginnings in Sintra: slow moonlit walks across the pale grass in Seteais, with long, silent pauses on the Penedo da Saudade to look out over the valley and the beaches beyond, lit by a white, nostalgic, idealising light; and the hot afternoons spent in the shade of the Penha Verde, listening to the cool, dripping murmur of water on stone; the evenings spent in the valley below Colares, rowing in an old boat on waters made dark by the shadows cast by the ash trees – and how they laughed when they ran aground in the tall reeds or when her straw hat caught on the low branches of the poplars!

She had always loved Sintra! The dark, whispering groves of Ramalhão at the entrance to the town filled her with happy melancholy!

They were left almost entirely free, she and cousin Bazilio. Her mama, poor thing, nervous, rheumaticky and self-absorbed, would smile and nod off and leave them to their own devices. Bazilio was rich then; he used to call her mother 'Aunt Jojó' and bring her little bags of sweets . . .

Winter came, and their love found shelter in the old room lined with dark red paper in Rua da Madalena. What delicious evenings they had spent there! Mama would be snoring softly, her feet wrapped in a blanket, and a volume from *The Ladies' Library* open on her lap. And they would sit contentedly, very close, side by side on the sofa. Ah, the sofa! What memories! It was a low, narrow sofa, upholstered in a pale woollen fabric, with a panel down the middle which she herself had embroidered with yellow and purple pansies on a black background. Then one day came 'the end'. João de Brito, who formed part of Bastos & Brito, went bankrupt. The house in Almada and the estate in Colares were both sold.

Finding himself suddenly penniless, Bazilio had left for Brazil. How she had missed him! She spent the first few days sitting on their beloved sofa, sobbing softly, with his photograph clasped in her hands. Then came the agonising wait for letters, the impatient messages sent to the shipping company when the steamship was delayed . . .

A year passed. And one morning, after some weeks of silence from Bazilio, she received a long letter from Bahia which began: 'I have been thinking long and hard lately and I believe that we should consider our feelings for each other to have been mere childish nonsense . . .'

14

Luiza fainted. In the ensuing two pages of explanations, Bazilio affected to feel great sorrow: he was still poor; he would have to struggle hard before he would ever earn enough for two to live on; the climate was horrendous; he did not want her to suffer, poor angel; he called her 'my dove' and signed his whole name, using a very elaborate signature.

For months, she was plunged in sadness. It was winter and, as she sat on the window seat with her wool embroidery to hand, she was, she thought, utterly without illusions now; she even considered entering a convent, as she glumly watched the dripping umbrellas pass by below in the teeming rain; or else, in the evening, she would sit at the piano and sing that song by Soares de Passos:

> Ah, farewell, farewell!
> Gone now are the days
> When I lived happy by your side . . .

or the final aria from *La Traviata* or the sad, sad *fado* that Bazilio himself had taught her.

But then her mother's heart condition worsened; there were anxious, sleepless nights. During her mother's convalescence they went to Belas: there she became friends with the tall, skinny, frivolous Cardoso sisters, who went everywhere together, trotting along beside each other like a pair of greyhounds. Goodness, how they laughed! And the things they said about men! A lieutenant in the artillery had fallen in love with her. He had a squint and wrote her a poem entitled 'To the Lily of Belas':

> On the side of the hill
> Grows the virginal lily . . .

It was a very happy time, full of consolations.

When they returned to Lisbon in the winter, her figure had filled out and she had a healthy glow in her cheeks. And one day, on opening a drawer and finding a photograph of Bazilio in white trousers and panama hat – a photograph he had sent her from Bahia when he first arrived there – she had looked at it hard and shrugged.

'And to think I tormented myself over the likes of him! What a fool I was!'

Three years had passed by the time she met Jorge. She had not, at first, felt drawn to him. She did not like bearded men; then she realised that it was his first beard, fine, close-cropped and doubtless very soft; she began to admire his eyes, his youthfulness. And, although she did not love him, whenever she was near him, she felt a weakness, a dependency and a lassitude, a desire to fall asleep on his shoulder and to stay there comfortably for many years, fearing nothing. What a shock when he had said to her: 'Let's get married, shall we?' She had suddenly seen that bearded face, those shining eyes, on the same pillow next to her, and she had blushed scarlet. Jorge had clasped her hand, and she was aware of the warmth of that broad hand penetrating and possessing her; she had said 'Yes' and stood there like an idiot, but beneath her merino wool dress, her breasts swelled slightly. She was engaged, at last! How wonderful, and what a relief for her mama!

They were married at eight o'clock one misty morning. They had to light a lamp in order for her to be able to see to put on her circlet and her tulle veil. She remembered that whole day as being swathed in mist, with all the edges blurred, as if in some ancient dream, out of which emerged the flabby, sallow face of the priest and the terrifying figure of an old woman, who, with fierce insistence, held out her claw-like hand, pushing and cursing, as Jorge, somewhat shaken, stood at the church door distributing alms. Her satin shoes had been too tight. She had felt sick in the morning, and they had had to make her some very strong green tea. And how tired she had felt that night in her new home after unpacking her trunks! When Jorge hesitantly blew out the candle, luminous S's flickered and danced before her eyes.

But he was her husband, he was young, strong and cheerful, and she dedicated herself to adoring him. She took an immense interest in his person and in his things; she was always fussing with his hair, his clothes, his pistols and his papers. She studied other women's husbands, compared them with her own and felt proud of him. Jorge showered her with tender, loving attentions; he knelt at her feet, and he was so very charming. He was always good-humoured and full of fun, except, that is, when it came to anything to do with his profession or his personal pride, for then he could be extremely stern and became gruff and solemn in word and manner. A rather romantic friend of hers, who saw potential tragedies lurking everywhere, had said to her: 'He's just the sort of man who could stab his wife to death.' She, not yet fully aware of Jorge's essentially placid nature, believed her friend, and this belief added a thrilling edge to her love for him. He was 'everything' to her – her strength, her goal, her destiny, her religion, her man! She thought about what would have happened had she married cousin Bazilio. It would have been dreadful! What would have become of her? She grew absorbed in imagining other destinies: she saw herself in Brazil, amongst coconut palms, lulled to sleep in a hammock, surrounded by black slaves and watching the parrots flutter and fly.

'Dona Leopoldina is here,' Juliana announced.

Luiza sat up, greatly surprised.

'What? Dona Leopoldina? Why ever did you let *her* in?'

She hurriedly buttoned up her peignoir. Goodness, if Jorge were to find out . . . And he had told her so often that he did not want Leopoldina in the house! But if the poor woman was already there in the drawing room . . .

'All right, tell her I'll be with her shortly.'

She was Luiza's closest friend. They had been neighbours in Rua da Madalena before they were married and they had studied at the same school, in Rua da Patriarcal, taught by poor, lame Rita Pessoa. Leopoldina was the only child of the ancient, dissolute Visconde de Quebrais, who had been page to the usurper Prince Miguel. She had made an unhappy marriage to one João Noronha, a clerk in the Customs office. People called her 'that Quebrais woman'; they also called her 'The Ever-Open Door'.

It was well known that she had had lovers, and it was said that she had other vices too. Jorge loathed her. And he had often said to Luiza: 'You can see anyone you like, but not Leopoldina!'

Leopoldina was twenty-seven. She was not tall, but she was considered to have the best figure of any woman in Lisbon. She always wore very close-fitting dresses that emphasised and clung to every curve of her body, with narrow skirts gathered in at the back. Men rolled their eyes and said: 'She's like a statue, a Venus!' She had the full, softly rounded shoulders of an artist's model; and one sensed, even beneath the bodice of her dress, that her breasts had the firm, harmonious form of two lovely lemon halves; the luscious, ample line of her hips and certain voluptuous movements of her waist attracted men's lustful glances. Her face, though, was somewhat coarse; there was something too fleshly about her flared nostrils; and her fine skin, with its warm, olive glow, bore the marks of faded smallpox scars. Her greatest beauty lay in her intensely dark eyes, liquid and languid, and their very long lashes.

Luiza walked over to her with open arms and they embraced each other warmly. And Leopoldina, seated now on the sofa, slowly furling her pale silk parasol, launched into a litany of complaints. She had been unwell, in low spirits, and suffering from dizzy spells. The heat was killing her. And what had Luiza been up to? She seemed plumper.

Since she was rather short-sighted, Leopoldina screwed up her eyes slightly in order to confirm this, and opened her full, warm red lips.

'It seems that happiness brings everything, even rosy cheeks!' she said, smiling.

She had come to ask Luiza for the address of the French-woman who made her hats. Besides, it had been ages since she and Luiza had seen each other and she missed her!

'But you've no idea what this heat is like! I'm dead on my feet!'

And she slumped back against the sofa cushions as if over-come, smiling broadly and showing her large, white teeth.

Luiza told her the Frenchwoman's address and praised her work: she was very reasonable and had excellent taste. Then, since the room was in darkness, she went over to the window and opened the shutters just a crack. The upholstery and the curtains were all made from the same dark green fabric; the sprigged wallpaper and the carpet were of the same colour too, and this sombre décor highlighted the heavy, gilt frames of two engravings (Delacroix's *Medea* and Delaroche's *Martyr*), the scarlet bindings of two vast volumes of Dante illustrated by Doré and, between the windows, the oval mirror in which was reflected the bisque statuette on the console representing a Neapolitan dancing the tarantella.

Above the sofa hung the portrait in oils of Jorge's mother. She was seated and dressed in opulent black – very erect in her severe, corseted bodice: one of her heavily beringed hands, deathly pale, rested on her knees, the other was lost amongst the intricate lacework on her short satin cape; and that tall, gaunt figure, with her great dark eyes, was set against a scarlet curtain, drawn back to form copious folds and to reveal, beyond, blue skies and the round tops of trees.

'And how's your husband?' asked Luiza, moving still closer to Leopoldina.

'Oh, much the same. Not exactly fun,' replied Leopoldina, laughing. Then, looking very serious, her brow furrowed, she added: 'You know, of course, that I've finished with Mendonça?'

Luiza blushed slightly.

'Oh, really?'

Leopoldina immediately gave her all the details.

She was extremely indiscreet and talked a great deal about herself, her feelings, her boudoir and her accounts. She had never had any secrets from Luiza, and in her need to share confidences and to enjoy Luiza's somewhat scandalised admiration, she would describe her lovers, their opinions, their lovemaking, their eccentricities, their clothes – all, of course, wildly exaggerated. These whispered conversations on the sofa were always highly titillating and accompanied by much giggling; Luiza, pink-cheeked, used to listen with a somewhat pious air, fascinated and astonished, drinking it all in. She found it so very strange and interesting!

'This time I can honestly say that I was wrong, my dear!' exclaimed Leopoldina, looking at her bleakly.

Luiza laughed.

'But you nearly always are!'

It was true! She was a poor unfortunate wretch!

'Each time I think it's true love, and each time I'm disappointed.'

Prodding the carpet with the end of her parasol, she said:

'But one day I'll get it right.'

'See that you do,' said Luiza. 'It's about time.'

Sometimes, in her conscience, she felt that Leopoldina's behaviour was indeed 'indecent', but she had a soft spot for her; and she had always greatly admired the beauty of her body, which aroused in her a feeling almost of physical attraction. She would make excuses for her: she was, after all, so very unhappy with her husband. What the poor thing wanted was passion. And that glittering, mysterious word, from which happiness drips like water from an overflowing bowl, seemed to Luiza to be justification enough; she regarded her almost as a heroine, and she looked at her with amazed eyes as one might at someone returned from a marvellous and difficult voyage, full of thrilling incident. The only thing she did not like was the whiff of strong tobacco, mingled with cheap cologne, that clung to Leopoldina's clothes, for Leopoldina smoked.

'And what did he do, Mendonça?'

Leopoldina gave a bored shrug.

'Oh, he wrote me a really stupid letter, saying that, all things considered, it was best if we finished once and for all, because he didn't want to get too involved! The fool! Actually, I've probably got the letter with me.'

She felt in the pocket of her dress and pulled out a handkerchief, a small purse, some keys, a little box of face powder . . . but found only a programme from the circus.

She then talked about the circus. Dreadfully dull. The best thing had been the young trapeze artist. Terribly handsome and with a wonderful physique.

Then suddenly:

'I see your cousin, Bazilio, is coming to Lisbon.'

'So I read today in the newspaper. I was amazed.'

'Oh, there's one other thing I wanted to ask you before I forget. What edging did you use on that blue check dress of yours? I want to have the same thing.'

Luiza had had the dress edged in a slightly darker shade of blue.

'Come and have a look. Come inside.'

They went into the bedroom. Luiza opened the window and then the wardrobe. It was a small, pleasantly cool room, decorated with pale blue cretonne. There was a cheap rug on the floor, with blue designs on a white background. Positioned between the two windows was a tall dressing table adorned with a canopy of thick lace and crowded with cut-glass bottles. Between the curtains, the lush, healthy leaves of luxuriant plants, begonias and palms in glazed earthenware pots, drooped decoratively from small claw-footed tables.

This cosy décor doubtless reminded Leopoldina of tranquil pleasures. Looking around, she said slowly:

'And you're still in love with your husband, I suppose. And quite right, my dear, quite right.'

She stopped in front of the dressing table to dab some face powder on her throat and cheeks.

'Oh, yes, quite right,' she said again. 'But who could possibly feel fond of a husband like mine!'

She plumped herself down on the sofa, with an air of abandonment, and started on her usual complaints about her husband. He was so coarse! He was so selfish!

'You won't believe this, but lately, if I'm not home by four o'clock, he has taken to beginning his meal without me and leaving me nothing but the leftovers. And he's so slovenly and dirty, always spitting on the carpets . . . And his room – because, as you know, we have separate rooms – is an absolute pigsty!'

Luiza said sternly:

'That's awful, but, to be honest, it's as much your fault as his.'

'Mine!' Leopoldina sat up straight, her eyes glittering and seemingly even larger and darker. 'That's all I need, having to concern myself with his room as well!'

Oh, she was a poor wretch, the unhappiest woman in the world.

'He's not even jealous, the brute!'

At this point, Juliana entered the room and gave a cough; then, again fiddling nervously with her collar and her brooch, she said:

'Do you still want me to starch all the waistcoats?'

'Yes, I've told you already. They've all got to be packed into the trunk tonight before you go to bed.'

'What trunk is that? Is someone going away?' asked Leopoldina.

'Yes, Jorge. He's off to visit some mines in the Alentejo.'

'That means you'll be alone and I can come and see you. Good!'

And she sat down next to her, her eyes suddenly alight with love.

'I've got so much to tell you. If only you knew, my dear.'

'What's this? Not another grand passion,' said Luiza, laughing.

Leopoldina's face grew grave.

It was nothing to laugh about. She was in a terrible state. That was why she had come, in fact. She had felt so alone at home, so tense. 'I'll go and see Luiza, I thought to myself, and have a nice chat.'

And in a quiet, almost solemn voice:

'This time it's serious, Luiza!' She gave more details. He was a tall, fair, handsome lad. 'And so talented! He's a poet!' She spoke the word devoutly, emphasising the first syllable. 'He's a *po*et!'

She undid two buttons on her bodice and removed from her bosom a folded piece of paper. It was a poem.

And moving closer to Luiza, her nostrils flaring with delight and excitement, she read in hushed tones, proudly and slowly:

# To You

Farol da Guia, 5th June

When, at the sunset hour, I pause and think,
As I lean out over the rocks where the wild sea roars . . .

It was an elegy. In four-line stanzas, the young man described the long meditations during which he imagined he could see Leopoldina – that 'radiant vision slipping lightly by' – in the sleeping waters, in the red skies of sunset, in the white foam. It was a clumsy composition, full of lines that did not scan and with a sickly, vulgarly sentimental, very 'Lisbon' feel about it. And it closed by telling her that it was 'not in splendid salons' that he loved to see her, not at 'febrile dances'; it was there, amongst those rocks . . .

Where, each day, at sunset,
I watch the vast sea fall asleep.

'Lovely, isn't it?'

They both fell silent, feeling rather moved.

Leopoldina, her eyes wild, lovingly repeated the place and date: 'Farol da Guia, 5th June!'

But the clock in the room struck four. Leopoldina leapt anxiously to her feet, replacing the poem in her bosom.

She had to leave. It was getting late, and that other man would be sitting down to eat. They were having baked mullet for dinner. And there was nothing worse than cold fish.

'Goodbye, then, and see you soon.' While Jorge was away, she would visit often. 'Goodbye. And the Frenchwoman is in Rua do Ouro, above the tobacconist's, is that right?'

Luiza went out onto the landing with her. Leopoldina, when she was at the bottom of the stairs, shouted up:

'So you think I should edge the dress with blue, do you?'

Luiza leaned over the banister:

'That's what I decided, I think it's best.'

'Bye, then. Rua do Ouro, above the tobacconist's.'

'That's right. Rua do Ouro. Goodbye.' And in a shrill little voice: 'The door on the right, Madame François.'

★

Jorge returned at five o'clock, and no sooner had he entered the room and placed his cane in one corner than he said:

'I know about your visitor.'

Luiza turned, reddening slightly. She was standing at the dressing table, wearing a white linen dress trimmed with lace and with her hair carefully coiffed.

It was true, Leopoldina had called round. Juliana had shown her in. She had been most put out. Leopoldina had wanted the address of that Frenchwoman who makes hats. She had only stayed ten minutes. Who had told him?

'Juliana. And according to her, Dona Leopoldina was here all afternoon.'

'All afternoon! What nonsense, she was here for ten minutes, if that.'

Jorge was silently pulling off his gloves. He went over to the window and started brushing at the stiff leaves of a begonia which had unhealthy red spots on them and a kind of silvery slime. He was whistling softly and seemed entirely absorbed in rearranging an amaryllis bud, which nestled amongst its glossy foliage like a small, startled heart.

Luiza was threading a gold medallion onto a long black velvet ribbon; her hands were trembling and she was still blushing.

'This heat doesn't suit them,' she said.

Jorge did not respond. He merely whistled more loudly, went over to the other window, and flicked his fingers at the supple red- and green-tinged leaves of a palm, then, impatiently tugging at his collar as if he were suffocating, he said:

'Look, you've got to stop seeing that woman. Once and for all.'

Luiza blushed scarlet.

'It's for your own sake. And for decency's sake, because of what the neighbours might say.'

'But it was Juliana who . . .' stammered Luiza.

'You should simply have sent her away again. You should have said you were out or in China or ill!'

24

He stopped and, opening wide his arms, added in a sad voice:

'My dear girl, everyone knows her. She's "that Quebrais woman"! She's "The Ever-Open Door"! She's nothing but a shameless hussy!'

In exasperation, he listed her lovers: Carlos Viegas, that thin man with the droopy moustache who used to write plays for the Ginásio! Santos Madeira, with the pockmarked face and the great shock of hair! Melchior Vadio, a spineless good-for-nothing, with eyes like a dead sheep, and that ridiculously long cigarette holder! That very pretty young man, Pedro Câmara! And Mendonça, the martyr to his corns! *Tutti quanti*!

Then shrugging his shoulders, he said angrily:

'As if I wouldn't have known she had been here anyway! The smell is enough to give her away. That awful cheap cologne! I know you were brought up together, etc. etc., but, I'm sorry, if I meet her on the stairs, I'll send her packing! I mean it!'

He stopped for a moment and said tenderly:

'Tell me, Luiza, I'm right, aren't I?'

Luiza, her thoughts confused, was looking in the mirror, putting on her earrings.

'Of course,' she said.

'Well, then!'

He left the room angrily.

Luiza did not move. A small, clear, round tear trickled over one nostril. She mournfully blew her nose. That Juliana! That tattletale! And out of pure spite too! Just to cause trouble!

She was filled with anger. She went to the ironing room and flung open the door.

'Why did you have to say who had or hadn't been here?'

Juliana, greatly surprised, put down the iron.

'I didn't know it was a secret, madam.'

'Of course, it wasn't, you fool. No one said it was. But why did you show her in? How often have I told you that I don't receive Dona Leopoldina?'

'You've never told me any such thing,' Juliana replied, in offended, self-righteous tones.

'Shut up! You're lying!'

Luiza turned on her heel and went back to her bedroom, greatly agitated, and stood leaning at the window, looking out.

The sun had disappeared; the uniform darkness of a windless evening filled the narrow street; on the balconies of the unlit houses, which were all old buildings, stood red earthenware pots containing the occasional miserable, shrivelled plant, a marjoram or a carnation; somewhere, on the melancholy keys of a piano, a little girl was playing 'A Virgin's Prayer', as befitted the indolent, sentimental, Sunday mood; and at the window opposite, Teixeira Azevedo's four skinny, curly-haired, hollow-eyed daughters were spending the evening of this day of rest gazing out at the street, at the air, at the neighbouring windows, whispering if they saw a man walk past, or else leaning out, and with an absurd degree of concentration, aiming their gobs of spit at the pavement below.

Jorge was right, poor love, thought Luiza. But what more could she do? She no longer went to Leopoldina's house, she had removed her photograph from the album in the living room, she had felt obliged to tell her of Jorge's dislike for her, they had both even wept together about it. The poor thing! She hardly ever received her, or only very rarely, and then only for a moment! And since she had already been shown into the drawing room, she could scarcely have pushed her down the stairs!

A thickset, bow-legged man, hunched over a hurdy-gurdy, appeared at the end of the street; he had a fierce-looking black beard; he stopped where he was and began turning the handle of the machine, gazing up at the windows with a sad smile that revealed white teeth; 'Casta Diva', in harsh, tremulous, metallic strains, rang out along the street.

Gertrudes, the mathematics teacher's housekeeper and mistress, immediately appeared at her narrow window and rested her broad, swarthy face – the face of a plump, contented forty-year-old – against the window frame; further along, on the open balcony of a second-floor apartment, the gaunt figure of Cunha Rosado leaned out, clutching his dressing gown to his belly with hands so thin they looked almost transparent; he wore a cap with a tassel on it and the disconsolate look of a man with digestive problems. Other bored faces looked out from behind cotton curtains.

In the street, the woman who owned the tobacconist's came to her door, dressed in deep mourning; she peered out with her ugly, widowed face, her arms folded over her black-dyed shawl, a lanky, scrawny figure in her narrow skirts. From the shop beneath Azevedo's house emerged the coal merchant's wife, hugely, bestially pregnant, her dry, thinning hair all dishevelled, her face greasy and grimy with coal, with three half-naked, almost black children, snivelling and hirsute, clinging to her cotton print skirts. Senhor Paula, who owned the junk shop, strode out into the middle of the street; the polished peak of his black cloth cap was never raised to reveal his eyes and, as if to appear still more reserved, he always hid his hands behind his back beneath the tails of his thin jacket; the grubby heel of his socks showed above his bead-embroidered slippers; and chronic catarrh meant that he was constantly, angrily clearing his throat. He hated kings and he hated priests. He was enraged by the state of public amenities. He often whistled revolutionary songs and in his every word and attitude revealed himself to be a patriot at the end of his tether.

The man with the hurdy-gurdy took off his broad slouch hat and, still playing, held it out to the windows, with a pleading look in his eye. The Azevedo girls immediately slammed the window shut. The coal merchant's wife gave him a few copper coins, but she asked him questions too; she wanted to know what country he was from, what roads he had travelled and how many tunes the instrument could play.

People in their Sunday best were wending their way home, with the exhausted air of those returning from a long walk, their boots all dusty; women in shawls, were coming back from their vegetable plots, carrying children lulled to sleep by the walking and by the heat; placid old men in white trousers, hat in hand, were enjoying the cool, taking a turn about the neighbourhood; people stood at their windows yawning; the sky was taking on the blue, polished sheen of porcelain; a bell was tolling in the distance at the end of some church festival; and Sunday was drawing to a close in an atmosphere of tired, sad serenity.

'Luiza,' said Jorge's voice.

She turned round and uttered a vague: 'Hm?'

'Let's have supper, my dear. It's seven o'clock.'

In the middle of the room, he put his arms about her waist and spoke very softly, his lips brushing her cheek:

'Were you angry with me just now?'

'No, you're right. I know you're right.'

'Aha!' he said in a victorious tone, very pleased with himself: 'So it's a case of:

> What better friend and counsellor
> Than the husband of my own soul's choosing.'

Then he added, tenderly and gravely:

'My love, our little house is so honest and decent that it pains my soul to see that woman come in here, smelling of cheap cologne, cigarettes and all the rest! *Mà, di questo non parlaremo più, o donna mia!* Our soup awaits!'

# II

On Sunday nights there was always a small gathering at Jorge's house, an 'at-home', in the drawing room, around the old pink porcelain oil lamp. Only close friends were invited. 'The Engineer', as he was known to the neighbours, kept himself very much to himself and did not normally have visitors. It was an occasion for tea and talk. There was a student air about it all. Luiza did her crocheting, and Jorge puffed away on his pipe.

The first to arrive was always Julião Zuzarte, a distant relative of Jorge and a fellow student during their first years at the Politécnica. He was a thin, nervous man, who wore blue-tinted spectacles and hair so long that it brushed his collar. He had qualified as a surgeon. He was extremely intelligent and studied constantly, but he was, as he said, 'jinxed'. At thirty, poor and in debt and with no clientele, he was beginning to grow weary of his fourth-floor room in the Baixa, of cheap suppers and of his old-fashioned, threadbare overcoat; trapped in his narrow life, he watched as others, the mediocre and the superficial, 'forged ahead,' 'climbed the ladder' and settled into a life of prosperity. 'Lack of opportunity,' he used to say. He could have accepted a municipal post in a provincial town, with the possibility of taking on private patients, with a house of his own and even some livestock. But he was proud and stubborn and had complete faith in his own abilities and knowledge, and he did not want to go and bury himself in some sleepy, gloomy backwater where pigs rooted in its three streets. Everything about the provinces terrified him; he imagined himself living an obscure life, playing cards at the local club and dying of sheer tedium. That was why he did not budge; and with the tenacity of the ambitious plebeian he waited for a wealthy clientele, a chair at the School of Medicine, a coupé in which to make his calls, and a blonde wife with a dowry. He was convinced of his right to such good fortune, but since it was taking some time to arrive, he was becoming sour and resentful; he was at odds with life; each day his angry, nail-biting silences grew longer; and even on his better days, he was always coming out with sharp remarks and bitter tirades, during which his unpleasant voice cut through the air like an icy blade.

Luiza did not like him; she thought he looked provincial; she hated his pedagogical tone, the dark glint of his spectacles, the too-short trousers that revealed the frayed elastic of his boots. But she disguised these feelings behind a smile because Jorge admired him. 'He's got great spirit,' he would say, 'great talent! An excellent fellow!'

Since Julião always arrived early, he used to go into the dining room to drink his coffee, looking askance at the silver on the sideboard and at Luiza's new outfits. The fact that Jorge, his relative – another 'mediocrity' with a comfortable life and a nice wife, with all his fleshly desires satisfied – should be respected by everyone at the Ministry and own a few *contos de réis'* worth of government bonds, seemed to him an injustice and weighed on him like a humiliation. He nevertheless pretended to admire him and went to his house every Sunday evening; he concealed his anxieties and chatted and made jokes, constantly running his fingers through his long, dry, scurf-ridden hair.

Dona Felicidade de Noronha would normally arrive at nine o'clock. She would come in, arms outstretched, smiling her broad, kindly smile. She was fifty years old and very plump, and since she suffered from dyspepsia and wind, she could not, at that hour, wear corsets and so her opulent figure remained unconstrained. There were a few grey threads in her slightly curly hair, but she had a smooth, round, full face and the soft, dull white complexion of a nun; beneath her fleshy eyelids, the skin around which was already lined, shone two dark, moist, very mobile pupils; and the few soft hairs at the corners of her mouth looked like two faint circumflexes drawn with the finest of quills. She had been Luiza's mother's closest friend and had got into the habit of visiting 'little Luiza' on Sundays. Born into a noble family – the Noronhas of Redondela – and with influential relatives in Lisbon, she was rather devout and often to be seen at the convent church of the Incarnation.

As soon she arrived, she would plant a loud kiss on Luiza's cheek and ask in a soft, anxious voice:

'Is he coming?'

'The Councillor? Yes, he is.'

Luiza knew this because the Councillor, Councillor Acácio, never came to 'Dona Luiza's teas', as he called them, without first going to the Ministry of Public Works the day before in order to seek out Jorge and declare gravely, with a slight inclination of his tall figure:

'Jorge, my friend, I will be coming tomorrow to demand from your good wife my cup of tea.'

He would normally add:

'And how is your valuable work progressing? So glad. If you see the Minister, give him my respects. Yes, give my respects to that formidable talent!'

And with that he would leave, stepping solemnly away down the grimy corridors.

Dona Felicidade had been in love with the Councillor for five years. In Jorge's house, they laughed about this 'grand passion'. Luiza would say: 'It's just a silly fancy of hers!' They saw only her plump, pink exterior and never suspected the intensity of her feelings, which were inflamed once a week and which burned unspoken, eating away at her like an illness, as corrupting as a vice. All her previous passions had come to nothing. She had loved an officer in the lancers, but he had died, and all she retained of him now was his daguerrotype. Subsequently, although she had never said a word to anyone, she had fallen in love with a local baker, only to see him marry someone else. Then she had lavished all her love on a dog, Bilro, upon whom a dismissed maid took her revenge by feeding him boiled cork; Bilro burst, and his stuffed remains now graced the dining room. One day, the Councillor had appeared in her life and ignited those desires, piled one on top of the other like so much firewood. Acácio had become her obsession: she admired his figure and his grave manner, she listened wide-eyed to his eloquence, he had, she thought, 'a

31

splendid position in society'. The Councillor was both her ambition and her vice! There was one particular aspect of his beauty – his bald head – prolonged contemplation of which went to her head like strong wine. She had always shared the perverse liking some women have for bald men, and that desire, unslaked, had only grown with age. When she gazed on the Councillor's bald pate, broad, round, polished and glinting in the light, her back became damp with nervous perspiration, her eyes glittered, and she felt an absurd, desperate impulse to place her hands on it, to touch it, feel it, knead it, penetrate it! However, she managed to disguise this longing by talking loudly, with a foolish smile on her face, fanning herself furiously, while the sweat ran over the rolls of fat around her neck. She would go home and say her rosary, impose a penance on herself to say ten Our Fathers and seventy Hail Marys; but as soon as her prayers were ended, those lubricious feelings would resurface. And poor, good Dona Felicidade was now tormented by lewd nightmares and the melancholic moods of the ageing hysteric! The Councillor's indifference only made matters worse: no glance, no sigh, no amorous confession could move him. With her, he was glacial and polite. They had occasionally found themselves alone in the safe haven of a window seat, in the ill-lit solitude of one corner of a sofa, but as soon as she made the slightest attempt to reveal her feelings, he would start to his feet and move away, stern and very proper. One day, she thought she could see the Councillor casting an appreciative eye, from behind his tinted glasses, over her abundant bosom; she had spoken then more openly, more urgently, she had mentioned the word 'passion', had softly pronounced his name: 'Acácio!' But he had frozen her with a gesture and, getting up, had said gravely:

'My dear lady,

> The snows that gather on the brow
> Fall, at last, upon the heart . . .

It is pointless, dear lady!'
Dona Felicidade's suffering was kept hidden and carefully

disguised; no one knew about it; they knew of her unrequited feelings, but they knew nothing of the torments of her desire. One day, Luiza was taken aback when Dona Felicidade suddenly grabbed her wrist with one moist hand and said in a low voice, her eyes fixed on the Councillor:

'What a man!'

That night, they were talking about the Alentejo, about the treasures to be found in Évora, about the Chapel of Bones, when the Councillor came in with his coat over his arm. He placed it carefully on a chair in one corner and then made his prim, officious way over to Luiza, took both her hands in his and said in lofty, sonorous tones:

'I hope I find my dear, good Senhora Dona Luiza in perfect health. Jorge told me as much. So glad! So very glad!'

He was tall, thin and dressed all in black, with a high collar tight around his neck. His face, with its pointed chin, grew wider and wider until it reached his vast, gleaming bald pate, which had a slight dent on top; the fringe of hair, that formed a kind of collar around the back of his head, from ear to ear, was dyed a lustrous black, and this only made his bald head, by contrast, appear even glossier; he did not, however, dye his abundant, greying moustache, which grew down around the corners of his mouth. He was extremely pale and never removed his dark glasses. He had a cleft in his chin and large, protruding ears.

He had once been director-general of what was known at the time as the King's Ministry, in charge of political and civil administration and public education, and whenever he mentioned the king, he would sit more erectly in his chair. His every gesture was measured, even when taking a pinch of snuff. He never used trivial words; he would never say 'vomit', for example, but would instead make an appropriate gesture and use the word 'regurgitate' instead. If he mentioned a Portuguese writer, he would speak of 'our Garrett' or 'our Herculano'. He was always quoting writers. Indeed, he was himself an author. He had no family, and lived in concubinage with his maidservant in a third-floor apartment in Rua do Ferregial, and devoted his time to political economy: he had compiled a book entitled: *Generic Elements of the Science of Wealth and its Distribution according to the Best Authorities*, sub-titled *'Fireside Reading'*. Only a few months before, he had published *A List of all the Ministers of State from the Great Marquês de Pombal to the Present Day, with the Dates of their Birth and their Passing Scrupulously Verified*.

'Have you ever been to the Alentejo, Councillor?' asked Luiza.

'Never, my dear lady.' And he bowed. 'Never! And I deeply regret it. I have always wanted to go there, for they tell me that its curiosities are of the very first order.'

From a gold box, he delicately took a pinch of snuff between his fingers and added grandly:

'It is also, of course, an area of great porcine wealth!'

'Jorge, find out how much the post of municipal doctor in Évora pays,' said Julião from one end of the sofa.

The Councillor, bursting with information, his pinch of snuff still poised in the air, said:

'It must be about six hundred *mil réis*, Senhor Zuzarte, plus the option to take on private patients. I have it in my notes somewhere. But why do you want to know, Senhor Zuzarte? Do you wish to leave Lisbon?'

'Possibly.'

Everyone voiced their disapproval.

'Ah, there's nowhere like Lisbon,' sighed Dona Felicidade.

'City of marble and of granite, to quote the sublime words of our great historian!' intoned the Councillor solemnly.

And he finally took his pinch of snuff, fanning out three lean, manicured fingers as he did so.

Then Dona Felicidade said:

'One person who could never leave Lisbon, not even if God our Father led him by the hand, is the Councillor!'

The Councillor turned to her languidly, bowing slightly, and replied.

'I was born in Lisbon, Dona Felicidade. I am a Lisbonite to my soul!'

'You were born in Rua de São José, weren't you?' said Jorge.

34

'Number seventy-five, Jorge. Right next door to the house where my poor, dear Geraldo lived until his marriage.'

Geraldo, his poor, dear Geraldo, was Jorge's father. Acácio had been his best friend. They were neighbours. In those days, Acácio used to play the violin, and since Geraldo played the flute, they would perform duets together, and even belonged to the local music society in Rua de São José. When Acácio began working in government departments, he decided, out of a sense of delicacy and dignity, to bid farewell not only to the violin, but also to all tender feelings and to those jolly evenings spent at the music society. He devoted himself entirely to statistics. But he remained very loyal to Geraldo and extended that same vigilant friendship to Jorge; he had been best man at his wedding, he visited him every Sunday, and, on his birthday, as well as a congratulatory card, he always sent him a large cake.

'I was born here,' he said again, unfurling his beautiful Indian silk handkerchief, 'and here I will die.'

And he blew his nose discreetly.

'But that's a long way off yet, Councillor!'

With grave melancholy, he replied:

'I do not fear death, my dear Jorge. I have even gone so far as to have my last dwelling place built in the cemetery of Alto de São João. A modest affair, but decent enough. It's on the right as you go in, a nice, sheltered spot, near the humble abode of my friends the Veríssimos.'

'And have you already composed your epitaph, Councillor?' asked Julião ironically from the sofa.

'I do not want one, Senhor Zuzarte. I want no words of praise on my tomb. If my friends and my fellow countrymen feel that I have been of some service, then there are other means of commemorating this; there is the press, official despatches, the obituary column, even poetry! For myself, all I want to have engraved – in black letters on the otherwise bare stone – is my name, with the title of Councillor, the date of my birth and the date of my passing.'

And then slowly and thoughtfully, he added:

'I would have no objection, however, if the words, "Pray for him" were to be engraved underneath in smaller letters.'

There was an emotional silence, then, at the door, a shrill voice said:

'May I?'

'Ernestinho!' cried Jorge.

Ernestinho entered the room, taking short, rapid steps, and flung his arms around Jorge.

'I heard that you were leaving, cousin Jorge. How are you, cousin Luiza?'

He was Jorge's cousin. A slight, listless figure, whose slender limbs, still barely formed, gave him the fragile appearance of a schoolboy; his sparse moustache, thick with wax, stood up at either end with points sharp as needles; and in his gaunt face, beneath fleshy lids, his eyes looked dull and lethargic. He was wearing patent leather shoes with large bows on them; and dangling from his watch chain over his white waistcoat was a huge gold medallion bearing a bas relief of enamelled fruits and flowers. He lived with an actress from the Ginásio – a scrawny, sallow-skinned woman with very curly hair and a tubercular look about her – and he wrote for the theatre. He had done translations, written two original one-act plays and a comedy full of puns. Lately he had been rehearsing a longer work at the Teatro das Variedades, a drama in five acts, entitled *Honour and Passion*. It was his first serious play. With his pockets stuffed with manuscripts, he was now constantly having to deal with journalists and actors, buying coffees and cognacs for everyone, his hat awry, his face pale, telling all and sundry: 'This life will be the death of me!' He wrote out of a deep love of Art, for he was an employee in the Customs Office, with a good salary and five hundred *mil réis* in government bonds. It was Art, he said, that was obliging him to spend money: for the ball scene in *Honour and Passion*, he had, at his own expense, ordered patent leather boots for the leading man and for the actor playing the father. His family name was Ledesma.

They made room for him, and Luiza, putting down her embroidery, immediately remarked on how tired he looked!

He listed his complaints: the rehearsals were destroying him, he was in dispute with the impresario. The night before, he had been forced to rewrite the final scene of one act, the whole scene!

'And all because,' he added in a state of great excitement, 'the man is a jumped-up little fool. He wants the scene to take place in a drawing room rather than in an abyss!'

'In a what?' asked Dona Felicidade, surprised.

The Councillor very courteously explained:

'In an abyss, Dona Felicidade, a gorge. Another excellent word for it is "vortex".' And he recited: 'He hurls himself into the churning vortex . . .'

'In an abyss?' everyone asked. 'But why?'

The Councillor too wanted to know the precise situation.

A jubilant Ernestinho launched into a long description of the plot. The heroine was a married woman. In Sintra, she has met an *homme fatal*, the Count of Monte Redondo. Her ruined husband has gambling debts amounting to one hundred *contos de réis*. He has been dishonoured and is on the point of being arrested. The woman, mad with worry, runs to the ruined castle where the count lives, tears off her veil and tells him of the impending disaster. The count throws his cloak over his shoulders and sets off, arriving just as the police are about to take the man away. 'It's a terribly moving scene,' he said. 'It is a moonlit night. The count reveals himself and throws a bag of gold at the feet of the police, crying: "Sate yourselves on that, you vultures!"'

'A fine ending!' murmured the Councillor.

'Anyway,' said Ernesto, summing up, 'the plot thickens: the Count of Monte Redondo and the wife have an affair; the husband finds out, hurls the gold at the count's feet and kills his wife.'

'How?' they all asked.

'He throws her into the abyss. That's in the fifth act. The count sees this and hurls himself in after her. The husband folds his arms over his chest and gives a diabolical laugh. That, at least, is how I had imagined it.'

He fell silent, his chest heaving; then, fanning himself with his handkerchief, he looked around him with languorous eyes that had the silvery sheen of the eyes of a dead fish.

'It's clearly a pioneering work, full of grand passions!' said the Councillor, stroking his bald head. 'My congratulations, Senhor Ledesma!'

'But what does the impresario want you to do?' asked Julião, who had been standing, listening in astonishment. 'What does he want? Does he expect you to put the abyss in a first-floor apartment, furnished by Gardé?'

Ernestinho turned and said fondly:

'No, Senhor Zuzarte,' his voice was almost tender now, 'he wants the scene to take place in a drawing room. And so I . . .' and he made a resigned gesture, 'well, sometimes one has to give in, and so I had to rewrite the ending. I sat up all night. I drank three cups of coffee!'

The Councillor held up one hand and said:

'Be careful, Senhor Ledesma, be very careful! Use such stimulants with great caution, oh yes, my dear fellow, with great caution.'

'Well, they certainly did me no harm, Councillor,' said Ernestinho, smiling. 'I wrote it in three hours! I've just been to see him with it now. I've got it here with me.'

'Oh, read it, Senhor Ernesto, read it!' Dona Felicidade exclaimed.

Yes, they all cried, read it, read it! Why didn't he read it?

No, he mustn't bore them with it! It was just a draft! Oh, all right, if they insisted! And, smiling radiantly in the ensuing silence, he unfolded a large sheet of lined blue paper.

'I ask your forgiveness in advance. This *is* just a rough draft. I haven't yet dotted all the i's and crossed all the t's.' Then in a theatrical voice, he said: 'Agatha! She's the wife, this is the scene with the husband, who now knows everything . . .

AGATHA: *(falling on her knees at Júlio's feet)*
Kill me, kill me, for pity's sake, kill me. Rather death than have my heart torn apart fibre by fibre by your scornful words!
JÚLIO:
And did you not tear my heart apart too? Did you show

any pity? No. You cut it into pieces. Dear God, and to think I thought you a pure woman, when you were, in fact . . .'

The door curtain was drawn aside. There was the faint tinkle of cups. It was Juliana, in a white apron, bringing the tea.

'Oh, what a shame!' exclaimed Luiza. 'Read it after tea, yes, after tea.'

Ernestinho folded up the piece of paper and, casting a rancorous eye in Juliana's direction, said:

'No, it's not worth it, cousin Luiza.'

'Not at all. It was lovely,' said Dona Felicidade.

Juliana was placing on the table a plate of toast, biscuits from Oeira and cakes from Cocó's.

'A cup of weak tea for you, Councillor,' Luiza was saying. 'Help yourself, Julião. Toast for Senhor Julião! More sugar? Who wants some? Some toast, Councillor?'

'I am amply provided for, my dear lady,' he replied, bowing.

And then, turning to Ernestinho, he declared that he had found the dialogue magnificent.

But, they all burned to know, what more did the impresario want, now that he had his drawing room?

Ernestinho, standing up, very excited, a small cake clasped between his finger tips, explained:

'What the impresario wants is for the husband to forgive her.'

There were various shocked cries:

'Really! How extraordinary! But why?'

'Exactly!' exclaimed Ernestinho, with a shrug. 'He says that audiences don't like that kind of thing. That it's not right for Portugal.'

'To be perfectly honest, Senhor Ledesma,' said the Councillor, 'audiences here are not great lovers of bloodthirsty scenes.'

'But there is no blood, Councillor!' protested Ernestinho, rising up onto the tips of his toes. 'There is no blood! There's just a gunshot. He shoots her in the back, Councillor.'

Luiza hissed at Dona Felicidade:

'Have one of these cakes. They're fresh today!'

Dona Felicidade replied in mournful tones:

'No, my dear, really, I mustn't!'

And she glumly patted her stomach.

Meanwhile, the Councillor was urging clemency on Ernestinho; he had placed one paternal hand on his shoulder and was saying in persuasive tones:

'It brings a cheerful note to the play, Senhor Ledesma. The audience leaves with a light heart. Why not allow them that?'

'Another cake, Councillor?'

'I am quite replete, dear lady.'

And then he asked for Jorge's views on the subject. Did he not think that good Ernesto should forgive the wife?

'Me, Councillor? Certainly not. I'm all in favour of her dying. Oh, absolutely. I demand that you kill her, Ernestinho!'

Dona Felicidade said in kindly fashion:

'Take no notice of him, Senhor Ledesma. He's only joking. He's got the heart of an angel.'

'That's where you're wrong, Dona Felicidade,' said Jorge, standing before her. 'I'm perfectly serious. I mean it. If she deceived her husband, then I think she should die. In the abyss, in the drawing room, in the street, wherever, but she deserves to be killed. I can't allow a cousin of mine, someone from my own family, of my own blood, to take the namby-pamby decision to forgive such a thing. No, kill her! It's a matter of family principle. Kill her and be done with it!'

'Here's a pencil, Senhor Ledesma,' cried Julião, holding out a pencil box.

The Councillor intervened gravely:

'No,' he said, 'I cannot believe that our Jorge is serious. He's too educated to have ideas which are so . . .'

He hesitated, searching for the right adjective. Juliana appeared in front of him bearing a tray on which a silver monkey was crouched in comical fashion beneath a vast sunshade bristling with toothpicks. He took one, bowed and concluded:

'. . . so uncivilised.'

'Well, that's where you're wrong, Councillor, I do,' affirmed Jorge. 'Those are my ideas. And if, instead of the final act of a play, this were a real-life case, if Ernesto came to tell me: "Do you know, I found my wife . . ." '

'Jorge!' everyone cried in disapproval.

'All right, but just suppose he said that to me, I would respond in the same way. I give you my word of honour that I would respond in exactly the same way: "Kill her!" '

Everyone protested. They called him 'Barbarian', 'Othello', 'Bluebeard'. He laughed and calmly filled his pipe.

Luiza carried on with her embroidery, and said nothing: the light from the oil lamp, dimmed by the lampshade, lent a warm golden light to her fair hair and slipped over her pale forehead as if over highly polished ivory.

'What do you say to that?' asked Dona Felicidade.

Luiza looked up, smiling, and shrugged.

And the Councillor said:

'Dona Luiza is merely saying with pride what any true wife would say:

The impurities of the world do not touch me,
They do not touch so much as the hem of my garment.'

'Good evening,' said a deep voice from the door.

Everyone turned round.

'Sebastião! Senhor Sebastião!'

It was Sebastião, the great Sebastião, strong-as-a-tree-Sebastião – Jorge's best friend and inseparable companion ever since they attended Father Libório's Latin classes at the Paulist school.

He was a short, thickset man, all dressed in black, carrying a soft, broad-brimmed hat in his hand. His fine, brown hair was thinning slightly at the temples. He had very white skin and a short, fair beard.

He went over and sat down next to Luiza, who asked:

'So, and where have you come from?'

He had come straight from the circus. How he had laughed at the clowns. They had performed that trick with the pipe.

41

In the light, his face had an honest, straightforward, open expression; his small, very pale blue eyes were grave and gentle, and softened when he smiled; and his firm, smooth, red lips and shining teeth were evidence of healthy living and chaste habits. He spoke slowly and softly, as if afraid of revealing himself or of becoming wearisome. Juliana brought him his cup of tea, and Sebastião sat stirring the sugar in with a teaspoon, his eyes still laughing and a kindly smile on his lips:

'It really is very funny that trick with the pipe, very funny indeed!'

He took a sip of tea and said to Jorge:

'So, you rascal, you're still off tomorrow, are you? And you, my dear friend, are you not the slightest bit tempted to go with him?'

Luiza smiled. She would love to! If only she could. But it was such an awkward journey. And she couldn't possibly leave the house alone, one couldn't necessarily trust the servants . . .

'Of course, of course,' he said.

Then Jorge, who had opened the door to his study, called him:

'Sebastião, would you mind coming in here a moment?'

Sebastião ambled heavily over, his broad back slightly bent; his ill-cut jacket was almost ecclesiastical in length.

They went into the study.

It was a small room with a tall display case, on top of which was perched an old, dusty plaster statue of an enraptured bacchante. By the window was a desk, on which there was a silver inkwell that had belonged to his grandfather; in one corner of the room, stood pristine white piles of government gazettes; above a dark morocco armchair, in a black frame, hung a large photograph of Jorge himself; and above that glinted two crossed swords. A door, on the far wall, covered by a heavy scarlet curtain opened onto the landing.

'Do you know who was here this afternoon?' Jorge said, lighting his pipe. 'That slut Leopoldina! What do you think of that, eh?'

'Did she actually come in?' asked Sebastião quietly, drawing the curtain to behind him.

42

'She came in, sat down and stayed! She did just as she wanted to! Leopoldina – the Ever-Open Door!'

And violently throwing down his match, he went on:

'When I think of that hussy coming into my house. A woman with more lovers than she has chemises, who mingles with the hoi polloi, and who appeared at dances this year in fancy dress, accompanied by a tenor! The wife of that libertine who falsified a bill of exchange!'

And then almost in Sebastião's ear:

'A woman who slept with Mendonça, you know, the one with the corns! Yes, grimy, corn-ridden Mendonça!'

He made an angry gesture and exclaimed:

'And she comes here, sits in my chairs, embraces my wife, breathes my air . . . I swear to you, Sebastião, if I ever catch her here,' eyes glinting, he groped for an appropriate punishment, 'I'll have her whipped!'

Sebastião said slowly:

'And, of course, in this neighbourhood . . .'

'Precisely!' cried Jorge. 'Everyone in the street knows who she is! They know all her lovers, they know where she goes. She's "the Ever-Open Door"! Everyone knows her!'

'Yes, it is a bad neighbourhood,' said Sebastião.

'Terrible!'

But then he was used to the house, it was his home, he had decorated it himself, it was cheap . . .

'Otherwise, I wouldn't stay here another day!'

It was a ghastly street! Small, narrow, all crammed in together! A place where people were always on the look out, greedy for gossip! At the slightest noise, a cab trotting by, for example, a pair of prying eyes would appear at every window! And then, all down the street, there would immediately be a clamour of tongues, confabulations, opinions! So-and-so's no better than she should be, so-and-so's a drunk!

'It's a devilish place!' said Sebastião.

'Luiza is an absolute angel, poor love,' said Jorge, pacing up and down the room, 'but she's such a child about some things! She doesn't see the bad in people. She's very kind and easily led. Leopoldina's a case in point; they were brought up

43

together, they were friends, and she doesn't have the courage now to send her packing. It's shyness on her part, kindness. It's understandable really. But the laws of life make certain demands . . .'

And after a pause:

'That's why, Sebastião, if, while I'm away, you find out that Leopoldina has been coming here, then I want you to talk to Luiza. Because that's the way she is, she forgets, she doesn't think. She needs someone to warn her, to say to her: "Now, stop right there, you can't do that!" Then she immediately sees sense; she's the first one to admit it. Come and see her, keep her company, play some music with her, and if you see Leopoldina appearing round the corner, all you have to say is: "My dear lady, be careful, this simply isn't on!" Because, with someone else's backing, she can stand firm. Otherwise, she'll simply cave in and let her visit the house. It's difficult for her, but she doesn't have the courage to say to her: "I don't want to see you, go away!" She doesn't have it in her: her hands start to shake, her mouth goes all dry . . . She's a woman, very much a woman. You won't forget, will you, Sebastião?'

'Of course I won't.'

They heard the piano in the drawing room and Luiza's voice rising up, clear and fresh, singing the 'Mandolinata':

> *Amici, la notte é bella,*
> *La luna va spontari . . .*

'She'll be so alone, poor love,' said Jorge.

He took a few steps about the room, smoking, his head bowed:

'Every well-organised couple, Sebastião, should have two children! Or at least one!'

Sebastião scratched his beard in silence, and Luiza's voice, straining slightly on the high notes, sang:

> *Di cà, di là, per la città*
> *Andiami a transnottari . . .*

It was Jorge's secret sorrow – not having a child! He so wanted one! Even when he was still single, on the eve of his marriage, he used to dream of the joy of having a child! He imagined such a child in all kinds of situations: crawling about with his chubby little red legs, his curly hair, fine as silk; or a strapping lad, eyes shining, arriving gaily back from school with his books and showing him the good marks his teachers had given him; or, even better, a young girl, all radiant and pink, in a white dress, her two plaits hanging loose, coming and resting her hands on his greying locks.

He had sometimes been assailed by a fear of dying without ever having experienced that culminating happiness.

Now, from the drawing room, came Ernestinho's shrill, pontificating tones; then, at the piano, Luiza began singing the 'Mandolinata' again, with great jollity and brio.

The study door opened and Julião came in:

'What are you two plotting in here? I've got to be off now, it's getting late. See you when you get back, old man. I wish I could go with you to breathe some fresh air and see the countryside, but . . .'

He gave a bitter smile. '*Addio*! *Addio*!'

Jorge lit his way out to the landing and embraced him again. If he needed anything from the Alentejo . . .

Julião pulled on his hat.

'Give me another cigar, as a farewell gift. No, give me two!'

'Take the whole box! I only smoke a pipe when I'm travelling. Take the box, man!'

He wrapped it in a sheet of newspaper. Julião put it under his arm and as he was going down the stairs, he called back:

'Mind you don't catch a fever, and make sure you find that gold mine!'

Jorge and Sebastião went into the drawing room. Ernestinho was leaning on the piano, twirling the ends of his moustache, and Luiza had started playing a Strauss waltz, 'The Blue Danube'.

Laughing and holding out his arms, Jorge said:

'Would you care for a waltz, Dona Felicidade?'

She turned to him, smiling. Why not? As a young girl, she

had been noted for her dancing. She described a waltz she had danced with Don Fernando, in the time of the Regency, in the Palácio das Necessidades. It was a charming waltz of the time: 'The Pearl of Ophir'.

She was sitting next to the Councillor on the sofa. And as if returning to a topic closer to her heart, she went on, in a low, tender voice:

'You know, you're looking in excellent health. You have a very good colour.'

The Councillor was languidly rolling up his Indian silk handkerchief.

'I always feel better in the warmer weather. And what about you, Dona Felicidade?'

'Oh, I'm a new woman, Councillor. Excellent digestion and very little wind. Yes, I'm a new woman!'

'I certainly hope so, dear lady, I certainly hope so,' said the Councillor, slowly rubbing his hands.

He coughed and was about to get up, but Dona Felicidade said:

'I hope your interest in me is genuine.'

She blushed. The loose bodice of her black silk dress filled as her chest rose.

The Councillor lowered himself slowly back onto the sofa, and with his hands on his knees, he said:

'You know you have in me a sincere friend, Dona Felicidade.'

She raised weary eyes to him, eyes that blazed with passion and pleaded for happiness:

'As you have in me, Councillor!'

She gave a great sigh and covered her face with her fan.

The Councillor got abruptly to his feet, and with head held high, his hands behind his back, he went over to the piano and, bowing, asked Luiza:

'Is that a song from the Tyrol, Dona Luiza?'

'It's a waltz by Strauss,' Ernestinho murmured in his ear, standing on tiptoe.

'Oh, yes, he's very famous, isn't he? A great composer!'

He then took out his watch. It was time, he said, for him to go home and sort out some notes. He went solemnly over to Jorge.

'Jorge, my dear good Jorge, farewell! Be careful in the Alentejo! The climate is injurious, the season treacherous.'

And he clasped Jorge to him, greatly moved.

Dona Felicidade had put on her black lace shawl.

'Are you leaving already, Dona Felicidade?' asked Luiza.

Dona Felicidade whispered in her ear:

'Yes, my dear, I've been feeling so terribly bloated, I ate some green beans and they disagreed with me. And that man, that block of ice! Senhor Ernesto, you're going my way, aren't you?'

'I'll be with you in a flash, dear lady!'

He had donned his light alpaca overcoat and was inhaling deeply, cheeks sucked in, from an enormous cigarette holder, on which a Venus was writhing about on the back of a tame lion.

'Goodbye, cousin Jorge, good health and plenty of money, eh? Goodbye. When *Honour and Passion* opens, I'll be sure to send cousin Luiza tickets for a box at the theatre. Goodbye. Take care!'

They were about to leave, but the Councillor, having hurried back up the stairs, was at the door, the tails of his overcoat pushed back, one hand resting ostentatiously on the silver Moor's head that formed the handle of his walking stick. He said gravely:

'There was something I forgot to say, Jorge. Make a point, in both Évora and Beja, of visiting the civil governors! I say this because you owe it to them as the principal functionaries in the district, and they could be of great use to you in your scientific pilgrimages.'

Then bowing low:

'*Al rivedere*, as they say in Italy.'


Sebastião had stayed behind. To get rid of the smell of tobacco, Luiza went and opened the windows; it was a hot, still, moonlit night.

Sebastião sat down at the piano and, with head bent, ran his fingers slowly over the keys.

He played admirably, with a very fine understanding of the music. Once, he had even composed a 'meditation', two waltzes and a ballad, but they were overwritten, derivative and with no real style. He used to say good-naturedly, tapping his head: 'I can't get anything out of the old grey matter, but my fingers, now that's another thing entirely!'

He started playing one of Chopin's *Nocturnes*. Jorge joined Luiza on the sofa.

'The food for your journey is all ready!' she said.

'All I need are a few biscuits, my love. What I really want is a flask of cognac.'

'And don't forget to send me a telegram as soon as you arrive!'

'Of course, I won't forget.'

'And I want you back here within a fortnight!'

'Possibly . . .'

She looked put out.

'Well, if you don't come back, I'll come and get you! It's your choice.'

Then looking around:

'I'm going to be so lonely!'

She bit her lip and stared at the carpet. Then, suddenly, in a still melancholy voice, she said:

'Sebastião, play the *malagueña*, will you?'

Sebastião began playing the *malagueña*. She loved that warm, languid melody. It made her feel as if she were in Málaga, or perhaps Granada: she is walking through the orange groves, and a thousand tiny stars are shining; it is a hot night, and the air smells good; beneath a lamp suspended from a branch, a singer sitting on a three-legged Moorish stool is strumming a guitar; around him women wearing scarlet velvet bodices are clapping rhythmically; and in the distance sleeps the Andalusia of romances and operettas, warm and sensual, filled with white arms opening wide for love, romantic cloaks brushing past walls, dark alleyways where the candles in little shrines flicker and where a guitar thrums softly, and where nightwatchmen invoke Our Lady as they call out the hours . . .

'That was wonderful, Sebastião. *Gracias!*'

He smiled, got to his feet, carefully closed the piano lid and went in search of his broad-brimmed hat.

'I'll be here tomorrow at seven, then, and I'll go with you to Barreiro.'

Good old Sebastião!

They went out and leaned over the balcony to watch him leave. The night was filled by a lofty silence, a placid melancholy; the gas in the streetlamps seemed about to sputter out; the sharp, intense shadows in the street looked warm and soft; there were brilliant pools of light on the white façades of the houses, and the cobbles glittered like glass; a skylight in the distance glinted like a dull sheet of silver; nothing was moving; and instinctively they lifted their eyes up to the sky, looking for the grave, white moon.

'What a lovely night!'

The street door closed, and from down below in the shadows, Sebastião said:

'A nice night for a walk, eh?'

'Lovely!'

They lingered lazily on the balcony, captivated by the quiet and by the moonlight. They started talking softly about the journey. Where would he be this time tomorrow? In Évora, in a room in some inn, pacing monotonously up and down its tiled floor. But he would soon be back; he was hoping to do a good deal with Paco, the Spaniard who owned the mines at Portel, perhaps bring back a few hundred *mil réis*, and then they would have the whole sweet month of September; they could go north, visit Buçaco, climb the hills, drink cool water from rocky streams, beneath the dense, damp leaves of trees; they could go to Espinho and sit on the beach, in the good, nitrogen-rich air, watching the shimmering, metallic blue sea, the summer sea, with a few steamships heading south towards the slender, distant horizon. Leaning together, shoulders touching, they made other plans; a delicious sense of abundant happiness filled them. And Jorge said:

'You wouldn't be so lonely if we had a baby!'

She sighed. She too so wanted a baby! He would be called Carlos Eduardo. And she could see him asleep in his crib, or lying naked in her lap, grasping his toes with his little hand, sucking at her rosy nipple . . . A tremor of infinite delight ran through her body. She put her arm around Jorge's waist. One day, yes, one day, they would have a child! And she did not for a moment imagine her son a grown man or Jorge old: she saw them both exactly the same: one eternally young, strong, loving; the other always suckling at her breast, or crawling and babbling, fair and pink. And life seemed to her then unending and uniformly sweet, imbued with the same loving tenderness, as warm, calm and bright as the night that wrapped around them.

'What time would you like me to wake you, madam?' said Juliana's harsh voice.

Luiza turned round:

'I told you just now, at seven o'clock.'

They closed the window. A white moth was fluttering around the candles. It was a good omen.

Jorge took her in his arms.

'So you're going to be left without your little husband, eh?' he said sadly.

She leaned back against his entwining arms and gazed at him with eyes that grew misty and dark, then, putting her arms around his neck in one slow, harmonious, solemn gesture, she placed a long, grave kiss upon his lips. Her breast rose with a slight sob.

'Oh, Jorge, my love!' she murmured.

# III

It had been twelve days since Jorge had left and, despite the heat and the dust, Luiza was getting dressed in order to go to Leopoldina's house. If Jorge found out, he wouldn't be at all pleased. But she had had enough of being alone. She was so bored! In the morning, there were the household arrangements, her sewing, getting dressed, perhaps reading a novel . . . but the afternoons!

At the hour when Jorge usually came back from the Ministry, solitude seemed to grow and spread around her. She so missed his ring at the doorbell, his footsteps in the corridor . . .

In the evening, as the light faded, she would grow sad for no reason; she would fall into a mood of vague sentimentality: she would sit down at the piano and, beneath her indolent fingers and the languid movement of her listless arms, sad *fados* and passionate cavatinas would spring instinctively from the keys. And the foolish thoughts that went through her mind! At night, alone in the large double bed, unable to sleep because of the heat, she would be assailed by a sudden dread, by presentiments of widowhood.

She was simply unaccustomed to being alone, she couldn't bear it. She even thought of summoning Aunt Patrocínio, an ancient poor relation of hers who lived in Belém: she was at least *someone*; but she feared that she might feel even more bored in the proximity of that angular, taciturn widow, who knitted constantly and wore huge tortoiseshell glasses perched on the end of her aquiline nose.

That morning she had thought of Leopoldina, who was more than happy to while away the heat of the day chatting and laughing and sharing whispered confidences. Luiza was sitting in her corset and white petticoat, arranging her hair; her low-cut chemise revealed smooth, round, pale shoulders and her soft, white décolleté with its fine blue veins; and as she raised plump arms, slightly reddened at the elbows, to pin in place her plaited hair, she revealed two nests of fine blonde threads. Her skin was still damp and pink from the cold water bath; the acrid smell of toilet water hung in the air; the white linen blinds let in a dull, milky light.

She really must write to Jorge and tell him to come back soon! What would be really fun would be to make a surprise visit to Évora, to arrive at the Tabaquinho Inn at three o'clock one afternoon! And when he came back from work, hot and dusty, wearing his blue-tinted spectacles, she would rush into his embrace. And in the evening, still exhausted from the journey, having put on a fresh dress, she would go for a stroll with him, arm in arm about the city. She would be much admired in the narrow, gloomy streets. Men would come to the doors of the shops. Who is she? She's from Lisbon. She's the engineer's wife. And sitting at the dressing table, fastening the bodice of her dress, she smiled at these imaginings and at her own face in the mirror.

The bedroom door creaked slowly open.

'What is it?'

Juliana's plangent voice said:

'May I go to the doctor's, madam?'

'Of course, but don't be long. Help me do up my petticoat, will you? Tighter. What's wrong with you, anyway?'

'I feel sick, madam. And it's as if I had a kind of weight on my heart. I didn't sleep a wink last night.'

She did indeed look more sallow than usual; there were dark circles under her eyes and her face seemed older. She was wearing a faded black merino dress and the rather old topknot of false hair that she affected during the week.

'All right then, off you go,' said Luiza. 'But do all your jobs first. And don't be long.'

Juliana went straight back up to the kitchen. It was on the second floor and had two windows with a balcony that gave on to the back of the house; it was a large room, with a tiled floor around the oven.

'She says it's all right for me to go, Senhora Joana,' she told the cook, 'I'll go and get dressed. She's about to go out too, so you'll have the house to yourself!'

The cook blushed and started singing, then stepped onto the balcony to shake out an old fraying rug and hang it on the line; and all the while, her eyes never left the low, yellow stucco house opposite with its broad front door – João Galho's joinery where Joana's lover, Pedro, worked. Poor Joana was mad about him. He was a pale, surly-looking lad, and Joana, from Avintes, in the Minho, the daughter of farm labourers, had fallen violently and passionately for this thin, anaemic Lisbon lad. Since she was not allowed out during the week, she let him into the house through the back door whenever she was alone, and the signal was that faded rug on which one could still just make out the antlers of a deer.

She was a robust young woman, with breasts worthy of a wetnurse and jet-black hair made glossy by the application of sweet almond oil. She had the blunt head of the stubborn plebeian, and her thick eyebrows made her eyes seem even darker.

'Ah, well!' sighed Juliana. 'You get the benefit, of course!'

The girl blushed scarlet.

But Juliana immediately added:

'Not that there's anything wrong in that! I'd do the same. You carry on.'

Juliana always praised the cook; she needed her; Joana made her broth when she was feeling weak or, when she was more seriously indisposed, cooked her a bit of beef steak behind their mistress's back. Juliana had a terrible fear of 'having a turn' and was in constant need of 'sustenance'. Obviously, as an ugly spinster, she was outraged by that 'scandalous affair with the carpenter', but she kept quiet about it because, in that way, she ensured a continuous supply of the titbits for which she had such a weakness.

'I'd do the same,' she said again. 'I'd give him only the very best. It would be a fine thing if we were to start having moral scruples because of our master and mistress! I mean look at them! They see a person dying and she might as well be a dog, for all they care.'

She gave a bitter laugh and added:

' "Don't be too long at the doctor's", she says. It's like saying to someone: Look, either get well quickly or hurry up and die!'

She went to fetch the broom from a corner, and with a deep sigh, added:

'They're all the same, the whole wretched lot of them!'

She went downstairs and started sweeping the corridor. She had been feeling ill all night; indeed, in the suffocating attic room immediately under the roof, with its smell of baked tiles, she had been suffering from nausea and breathlessness ever since the summer began; yesterday evening, she had actually vomited. She had been up since six o'clock that morning and had not stopped once: cleaning, ironing, tidying, and with that constant pain in her side and her stomach all upset. She flung open the front door and, all the while uttering loud sighs, was furiously sweeping, banging the broom against the banister railings as she did so, when a voice said:

'Is Dona Luiza at home?'

She turned round. At the bottom of the stairs stood a man, who, to her eyes, looked distinctly foreign. He was tall and tanned, had a small waxed moustache, a flower in the button-hole of his blue frock coat and gleaming patent leather shoes.

'She's just about to go out,' she said, studying him hard. 'And who may I say wishes to speak to her?'

The man smiled.

'Tell her it's about business, about the mining business.'

Luiza, still sitting at her dressing table, though with her hat on now, was slipping two rosebuds into a buttonhole on her bodice.

'Business!' she said, greatly surprised. 'It must be a message for Senhor Jorge! Tell him to come in. What sort of a man is he?'

'A real dandy!'

Luiza lowered her white veil, slowly pulled on her light suede gloves, gave a quick glance in the mirror, fluffed out her lace bow, then opened the living room door. She immediately drew back with a little cry, her face scarlet. She had recognised him at once. It was cousin Bazilio.

★

54

They exchanged a long, somewhat tremulous handshake. Neither of them said anything – she, red-faced, smiling vaguely; he staring at her in frank admiration. Then came a rush of words and questions: When had he arrived? Had she known he was in Lisbon? How had he found her address?

He had arrived the night before on the steamship from Bordeaux. He had asked at the Ministry; they had told him that Jorge was in the Alentejo and had given him their address.

'Goodness, you've changed!'

'Older, you mean?'

'No, prettier.'

'Really now!'

And what had he been up to. Was he staying long?

She opened a window to allow in more light. They sat down, he very languidly on the sofa, she perched lightly on the edge of an armchair, in a state of great agitation.

He had returned from 'exile', he said. He had come to breathe a little of the air of old Europe. He had been in Constantinople, in the Holy Land, in Rome. He had spent the last year in Paris. He had just come from there, straight from 'the little village of Paris'! He spoke slowly, leaning back nonchalantly, his patent leather shoes planted comfortably on the carpet.

Luiza was looking at him. She thought him more manly, more tanned. There were a few grey threads in his curly black hair now, but his small moustache had the same proud, youthful, fearless air about it; and his eyes, when he smiled, had the same soft, liquid sweetness. She noticed the pearl horseshoe pinned to his black satin cravat and the tiny white stars embroidered on his silk socks. Bahia had certainly not coarsened him. His travels had only made him more interesting.

'But tell me about yourself,' he said with a smile, leaning towards her. 'You're happy, you've got a baby . . .'

'No, I haven't,' exclaimed Luiza, laughing. 'Who told you that?

'Oh, someone or other. And will your husband be away for long?'

'Three or possibly four weeks.'

Four weeks! It was like being widowed! He immediately offered to come and see her more often, to talk for a while, in the mornings . . .

'Oh, would you? You're the only relative I have now.'

It was true. And their conversation took on a kind of melancholy intimacy: they talked about Luiza's mother, or Aunt Jojó, as Bazilio used to call her. Luiza described how she had slipped quietly away in her armchair, without so much as a murmur.

'Where is she buried?' Bazilio asked earnestly, then tugged at the cuffs of his cotton shirt and added: 'Is she in the family vault?'

'She is.'

'I must go and visit. Poor Aunt Jojó!'

There was a silence.

'But I'm keeping you!' said Bazilio suddenly, making as if to get up.

'No!' she cried. 'No. I was bored and had nothing to do. I was going for a walk, but I won't bother now.'

He said again:

'Are you sure?'

'What nonsense! I was just popping over to a friend's house for a moment.'

She took off her hat, and that movement of raising her arms drew the fabric on her bodice taut, emphasising the soft swell of her breasts.

Bazilio slowly twirled one end of his moustache, and seeing her removing her gloves, said:

'I used to be the person to put on and take off your gloves, do you remember? I think I still have that exclusive privilege.'

She laughed.

'You certainly do not.'

Then staring down at the floor, Bazilio said:

'Ah, the old days . . .'

And he started talking about Colares. His first thought, when he arrived, had been to hire a carriage and go straight there; he wanted to see the old garden. Would the swing under the chestnut tree still be there? And that summerhouse covered in white roses, next to the plaster cupid with the broken wing?

Luiza had heard that the place was owned by a Brazilian now: above the road there was a mirador with a Chinese-style roof, decorated with glass balls; and the old house had been completely renovated and furnished by Gardé.

'Our poor billiards room, with its yellow stucco and garlands of roses!' said Bazilio. And looking at her, he asked: 'Do you remember our games of billiards?'

Luiza, slightly flushed, was playing with the fingers of her gloves. She looked up at him and said, smiling:

'We were just children!'

Bazilio shrugged sadly and stared down at the floral pattern on the carpet; he seemed immersed in far-off thoughts of the past. And in a mournful voice, he said:

'They were good times, well, for me at least!'

She saw his shapely head, bowed by the melancholy thought of past happiness, the neat parting, the scattering of grey hairs, the latter clearly the product of their separation. She too felt a vague nostalgia fill her breast: she got up and went to open another window, as if the strong, bright light would dissipate her troubled mood. She asked him about his travels, about Paris and Constantinople.

She had always wanted to travel, she said, to visit the Orient. She would like to ride in a caravan, on the swaying back of a camel; and she wouldn't be afraid, not of the desert, nor of the wild beasts . . .

'Aren't you the brave one!' said Bazilio. 'You used to be such a sissy, you were afraid of everything. You were even scared of the cellar in papa's house, in Almada!'

She blushed. She well remembered the subterranean chill of that cellar, cold enough to send a shiver down your spine! The oil lamp hanging on the wall used to cast a smoky, reddish light on the great cobwebbed beams and the dark ranks of big-bellied barrels. Down there, in the dark corners, they had exchanged occasional furtive kisses.

She asked him then what he had got up to in Jerusalem, if it was very beautiful.

It was a strange place. He used to visit the Holy Sepulchre in the morning, then go horseriding after lunch. The hotel wasn't bad either, and there were some very pretty English-women there. He had made a few eminent acquaintances.

He crossed his legs and spoke languidly of his friend, the Patriarch of Jerusalem, of another old friend, the Princesse de La Tour d'Auvergne. The best part of the day, though, was the evening, he said, in the Garden of Olives, with the walls of the Temple of Solomon opposite, next to the obscure little village of Bethany where Martha had sat at Jesus's feet doing her spinning, and farther off, glittering in the sunlight, lay the still waters of the Dead Sea! And there he used to sit on a bench, calmly smoking his pipe!

Had he encountered any dangers?

Oh, yes. A sandstorm in the desert of Petra! Awful! But what a journey that had been: the caravan, the encampments! He described the outfit he used to wear: a black-and-red-striped camel-skin cloak, a dagger from Damascus, a belt from Baghdad, and a long Bedouin spear.

'It must have suited you!'

'It did! And I have the photographs to prove it!'

He promised to bring her one, then added:

'I've got some presents for you, you know.'

'Really?' And her eyes shone.

The best present was a rosary.

'A rosary?'

'A relic! It was blessed first by the Patriarch of Jerusalem on the tomb of Christ and then by the Pope.'

Oh, yes, he had visited the Pope too. A very clean old gentleman, his hair completely white now, and entirely dressed in white as well, a delightful man.

'As I remember, you were never particularly devout,' he said.

'No, I'm not exactly the most conscientious person in that respect,' she replied, laughing.

'Do you remember the chapel at our house in Almada?'

They had spent such lovely afternoons there. There was an ancient graveyard next to the chapel, full of very tall wild flowers, and in the breeze the poppies used to flutter like the wings of red butterflies.

'And do you remember the lime tree where I used to do my gymnastics?'

'Oh, don't let's talk about the past!'

What did she want him to talk about then? His youth had been the best part of his life.

She smiled and asked:

'And what about Brazil?'

Awful! He had even been reduced to courting a mulatto woman.

'And why didn't you marry her?'

She must be joking! A mulatto woman!

'And besides,' he said in a remorseful voice, 'since I didn't marry when I should have done,' he gave a melancholy shrug, 'that's that. I missed my chance. I'll stay a bachelor.'

Luiza turned bright red. There was a silence.

'And what's the other present, apart from the rosary?'

'Gloves! Summer gloves made out of suede and with eight buttons! Decent gloves. Here you use those skimpy gloves with only two buttons, that show the wrist. Ghastly!'

As far as he could see, the women in Lisbon were becoming more badly dressed by the day! It was appalling. He didn't mean her, of course, her dress was chic, simple, demure. But generally speaking, the standard was terrible. In Paris, on the other hand, this summer's dresses were so delicious, so cool! But, of course, that was Paris, where everything was so superior. For example, since he arrived in Portugal, he had simply not been able to eat. Not at all!

'The only place one can eat well is in Paris,' he said.

Luiza was toying with the gold locket which she wore round her neck on a black velvet ribbon.

'And were you in Paris for a whole year?'

Yes, for one whole divine year. He had lived in a beautiful apartment in Rue Saint-Florentin, belonging to Lord Falmouth, and he had kept three horses.

And leaning back further, with his hands in his pocket, he said:

'But then one has to make this vale of tears as comfortable as one can. Tell me, have you got someone's picture in there?'

'Yes, it's a picture of my husband.'

'Oh, let me see!'

Luiza opened the locket. He bent over, his face almost brushing her breast. Luiza could smell the delicate perfume emanating from his hair.

'Hm, excellent!' said Bazilio.

They fell silent.

'It's so hot!' said Luiza. 'It's hard to breathe!'

She stood up and opened one of the balcony doors slightly. The sun had left the balcony now. The thick folds of the curtains billowed in the gentle breeze.

'It's as hot as Brazil,' he said. 'You've filled out, you know.'

Luiza was standing up. Bazilio ran his eyes over the lines of her body, and then, his elbows resting on his knees, his face raised to her, he added in a more intimate tone:

'But, tell me honestly, did you think I would come and see you?'

'Of course! I would have been angry if you hadn't. You're the only family I have left. It's just such a shame my husband isn't here.'

'I . . .' began Bazilio, 'actually, it was precisely because he wasn't here . . .'

Luiza blushed again. Bazilio quickly corrected himself, slightly red-faced.

'I mean . . . perhaps he knows that we were once . . .'

She interrupted him:

'What nonsense! We were mere children. And those days are gone now.'

'I was twenty-seven,' he remarked, bowing.

They fell into a slightly embarrassed silence. Bazilio smoothed his moustache and looked vaguely around him.

'You've got a very nice house here,' he said.

Yes, she said, it wasn't bad. Small, but very comfortable, and it was theirs.

'It couldn't be better! Who's that lady with the gold spectacles?'

And he pointed to the portrait above the sofa.

'She's my husband's mother.'

'Ah. Is she still alive?'

'No, she died.'

'That's the most decent thing a mother-in-law can do.'

He yawned slightly, studied the very pointed toes of his shoes, and then got abruptly to his feet and picked up his hat.

'Are you leaving already? Where are you staying?'

'At the Hotel Central. When shall we see each other again?'

'Whenever you like. Didn't you say you would be coming tomorrow to bring the rosary?'

He took her hand and bowed:

'May I kiss the hand of an old cousin?'

'Why not?'

He planted a very long, gentle kiss on her hand.

'Goodbye,' he said.

And he turned at the door, holding back the curtain:

'You know, as I was coming up the stairs, I was wondering to myself how things would turn out.'

'What things? Do you mean seeing each other again? What did you expect would happen?'

He hesitated, then smiled:

'I didn't expect you would be so . . . forgiving. Goodbye. See you tomorrow.'

At the bottom of the stairs, he slowly lit a cigar.

'She really is *very* pretty!' he thought, flinging down the match. 'And to think that I, great fool, had almost decided not to bother to come and see her. She's gorgeous! Much better than she was! And alone in the house too, probably bored.'

Near the gardens in Rua da Patriarcal, he hailed an empty cab and, lolling back in the seat, his hat on his knees, while the two exhausted horses set off at a trot, he thought:

'And she seems very clean, too, a rare thing here! She takes care of her hands as well. And she's got very pretty feet!'

He imagined her small feet, and began, from there, to create a mental picture of other beauties, undressing her, trying to guess what she would look like. The lover he had left behind him in Paris was very tall and thin, with a kind of tubercular elegance; when she wore a low-cut dress, you could see her ribs. Luiza's rounded figure decided him.

'I'll lay siege to her!' he exclaimed gleefully. 'The way Santiago laid siege to the Moors!'

When Luiza heard the street door close, she went back into her bedroom, threw her hat down onto the chaise longue and immediately went to look at herself in the mirror. Thank heavens she had been dressed to go out! What if he had caught her still in her peignoir or with her hair all over the place! Her face was still very red, and so she applied some more powder. She went over to the window and gazed out at the street, where the sun was still beating down on the houses opposite. She felt tired. Leopoldina would doubtless be having dinner now. She considered writing to Jorge 'to kill some time', but she felt too lazy; it was so hot! And, besides, she didn't have anything to say to him. She started slowly getting undressed in front of the mirror, studying her own image, pleased with her whiteness, stroking her soft skin and yawning languidly, filled by a weary contentment. It was seven years since she had last seen cousin Bazilio! He was darker and more sunburned, but it suited him.

After dinner, she lounged in the wing chair by the window, with a book lying forgotten in her lap. The wind had dropped, and the air, intensely blue high up, was utterly still; the heavy dust had settled, and there was a transparent calm about the afternoon, brilliant with light; birds chattered in the fig tree; from the nearby forge came the sound of loud, continuous hammering. Gradually the blue faded; above the setting sun, the sky was smeared with pale orange, like clumsy brush-strokes. Then everything became submerged in diffuse shadow, silent and warm, with one bright, tiny star that shimmered and shivered. And Luiza sat on in the chair, oblivious, absorbed, not even bothering to call for a lamp to be brought.

'What an interesting life cousin Bazilio has led,' she was thinking. The things he had seen. If only she too could pack her bags and set off to see new and unfamiliar landscapes, snowy mountains, sparkling waterfalls! How she would love to visit the countries she had read about in novels: Scotland and its gloomy lakes, Venice and its tragic palaces; to come ashore in bays where luminous, glittering waves come to die on golden sands; and from the flat-roofed huts of fishermen, inhabited by Grazielas, to see the blue outline of distant islands with strange and beautiful names! And to go to Paris. Oh, yes, Paris! But what was she thinking! She would probably never travel; they were poor; Jorge, a typical Lisbonite, preferred to stay at home.

What would the Patriarch of Jerusalem look like? She imagined an old man, all adorned with gold and with a long, white beard, surrounded by solemn music and spiralling clouds of incense! And what about the Princesse de La Tour d'Auvergne? She would be beautiful, with a regal bearing and an entourage of pages; she and Bazilio had doubtless been lovers. The night was growing dark, more stars were coming out. But what was the point of travelling, being seasick on steamships, yawning in trains, being jolted about in a stage-coach, and only nodding off to sleep as one drove through mountains in the chill of dawn? Wasn't it better to live in comfort, with a loving husband, a cosy little house, soft mattresses, the occasional night at the theatre, and a hearty breakfast on bright mornings when the canaries were singing? That was what she had, and she was very happy! She missed Jorge intensely then; she wanted to embrace him, for him to be there, or, when she came downstairs, to find him in his study in his double-breasted velvet jacket, smoking a pipe. He had all the necessary qualities to make a woman happy and proud: he was handsome, he had splendid eyes, he was loving and faithful. She wouldn't want a husband with a stolid, sedentary career; Jorge's work was interesting; he went down dark mine-shafts; one day he had fended off a mutinous crowd with his pistols; he was brave, he had talent! Involuntarily, though, the image of cousin Bazilio, fluttering across the plains of the Holy Land in his white robes, or, in Paris, sitting upright in his carriage, in cool control of his spirited horses, awoke in her the idea of a more poetic existence, one more suited to affairs of the heart.

A diffuse light fell from the starry sky; brightly-lit windows stood out in the distance, open to the hot night; bats flitted past outside.

'Don't you want a light on, madam?' asked Juliana's weary voice from the door.

'Put it in the bedroom.'

She went downstairs, yawning widely. She felt exhausted.

'It feels like thunder,' she thought.

She went into the drawing room, sat down at the piano and played, at random, snatches from *Lucia di Lammermoor* and *La Sonambula*, she played a *fado*, then, fingers poised lightly on the keys, she remembered that Bazilio would be coming to see her the next day: she would wear her new brown foulard peignoir! She began playing the *fado* again, but her eyes were growing heavy.

She went to her bedroom.

Juliana brought her the household lists and a nightlight. Hunched and lugubrious, she shuffled along in her slippers, a jacket over her shoulders. That figure, with its air of the infirmary, irritated Luiza.

'Good grief, woman, you look like death!'

Juliana did not reply. She set down the lamp; picked up, coin by coin, from the sideboard the money for the next day's shopping, and with eyes lowered, said:

'You won't be needing anything more, will you, madam?'

'Go away, woman, go away!'

Juliana fetched the oil lamp and went upstairs to bed. She slept at the top of the house, in the attic, near the cook's bedroom.

'So I look like death, do I!' she muttered furiously.

Her room was very low and narrow, with a sloping wooden roof; after the sun had been beating down on it all day, the room was like an oven; and at night there was always the scorched smell of baked tiles. She slept in an iron bed, on a straw mattress with a cotton coverlet; from the bedhead hung her scapulary and her grubby hairnet; at the foot of bed stood her most precious possession, a large wooden, blue-painted chest with a heavy lock. On the pine table was a small mirror with a drawer beneath it, a blackened, balding hair brush, a comb made out of bone, her medicine bottles, an ancient, yellow satin pin cushion, and, wrapped in newspaper, the false hairpiece she wore on Sundays. And the only decorations on the dirty walls, which bore the marks of struck matches, were, above the bed, a lithograph of Our Lady of Sorrows and a daguerrotype in which, in the mirror-like surface of the glass, one could just make out the waxed moustaches and the three stripes of a sergeant.

'Has the mistress gone to bed, Senhora Juliana?' asked the cook from the room next door, from where a bright line of light emerged, cutting through the darkness in the corridor.

'Yes, she has, Senhora Joana. She's in a foul mood today. She's missing her husband!'

Joana made the old wooden struts of the bedstead creak with her tossing and turning. She couldn't sleep! It was suffocatingly hot!

'It's the same in here,' said Juliana.

She opened the skylight to let some air in; she put on her carpet slippers and went to Joana's room. But she did not go in, she remained at the door; she was, after all, an upstairs maid and she avoided familiarities. She had removed her hairpiece, and with a black and yellow scarf tied around her head, her face looked even gaunter, her ears more prominent; her low-cut chemise revealed bony clavicles, and her short petticoat showed her very white, scrawny shins. With her jacket over her shoulders, she stood, slowly scratching her sharp elbows, and asked discreetly:

'Tell me, Senhora Joana, that man who was here, did he stay long? Did you notice?'

'He'd just left when you got back. Ooh, it is hot!'

Sweltering, with the sheets thrown back and her legs flung wide, Joana was furiously scratching herself under the coarse ruffled nightshirt that revealed her breasts. She was being driven mad by bed bugs. The wretched room had whole nests of them! It made her feel quite sick.

'Yes, it's a real hellhole!' said Juliana feelingly. 'I only manage to drop off by the time it's nearly light. I've just noticed that picture of St Peter above your bed. Is he your patron saint?'

'No, he's my young man's saint,' said Joana. She sat on the side of the bed. She got so thirsty in the night!

She then slid out of bed and, with heavy steps that made the floorboards tremble, went over to the water jug, held it to her mouth and took a long, gulping drink. Her skimpy, close-fitting nightdress revealed her strong, sturdy form.

'Anyway, I went to the doctor,' said Juliana. And with a great sigh: 'Ah, Senhora Joana, only God can help me now, yes, only God can help me!'

But why did Senhora Juliana not go to the healer, asked Joana. She would put her right. She lived in Poço dos Negros; she had prayers and unguents for everything. She charged half a *moeda* per remedy.

'Because what you've got, Senhora Juliana, are humours. That's what you've got.'

Juliana took a couple of steps into the room. When the talk turned to illnesses and medicines, she grew more familiar.

'Yes, I had thought about going to see her, I had thought about it. But half a *moeda*!'

And she stood there sadly, looking and thinking.

'That's how much I've got saved up for a new pair of boots with a high vamp.'

Boots were her one vice! She spent all her money on them: she had a serge pair with patent leather toecaps, a laced pair made of Cordovan leather, and another made of kid with coloured stitching, all wrapped up in tissue paper and stowed away in the chest, ready to be taken out on Sundays.

Joana told her off.

'When it comes to a choice between that and your body and your insides, you can keep your fripperies!'

She too complained of a lack of money. She had asked the mistress for a month's pay in advance! She had no night-dresses! The two she had were in tatters. Falling to pieces, like the one she had on now!

66

'And then, of course,' she sighed, 'my young man needed some money . . .'

'You see, you too, Senhora Joana, are letting yourself be duped by a man!'

Joana smiled.

'Even if I was reduced to gnawing bones, Senhora Juliana, my last crumb would go to him!

Juliana gave a short laugh and drawled:

'Well, I hope he's worth it!'

But she deeply envied the cook her love and its pleasures. She said again, this time in a more constrained voice:

'Yes, I hope he's worth it!'

Then she went on:

'He was a handsome fellow, the one who came to see the mistress today! Better than the master!'

And after a pause:

'So he stayed more than two hours, did he?'

'He'd just left when you came back.'

But the oil lamp was going out, giving off a fetid smell and a lot of black smoke.

'Goodnight, Senhora Joana. I'm going to say my rosary before I go to bed.'

Oh, Senhora Juliana!' said Joana from between her sheets. 'If you'll say three Hail Marys for the health of my young man, who's been ill lately, I'll say three for your chest to get better.'

'All right, Senhora Joana!'

Then, on further thought:

'Actually, my chest's not so bad at the moment. Perhaps you could try praying to Saint Engrácia for my headaches to go away.'

'Whatever you say, Senhora Juliana!'

'Thank you. Goodnight, then. Heavens, the smell in here is terrible now.'

She went into her own room. She prayed and put out the light. The roof gave off a continuous, enervating heat; she began to feel as if she were suffocating; she opened the sky-light wider, but the hot breath given off by the tiles made her dizzy; and it had been like this every night since the beginning of summer! And all the old wood was seething with insect life! It was the worst room she had ever had in the many other houses she had served in.

In the next room, the cook began to snore. Juliana, unable to sleep, turning this way and that, and afflicted by pains in her heart, felt life weigh on her even more bitterly than usual.

She had been born in Lisbon. Her name was Juliana Couceiro Tavira. Her mother's job had been starching and ironing clothes; and she had been aware from early childhood of a particular male visitor, whom people in the neighbourhood referred to as 'the gentleman', and whom her mother called Senhor Dom Augusto. He came every day, in the afternoon in summer and in the morning in winter, to the small room where her mother did her work, and he would spend hours sitting on the bench by the window that opened out onto the small garden, smoking his pipe and silently smoothing his enormous black moustache. The bench was made of stone, and so, very methodically, he would place upon it an air-cushion, which he himself would inflate. He was bald and usually wore a tall, white hat and a light jacket made of brown velvet. At six o'clock, he would get up, deflate the air-cushion, painstakingly smooth the creases from his trousers and then saunter out, carrying his thick Indian cane walking stick beneath his arm. She and her mother would have dinner at the narrow pine table in the kitchen beneath the small window, through which, summer and winter, they could watch the thin, swaying branches of one sad tree.

Dom Augusto would return at night; he always brought a newspaper with him; her mother would serve him tea and toast and gaze at him adoringly. Juliana had often seen her weep jealous tears.

One day, a nasty neighbour, whom Juliana had declined to help with her washing, suddenly flew into a rage and, standing on the front doorstep, heaped insults on her, declaring loudly that her mother was no better than she should be, and that her father had long ago been sent to Africa for killing her mother's 'fancy man'.

Shortly afterwards, Juliana had gone into service. Her mother died a few months later from a disease of the womb. Juliana only saw Senhor Dom Augusto again once, one afternoon, looking morose in a purple surplice in the Procession of the Stations of the Cross.

She had been a servant for twenty years. As she herself said, she had changed masters, but never her luck. Twenty years of sleeping in dark, cramped rooms, of getting up at dawn, eating leftovers, wearing old clothes, putting up with being pushed around by children and insulted by the mistress of the house, emptying chamber pots, going to the public hospital whenever she was ill, only to wear herself out again as soon as her health returned! It was too much. There were days now when the mere sight of the slop bucket or the iron made her stomach churn. She had never really got used to being a servant. Ever since she had been a girl, her ambition had been to own a small business, a tobacconist's, a haberdasher's or a shop selling knick-knacks, to plan, to manage, to be her own mistress: but after years of scrimping and saving and furious calculations, she had still only managed to scrape together seven *moedas*; then she had fallen ill. Terrified of going into hospital, she had gone to recover at a relative's house; and her money, alas, had melted away! On the day that she had to break into her last *libra*, she had lain for hours with her head under the bedcovers, weeping.

She had been ill ever since and had lost all hope of ever being well again. She would have to be a servant for the rest of her working life, going from employer to employer, until she was an old woman. That certainty filled her with a constant feeling of affliction. She began to grow embittered.

And she was no good at getting the best out of the houses where she worked: she saw her fellow servants having fun, making friends, watching from the window, gossiping, going out on Sundays to their allotments or to some quiet little nook somewhere, spending all day singing, and, when the master and mistress went to the theatre, opening the door to their lover and having a good time in the bedrooms! Not her though. She was always in a bad mood. She did her duty, ate her meals, then went and lay down on her bed; and on the Sundays when she did not go out for a walk, she would sit at a window, with a handkerchief on the sill so as not to dirty her sleeves, and there she would stay, wearing her filigree brooch and the false hairpiece she only wore on high days and holidays, watching. Some of her fellow servants were very close to their mistress, humbling themselves before her, always flattering her and bringing her gossip from the street, delivering notes and running errands, in and out all the time, very much the confidante, and getting well rewarded with presents! She was simply incapable of doing that. It was, Yes, madam, No, madam, and then they went their separate ways. It was all a question of temperament!

Ever since she first became a maid, she could sense the hostility and malevolence as soon as she entered a new house: the mistress would address her sharply, coolly; the children would take against her; if the other servants were talking, they would stop the moment her long, lean figure came into view; they gave her nicknames: the Smoked Herring, the Dried Prune, the Corkscrew; they imitated her tics; there would be giggling and whispering in corners; and the only fellow feeling she had ever found had been in the taciturn, homesick, heavy-footed Galicians, who would arrive in the mornings when all the rooms were still in darkness, to fill the water barrels and polish the shoes.

She gradually became very wary and suspicious, as cutting as a north-east wind; she was always ready with a sharp response and she quarrelled with the other servants; she wasn't going to let them get the better of her.

The antipathy with which she was surrounded made her fierce, just as a circle of rifles enrages the wolf. She became very spiteful; she would pinch children until their skin bruised; and if she was told off, her anger would burst forth like a storm. She began to be dismissed from jobs. In one year alone, she had posts in three different houses. She kicked up an enormous fuss when she left, shouting and banging doors, leaving her mistresses looking pale and nervous.

Her old friend, Tia Vitória, who ran a kind of agency that found places for servants and who often recommended her for jobs, said to her:

'If you carry on like this, you'll end up with nowhere to go and with no bread on the table!'

Bread! That word, which is the terror, the dream and the great difficulty of the poor, frightened her. She was clever and so she mended her ways. She pretended to be 'a poor soul', and, with eyes downcast, affected a zealous, long-suffering air. Inside, though, she was being eaten away: her disquiet showed itself in her facial muscles, in the nervous tic she had of always wrinkling her nose; her skin took on a bilious hue.

The need for constant constraint brought with it the habit of hatred: most of all she hated her mistresses, with an irrational, puerile hatred. She had known rich mistresses who lived in mansions and the poor wives of minor civil servants, but old or young, irascible or patient, she hated them all equally. They were her bosses and that was that! She hated them for the merest word, for the most trivial act! If she saw them sitting down, she would think: 'Go on, you enjoy yourself and let your slave work!' If she saw them going out, it was: 'Go on and leave your lackey stuck here in this hole!' Every peel of laughter was an offence to her morbid sadness; each new outfit was an affront to her old dyed merino wool dress. She hated them for their happy children and their prosperous houses. She called down plagues upon them. If her master and mistress ever had a problem or looked sad, then she would sing to herself all day in her falsetto voice, Offenbach's 'O beloved letter', and with what glee she would bring in the unpaid invoice of some impatient creditor, when she sensed economic difficulties in the household! 'It's a note for you!' she would declare in a strident voice. 'He says he won't leave without a reply!' Any period of mourning was a source of delight, and beneath the black shawl specially bought for her, her heart beat fast with joy. She had seen tiny babies die and not even the mother's grief had moved her; she would simply shrug and think: 'She can always make another one, the bitch!'

Even kind words and compliance were lost on her, like drops of water thrown on a fire. She summed all mistresses up in one word – scum. And she hated the kind ones for the vexations the bad ones has caused her. To her, the mistress was the Enemy, the Tyrant. She had seen two die, and, without quite knowing why, each time she had felt a vague sense of relief, as if part of the great weight suffocating her life had broken off or evaporated.

She had always been envious and, with age, that feeling had grown increasingly bitter. She envied everything in the house: the desserts that the master and mistress ate, and even their underwear. Soirées and visits to the theatre infuriated her. If it rained on a day when a walk had been planned, she was over-joyed. The sight of the ladies all dressed up and with their hats on, staring miserably out of the window, delighted her and made her almost loquacious:

'Oh dear, madam! What a downpour! It's absolutely pelting. It looks set in for the day too. What a shame!'

She was also extremely nosy: she could often be found pressed against the wall behind a door, broom to attention, eyes peeled. She would sniff all letters delivered and turn them this way and that. She would rummage discreetly in any open drawer and scrutinise any discarded bits of paper. She had a light, stealthy way of walking. She examined every visitor. She was looking for a secret, a really good secret. If ever such a secret were to fall into her hands . . .

She also loved good food. She nursed an eternally unsatis-fied desire to eat well, to enjoy tasty titbits and desserts. At supper in the houses where she served, she would follow with eager, bloodshot eyes the portions cut ready for the table; and she was enraged by any healthy appetite that demanded sec-onds because this diminished her rightful share. A diet of leftovers had given her a lacklustre look, her hair became dull, rat-brown. She had a sweet tooth and she liked wine; on some days, she would buy a bottle of wine for 80 *réis* and, gleefully shut up in her room, smacking her lips, would sit and drink it all herself, with the hem of her dress slightly raised so that she could gaze with pleasure on her feet.

She was also a virgin; she had never had a man. She had always been ugly, and no one had ever tried to tempt her; and, out of pride and obstinacy, and a fear of rejection, she had never offered herself up, as she had seen other women do. The only man who had eyed her with desire had been a filthy, thickset stableman who looked like a criminal: her thinness, her false hair, her Sunday clothes had excited the brute. He used to leer at her like a bulldog. He aroused in her feelings of horror, but awoke her vanity too. And the first man for whom she had felt affection, a handsome, blond servant, had laughed at her and given her the nickname, 'The Smoked Herring'. She did not bother with men after that, out of spite, and because she did not trust herself. She suppressed nature's rebellions; they were flickering flames, brief passions. They passed. But inside she became even more shrivelled, and the lack of that one great consolation only made her life more wretched.

One day, at last, a great hope appeared. She had entered the service of Jorge's aunt, Senhora Dona Virgínia Lemos, a rich widow, who was seriously ill, in fact, close to death, with various bladder problems. Tia Vitória, who had found her the job, warned her:

'Take good care of the old lady and spoil her, because all she wants is a nurse who will put up with her. She's rich and she's not stingy either; who knows, she might leave you an inheritance!'

For a year, Juliana, consumed with ambition, was the old woman's nursemaid. What zeal, what care she lavished on her!

Virgínia was extremely cantankerous, and the idea of dying filled her with rage; the more she railed at Juliana in her guttural voice, the more helpful Juliana became. In the end, the old woman softened: she would sing her praises to the people who came to see her, and refer to her as her 'providence'. She had spoken glowingly of her to Jorge.

'There's no one like her, no one!' she exclaimed.

'You're in!' said Vitória. 'She's bound to leave you some money, one *conto de réis* at least!'

73

One *conto de réis*! At night, while the old woman lay moaning in her ancient bed made of lignum vitae, in the sickly light cast by the oil lamp, Juliana could imagine the money, could see glinting, inexhaustible, prodigious piles of gold. What would she do with the money? And as she sat at her patient's bedside, a blanket around her shoulders, her eyes wide and staring, she would make plans: she would open a haberdashery! Other happinesses flashed brightly before her: one *conto de réis* could serve as a dowry, she could marry and have a man of her own!

Her struggles were over. She would finally be able to choose what to eat for supper. She would finally have her own maid to order about! A maid of her own! She could see herself summoning her and saying haughtily: 'Do this, go there, tidy that, go away!' Her stomach contracted with sheer happiness. She would be a good mistress. As long as they behaved themselves! She wouldn't put up with any sloppy work or impudence! And impelled forward by these imaginings, she would quietly pace her room, talking to herself, her slippers dragging. Oh no, she wouldn't put up with any sloppy work! She would pay them decently though, because workers need to be able to put something aside. But they would have to work hard. Oh, yes, they would have to behave themselves! At that moment, the old woman would utter a more heartfelt moan.

'Now!' Juliana thought. 'She's dying!'

And her eager eye went straight to the drawer in the sideboard where the money and the papers were doubtless kept. But no, the old woman only wanted something to drink or to be helped to turn over in bed.

'How are you feeling?' Juliana would ask plaintively.

'Better, Juliana, better,' the old woman would murmur.

She always thought she was feeling better.

'But you've been so restless,' Juliana would say, exasperated by this improvement.

'No,' the old woman sighed, 'I slept well.'

'But you haven't been asleep! I've heard you moaning. You've been moaning all night!'

She wanted to argue with her, to convince her that she was,

in fact, worse, to convince herself that this respite was only temporary and that she would soon die. And every morning, arms folded, face grave, she would follow Dr Pinto to the front door.

'Is there no hope, then, doctor?'

'It's only a matter of days now.'

She wanted to know how many days. Two? Five?

'Yes, Senhora Juliana,' the old doctor would say, drawing on his black gloves, 'a few days, seven or eight!'

'Eight days!'

And as happiness approached, she already had her eye on three pairs of boots she had seen in Manuel Lourenço's shop window.

The old woman did finally die. And she did not even mention Juliana in her will!

Juliana succumbed to a fever. Jorge, grateful for the way she had cared for his Aunt Virgínia, paid for her room in the hospital and promised to take her on as an upstairs maid. The maid they had, the very pretty Emília, was about to marry.

When she left hospital and went to Jorge's house, she began to complain more frequently about her heart. She was deeply disillusioned with everything, and sometimes she wished she could die. Her sighs filled the house all day long. Luiza found her positively funereal.

After only two weeks, she wanted to get rid of her, but Jorge would not agree, he was in her debt, he said. But Luiza could not disguise her antipathy, and Juliana began to hate her; she even gave her a nickname: the 'dumpling'! Then, a few weeks later, she saw the upholsterers arrive: they were renovating the furniture in the drawing room! Aunt Virgínia had left Jorge three *contos de réis*, and she, she who had nursed her for a whole year, humble as a dog and steadfast as a shadow, putting up with the old monster, had been paid for all those sleepless nights and all that work with a visit to the hospital, with a fever! She had a vague sense of having been robbed. She began to hate the house.

She had, she said, more than enough reasons to hate it: she slept in an airless attic room; for supper they gave her neither wine nor dessert; there was an enormous amount of starching and ironing to do; both Jorge and Luiza bathed every day, and it was a real labour having to fill up and empty out those large tin baths; their mania for splashing about in water every God-given day seemed to her ludicrous; she had served in twenty houses and had never seen anything so ridiculous! The only advantage – as she told Vitória – was that there were no small children; she had a horror of children! Apart from that, it was a salubrious area; and since she had the cook, as she put it, in the palm of her hand, there was the added benefit of those bowls of soup and the occasional decent meal. That is why she stayed, otherwise, she simply would not have put up with it!

Meanwhile she did her work, and no one had any complaints about that. And she kept her eyes open and her ears pricked. Since she had lost all hope of setting up her own business, she no longer subjected herself to the rigour of saving: that is why she consoled herself from time to time with a drop of wine, and satisfied her vice, which was to be elegantly shod. Her feet were her pride, her obsession, her one extravagance. She had very small, pretty feet.

'Unusually pretty,' she would say. 'There's not a prettier foot in the whole Passeio Público!'

She squeezed them into tight shoes that pinched; she wore her dresses slightly short and made a point of showing her feet as she walked. Her one joy was to go for a Sunday walk in the Passeio Público and there, with the hem of her dress slightly raised, her face hidden beneath a dainty silk sunshade, she would spend the whole afternoon in the dust and the heat, utterly still and happy, displaying her feet and exposing them to view!

# IV

About three o'clock one afternoon, Juliana went into the kitchen and collapsed into a chair, exhausted. She felt so weak she could barely stand. She had been cleaning the drawing room since two o'clock! It was filthy! That dandified fellow who had visited the previous day had dropped ash on the tables. And, of course, she was the one who had to clear it up. And the heat! It was sweltering!

'Is the soup ready yet?' she said, softening her voice. 'Pour me some out, will you, Senhora Joana?'

'You look different today,' said the cook.

'Oh, I feel a new woman, Senhora Joana! But you know I didn't sleep a wink all night. When I finally managed to drop off, it was getting light!'

'Same here!' said Joana, and she had had such strange dreams. Heavens! A fiery ghost was striding about over her body and stamping on her stomach like someone treading grapes!

'Indigestion,' remarked Juliana gravely, then said again: 'Yes, I feel a new woman. I haven't felt so well in months!'

She was smiling, showing her yellow teeth. The delicious smell emanating from the thick vegetable soup that Joana was pouring into the white bowl filled Juliana with greedy joy. She stretched out her legs and leaned back, revelling in the bright, afternoon warmth pouring in through the two open windows.

The sun had left the balcony, and on the stone slabs, a few pathetic plants drew in their parched leaves; on a table in the corner, in an old, potbellied saucepan, was the brilliant green of a well-watered parsley plant; the cat was asleep on a large mat; floorcloths were drying on the line; and beyond, stretched the blue sky, glowing like some incandescent metal; the trees in the gardens glittered in the sun; the tawny roofs and the tall weeds growing on them baked in the heat; and here and there, patches of whitewashed walls gave off a harsh, dazzling light.

'It's delicious, Senhora Joana, absolutely delicious!' said Juliana, slowly, greedily stirring the soup. The cook, standing up, arms folded over her ample bosom, said proudly:

'We aim to please.'

'It's perfect.'

They smiled, enjoying the camaraderie and the kind words. And the doorbell, which had already rung once, rang again discreetly.

Juliana did not move. Gusts of warm air blew in; there was the sound of a saucepan boiling on the hob and, outside, the incessant hammering from the forge; occasionally the sad cooing of the two doves who lived in a wicker cage on the balcony lent a sudden sweetness to the scorching afternoon.

The bell rang again, this time impatiently.

'Try knocking with your head, you idiot!' said Juliana.

They laughed. Joana went over and sat by the window, in a low chair; she stretched out her large, slippered feet and scratched her armpits in a slow, leisurely fashion.

The bell rang violently this time.

'Oh, go away!' growled Juliana calmly.

But Luiza's angry voice rose up from below:

'Juliana!'

'Honestly, what a place! A person can't even eat her food in peace!'

'Juliana!' called Luiza.

The cook turned to her, worried now.

'The mistress is getting annoyed, Senhora Juliana.'

'Oh, devil take the creature.'

She wiped her greasy lips on her apron and stormed downstairs.

'Didn't you hear, woman? They've been ringing for ages!'

Juliana opened wide, astonished eyes: Luiza was wearing her new brown foulard peignoir, with yellow polka dots.

'Something's going on here, something big!' thought Juliana as she walked down the corridor.

The bell was still clattering. And on the landing, dressed in a light-coloured suit, with a rose in his buttonhole and a package under his arm, was 'the man from the mines'!

'It's that man again, the one who came yesterday,' she told Luiza in amazed tones.

'Tell him to come in.'

'Well!' Juliana thought.

She ran upstairs to the kitchen and announced from the door, her voice shrill with excitement:

'It's the dandified fellow who was here yesterday. He's here again! He's brought a package with him! What do you think, Senhora Joana, what do you think?'

'A visitor, I suppose,' said the cook.

Juliana gave a wry laugh. She sat down and hurriedly finished her soup.

Joana, oblivious, walked about the kitchen, singing; outside, the doves kept up their faint, languorous cooing.

'There's something fishy going on here,' said Juliana.

She sat for a moment, running her tongue over her teeth, staring into space, thinking. She smoothed her apron and went down to Luiza's bedroom: her probing eye immediately spotted the pantry keys abandoned on the dressing table; she could go upstairs, have a drink of good wine and eat some quince jelly . . . but she was gripped by an urgent curiosity and so, instead, she tiptoed over to the drawing-room door where she crouched and listened. The door curtain was drawn inside: she could hear only the man's deep, jovial voice. She walked round via the corridor to the other door, next to the stairs; she put her eye to the keyhole, then pressed her ear to the crack. There too the door curtain was drawn.

'They've sealed themselves in, the devils!'

She thought she could hear a chair being dragged across the floor, then a window being closed. Her eyes glittered. There was a burst of laughter from Luiza, followed by a silence, then the voices began talking again in a calm, continuous tone. Suddenly, the man spoke more loudly, and amongst the words he said, doubtless as he paced about, Juliana clearly heard: 'No, Luiza, it was you!'

'The hussy!'

The bell beside her rang timidly, startling her. She went to open the front door. It was Sebastião, his face red from the heat, his boots covered in dust.

'Is your mistress in?' he asked, mopping the sweat from his brow.

'She's got a visitor, Senhor Sebastião!'

And closing the door behind her, she said in a low voice:

'A young man who was here yesterday, a real dandy! Shall I tell her you're here?'

'No, no, it's all right. Goodbye!'

He went discreetly back down the stairs. Juliana immediately resumed her post at the door, her ear pressed against the wood, her hands behind her back: but the conversation was just a vague, tranquil murmur now, with no loud outbursts. She went upstairs to the kitchen.

'He calls her "Luiza"!' she exclaimed. 'He calls her "Luiza", Senhora Joana!' And she added excitedly:

'Goodness, things are moving fast! That's what I like to see!'

The man left at five o'clock. As soon as Juliana heard the front door open, she ran to see. There was Luiza on the landing, leaning over the banister, calling down, in very friendly tones:

'All right, I'll be there. Goodbye.'

Juliana was gripped then by a curiosity that burned her like a fever. All afternoon – in the dining room and in the bedroom – she kept shooting Luiza searching sideways glances. But Luiza, wearing an old linen robe now, seemed calm and indifferent.

'She's a sly one!'

Such nonchalance provoked Juliana's need for intrigue.

'I'll catch you out yet, you shameless creature!' she thought.

It seemed to her that Luiza had faint shadows under her eyes! She studied the way she stood, the way she spoke. She noticed that she asked for a second helping of the roast and Juliana immediately thought: 'It's given her an appetite!'

And when, after supper, Luiza sat down in the wing chair, looking tired, Juliana said to herself: 'She's exhausted!'

That evening, Luiza, who never drank coffee, asked for 'half a cup, but strong, very strong'.

'She wants coffee!' she told the cook, all excited. 'No stinting either. She wants it strong! Who would think it!'

She was furious.

'They're all the same. Bitches on heat, the lot of them!'

The next day was Sunday. Early in the morning, as Juliana was going out to mass, Luiza called to her from the bedroom door and gave her a letter to take to Dona Felicidade. Usually she sent a verbal message, and Juliana's curiosity was immediately aroused by that envelope bearing Luiza's own seal, a gothic L surrounded by a garland of roses.

'Do you need an answer?'

'I do.'

When Juliana returned at ten o'clock with a note from Dona Felicidade, Luiza asked if it was still very hot, if there was a lot of dust about. On the table was a dark straw hat, which she was decorating with two musk roses.

There was a bit of a breeze, but it would probably die down by the evening. And she thought: 'So she's going for a stroll, is she? She's going to meet that man.'

But during the day, Luiza, still in her robe, stayed in her bedroom or in the drawing room, and either lounged for a while on the chaise longue, reading, or distractedly played fragments of waltzes on the piano. She dined at four o'clock. The cook went out, and Juliana settled down to spend her afternoon at the dining-room window. She was wearing her new dress, its petticoats stiff with starch, and her best hairpiece, and she solemnly rested her elbows on a handkerchief spread out on the balcony balustrade. Opposite, the birds were chirruping in the fig tree. On either side of the fence surrounding the empty plot crouched the dark roofs of the houses in the two narrow streets that ran parallel: they were poor houses inhabited by women with oiled hair who sat at their windows in the evenings, wearing a peignoir or a loose blouse, knitting, talking to men, or singing to themselves in sad, bored voices. The leafy gardens and the white walls on the other side of the plot gave the place a sleepy, village air. Almost no one walked past. There was a weary silence; very occasionally, the distant sound of a hurdy-gurdy, playing tunes from *Norma* or *Lucia di Lammermoor*, lent a melancholy note to the evening. And Juliana sat on, unmoving, until the hot sounds of the afternoon were beginning to fade and the bats were beginning to fly.

At about eight o'clock, she went into Luiza's room and was astonished to find her dressed entirely in black and with her hat on! She had lit the lamps on the wall and the candles on her dressing table, and she was sitting on the edge of the chaise longue, slowly drawing on her gloves, her eyes bright, a very serious look on her soft, lightly powdered face.

'Has the breeze died down?' she asked.

'Oh, yes, it's a lovely night, madam.'

Shortly before nine o'clock, a carriage stopped at the door. It contained a very hot Dona Felicidade. She had been positively suffocating all day! And there wasn't a breath of air tonight. She had even ordered them to find her an open carriage, because, goodness, one would just die inside a coupé!

Juliana bustled about the room putting things in their place, consumed by curiosity. Where were they going? Dona Felicidade, amply seated, still with her hat on, was chattering away about a terrible bout of indigestion she had had the night before because of some beans; about the cook who had tried to 'diddle' her out of four *vinténs*; about a visit she had received from the Countess de Arruela . . .

Finally, Luiza lowered her white veil and said:

'Come along, my dear. It's getting late.'

A furious Juliana lit the way. The idea of it, two women going out alone in an open carriage! And the fuss that would be made if a maidservant spent so much as half an hour in the street! The great hussies!

She went into the kitchen to vent her spleen on Joana. But the girl was dozing, sprawled in a chair.

She had been to the cemetery of Alto de São João with her Pedro. And they had spent the whole afternoon together there, admiring the tombs, clumsily reading out the epitaphs, exchanging loving kisses in the shady nooks afforded by the weeping willows, and enjoying the breeze from the cypresses and the lawns of the dead. They had returned by way of Serena's house and stopped for a sip of wine at Espregueira's . . . A full afternoon! And she was worn out from the midday sun, from the dust, from admiring so many wealthy tombs, from being with her man and from that drop of wine.

She was just about ready to fall into bed!

'Honestly, Senhora Joana, you're becoming a real sleepy-head! Heavens, it doesn't take much to wear you out!'

She went down to Luiza's room, put out the lights, opened the windows, and dragged the armchair over to the balcony; then she folded her arms, made herself comfortable and prepared to spend the rest of the evening there.

The tobacconist's had not yet closed, and the faint light from the shop, as dreary as its owner, fell sadly onto the cobbles in the street; the windows nearby were open; some, dimly lit, revealed melancholy gatherings; in others, full of static shapes, there would be the occasional glow of a cigarette end; now and then someone coughed; and the baker's boy, in the hot silence of the night, strummed softly on his guitar.

Juliana was wearing a dress of pale cotton; two men standing at the door of the tobacconist's were laughing and kept looking up at the window, at that white, female figure. Juliana was thrilled. They doubtless took her for her mistress, for the engineer's wife; they made eyes at her, made suggestive remarks . . . One of the men was wearing white trousers and a tall hat, both were dandies. And Juliana, her feet outstretched, her arms folded, her head on one side, revelled in that attention.

Heavy footsteps came up the street and stopped at the door; the bell jingled faintly.

'Who is it?' she called impatiently.

'Is your mistress there?' said Sebastião's deep voice.

'She's gone out with Dona Felicidade, in a carriage.'

'Ah!' he said.

And added:

'It's a lovely night!'

'Wonderful, Senhor Sebastião, wonderful!' she exclaimed loudly.

And when she saw him heading off down the street, she called after him in an affected way, as if they were close friends and she were the mistress, and all the while making eyes at the two men: 'Give my regards to Tia Joana! Don't forget, now!'

At that hour, Dona Felicidade and Luiza were just arriving at the Passeio Público.

A charity event was being held that night; from outside, one could already hear the slow, monotonous hubbub of voices and see a high cloud of yellowish, luminous dust.

They went in. By the pool, they met Bazilio. Feigning great surprise, he exclaimed:

'Well, this is a happy coincidence!'

Luiza blushed and introduced him to Dona Felicidade.

The excellent lady was all smiles. She remembered him, but if they hadn't been introduced, she would never have recognised him! How he had changed!

'The effects of hard work, madam,' said Bazilio, bowing.

And then he added, laughing and striking the stone edge of the pool with his stick:

'It's old age, really, old age!'

The shifting reflections from the gaslights penetrated down into the depths of the dark, murky water. In the still air, the leaves around them were motionless and of a livid, artificial green. Between the long, parallel ranks of mean little trees, interspersed with gaslights, a dark, compact crush of people were crammed together on the dusty macadam path; and above the deep hum of conversation, the metallic notes of the music sent the lively rhythms of a waltz floating off through the heavy air.

They had stopped to talk.

Wasn't it hot? But such a lovely evening! Not a breath of wind! And what a crowd!

And they looked at the people arriving: young men with carefully curled hair and wearing mauve trousers, ceremoniously smoking their Sunday cigars; an officer cadet with corseted waist and padded chest; two young women with ringlets and a swaying gait that revealed the line of their shoulder blades beneath the fabric of their hastily made dresses; a sallow-skinned cleric with a languid air, a cigarette in his mouth and wearing tinted glasses; a Spanish woman with vast starched white petticoats rustling through the dust; sad Xavier, the poet; a nobleman with a double-breasted overcoat and a stout walking stick, hat pushed back on his head and a vinous look in his eyes; and Bazilio roared with laughter at the sight of two small children being led along by their proud, joyful father – the foolish, dazed creatures were dressed in pale blue, with scarlet sashes, lancer's helmets and Hungarian-style boots.

A tall man passed close by them and, turning, looked Luiza up and down with large, languorous, silver-grey eyes: he had a long, pointed goatee beard; he was wearing a waistcoat cut low to reveal his fine shirt front, and he brandished a huge cigarette holder in the shape of a zouave.

Luiza wanted to sit down.

A lad in a filthy smock ran off to find them some chairs, and they sat down near a dour, taciturn family group.

'What did you do today, Bazilio?' asked Luiza.

He had been to see a bullfight.

'And how was it? Was it fun?'

'No, very insipid stuff. If it hadn't been for Peixinho falling over, one would have died of boredom. Useless bulls, terrible horsemen, a complete waste of time. Now Spain, that's the place for bullfighting!'

Dona Felicidade protested, horrified. She had been to a bullfight in Badajoz, when she was visiting her Aunt Francisca in Elvas, and she had almost fainted. The blood, the poor disembowelled horses! Ugh! It was so cruel!

Bazilio said with a smile:

'Whatever would you do if you saw a cockfight, madam?'

Dona Felicidade had heard of such things, but she found all such entertainments both barbarous and irreligious.

Then, recollecting a pleasure that put a smile on her plump face, she said:

'In my opinion, there is nothing like a good night at the theatre! Nothing!'

'But the standard of acting here is appalling!' replied Bazilio desolately. 'Absolutely awful, my dear lady!'

Dona Felicidade did not respond; she had half raised herself up from her chair, waving desperately, her eyes shining.

'Gone,' she said disconsolately.

'Who was it? The Councillor?' asked Luiza.

'No, it was the Countess de Alviela. She didn't see me. She often goes to the convent church of the Incarnation. I'm a close acquaintance of hers. She's an absolute angel. She didn't see me, though. She's with her father-in-law.'

Bazilio did not take his eyes off Luiza. Beneath her white veil, in the false glow of the gaslights, in the dusty air, her face was a smooth, white shape to which her eyes, made darker by the night, lent passion; her blonde curls made her head appear smaller and gave her a sweet, childish grace; and her pearl-grey gloves against the black of her dress emphasised the elegant shape of her hands, which lay in her lap holding her fan, her slender wrists adorned by a ruff of soft white lace.

'And what did you do today?' Bazilio asked.

She had been mortally bored. She had spent the whole day reading.

He had spent the morning reading too, a book entitled *Woman of Fire* by Belot. Had she read it?

'No, what is it?'

'It's a novel, just out.'

Then he added, smiling:

'It's perhaps a bit *risqué* for you. I wouldn't really recommend it!'

Dona Felicidade was reading *Rocambole*. So many people had told her how wonderful it was! But it was so convoluted! She got lost, she forgot the plot . . . In fact, she was going to abandon it altogether, having noticed that reading seemed to exacerbate her indigestion.

'Do you suffer much from indigestion?' asked Bazilio out of polite interest.

Dona Felicidade launched into an account of her dyspepsia. Bazilio recommended using ice. And he congratulated her, because, lately, illnesses of the stomach had become positively chic. He asked after hers and requested more details.

Dona Felicidade provided them in abundance, and, as she spoke, her growing fondness for Bazilio was evident in her voice and eyes. She would definitely try ice!

'With wine, I assume?'

'With wine, dear lady!'

'It's certainly worth a try,' exclaimed Dona Felicidade, tapping Luiza's arm with her fan, suddenly filled with hope.

Luiza smiled and was about to respond, when she saw the pale man with the long goatee staring obstinately at her again with his languorous eyes. She turned away, annoyed. The man moved off, tugging at his beard.

She felt strangely indolent; the monotonous murmur and bustle of people, the hot night, the crowds, the sense of being surrounded by greenery, all filled her homely self with a pleasant torpor; an inert sense of well-being wrapped her in the emollient sweetness of a warm bath. She gazed around her with a vague smile on her lips, her eyes languid; she felt almost too lazy to move her hands, to open her fan.

Bazilio noticed her silence. Was she sleepy?

Dona Felicidade smiled slyly.

'She hasn't got her husband with her, you see! She's been in a bad mood ever since he left.'

Glancing instinctively at Bazilio, Luiza retorted:

'What nonsense! I've actually been feeling rather cheerful these last few days!'

But Dona Felicidade insisted:

'Don't you believe her! That little heart of hers is in the Alentejo!'

Luiza said tartly:

'Well, you can hardly expect me to go skipping through the park, guffawing.'

'Now, now, don't get angry!' exclaimed Dona Felicidade. And to Bazilio: 'What a temper, eh?'

Bazilio burst out laughing.

'Cousin Luiza always used to have a sharp tongue on her. Nowadays, I don't know . . .'

Dona Felicidade was quick to say:

'Oh, she's a lamb, poor thing, an absolute lamb. No, really.'

And she enfolded Luiza in a maternal gaze.

The taciturn family rose noiselessly to their feet at this point, and, with the little girls first and the parents following, they moved off in dreary, sullen silence.

Bazilio immediately moved to the chair next to Luiza and, when Dona Felicidade was looking in the other direction, said softly:

'I nearly came to see you this morning.'

She said in a normal, almost indifferent tone of voice:

'Why didn't you, then? We could have played some music together. It was wrong of you not to come. You should have.'

Dona Felicidade asked what time it was. She was beginning to grow bored. She had hoped to see the Councillor; indeed, in order to look her best, she had sacrificed herself for his sake and worn her corset; Acácio had not appeared, and she was beginning to be troubled by wind; and the disappointment caused by his absence was only exacerbating her digestive torments. Sitting limply in her chair, she watched as the crowd moved ceaselessly about in a fog of dust.

Then with a great blare of brass, the music on the bandstand suddenly struck up loudly, the compelling opening notes of the march from *Faust*. This revived her. It was a medley of music from the opera, and there was no music she enjoyed more. Would Senhor Bazilio be there for the opening night at the Teatro de São Carlos?

Turning to Luiza, Bazilio said meaningfully:

'I don't know, madam, that depends . . .'

Luiza looked at him and said nothing. The crowds were growing. Only the shy, the bereaved and those with threadbare clothes strolled along the cooler, more spacious paths off to the side, beneath the shadows of the trees. The whole Sunday bourgeoisie had crammed themselves into the main avenue, along the corridor formed by the closed ranks of chairs: and there they moved along, wedged together, with the thick slowness of a barely molten mass, dragging their feet, scuffing the macadam surface, looking crumpled and plebeian, throats dry, arms hanging loose by their sides, barely speaking. They came and went incessantly, shuffling gracelessly along, accompanied by a deep murmur of voices, devoid of joy and bonhomie, caught up in the kind of passive excitement favoured by indolent races; in the midst of that abundance of light and the gaiety of the music, there was an air of tedium, penetrating as mist; a fine dust enfolded the figures, reducing them all to the same neutral tones; and in the most brightly lit areas, on the faces that passed beneath the street lamps, one saw the discontent of the weary and the monotonous gloom of Sundays.

Opposite, the façades of the houses in Rua Occidental were bathed in the reflected glow from the Passeio; a few windows were open; the dark curtains stood out against the bright, lamp-lit interiors. Luiza felt a kind of nostalgia for other summer nights and for intimate evenings. But where? She could not remember. Her eyes were drawn back to the crowd, and she found herself face to face again with the man with the long goatee beard, who was staring at her moodily. Beneath her veil, she felt the dust burning her eyes; all around her, people were yawning.

Dona Felicidade proposed that they should go for a stroll. They got up and slowly pushed their way through the crowd; the rows of chairs were packed tightly together, and an infinity of bored faces, bathed by the gaslight in the same uniformly yellowish tone, stared fixedly ahead, plunged in torpid gloom. The sight irritated Bazilio, and since it was difficult even to walk, he suggested 'leaving the wretched place'.

They left. While he went off to buy some tickets, Dona Felicidade, collapsing onto a bench beneath the shade of a weeping willow, cried plaintively:

'Oh, my dear, I'm almost bursting!'

She stroked her stomach, her face suddenly older.

'And then there's the Councillor! What bad luck! The one day when I come to the Passeio Público . . .'

She sighed, fanning herself. Then with her kindly smile, she said:

'Your cousin's awfully nice. Such lovely manners. A real gentleman. One can always tell, my dear.'

As soon as they had gone out through the gates, she declared herself greatly fatigued. It would be best to get a carriage.

Bazilio thought it preferable to walk as far as Largo do Loreto. It was such a pleasant evening! And the walk would do Dona Felicidade good!

Outside the Café Martinho, he suggested they stop and have a sorbet; but Dona Felicidade was afraid of the effects of the cold on her stomach, and Luiza felt too embarrassed. Through the open doors of the café could be seen much-thumbed newspapers lying on tabletops, and the odd individual, in white trousers, placidly eating a strawberry ice.

People were walking about under the trees in the Rossio; on the benches, motionless figures appeared to be sleeping; here and there a lighted cigarette glowed; men walked by, waistcoat undone, hat in hand, fanning themselves; and on every corner someone was selling cool water 'from the Arsenal'; open carriages drove slowly round the square. The sky hung heavy, and in the dark night, the column bearing the statue of Dom Pedro had the dull pallor of a vast, extinguished candle.

At Luiza's side, Bazilio was silent. 'What a ghastly city,' he was thinking. 'What a grim place!' And he thought of Paris in the summer, and how he used to ride slowly up the Champs-Elysées in his phaeton: there, hundreds of victorias trot discreetly and blithely up and down; and the carriage lamps fill the whole avenue with a jolly to-and-fro of little points of light; the charming white figures of women recline on sprung, cushioned seats; the air round about has a velvety softness, and the chestnut trees give off a subtle perfume. On either side, between the trees, one is regaled with the brash lights of cafés-concerts, full of the happy buzz of multitudes and the musical verve of orchestras; the restaurants glow; there is a sense of loving, happy life being intensely lived; and beyond, from behind the silk blinds of mansion windows comes the discreet, veiled light of opulent lives. Ah, if only he was there now! But as he passed beneath the street lamps, he glanced sideways at Luiza: beneath her white veil, her delicate profile looked so sweet; her dress neatly highlighted the curve of her breast; and there was a lassitude in her gait that gave a languid, alluring sway to her hips.

An idea struck him and he began to say: 'What a shame there is nowhere in the whole of Lisbon where one can dine on partridge washed down by a bottle of *champagne frappée!*'

Luiza did not reply. She merely thought: 'How delicious!' But Dona Felicidade exclaimed:

'Partridge at this hour!'

'Yes, partridge or something else.'

'Heavens! Whatever it was, I would simply explode!'

They walked up Rua Nova do Carmo. The street lamps gave off a dim light; the tall, darkened houses pressed in on either side, making the shadows still darker; and the heavily armed night patrol walked slowly and silently down the street, sinister and subtle.

In the Chiado, a boy in a blue beret pursued them, trying to sell them lottery tickets; his shrill, mournful voice promised them a fortune, many *contos de réis*. Dona Felicidade stopped, almost tempted . . . But at that point, the two ladies were much alarmed by the sight of a band of drunken youths coming unsteadily down the hill, their hats pushed back on their heads, and talking loudly. Luiza moved closer to Bazilio, Dona Felicidade anxiously grabbed his arm and wanted to find a carriage immediately; and all the way to Largo do Loreto, without once letting go of Bazilio's arm, she was anxiously explaining her great fear of drunks and retailing various violent incidents and knifings. From out of the line of old carriages beside the railings in Praça de Camões, an excitable coachman driving an open caleche suddenly emerged, standing up on the seat, hurriedly catching up the reins, wildly whipping the horses, and shouting:

'Here, sir, here!'

Bazilio and the two ladies stood for a moment talking. A man passed by and looked at them, and Luiza, in despair, recognised the ogling eyes of the man with the goatee beard.

They got into the caleche. Luiza turned round once to see Bazilio standing motionless in the square, his hat in his hand; then she settled back in her seat, placed her small feet on the seat opposite and, lulled by the easy trotting of the horses, she watched in silence as they passed the dark houses in Rua de São Roque, the trees in São Pedro de Alcântara, the narrow façades of Rua do Moinho do Vento, the sleeping gardens in Rua da Patriarcal. The soft, warm night was utterly still: and though she did not quite know why, she would have liked to have driven endlessly on like this along the streets, past railings revealing the leafy grounds of splendid houses, with no aim, no worries, towards some happy thing she could not quite discern! A group of young men outside the Politécnica were playing a *fado*, and the sound wafted into her soul like a soft breeze, gently stirring up all kinds of long-lost feelings; she sighed softly.

'A little sigh winging its way to the Alentejo,' said Dona Felicidade, patting her arm.

Luiza felt the blood rush to her face. The clocks were chiming eleven when she went into the house.

Juliana came to light her way. The tea was ready whenever madam wished.

Luiza went upstairs shortly afterwards wearing a loose, white robe, and sat down wearily in the wing chair; she felt sleepy, her head kept nodding, her eyes closing . . . And Juliana was taking so long with that tea. She called her. Where was she? Honestly!

Juliana had tiptoed downstairs to Luiza's room. And picking up the dress and the starched petticoats that Luiza had removed and thrown down on the chaise longue, she smoothed, scrutinised, examined them, and, with a particular idea in mind, she even sniffed them! There was a vague smell of warm, freshly washed skin, with just a hint of sweat and eau-de-cologne. When she heard her mistress's impatient calls, she raced upstairs to her. She had just gone downstairs to tidy up a little. Was it her tea she wanted? It was ready now.

And bringing in the toast, she said:

'Senhor Sebastião called, it must have been about nine o'clock.'

'What did you tell him?

'That madam had gone out with Senhora Dona Felicidade. I couldn't tell him where because I didn't know.'

And she added:

'Senhor Sebastião stayed here chatting to me. He was chatting to me for more than half an hour!'

The following morning, Luiza received a bouquet of magnificent, dark magenta roses from Sebastião. He grew them on his estate in Almada, and they were known as 'Dom Sebastião's roses'. She ordered them to be put in vases in the drawing room, and since, although the day was overcast, it was still suffocatingly hot, she said to Juliana:

'Open the windows, will you?'

'Aha,' thought Juliana, 'so Mr Slyboots is coming.'

'Mr Slyboots' duly arrived at three o'clock. Luiza was in the drawing room, playing the piano.

'It's that man again,' said Juliana.

Luiza turned round, blushing, shocked by the expression.

'Oh, you mean my cousin Bazilio. Ask him to come in.'

And she called after her:

'And if Senhor Sebastião comes or anyone else, be sure to send them in.'

So it was her cousin! The 'man' and his visits suddenly lost all their piquant interest. Her full-blown, fully inflated malice, crumpled like a sail when the wind drops. That was that, then. It was her cousin.

She went slowly up to the kitchen, a disappointed woman.

'Well, the big news, Senhora Joana, is that the fop turns out to be her cousin. She says it's her cousin Bazilio.'

And with a giggle, she added:

'Bazilio. Yes, it turns out that Bazilio is her cousin! Who'd have thought it!'

'Well, he was bound to be a relative of hers, wasn't he?' remarked Joana.

Juliana did not respond. She wanted to know if the iron was

ready because she had a mound of ironing to do. And she sat down at the window, waiting. The low, grey sky was heavy with electricity; an occasional sharp, sudden breeze sent a tremor through the trees in the gardens.

'Her cousin, huh!' she was thinking. 'And of course he just happens to visit when her husband's away. And she's all head-in-the-clouds when he leaves, and she's always demanding fresh underwear, here, there and everywhere, and then there's a new peignoir and a carriage to go out in, and the sighing and those dark shadows under her eyes! The slut! And it's all in the family!'

Her eyes glinted. She no longer felt quite so disappointed. There was still much to see and listen out for. Was the iron ready?

But the doorbell rang downstairs.

'Good grief, it never stops around here. And we're expected to do everything!'

She went downstairs and, seeing Julião standing there with a book under his arm, she exclaimed:

'Come in, Senhor Julião! Madam is with her cousin at the moment, but she said to show anyone else who called straight in!'

She flung open the drawing room door, without warning.

'Senhor Julião is here,' she said with satisfaction.

Luiza introduced the two men.

Bazilio rose languidly from the sofa and gazed in near hor- ror at Julião, taking in at a glance everything from his unruly hair to his scuffed boots.

'What a sloven!' he thought.

Luiza was acute enough to notice and she blushed, feeling ashamed of Julião, of this man with the grimy collar and the ancient, ill-made, black cloth jacket. What would Bazilio think of the people she knew, of the friends who visited the house! She felt her own chic drastically diminished. And instinctively, her face took on a reserved expression, as if she were surprised by this visit and appalled by the visitor's clothes!

Julião saw her embarrassment and said, awkwardly, adjust- ing his glasses:

'I was just passing and I dropped in to ask if you'd heard from Jorge.'

'Thank you. Yes, he says in his letters that he's fine.'

Bazilio lounged on the sofa with all the nonchalance of a close relative; he examined his own silk socks embroidered with small scarlet stars, and indolently smoothed his moustache, slightly cocking one little finger, on which glittered two thick gold rings, each set respectively with a sapphire and a ruby.

His affected pose and the flashing jewels irritated Julião.

Wanting to establish that he too was a close friend with his own rights, he said:

'I haven't been to see you before because I've been so busy.'

Luiza hurriedly tried to undermine this attempt at familiarity.

'I haven't been well myself. In fact, I haven't been receiving visitors at all, apart from my cousin, of course!'

Julião felt rejected and betrayed. He said nothing, but sat bouncing one leg up and down, the book still resting on his knee, his face bright red with surprise and indignation; his trousers were too short and revealed the fraying elastic on his old boots.

There was a constrained silence.

'Lovely roses!' Bazilio drawled.

'Yes, aren't they?' replied Luiza.

She felt sorry for Julião now and struggled to find something to say; at last she blurted out:

'And it's been so hot! Unbearable! Has there been a lot of illness?'

'A bit of nausea and diarrhoea,' said Julião. 'Mostly from eating too much fruit. Stomach upsets.'

Luiza lowered her eyes. Bazilio then started talking about the Viscountess de Azeias: she had aged terribly, he thought; and what had become of her older sister?

This conversation about aristocrats whom he did not know made Julião feel even more excluded; he felt the sweat trickling down his neck; he tried to come up with some aphorism, some ironic remark, some witty saying, and meanwhile kept mechanically opening and closing the fat book with its yellow covers.

'Is that a novel?' Luiza asked him.

'No, it's a treatise by Dr Lee on diseases of the womb.'

Luiza turned scarlet, as did Julião, furious with himself for uttering that word. Bazilio smiled and then asked after one Dona Rafaela Grijó who used to be a regular visitor to Rua da Madalena; she wore glasses and had a brother-in-law who stuttered . . .

'Oh, her husband died and she married her brother-in-law.'

'The one with the stutter?'

'Yes, they've got a little boy now, and he stutters too.'

'Their family conversations must be something to behold! And what about Dona Eugénia, the one from Braga?'

Exasperated, Julião got up and in a hoarse, nervous voice said:

'I'm in a hurry, I'm afraid, I can't stop. Give Jorge my regards when you next write to him, won't you?'

He nodded briefly to Bazilio, but couldn't find his hat, which had rolled underneath the chair. He then got caught up in the door curtain, bumped into the door itself and finally flounced out, feeling desperate and vengeful, hating Luiza, Jorge, luxury, life, and brimming now with ironic remarks, aphorisms and witty ripostes. He should have crushed them, the ass and the ninny . . . But absolutely nothing had occurred to him!

As soon as Julião had closed the door, Bazilio stood up and, folding his arms, asked:

'Who is that slovenly individual?'

Luiza flushed and stammered:

'He's a young doctor . . .'

'How ridiculous, you mean he's a student!'

'Poor thing, he doesn't have much money.'

But you didn't need money to brush your jacket and rid yourself of dandruff! She should not receive such a man! It brought shame on the house. If her husband was so very fond of him, then he should receive him in his study!

He was striding agitatedly about the room, his hands in his pockets, jingling his money and his keys.

'You certainly have some rather louche friends!' he went on. 'Damn it, this isn't how you were brought up! You never had people like that visiting Rua da Madalena.'

It was true, they had not, and it seemed to her that, since her marriage, her circle of acquaintances had become more plebeian. But respect for Jorge's opinions and tastes prompted her to say:

'They say he has great talent . . .'

'He'd be better off with a new pair of boots.'

Luiza, out of cowardice, agreed.

'I must admit I do find him a bit odd,' she said.

'He's absolutely ghastly, my dear!'

Those last two words made her heart beat faster. That is what he used to call her, before. There was a moment's silence, then the door bell rang loudly.

Luiza was terrified. Oh no, what if it was Sebastião? Bazilio would find him even more vulgar. But Juliana announced:

'It's Councillor Acácio, madam. Shall I ask him to come in?'

'Yes, of course,' Luiza exclaimed.

And the tall figure of Acácio entered, with the lapels of his alpaca jacket thrown back and his stiff white trousers neatly covering the tops of his lace-up shoes.

As soon as Luiza introduced cousin Bazilio to him, Acácio said respectfully:

'I knew of your arrival already, sir, I read about it in one of the many interesting news items furnished by our society columns. But tell me, madam, how is Jorge?'

Jorge was in Beja. Terribly bored.

Bazilio, in more friendly mode, remarked:

'I really have no idea what one could possibly do in Beja. It must be horrendous!'

The Councillor, smoothing his moustache with one white hand, the hand that bore his signet ring, replied:

'It is, nevertheless, the district capital!'

But there was nothing to do even in Lisbon, and that was

the national capital! Bazilio, leaning back, tugged at the cuffs of his shirt. One could die of boredom here.

Pleased to find Bazilio so affable, Luiza laughed:

'Don't say that in front of the Councillor. He's a great admirer of Lisbon.'

Acácio bowed.

'Yes, dear lady, I was born in Lisbon and have a deep regard for the city.'

Then he went on with great bonhomie:

'I recognise, however, that it cannot compare with the Parises, Londons and Madrids of this world . . .'

'Naturally,' said Luiza.

And the Councillor continued grandly:

'Lisbon, however, enjoys certain unrivalled beauties! The entrance from the sea, they say (although I myself have never entered the city from that direction) offers a magnificent panorama to rival that of the Constantinoples and the Naples of this world. Worthy of the pen of a Garrett or a Lamartine! Enough to inspire a great genius!'

Fearing a flood of literary quotations and opinions, Luiza interrupted him and asked what he had been up to. She and Dona Felicidade had been to the Passeio Público on Sunday, hoping to see him, but not a sign.

He never went there on a Sunday, he said. It was, he agreed, most pleasant, but the crowd made him positively dizzy. He had noticed – and he spoke in the measured tones of one about to make some astonishing revelation – he had noticed that being in the presence of a great many people all in one place often provoked feelings of dizziness in men of a studious bent. He complained too of his health and of pressure of work. He was compiling a book and taking Vichy water.

'You can smoke, if you like,' Luiza said suddenly, smiling at Bazilio. 'Do you need a match?'

She herself sprang lightly and gaily to her feet to fetch him one. She was wearing a pale-coloured dress, slightly transparent and very cool. Her hair looked fairer and her skin softer.

Bazilio exhaled the smoke from his cigar, leaned back and declared:

'The Passeio Público on a Sunday is quite simply idiotic!'

The Councillor pondered and replied:

'I would not put it in quite such severe terms, Senhor Brito!' However, it did seem to him that it had once been a more pleasant experience. In the first place – he exclaimed with great conviction, drawing himself up – because nothing, absolutely nothing, could beat the Navy band! Then there was the question of prices . . . Oh, he had studied the matter closely! Low prices were bound to encourage the subaltern classes to gather together. Not that he would dream of casting aspersions on that section of the population. He was known for his liberal views on the matter. 'You have only to ask Senhora Dona Luiza,' he said. But it was, after all, always so much more agreeable to find oneself amongst a select group! As for himself, he never went to the Passeio now. No, hard though it was to believe, not even when there were fireworks! Although he did go and stand outside the railings to watch. Not for financial reasons. Oh, no. He might not be rich, but he could afford that small expense. It was simply that he feared accidents. He feared them greatly. He told the story of a man, whose name escaped him now, whose skull had been pierced by a rocket. And nothing could be easier than for a spark to fall on one's face, or on one's new over-coat. 'It is always best to be prudent,' he concluded decisively, wiping his lips with a very crumpled Indian silk handkerchief.

They went on to discuss Lisbon in the summer; a lot of people had gone to Sintra; and, besides, Lisbon at that time of year was such a bore! And the Councillor affirmed that Lisbon only came into its true magnificent self when the government was sitting and the Teatro de São Carlos was open!

'What were you playing when I came in, Luiza?' Bazilio asked.

The Councillor immediately said:

'Oh, if you were playing music, then pray continue. I have been a subscriber to the Teatro de São Carlos for eighteen years . . .'

Bazilio broke in:

'Do you play yourself?'

'Oh, I used to. I certainly don't conceal the fact. Yes, as a young man, I played the flute.'

And he added with a benevolent gesture:

'Boyish larks! Were you playing something new, Dona Luiza?'

'No! It's an old favourite: "The Fisherman's Daughter" by Meyerbeer! I've got the translation of the words.'

She had closed the windows and sat down at the piano.

'Sebastião plays this beautifully, doesn't he, Councillor?'

'Our Sebastião,' said the Councillor authoritatively, 'is a rival to all your Thalbergs and Liszts. Do you know our Sebastião?' he asked Bazilio.

'No, I don't.'

'A pearl amongst men!'

Bazilio had gone slowly over to the piano, twirling his moustache.

'Do you still sing?' Luiza asked him, smiling.

'Only when I'm on my own.'

But the Councillor immediately asked him to sing something. Bazilio laughed. He was afraid he might scandalise an old subscriber to the Teatro de São Carlos.

The Councillor urged him, adding paternally:

'Courage, Senhor Brito, courage!'

Luiza played the opening notes.

And Bazilio began singing in a full, rich, baritone voice, and the room rang with the top notes. The Councillor, sitting upright in his armchair, was listening with great attention; his forehead, creased into a frown, seemed bowed beneath the responsibilities of a judge; and the tinted lenses of his spectacles stood out darkly against his bald physiognomy, made paler by the heat.

Bazilio sang the song's long first phrase with a melancholy gravity:

> Just like the dark, dark sea
> My heart too has its deeps . . .

A poet, out of some obscure sense of devotion, had translated the words for the *Women's Journal*. Luiza had added them to the music in her own hand. Bazilio, bent over the pages, still twirling the ends of his moustaches, sang:

> It has its storms and rages
> And tears like pearls it weeps!

Luiza kept her large eyes firmly on the music, occasionally glancing up at Bazilio. When it came to the long, final note, like the complaint of a supplicant lover, Bazilio sang pleadingly:

> Come, come,
> O my best beloved,
> Press thy breast to mine . . .

and his eyes fixed on her with such a look of desire that Luiza's breast rose and fell very fast, and her fingers fumbled over the keys.

The Councillor applauded.

'Admirable!' he cried. 'Admirable!'

Bazilio modestly demurred.

'No, sir!' protested Acácio, getting up. 'You have a very fine organ there; indeed, I would go so far as to say that you have the finest organ in Lisbon society.'

Bazilio laughed. Since he had made such a good impression, he would sing them a Brazilian *modinha* from Bahia. He sat down at the piano, and after playing the opening notes of a swaying, rhythmic, tropical melody, he began:

> My skin may be black, but my black heart
> feels more than any white heart can . . .

Breaking off, he said:

'This was all the rage at parties in Bahia when I left.'

It told the story of a young black woman born in the countryside and who, in rather clichéd lyrical terms, recounts her passion for a white farm manager.

Bazilio parodied the sentimental tones of a young Bahian woman, and his voice took on a wonderfully comic note when he sang the tearful refrain:

> And the black girl's eyes
> Gaze out at the waves so strong;
> While in a tall palm tree
> The bellbird sings its song.

The Councillor found it 'delicious'; but the song set him off, as he stood there in the drawing room, on the lamentable condition of slaves in Brazil. Brazilian friends assured him that the blacks were treated very well, but civilisation was civilisation, and slavery was a blot on any civilised society. He had, nevertheless, every confidence in the emperor.

'A monarch of rare enlightenment,' he added respectfully.

He went to get his hat and pressing it to his chest, he bowed, declaring that it had been a long time since he had spent such a satisfying afternoon. There was nothing like good conversation and good music.

'Where are you staying, Senhor Brito?'

Oh, please, he mustn't worry about him. He was staying at the Hotel Central.

Nothing would prevent him from fulfilling his social duties, declared Acácio. Nothing! He was a man of little account, as Senhora Dona Luiza well knew. 'But if you need anything, information, an introduction to some regional official, permission to visit a public amenity, I am at your service!'

And still holding Bazilio's hand in his, he added.

'Rua do Ferregial de Cima, number 3, third floor. A hermit's modest refuge.'

He bowed once more to Luiza.

'And when you next write to our traveller, do please send him my sincerest wishes for the success of his enterprise. Your servant!'

And, very erect and very serious, he left.

'Well, at least he's clean,' muttered Bazilio, a cigar in the corner of his mouth.

He had sat down again at the piano and was running his fingers up and down the keys. Luiza went over to him.

'Sing something, Bazilio!'

Bazilio gave her a long look.

Luiza blushed and smiled; the soft, milky skin of her throat and arms was visible through the pale, sheer fabric of her dress; and there was a vibrancy and a kind of amorous excitement in her eyes and in the warm colour of her cheeks.

Bazilio said to her softly:

'You look very happy today, Luiza.'

His eager gaze troubled her; she said again:

'Sing something.'

Her chest rose and fell.

'No, you sing something.'

Very slowly, he took her hand. Their two slightly damp, slightly tremulous palms met.

Outside, the bell rang. Luiza quickly withdrew her hand.

'There's someone at the door,' she said anxiously.

Low voices could be heard on the landing.

Bazilio gave an irritated shrug and picked up his hat.

'You're not going, are you?' she cried desolately.

'I certainly am! I can't get a moment alone with you!'

The door banged shut.

'It wasn't anyone important,' said Luiza, 'they've gone.'

They were standing up in the middle of the drawing room.

'Don't go, Bazilio!'

Her deep eyes looked at him sweetly, imploringly.

Bazilio put his hat down on the piano; he was nervously biting his moustache.

'And why do you want to be alone with me?' asked Luiza. 'What does it matter if there are other people here?' But she immediately regretted her words.

Bazilio, in one brusque movement, put his arm about her shoulders, took her face in his hands and covered her forehead, eyes, hair with voracious kisses.

She pulled away, trembling, her cheeks scarlet.

'Forgive me,' he cried passionately. 'Forgive me. I didn't mean to, but I adore you, Luiza!'

He took her hands masterfully, almost proprietorially in his.

'No, you must hear me out. From that first day when I saw you again, I've been mad about you, just as I used to be, exactly the same. I've never stopped loving you. But, as you well know, I had no money, and I wanted you to be rich and happy. I couldn't take you with me to Brazil. It would have killed you, my love! You can't imagine what it's like out there. That's why I wrote you that letter, but how I've suffered, the tears I've shed!'

Luiza was listening to him, motionless, her head bowed, looking at nothing in particular; that warm, strong voice, which touched her with its loving breath, was controlling her, subduing her; and Bazilio's hands filled hers with their fever-ish heat; she was overwhelmed by a sense of lassitude, almost as if she were about to fall asleep.

'Speak! Answer!' he said urgently, shaking her hands, eagerly seeking her eyes.

'What do you want me to say?' she murmured.

Her voice had the abstract sound of one barely awake.

And slowly detaching herself from him, she turned away:

'Let's talk about something else!'

Reaching out his arms to her, he stammered:

'Luiza! Luiza!'

'No, Bazilio, no!'

And in her voice there was just the slightest trace of a lament, the softness of a caress.

He did not hesitate; he took her in his arms.

Luiza remained inert, her lips white, her eyes closed, and Bazilio, placing one hand on her forehead, leaned her head back and slowly kissed her eyelids, her cheek, then kissed her long and deep upon her lips; her lips half-opened, her knees gave beneath her.

Then suddenly her whole body stiffened indignantly, and she turned away, gasping:

'Stop it, stop it!'

She was filled by nervous energy; she extricated herself from his embrace, pushing him away; passing her hands over her head and her hair, she muttered:

'Oh my God, how awful! Leave me alone! It's too awful!'

He walked towards her, teeth gritted, but Luiza drew back, saying:

'Go away! What do you want? Go away! What are you doing here? Leave me alone!'

He tried to calm her, his voice suddenly serene and humble. He didn't understand. Why was she so angry? What did a kiss matter? He asked for nothing more. Whatever was she thinking? He adored her, it was true, but he adored her with a pure heart.

'I swear it!' he said vehemently, striking his chest.

He made her sit on the sofa and sat down next to her. He spoke very rationally. He saw how things were and he was resigned to it. They would be like brother and sister, nothing more.

She was listening to him as if in a daze.

His passion for her was a terrible torment to him, but he was strong, he would learn to bear it. All he wanted was to come and see her and talk to her. His would be an ideal love. And his eyes devoured her.

He turned her hand palm uppermost, bent over and kissed it hard. She shivered and sprang to her feet:

'No! Go away!'

'All right. I'll say goodbye, then.'

He got up sadly, reluctantly. Then, unhurriedly brushing the silk of his hat, he said again, in melancholy tones:

'Goodbye, then.'

'Goodbye.'

Bazilio said very tenderly:

'You're not angry with me, are you?'

'No!'

'Listen,' he murmured, approaching her once more.

Luiza stamped her foot.

'Please, leave me now and come back tomorrow. Goodbye. Go away! Tomorrow!'

'Tomorrow!' he said softly.

And with that he left.

Luiza went into her bedroom in a state of great agitation.

However, as she walked past the mirror, she was surprised at what she saw: she had never seen herself looking so lovely! She took a few more steps in silence.

Juliana was sorting out underwear in one of the wardrobe drawers.

'Who was it who rang just now?' asked Luiza.

'It was Senhor Sebastião. He didn't want to come in; he said he would come back.'

He had indeed said that he would come back. But he was beginning to feel almost embarrassed by the fact that he had been to see her every day and found each time that she had 'a visitor'.

He had been surprised the first time when Juliana said: 'She's with a man, a young man. He was here yesterday too.' Who could he be? He knew all the friends of the house. Perhaps it was some clerk from the Ministry or the owner of a mine, Alonso's son perhaps, doubtless something to do with Jorge . . .

Then on Sunday night, he had brought her the score of Gounod's *Romeo and Juliet* that she had so wanted to hear, and when Juliana told him from the balcony that 'she had gone out with Dona Felicidade in a carriage', he had felt very foolish standing there, slowly scratching his beard, with the large score clasped beneath his arm. Where could they have gone? He remembered Dona Felicidade's enthusiasm for the Teatro de Dona Maria. But they would hardly go to the theatre alone, in this July heat! But it was possible. He went there just in case.

The half-deserted theatre presented a gloomy picture; there was the occasional ugly family occupying one of the boxes, the women with their very black hair bulked out with false topknots, taking grim pleasure in their Sunday night out; in the stalls, along the largely empty benches, prematurely aged people with inexpressive faces sat looking hot and bored, occasionally wiping the sweat from their necks with silk handkerchiefs; in the gallery sat swarthy, oily-skinned workers with wide, dark eyes; even the light seemed half-asleep;

there was much yawning. The scene on stage was a yellow ballroom where a bemedalled old man was addressing a thin young girl with curly hair, talking on and on in the dilute tones of warm, greasy water being poured out of a jug.

Sebastião left. Where could they be? He found out the following day. He was walking down Rua do Moinho do Vento just as one of his neighbours, Neto, was walking up, hunched beneath his sunshade, and with a cigar protruding from one corner of his greying moustache. Neto stopped him to say:

'Do you know, last night I saw Dona Luiza with a young man I'm sure I know, but I can't for the life of me think where I know his face from.'

Sebastião shrugged.

'A tall, handsome young man, with a foreign look about him. I know him from somewhere. I saw him going into the house the other day. Have you any idea who he is?'

Sebastião did not.

'I know that face. I've been racking my brain to remember.' He stroked his head with one hand. 'I know that face! He's from Lisbon. He's definitely from Lisbon!'

And after a silence, he twirled his parasol and asked:

'So, have you any other news, Sebastião?'

Sebastião did not.

'No, nor me!'

He yawned loudly:

'God, this is a boring place!'

That afternoon, at four o'clock, Sebastião had gone back to Luiza's house. The 'man' was there again! Sebastião was genuinely worried now. It must be something to do with Jorge's work; for Sebastião could not imagine that Luiza could talk about, feel or experience anything that was not in the interests of the house and of Jorge's greater happiness. But it must be very serious indeed to require so many visits, meetings and reports. Jorge must have important deals about which he knew nothing. This struck him as ungrateful on Jorge's part and as a diminution of their friendship.

His housekeeper Tia Joana found him sunk in gloom.

The next day he learned that 'the man' was cousin Bazilio, Bazilio de Brito. His vague displeasure vanished, but a more clearly defined fear took its place.

Sebastião did not know Bazilio personally, but he was familiar with the chronicle of his youth. It did not, it is true, involve any great scandal or poignant romance. Bazilio had merely been something of a hellraiser and, as such, had worked his way methodically through all the usual episodes of Lisbon debauchery: games of monte until dawn with some nabobs from the Alentejo; a horse-drawn cab wrecked one Saturday at the bullfight; frequent suppers with an ancient Spanish Lola and an equally ancient lobster salad; a bit of derring-do in the bullring in Salvaterra or in Alhandra for which he won applause; nights spent in rough taverns, eating salt cod and drinking Colares wine; much playing of the guitar; a couple of well-placed blows delivered to the astonished face of a police officer; and plenty of raw eggs thrown during the height of carnival. The only actual women who appeared in this saga, apart from the usual aforesaid Lolas and Carmens, were Pistelli, a German dancer who had the muscled legs of an athlete, and the mad Countess de Alvim, a great horsewoman, who had left her husband, after first whipping him soundly, and who had dressed up as a man so that she could herself drive a carriage from Rossio to Dafundo. This was quite enough for Sebastião to consider Bazilio a debauchee and a roué; he had heard that Bazilio had gone to Brazil in order to flee his creditors, that he had got rich purely by chance, in some speculative deal in Paraguay, and that, even in Bahia, when he was on his uppers, he had never been a hard worker; and he imagined that, for a man like Bazilio, the possession of a fortune would mean only a proliferation of his vices. And this same man was now going to visit Luiza every day and spending hours and hours there and following her to the Passeio Público.

But why? Obviously in order to lead her astray.

He was walking down the street, bent beneath the heavy weight of these ideas, when a voice husky with catarrh said respectfully:

'Senhor Sebastião!'

It was Senhor Paula from the junk shop.

'Greetings, Senhor João.'

Senhor Paula spat out a dark stream of saliva onto the cobbles and, with his hands clasped behind him, beneath the tails of his long cotton jacket, he said gravely:

'Is someone ill at the Engineer's house, Senhor Sebastião?'

Much surprised, Sebastião said:

'No. Why?'

Paula snorted and spat again.

'It's just that I've seen a man going in there every day. And I assumed he was a doctor.'

Clearing his throat once more, he went on:

'You know, one of those new homeopathic ones.'

Sebastião had coloured.

'No,' he said. 'He's Dona Luiza's cousin.'

'Oh,' said Paula. 'I thought ... Forgive me, Senhor Sebastião.'

And he bowed respectfully.

'So, the gossip has started already!' Sebastião was thinking.

He went into his own house, feeling most unhappy.

He lived at the bottom of the street, in an old house with a garden.

Sebastião was all alone in the world. He had a modest fortune in government bonds, some agricultural land near Seixal and the Rosegal estate in Almada. His two maid-servants had worked for the family for years. Vicência, the cook, was a black woman from São Tomé and had originally worked for his mother. Tia Joana, his old nanny, had served him for thirty-five years; she still referred to him as Master Sebastião; she could sometimes be as giddy as a girl, but he always treated her with as much respect as if she were his grandmother. She was from Oporto, or Opooartoo, as she pronounced it, for she had never lost her Minho accent. Sebastião's friends said she was like a character out of a play. She was short and stout, and had a very kindly smile; her hair, white as flax, was caught up in a bun on top of her head and held in place with an old tortoiseshell comb; she always wore a large, spotlessly clean shawl tied across her chest. And she spent all day shuffling about the house, rattling her bunch of keys, muttering proverbs and taking snuff from a round box on which was carved a tiny image of the suspension bridge in Oporto.

The house itself had a gentle, old-fashioned air: in the visiting room, which was only rarely used, the vast sofa and armchairs had the stiff appearance of the days of Dom José I, and the faded red damask upholstery was reminiscent of the grandeur of a decadent court; the dining room walls were hung with engravings depicting Napoleon's first battles, all of which included a white horse standing on a hill towards which a hussar was galloping at breakneck speed, brandishing a sabre. Sebastião slept his dreamless seven hours' sleep in an ancient bed made from carved blackwood; and in a dark little room, beneath the subtle sounds of mice scrabbling in the rafters, on a chest of drawers with gold metal handles, there stood, as he had for years, the patron saint of the house, St Sebastian, bristling with arrows and struggling against the cords that bound him to the tree trunk, and lit by an oil lamp carefully tended by Tia Joana.

House and owner were perfectly suited. Sebastião was an old-fashioned fellow. He was solitary and shy. In Latin classes they used to call him 'the Mouse'; they pinned tails on him and brazenly stole his food at mealtimes. Though possessed of a gymnast's strength, Sebastião had the resigned nature of a martyr.

In secondary school, he failed all his exams. He was an intelligent enough boy, but a single question, the glitter of the teacher's spectacles, the great expanse of blackboard, made him freeze; he would remain stubbornly silent, scratching his knees, his face swollen and red, his eyes vacant.

His mother, who came from a village where she had worked as a baker, and was very proud of her government bonds, her garden, her damask furniture, her silk dresses and her beringed fingers, used to say:

'He's got enough to eat and drink, so why torment the child with studying! Leave him be!'

Sebastião was very drawn to music. On the advice of Jorge's mother – her neighbour and close friend – Sebastião's mother found him a piano teacher; from the very first lessons, which she attended, adorned in red velvet and jewels, the old teacher Aquiles Bentes, with his owl-like face and round spectacles, had exclaimed excitedly, in his nasal voice:

'My dear lady, your child is a genius! A genius! He'll be another Rossini! He must be encouraged! We must urge him on!'

But that was precisely what she did not want; she did not want to urge him on to do anything, poor love. And that is why he did not become another Rossini; still, out of habit, old Bentes continued to say:

'He'll be another Rossini! He'll be another Rossini!'

Except that, instead of shouting it out and brandishing his sheet music, he would mutter it to himself, meanwhile yawning widely like a bored lion.

Even then, the two young neighbours, Jorge and Sebastião, were the best of friends. Jorge was the livelier and more inventive of the two, and he it was who dominated Sebastião. When they played in the garden, Sebastião was always the horse to Jorge's driver and carriage, and, in any wars, he was always the side that lost. Sebastião it was who carried any heavy weights, offered his back for Jorge to climb on and, at picnics, he ate all the bread, while Jorge ate all the fruit. They grew up, and that unchanging friendship, with never a falling-out, became an essential, permanent feature in the lives of both men.

When Jorge's mother died, they even thought of moving in together; they would live in Sebastião's house, which was more spacious and had a garden; Jorge had even planned to buy a horse; but then he met Luiza in the Passeio Público and, two months later, he was spending nearly all his time at her house in Rua da Madalena.

The whole jolly 'Sebastião and Jorge Society', as they laughingly used to call it, collapsed, like a house of cards. Sebastião was deeply saddened.

And yet he was the one who, later on, provided the

bouquets of roses for Jorge to take to Luiza, lovingly wrapped in tissue paper and with the thorns carefully removed. He was the one who took charge of decorating their 'nest', who chivvied the upholsterers, discussed the price of bedlinen, oversaw the work of the carpet-fitters, found servants, and sorted out all the paperwork for the wedding.

And at night, like a weary, devoted procurator, he would then have to listen with a smile on his face to Jorge's happy outpourings, as he paced about the room in his shirtsleeves until two o'clock in the morning, lovesick, loquacious and flourishing his pipe!

After the marriage, Sebastião felt very alone. He went to Portel to visit an uncle, an eccentric old man with wild eyes, who spent all his time grafting fruit trees and reading and re-reading Alexandre Herculano's novel *Eurico the Priest*. When he returned a month later, Jorge declared joyfully:

'This is your home now, you know. This is where you live.'

But he never managed to convince Sebastião that it truly was his home. Sebastião would knock timidly at the door. He would blush in Luiza's presence; the old Mouse of the Latin classes resurfaced. Jorge had to struggle to make him relax enough to cross his legs and smoke his pipe in front of her, and not to be constantly half getting up from his seat and addressing her as 'madam'.

He had to be coerced into coming to supper. When Jorge was not there, his visits were brief and full of silences. He felt clumsy and ill-dressed and was afraid he might bore her.

That afternoon, when he went into the dining room, Tia Joana came to ask after Luiza.

She adored her and thought her an 'angel', a 'lily'.

'How is she? Did you see her?'

Sebastião blushed, he did not want to say, as he had on the previous night, that he had not gone in because she had a visitor; instead, bending down and stroking the ears of his old pointer 'Trajan', he said:

'She's fine, Tia Joana, fine. Why shouldn't she be? She's in excellent form.'

★

112

At that same hour, Luiza had received a letter from Jorge. It was from Portel, full of complaints about the heat, about the bad inns he was obliged to stay at, and tales about Sebastião's eccentric uncle, and it closed with much love and many kisses.

She had not expected the letter, and that sheet of paper covered in tiny, neat writing, which brought Jorge so vividly to life before her – the way he stood, the way he looked at her, his tenderness towards her – filled her with a sensation akin to pain. The shame of her cowardly, swooning acquiescence to Bazilio's kisses welled up in her and made her cheeks flame! How could she have allowed herself to be embraced and held like that! The things he had said to her on the sofa, his eyes almost devouring her! She remembered it all: how he had sat, the warmth of his hands, the tremor in his voice . . . And, mechanically, gradually, her eyes languid, her arms limp by her sides, she allowed herself to become immersed in those memories, abandoning herself to the delicious lassitude they provoked in her. But then the idea of Jorge returned like the crack of a whip. She sat up suddenly and paced nervously around the room, feeling a vague desire to cry.

'No, this is awful, awful!' she was saying to herself out loud. 'It must end now!'

She decided not to receive Bazilio again, to write to him and ask him not to come back, to leave! She even pondered the words she would use; she would be brief and cold, she would not call him 'My dear cousin,' simply 'Cousin Bazilio'.

And what would he do when he got the letter? He would weep, poor love!

She imagined him alone in his hotel room, pale and unhappy; and from there, sliding down the slopes of sentiment, she went on to thinking about his actual person, his persuasive voice, his disquieting, dominating eyes, and her mind lingered on those memories with a feeling of happiness, like a hand absent-mindedly stroking the soft plumage of some rare bird. She shook her head impatiently, as if those imaginings were the stings of importunate insects; she forced herself to think only of Jorge, but the bad ideas kept biting her;

and she felt very sorry for herself, not knowing what she wanted, torn between confused desires to be with Jorge, to consult Leopoldina, to run away somewhere, anywhere, far away. Oh, she was so unhappy! And from the depths of her lazy nature came an obscure sense of resentment against Jorge, against Bazilio, against feelings, against duties, against everything that upset her and made her suffer. If only they would leave her alone!

Sitting at the window after supper, she started re-reading Jorge's letter. She deliberately made herself remember all the things she loved about him, about his body, about his many qualities. And she piled up random reasons, some based on honour, others on sentiment, as to why she should love and respect him. This was all happening because he was away in the provinces! If he were there with her . . . But to go so far away and take so long to come back! And yet, at the same time, against her will, the certain knowledge of his absence gave her a sense of freedom; the idea of being able to move freely about amongst her desires and interests filled her breast with a great sense of contentment, like a gust of independence.

But then what use was it to her being free and alone? And suddenly everything that she could do, feel and possess appeared to her in the form of a broad, glowing prospect; it was like a door, suddenly opened and then closed, that allowed her a glimpse of something vague and marvellous that pulsated and glittered. Oh, she must be mad!

It had grown dark. She went into the drawing room and opened the window; outside, the night was hot and thick, the air electric with the promise of thunder and lightning. She found it hard to breathe, she looked up at the sky, wanting something intensely, but not knowing what that something was.

The baker's boy in the street down below was, as always, playing a *fado*; those banal sounds penetrated her soul with the softness of a warm breeze and the melancholy of a mournful cry.

She listlessly rested her head on her hand. A thousand tiny

thoughts rushed into her mind like the dancing, fading points of light on a burning piece of paper; she remembered her mother, the new hat Madame François had sent her, wondered what the weather would be like now in Sintra, and imagined the sweetness of those warm nights beneath the thickly leaved trees.

She closed the window and stretched; and then, in her bedroom, on the chaise longue, she sat utterly still, thinking about Jorge, about writing to him and asking him to come home. Very soon, however, this absorption began to fray like a piece of cloth being ripped slowly apart, and behind it, intensely bright and strong, appeared the idea of cousin Bazilio.

His travels and all the seas he had crossed had made his skin darker; the melancholy of separation had given him a few white hairs. He had suffered for her, he said. And where was the harm in it anyway? He had sworn to her that his love was chaste, that it resided entirely in his heart. He had come all the way from Paris, the poor boy, in order to see her for a week or two weeks; he had sworn that this was so. Was she to tell him: 'Don't come back, go away'?

'Whenever you're ready for your tea, madam . . .' Juliana said from the door.

Luiza gave a loud sigh as if just waking up. No tea, but Juliana should bring her the lamp later on.

It was ten o'clock. Juliana went to drink her tea in the kitchen. The fire was burning out, and the oil lamp cast a reddish light on the copper pots.

'Something happened today, Senhora Joana,' said Juliana, sitting down. 'She's all up in the air! And she keeps sighing! Oh, yes, something definitely happened, something big!'

Joana, sitting opposite, elbows on the table and her cheeks resting on her fists, was blinking sleepily.

'You always look for the bad in things, Senhora Juliana,' she said.

'But you'd have to be a fool not to see it, Senhora Joana!'

She stopped talking and sniffed the sugar; this was one of

her many gripes; she like refined sugar and hated this coarse muscovado stuff, which made the tea taste of ants.

'This sugar is even worse than last month's! But then, I suppose, poor wretches like me can expect no better!' she muttered bitterly.

And after a brief pause, she said again:

'You'd have to be a fool not to see it, Senhora Joana!'

The cook said lazily:

'Each person knows himself . . .'

'. . . and God knows all,' sighed Juliana.

And with that they fell silent.

Luiza rang the bell from downstairs.

'Now what? God, she's impatient!'

She went down and came back, greatly annoyed, carrying the watering can:

'She wants more water! What does she want to go splashing around at midnight for! Honestly, it has to be seen to be believed.'

She went to fill up the watering can, and while the water from the tap drummed on the tin bottom, she said:

'And tomorrow for breakfast she wants some fried ham, the salted kind. She fancies something savoury!'

She added scornfully:

'The things they come out with! She fancies something savoury!'

By midnight the house was asleep and in darkness. Outside, the sky had grown still blacker; there was a flash of lightning and an echoing crack of thunder.

Luiza started awake; a loud, pounding rain had begun to fall; the thunder was still rumbling somewhere off in the distance. She lay for a moment listening to the raindrops falling on the paving stones; it was so stiflingly hot in the bedroom that she pushed back the sheet; sleep had fled and she lay on her back with her eyes fixed on the faint light emanating from outside and from the nightlight, listening to the tick-tock of the clock. She yawned and stretched, and an idea, a vision, began to form inside her brain, an idea that took such clear, almost visible shape that she turned slowly over in bed, reached out her arms and put them around the pillow, her dry lips open . . . to kiss a dark head of hair in which shone a few white strands.

Sebastião had slept badly. He woke at six and went out into the garden in his slippers. The French windows in the dining room opened onto a small terrace, just big enough for three painted, wrought-iron chairs and a few pots of carnations; from there, four stone steps led down into the garden; it was a vegetable-plot-cum-flower garden, packed with flower beds and carefully watered lettuces, with climbing roses on the walls, a well, a pond beneath a vine trellis and some trees; at the far end was another terrace, shaded by a lime tree, with a balustrade that looked down onto a quiet street below; opposite was another whitewashed garden wall. It was a secluded place, which had about it an almost rustic peace. Sebastião would often go there early in the morning to smoke a cigarette.

It was a delightful day. The air was crisp and transparent; up above, the sky formed a dome – of a blue only to be found in certain old porcelain – dotted here and there with the occasional small, milk-white, cottony cloud, vaguely cylindrical in shape; the leaves were of a bright, newly-washed green; the water in the tank was cold and crystalline; birds chirruped and called as they flew swiftly about.

Sebastião was standing looking down at the street, when, cutting through the cool silence, came the regular sound of a walking stick and slow, hesitant steps. It was a neighbour of Jorge's, Cunha Rosado, the one with digestive problems; he was shuffling along, all hunched and bundled up in a scarf and a dark red overcoat, his greying beard uncombed and badly in need of a trim.

'Up already, my friend!' said Sebastião.

Cunha Rosado stopped and slowly raised his head.

'Oh, it's you Sebastião,' he said in a mournful voice. 'I'm just out for my constitutional.'

'On foot?'

'I used to ride on my donkey as far as the outskirts of the city, but apparently a little walk is better for me.'

He shrugged sadly, a look of doubt and dejection on his face.

'How are you?' asked Sebastião kindly, leaning further out over the balustrade.

A desolate smile appeared on Cunha's pale lips:

'Oh, on the downward slope.'

Sebastião coughed, embarrassed, unable to think of any consoling words.

But there was a sudden glimmer of interest in the ailing man's dull eyes, as he stood, both hands resting on his walking stick.

'By the way, Sebastião, that tall young man I've seen going into Jorge's house every day, isn't he Bazilio de Brito? Dona Luiza's cousin? João de Brito's son?'

'Yes, he is, why?'

Cunha gave a satisfied 'Aha!'

'That's what I said!' he exclaimed. 'That's what I said. But that stubborn woman just wouldn't have it, oh no!'

And then he went on to explain in a sudden torrent of words, pausing every now and then to catch his breath:

'My room looks out onto the street and every day, since I'm almost always at my window, just passing the time . . . I've seen this rather foreign-looking young man going in there . . . every day! "That's Bazilio de Brito!" I said. But my wife said no, it wasn't! "Don't be so stupid, man!" I was almost sure . . . And I should know! He was all set to marry Dona Luiza. I know the whole story . . . She used to live in Rua da Madalena!'

Sebastião said non-committally:

'Yes, it's Brito all right.'

'That's just what I said!'

He stood for a moment motionless, staring at the ground; then, resuming his usual mournful tones, he said:

'Oh, well, I'd better stagger back home, I suppose.'

He sighed and opened wide his eyes:

'I wish I had your health, Sebastião!'

And waving goodbye with a hand gloved in dark wool, he moved off, still hunched, keeping close to the wall, clutching his voluminous overcoat to his stomach with his free arm.

Sebastião went back into the house feeling very worried. Everyone was beginning to notice! Naturally! A young dandy turning up every day in a carriage and spending two or three hours there! And in a malicious neighbourhood like this, where everyone lived practically on top of each other!

He went out in the early afternoon. He wanted to go and see Luiza, but, for reasons he did not know, he felt overwhelmed by shyness, as if he were afraid he would find her different and with a changed look on her face. And so he walked slowly up the street, beneath his parasol, hesitating when a carriage came trotting by and stopped outside Luiza's door.

A man jumped down, discarded his cigar and went inside. He was tall, with waxed moustaches, and he wore a flower in his buttonhole; it must be cousin Bazilio, he thought. The coachman wiped the sweat from his brow, crossed his legs and began rolling himself a cigarette.

At the noise of the carriage drawing up, Senhor Paula immediately came to his door, his peaked cap pulled down low, his hands in his pockets, and all the time watching out of the corner of his eye; looking her usual grimy self, her body deformed by obesity and pregnancy, the coal merchant's wife opposite came outside to gawp, a look of imbecilic amazement on her oily face; the doctor's maid flung open her window. Then Senhor Paula walked quickly across the shining, sunlit street and, shortly afterwards, appeared at the shop door with the sour-faced tobacconist's wife; they exchanged whispered comments, their treacherous eyes fixed on Luiza's balcony windows and on the carriage. Senhor Paula then shuffled over in his carpet slippers to mutter something to the coal merchant's wife, provoking a laugh that shook her massive bosom; and finally, he returned to his own door where he stood between a portrait of Dom João VI and two old leather chairs, whistling joyfully. In the silent street, someone could be heard clumsily picking out on the piano the tune of *Prayer to a Virgin*.

Sebastião glanced mechanically up at Luiza's windows.

'Hot enough for you, Senhor Sebastião?' remarked Senhor Paula, bowing. 'It's certainly nice to be in the cool.'

Luiza and Bazilio were sitting calmly and contentedly in the drawing room, with the shutters pulled to, in the pleasant half-darkness. Luiza was wearing a very cool white peignoir and smelled of lavender water.

'You must take me as you find me,' she said. 'I'm not going to stand on ceremony.'

But she looked lovely like that! That is how he always wanted her to look! exclaimed Bazilio, greatly pleased, as if her peignoir were a promise of a nakedness to come.

He was perfectly at ease and spoke in the familiar tones of a close relative. He did not trouble her today with words of passion or gestures of desire; he spoke instead about the heat, about a comic opera he had seen the night before, about old friends he had met up with, only mentioning in passing that he had dreamed of her.

What had he dreamed? That they were in a far distant land, which must have been Italy, given the number of statues in squares and melodious fountains singing in marble basins; it took place in an old garden on a classical terrace; rare flowers spilled out of Florentine pots; on the carved balustrades, peacocks spread their tails; and she was walking slowly across the square flagstones, dragging behind her the long train of her blue velvet dress. In fact, it was a terrace very like that in San Donato, Prince Demidoff's villa – Bazilio never missed an opportunity to mention his illustrious friendships or to flaunt the glory of his many journeys.

And what had she dreamed about?

Luiza blushed. She had been frightened by the thunder. Had he heard the thunder?

'I was having a late supper at the Literary Club when the storm broke.'

'Do you usually dine so late?'

He smiled wryly. Dine! If one could call it dining, going to the club to chew on a leathery steak and drink a positively poisonous bottle of Colares wine!

Fixing her with his gaze, he said:

'And all because of you, you ungrateful woman!'

Her?

'Who else? Why else did I come to Lisbon? Why else did I leave Paris?'

'Because of your business dealings.'

He gave her a harsh look and, bowing low, said:

'Thank you!'

And he paced about the room, violently exhaling the smoke from his cigar.

Then he came over and sat down beside her. She really was most unfair. She was the reason he was in Lisbon, she alone!

He affected a sweet voice and asked if she didn't feel even the teeny tiniest bit of love for him, even this much . . . and he indicated the length of his fingernail.

They both laughed.

'Perhaps that much.'

Luiza's breast rose and fell.

He then admiringly examined her nails, advising her to use the kind of nail polish used by French *cocottes* to give their nails lustre; he gradually took hold of her whole hand, kissing the tip of each finger; he sucked her little finger and declared it very sweet; he shyly smoothed a few threads of hair that had worked their way loose from her coiffure and said he had a favour to ask her.

He was looking at her pleadingly.

'What is it?

'Will you come for a drive in the country with me? It must be lovely in the countryside just now!'

She said nothing; she was lightly tapping the soft folds of her gown.

'Nothing could be simpler,' he went on. 'You meet me somewhere, somewhere far from here of course. I wait for you in a carriage, you jump inside, and it's "Driver, don't spare the horses!"'

Luiza hesitated.

'Please, don't say no.'

'But where in the countryside?'

'Wherever you like. To Paço de Arcos, to Loures, to Que-luz. Say yes.'

There was an urgency in his voice now, he was almost kneeling before her.

'What's wrong with it? We're friends aren't we? Almost brother and sister.'

'No! Absolutely not!'

Bazilio got angry and accused her of being a prude. He made as if to leave. She took his hat out of his hand and very sweetly, almost submissively, said:

'Perhaps. We'll see.'

'Say yes!' he insisted. 'Be a good girl!'

'All right, we'll see, we'll talk about it again tomorrow.'

But the following day, Bazilio very cleverly did not mention going out for the day, or going into the country. Nor did he speak of his love or his desires. He seemed in excellent spirits and in frivolous mood; he had brought her *The Woman of Fire*, the novel by Belot. And sitting down at the piano, he sang her some of the saucy songs he had heard in *cafés-concerts* in Paris; he imitated the singers' harsh, coarse, rough voices; he made her laugh.

Then he talked at length about Paris, he recounted anec-dotes, told her about the latest amorous gossip, the fashionable love affairs. These always involved duchesses and princesses and were dramatic and moving, occasionally funny, but always full of piquant pleasures. And of every woman he described, he would lean back and say: '. . . an extremely distinguished woman, who, naturally enough, had a lover . . .'

Adultery thus appeared almost an aristocratic duty. Virtue, on the other hand, according to him, was a defect of the small-minded or the despicable concern of a bourgeois temperament.

And when he left, he said, as if suddenly remembering something:

'You know I'm thinking of leaving, don't you?'

She turned slightly pale and asked:

'Why?'

Bazilio said dully:

'Well, what's the point of my being here?'

He did not speak for a moment, but stared down at the carpet, then sighed deeply, as if struggling to master his emotions.

'Goodbye, my love.'

And with that, he left.

When Luiza entered the dining room that afternoon, her eyes were red.

The next day, she was the one who spoke of the countryside. She complained of the continual heat, said how tedious Lisbon was. It must be so lovely in Sintra!

'You're the one who doesn't want to go,' he said. 'We could have a lovely little trip out.'

She was afraid; they might be seen.

'How? In a closed carriage? With the blinds down?'

But sweltering inside a carriage would be worse than being in a drawing room!

It wouldn't be like that! They would go to a country estate. They could go to Alegrias, the estate of a friend of his who was currently living in London. The only people there were the caretakers; it was a delightful place, near Olivais! Lovely avenues of laurel bushes, delicious shade! They could take ice and champagne with them.

'Say you'll come!' he said, clasping her hands.

She coloured. Perhaps. She would see on Sunday.

Bazilio kept hold of her hands. Their eyes met and grew bright with tears. Greatly troubled, she withdrew her hands; she went over and opened both windows, letting in the bright, public light of day; she sat down on a chair by the piano, fearing the shadows, the sofa, their complicity; and she asked him to sing something, because now she feared words as much as she feared silences! Bazilio sang that sensual, disquieting melody by Gounod, 'Medjé'. The passionate notes blew through her soul like gusts of wind on a stormy night. And when Bazilio left, she remained where she was, exhausted, as after an excess of feeling.

Sebastião had spent the last three days in Almada, at the Rosegal estate, where he was having some work done. He had come back early on Monday morning and, at around ten o'clock, sitting on the seat by the window in the dining room that looked out over the terrace, he was whiling away the time until lunch by playing with his cat, Rolim, sleek as a prelate and ungrateful as a tyrant, and friend and confidant to the illustrious Vicência.

It was beginning to grow hot; the garden was already full of sun; the water in the pool beneath the vine trellis glittered with tremulous, reflected lights. In their two cages, the canaries were in strident voice.

Tia Joana, who was quietly setting the lunch table, began saying in her slow, Minho accent:

'Gertrudes was here yesterday, you know, the doctor's housekeeper, and she was telling me some tittle-tattle, some nonsense . . .'

'What about, Tia Joana?' asked Sebastião.

'About a young man who she says goes to Luiza's house every day.'

Sebastião immediately stood up.

'What did she say, Tia Joana?'

Tia Joana was slowly smoothing the table cloth with her plump hand.

'Oh, she talked on and on. Who could it be, who couldn't it be? She says he's very handsome. He visits every day. In a carriage too. On Saturday, he was there until nearly dark. And he was heard singing in the drawing room, too, and he's got a voice the like of which you wouldn't even hear in the theatre.'

Sebastião broke in impatiently:

'It's her cousin, Tia Joana. Who else would it be? It's her cousin just back from Brazil.'

Tia Joana smiled broadly.

'I knew he must be a relative. Because she says he's very handsome, and quite the dandy too!'

And shuffling out to the kitchen, she added:

'I knew he must be a relative, I told her so.'

Sebastião ate his breakfast feeling most uneasy. The neighbours had started gossiping good and proper now. It was causing a scandal. And, much alarmed, he decided to consult Julião about the matter.

He was walking down Rua de São Roque, when he saw Julião labouring up the hill towards him in the shade, looking hot and sweaty, carrying a roll of paper under his arm, and with his white trousers all begrimed.

'I was just coming to see you!' cried Sebastião.

Julião noticed the unusual note of excitement in his voice. Had something happened? What was it?

'A devilishly difficult situation!' exclaimed Sebastião softly.

They were standing outside a cakeshop. On the shelves in the window behind them stood bottles of malmsey wine with brightly coloured labels, transparent red jellies, the sickly egg-yolk yellow of *doces de ovos*, and dark brown fruit cake stuck with pathetic pink and white paper carnations. Stale, lurid custard tarts grew soft in their puff pastry cases; thick slabs of quince jelly sat melting in the heat; and the dried-up shells of seafood pasties were slowly melding into one. In the centre, prominently displayed, was a hideous, plump *lampreia de ovos*, a cake shaped like an eel, with a gaping mouth, a disgustingly yellow belly and a back blotched with arabesques of sugar; in its great head bulged two horrible chocolate eyes, and its almond teeth were sunk into a tangerine; and all around this rearing monster flies flitted.

'Let's go into the café,' said Julião. 'It's too hot to stand around in the street!'

'I've been really worried,' Sebastião was saying, 'very worried indeed. I need to talk to you.'

In the café, the dark blue wallpaper and the half-doors reduced the harsh glare of the light and afforded a sense of quiet coolness.

They went and sat at the rear of the café. On the other side of the street, the whitewashed façades of the houses shone with a glittering intensity. Behind the counter, where glass bottles glinted, a sleepy, tousled waiter in a double-breasted jacket was nodding off to sleep. A bird was twittering some-where inside; from behind a green baize door came the leisurely knock of billiard balls; from outside, they could hear

125

the occasional loud cry of a muleteer, and then, for a few moments, all these noises would be drowned out by the loud rumble of a carriage coming down the street.

Opposite them, a dissolute-looking man was sitting reading a newspaper; his grizzled locks clung to his yellowing skull; his moustache bore the marks of cigarette burns; and his red-rimmed eyes spoke of many late nights. Occasionally he would glance languidly up, launch a dark gob of spit onto the sand-strewn floor, give the paper a sad little shake and then fix it once more with mournful eyes. When they had entered the café and ordered two iced fruit drinks, he had nodded gravely at them.

'What's the problem, then?' asked Julião.

Sebastião moved closer to him.

'It's about our friends, about that cousin,' he said in a low voice.

Then he added:

'You've met him, haven't you?'

The sudden memory of his humiliation in Luiza's drawing room brought the colour to Julião's face. Proudly and succinctly, he said only:

'Yes, I have.'

'And?'

'He struck me as a complete and utter ass!' he exclaimed, unable to contain himself.

'He's a philanderer, isn't he?' said Sebastião in horror. 'Didn't you think so?'

'He just struck me as a complete ass!' Julião said again. 'So mannered and affected and pretentious, always looking at his socks, ridiculous socks, too, that would have looked better on a woman.'

And with a rather sour smile, he added:

'I gave him a good view of my boots. These,' he said, pointing to his scuffed shoes. 'I'm very proud of them, they're the boots of a worker.'

For in public he took pride in a poverty which, in private, was a constant source of humiliation.

Slowly stirring his fruit juice, he summed up by saying:

'An utter fool!'

'Did you know that he was Luiza's childhood sweetheart?' asked Sebastião softly, as if frightened by the gravity of this confidence.

And then, responding immediately to the look of surprise in Julião's eyes:

'Well, he was. No one knows about it. Not even Jorge. I only found out a short while ago. They were going to be married. When his father went bankrupt, he set sail for Brazil and wrote to her from there breaking off their engagement.'

Julião smiled and leaned his head back against the wall.

'This is like something out of *Eugénie Grandet*, Sebastião! What you're telling me is straight out of a Balzac novel. It is, it's *Eugénie Grandet!*'

Sebastião looked at him, horrified.

'It's impossible to have a serious conversation with you! I give you my word of honour that it's true!' he said angrily.

'Go on, Sebastião, go on!'

There was a silence. The bald man was now studying the ceiling, which was stained with cigarette smoke and the feet of many flies; and with one stubby, sticky hand he lovingly smoothed his sparse locks. From the billiard room came the sound of raised voices.

Then, as if he had taken a decision, Sebastião said brusquely:

'Well, now he goes there every day; he's there all the time!'

Julião moved further away from him on the bench and looked at him:

'What are you suggesting, Sebastião?'

And with almost jovial vivacity, he added:

'Do you mean this cousin is setting his cap at our Luiza?'

This expression scandalised Sebastião.

'Julião!' Then severely: 'This is no joking matter.'

Julião shrugged.

'But it's obvious that he is!' he exclaimed. 'Don't be so naïve! Of course he is. He courted her when she was single, and now she's married, he wants her back!'

'Keep your voice down!' said Sebastião.

But the waiter was dozing, and the bald man had resumed his gloomy reading.

Julião lowered his voice.

'That's the way it is, Sebastião. Cousin Bazilio is quite right to want pleasure without responsibility!'

And almost whispering in Sebastião's ear, he said:

'It's free, you see, Sebastião! It's free! You cannot imagine the influence this can have on affairs of the heart!'

He laughed. He was aglow; words and witticisms poured out of him:

'The husband keeps her clothed, shod and fed and makes sure she's well turned out; he's the one who watches over her when she's ill and puts up with her when she's in a bad mood; he's the one who takes on all the responsibilities, all the boring bits, all the children, however many happen to come along, you know the law. So all the cousin has to do is turn up, knock on the door and find her in a clean, fresh, appetising condition, all thanks to the husband, and . . .'

He giggled and leaned back with great satisfaction, gleefully rolling himself a cigarette, relishing the scandal.

'It's wonderful!' he went on. 'That's how all cousins think. Bazilio is a cousin therefore . . . You know the syllogism, Sebastião! You know the syllogism, my friend!' he cried, patting Sebastião's thigh.

'It's terrible,' muttered Sebastião, his head bowed.

Then rebelling against the suspicion gradually taking hold of him:

'But do you suppose that a decent woman . . .'

'I don't suppose anything!' replied Julião.

'Lower your voice, man!'

'I don't suppose anything,' repeated Julião more quietly. 'I'm simply stating what he's up to. Now she . . .'

And he added drily:

'. . . if she is a decent woman . . .'

'What do you mean "if"!' cried Sebastião, banging his fist down on the stone table top.

'Coming!' the waiter sang out sleepily.

The bald man immediately rose to his feet, but seeing that

the waiter was once more slouching back to the counter, yawning, and that the other two men were still stirring their fruit juice, he leaned his elbows on the table, spat, picked up his newspaper and stared at it with a desolate eye.

Sebastião said sadly:

'She's not the problem. The problem is the neighbours.'

They sat in silence for a moment. The altercation in the billiards room was growing louder.

'But,' Julião began, as if emerging from a long period of reflection, 'what's this about the neighbours? What have they got to do with it?'

'They see him going into the house. They see the carriage, it provokes a great uproar in the street. They're already talking about it. They've even been to Tia Joana with their gossip. I met Neto a few days ago and he had noticed too. Cunha as well. And the man who owns the junk shop downstairs doesn't miss a thing: there are some very vicious tongues about. Only a matter of days ago, I happened to be passing when this cousin of hers got out of his carriage and went into the house, and there were immediate confabulations in the street and inquisitive glances up at the window, it was terrible! He goes there every day. They know Jorge is away in the Alentejo. This cousin stays there for two or three hours at a time. It's very serious, very serious indeed.'

'She's a fool to carry on like that!'

'She probably doesn't see the wrong in it.'

Julião shrugged doubtfully.

The baize door to the billiards room opened, and a herculean man with a black moustache and a very red face came bursting into the café, then stopped and, holding the door open, shouted back to those inside:

'Just think yourself lucky I'm not a fighting man!'

A deep voice from the billiards room responded with an obscene remark.

The herculean man furiously slammed the door, and strode, apoplectic, through the café, breathing hard; a gaunt young man, wearing a winter jacket and white trousers, minced after him.

129

'What I ought to do,' exclaimed the giant, brandishing a fist, 'is to smash that scoundrel's face in!'

The gaunt young man swayed on his feet, then said in sweet, servile tones:

'Now fighting won't solve anything, Senhor Correia!'

'I'm too sensible, that's my trouble!' roared the Hercules. 'If I wasn't always thinking of my wife and children, I'd drink that man's blood!'

And with that, he left, and his thunderous voice was lost in the noise of the street.

The waiter had turned very pale and and was standing trembling behind the counter; and the bald man, who had looked up, merely gave a bored smile and returned sadly to his newspaper.

Then Sebastião said thoughtfully:

'Don't you think she should be warned?'

Julião shrugged and exhaled a cloud of smoke.

'Say something!' implored Sebastião. 'Would you go and speak to her?'

'Me?' cried Julião, with a look on his face that dismissed the idea. 'Me? You must be mad!'

'But what do you think I should do?'

There was real distress in Sebastião's voice.

Julião hesitated.

'Well, go if you want to. Tell her that people have begun to notice. Oh, I don't know.'

And he took a long pull on his cigarette.

His silence unsettled Sebastião, who said disconsolately:

'Look, I came to you for your advice.'

'What the devil do you want me to say?' Julião was getting angry now. 'It's her fault and hers alone!' he insisted, seeing the look in Sebastião's eye. 'She's twenty-five years old and has been married for nearly four, she should know that you don't invite a peacock like that into your house every day, in a small street, with the whole neighbourhood watching. If she does, it's because she likes him.'

'Julião!' said Sebastião sternly.

Then, controlling his feelings, he said urgently:

'You're wrong, you're wrong!'

He fell into a wounded silence.

Julião got up.

'Look, my friend, I can only say what I think, and you have to do what you think best.'

He called the waiter.

'No, it's all right,' said Sebastião quickly, paying the bill.

They were just about to leave when the bald man flung down his newspaper, raced over to the door, opened it, bowed, and held out to Sebastião a grubby piece of paper.

Taken by surprise, Sebastião mechanically read it out:

'I, the undersigned, a former servant of the nation, finding myself in reduced circumstances . . .'

'I was a close friend of the noble Duke of Saldanha!' the bald man muttered in a hoarse, tearful voice.

Sebastião blushed, nodded and discreetly placed two five-tostão coins in his hand.

The man bowed deeply and declared in cavernous tones:

'A thousand thanks to Your Excellency, thank you, Count!'

# V

It was a scorching hot day. Shortly after noon, Joana, in the kitchen, was stretched out in an old wicker chair from Madeira, having a nap. She got up so early that, during the hottest part of the day, she was always overcome by exhaustion.

The windows were closed to the glittering sun; the pans on the oven purred sleepily; and the whole silent house seemed to be drowsing in the intense, debilitating heat, when Juliana burst into the room, flung down an armful of dirty washing on the floor and yelled:

'God help me, but there's going to be trouble in this house one day!'

Joana started awake.

'If she wants everything just so, then she can damn well do it herself!' Juliana was shouting, her eyes red and bloodshot. 'Instead of spending all day in the drawing room chatting to her visitors!'

Much alarmed, the cook hurriedly closed the door.

'What happened, Senhora Juliana, what happened?'

'She's in a filthy mood! Her blood's up! I reckon she could do with a bloodletting, she could! She finds fault with everything I do! And I simply won't put up with it any more!'

And she stamped her foot hard.

'But what happened? What happened?'

'She started off by saying that there wasn't enough starch in the collars, and then she started ranting! And I just won't put up with it any longer! I'm up to here with her!' she bawled, pinching the wrinkled skin on her throat. 'She'd better not push me too far! I'll leave and I'll tell her to her face exactly why I'm leaving too! I'm not staying in this house with all these shameless goings-on! I'm not getting involved in intrigues!'

'Please, Senhora Juliana, please, be quiet!' Joana was clutching her head in her hands. 'If madam hears you . . .'

'Let her, I'll say it to her face! I've had enough! I've had enough!'

Suddenly she turned white as chalk and collapsed into the wicker chair, her two hands pressed to her heart, her eyes rolled back.

'Senhora Juliana!' cried Joana. 'Senhora Juliana! Speak to me!'

She sprinkled water on her face, shook her anxiously.

'Oh, my God! Oh, my God! Are you all right? Say something!'

Juliana gave a long, relieved sigh and closed her eyes. And she lay there breathing slowly, in a state of prostration.

'How are you feeling? Would you like a bit of broth? You've been overdoing things.'

'I had a sudden pain in my chest,' murmured Juliana.

These rages would be the death of her, said the cook, still very pale herself, as she stirred Juliana's soup. As far as employers were concerned, you just had to put up with them! She should drink a little soup and calm down.

At that moment, Luiza opened the door. She was still in her corsets and her white petticoat.

What was all the noise about?

Senhora Juliana had suffered a fainting fit.

'I-I had a pain in my chest,' stammered Juliana.

And struggling to her feet, she said:

'If you don't need anything else, madam, I'll go to the doctor's.'

'Yes, go, go,' said Luiza. And she went back downstairs.

Juliana sat eating her soup with agonising slowness. Joana kept muttering consoling words. Senhora Juliana did tend to get worked up over nothing. And the worst thing you can do if your health's not good is get yourself in a state . . .

'You don't know what it's like!' Juliana lowered her voice, at the same time opening her eyes very wide. 'She's been absolutely unbearable! She's getting all dressed up as if she was off to a party! She crumpled up a few collars and threw them on the floor and said I was useless at starching, that I was useless at everything. And I've had enough!' she said again. 'I've had enough!'

'It's just a question of being patient! We all have our cross to bear!'

Juliana smiled wanly, got to her feet with a great sigh, picked at her teeth, gathered up the bundle of dirty washing and disappeared off to her attic room.

Shortly afterwards, looking very pale, with her black gloves on, she went out.

As she was turning the corner, just opposite the tobacconist's, she stopped, uncertain what to do. It was a long walk to the doctor's. And her legs were shaking. But then she couldn't afford the three *tostões* for a carriage!

'Pst!' said someone softly.

It was the owner of the tobacconist's shop, wearing her long widow's weeds and her cheerless smile.

Where was Senhora Juliana going? Off for a little walk, eh?

And she admired her black sunshade with its bone handle. 'Such good taste,' she said. 'And how's your health been?'

Bad. She had been getting pains in her chest. She was going to the doctor now.

But Senhora Helena, the owner of the tobacconist's shop, had no faith in doctors. They were a waste of money. She spoke of her husband's illness, the huge amounts of money they had spent . . . And all for what? Just to see him fade away and die, just like that. She had always regretted spending that money!

And she sighed. But then, of course, it was God's will. And how were things at the Engineer's house?

'Much the same as usual.'

'Senhora Juliana, who is that young man who comes visiting every day?'

Juliana replied at once:

'He's madam's cousin.'

'They seem very friendly.'

'Yes, they do.'

She coughed, and with a little nod of her head, said:

'Good afternoon to you, Senhora Helena.'

And as she moved off, she muttered:

'Stick that in your pipe, you old crone!'

Juliana hated the neighbours; she knew they made fun of her and imitated her and called her 'the Old Prune'. Well, they weren't going to get anything out of her. They could die of curiosity for all she cared! They could wait till Kingdom come, but she was going to keep everything she had seen or suspected locked up inside her. 'Until the right moment!' she thought bitterly, as she walked off, swaying her hips.

The tobacconist stood at her door, a disappointed woman. And Senhor Paula, the owner of the junk shop, who had seen them talking, immediately sidled over in his carpet slippers.

'So did the Old Prune let anything slip, then?'

'Oh, you won't get anything out of her!'

Senhor Paula plunged his hands in his pockets and said dully:

'I expect the Engineer's wife greases her palm. She's the one who delivers the letters and the one who opens the door at night.'

'Well, really, I wouldn't go that far!'

Senhor Paula gave her a superior look:

'You're always stuck behind your counter, Senhora Helena, but I know what these high society women are like! I know them down to the tips of their fingers. They're nothing but riff-raff!'

And he went on to name names, including a few illustrious ones; they had innumerable lovers, some of whom were mere footmen! They smoked cigarettes and drank! And some did even worse things!

'And they ride around, all nicely ensconced in their carriages, and dare to flaunt their behaviour before decent people!'

'I put it down to a lack of religion!' sighed Senhora Helena.

Senhor Paula shrugged.

'It's religion I blame, Senhora Helena! It's all the fault of those priests!'

Then, angrily shaking his fist, he went on:

'Scum, the lot of them!'

'Please, Senhor Paula, don't say such things!'

And her large, pale, ugly face wore the stern expression of one whose beliefs have been deeply offended.

'Nonsense, Senhora Helena!' he exclaimed scornfully.

He plunged on:

'Why do you think all the convents and monasteries have closed down? Tell me that! Because of all the shameless goings-on!'

'Really, Senhor Paula, really!' spluttered Senhora Helena, recoiling and shrinking back.

But Senhor Paula was raining down impieties upon her now like knife blows.

'Absolutely shameless! At night, the nuns would walk through a tunnel to meet up with the friars. And they would spend the night drinking wine and dancing the fandango in their underwear! It's in all the books.'

And raising himself up onto the tips of his slippered feet, he went on:

'And as for the Jesuits, well . . .'

But just then he drew back and raised one hand to the peak of his cap:

'Your servant, madam,' he said respectfully.

It was Luiza going by, all in black, her veil down. They fell silent, watching her.

'She *is* awfully pretty!' murmured Senhora Helena admiringly.

Senhor Paula frowned.

'Not bad,' he said. Then he added scornfully: 'If you like that kind of thing.'

There was a silence. And Senhor Paula grumbled:

'It's not women I spend my time on or this!'

And he patted his jacket pocket, making his money jingle.

He coughed, noisily cleared his throat and, still in austerely critical mode, said:

'Give me some of that Xabregas tobacco, will you?'

Whistling and rolling himself a cigarette, he was just opening the door of the shop, when his eyes opened wide in indignation, for up at one of the open windows of the Engineer's house, he had glimpsed the scrawny figure of Pedro, the carpenter.

He turned to Senhora Helena, ostentatiously folded his arms and said:

'And now that the mistress is going her own sweet way, the lad's having fun with the maid!'

He exhaled a vast cloud of smoke and said darkly:

'That house is turning into a veritable sink of iniquity!

'Into a what, Senhor Paula?'

'A sink of iniquity, Senhora Helena, it means "a brothel".'

And the scandalised patriot strode away.


Luiza was finally going to the country with Bazilio. She had agreed the day before, stipulating that it was to be a half-hour ride and that they would at no point get out of the carriage. Bazilio had insisted, talking of 'shady avenues, a little picnic, long grass'. But she had stubbornly stuck to her guns, laughing and saying: 'Definitely no long grass!'

They had arranged to meet in the Praça da Alegria. She arrived late – just after half past two – looking very flustered, with her parasol held low over her face.

Bazilio was sitting, smoking, in a coupé stationed under a tree at one corner of the square. He flung open the door and Luiza clambered in, at the same time trying to furl her sunshade; her dress caught on the step and the silk ruffle on the hem tore; then, at last, she was there beside him, agitated and breathless, her face ablaze, muttering:

'This is madness, utter madness!'

She could barely speak. The coupé set off at a smart trot. The driver was Pintéus, an ex-footman.

'You poor thing, you're worn out!' said Bazilio tenderly.

He lifted her veil; her face was damp with sweat; her large eyes shone with excitement, haste, fear.

'It's so hot, Bazilio!'

He made to open one of the carriage windows.

No, no! People might see them. They should wait until they were outside the city.

'Where are we going?'

She lifted the blind slightly and peered out.

'I thought over towards Lumiar would be the best place. What do you think?'

She shrugged. What did it matter? She was beginning to calm down; she had removed her veil and her gloves; she was smiling, fanning herself with her handkerchief, which exuded a fresh perfume.

Bazilio took her wrist and planted many long, delicate kisses on her fine, blue-veined skin.

'You promised to behave!' she said with a warm smile, though looking at him askance.

What did a kiss on the arm matter? There was no need to be quite such a prude!

And he gazed at her with hungry eyes.

The old blinds on the coupé windows were made of red silk, and the light coming in through them wrapped her in a uniformly pink glow. Her lips were moist and red, with the healthy, satin smoothness of a rose petal; and one shining point of light gleamed in the corners of her liquid eyes.

Unable to help himself, he ran tremulous fingers over her temples and her hair, in one fleeting, hesitant caress; then he asked humbly:

'Can I not even kiss your cheek, just once?'

'Just once?' she said.

He kissed her delicately near her ear, but that contact painfully stirred his desires; there was a kind of sob in his voice; he grasped her passionately to him, showering wild kisses on her throat, her cheek, her hat . . .

'No, no!' she spluttered, resisting him. 'I want to get out. Tell him to stop!'

She beat on the windows; she tried desperately to open one, bruising her fingers on the hard, grimy chain.

Bazilio begged her forgiveness! But it was silly to get so angry over a kiss! She was driving him mad with her prettiness, but he promised that he would sit still, absolutely still.

The carriage, as it neared the outskirts of the city, rumbled and bounced over the gravel surface; in the fields on either side, the dusty green olive trees stood unmoving in the white light, and the searing sun blazed down on the scorched grass.

Bazilio had lowered one of the windows; the blind fluttered gently; he started talking tenderly about himself, about his love, about his plans. He had decided to settle in Lisbon, he said. He had no intention of marrying; he loved her and could think of nothing better than to live near her side for ever. He was disillusioned, he said, bored. What more did life have to offer him? He had experienced all the sensations that ephemeral love affairs had to offer, as well as the adventure of long journeys. He had accumulated some money of his own, and he now felt old before his time.

Gazing at her and taking her hands in his, he said:

'I am old, aren't I?'

'Not very.' And her eyes grew wet with tears.

Oh, he was, he was! What he wanted now was to live entirely for her, to find rest in her sweet company. She was all the family he had. He waxed very 'cousinly'. 'After all, one's family is what matters most. Do you mind if I smoke?' And he added as he lit his match:

'What really matters in life are deep affections like ours. Don't you agree? Besides, I can content myself with very little. Seeing you every day, talking to you, knowing that you respect me. Pintéus!' he bawled out of the window. 'Drive out into the countryside!'

The coupé proceeded slowly to Campo Grande. Bazilio raised the blinds; fresh air flooded in. The dazzling light of the sun fell through the branches of the trees, forming hot, leafy shadows on the dusty, white ground. Everything seemed parched and exhausted. The short grass growing in the cracked earth was scorched almost grey. A yellowish dust blew along the road beside them. Sleepy peasants sheltering beneath vast scarlet sunshades rode past on mules, legs joggling; and the sun from the oppressive, dark blue sky drew crude, dazzling reflections from the bright whitewashed walls, from water in an abandoned bucket, from the pale stones . . .

Bazilio went on:

'I'll sell all my assets abroad and rent a little house in Lisbon, in Rua Buenos Aires perhaps. Wouldn't you like that? Tell me.'

She said nothing; these words, these promises, to which his hoarse, metallic voice lent a kind of amorous vigour, had upon her much the same effect as a strong liqueur. Her breast rose and fell very fast.

Bazilio lowered his voice and said:

'Whenever I'm near you, I feel so happy, everything seems so good.'

'If only that were true,' she sighed, leaning back in her seat.

Bazilio put his arm around her waist; he swore that it was true. He was going to put his entire fortune into government bonds. He began to provide her with proof; he had already spoken to a lawyer, and he mentioned the name of a thin fellow with a very pointed nose . . .

And holding her close to him, his eyes devouring her, he said:

'If it were true, what would you do?'

'I don't honestly know,' she murmured.

They were entering Lumiar and so they prudently lowered the blinds. She peered out and, as they passed, saw dusty trees; the grubby pink wall around a garden; the façades of mean-looking houses; an omnibus without its horse; women sitting in a doorway in the shade, delousing their children; and a man all in white, wearing a straw hat, who stopped suddenly and stared at the closed blinds of the coupé. And she began to think how nice it would be to have an estate there, far from the main road; she would have a lovely little house with climbing plants round the windows, a vine trellis mounted on stone pillars, rose trees, charming little paths shaded by interlacing trees, a pool beneath a lime tree, where, each morning, the servants would soap and beat the clothes, talking all the while. And as it grew dark, he and she, still slightly weary from the pleasures of the siesta, would walk through the fields together, beneath a sky filling up with stars, and listen in silence to the sad croaking of the frogs.

She closed her eyes. The violent movement of the carriage, the heat, his presence, the touch of his hand, his knee, were all sapping her will. She felt desire swelling in her breast.

'What are you thinking about?' he asked very softly and tenderly.

Luiza blushed scarlet. She did not respond. She was afraid to speak, to tell him.

Bazilio slowly, carefully, respectfully took her hand, as if it were some precious, holy object; and he kissed it lightly, with all the servility of a black slave and the piety of a devotee. That caress, so humble, so poignant, was too much for her; her nerves gave way; she fell back in her seat and burst into tears.

What was wrong? What was the matter? He took her in his arms and kissed her, saying the maddest things.

'Shall we run away together?'

The round, bright little tears rolling slowly down that sweet face touched him and lent his desires an almost painful intensity.

'Come away with me. I'll take you away with me! We'll go to the ends of the earth together!'

She was sobbing now, and murmured almost sadly:

'Don't talk such nonsense!'

He fell silent and covered his eyes with his hands in an attitude of great melancholy, thinking: 'I am talking nonsense, she's quite right!'

Luiza was drying her tears and discreetly blowing her nose.

'It's my nerves!' she said. 'It's just my nerves. Shall we go back? I don't feel well. Tell him to take us back.'

Bazilio ordered the coachman to hurry back to Lisbon.

She complained of an incipient migraine. He had once more taken her hand in his and was repeating the same terms of endearment: he called her 'his dove', 'his ideal', all the while thinking: 'You're mine for the taking!'

They stopped in Praça da Alegria. Luiza looked out, then jumped down quickly, saying:

'Tomorrow, without fail, all right?'

She opened her parasol, lowered it over her face and walked swiftly in the direction of Rua da Patriarcal.

Bazilio opened the carriage windows and gave a sigh of satisfaction. He lit another cigar, stretched out his legs and shouted:

'To the club, Pintéus!'

In the reading room, his friend, Viscount Reinaldo, who had lived in London for years now, having spent many years in Paris as well, was sitting slumped in an armchair, languidly reading *The Times*. They had travelled from Paris together, on the condition that they would return via Madrid. The heat had a desolating effect on Reinaldo; he found the temperature in Lisbon 'vulgar'; he was wearing spectacles with smoked lenses and was drenched in perfume as a defence against 'the ignoble smells of Portugal'. As soon as he saw Bazilio come in, he let his copy of *The Times* slide to the floor and, arms hanging limply, said in a faint voice:

'How's this business with your cousin going, then? Is it on or off? It's just ghastly here, old man! I'm dying! I need the north! I need Scotland! Let's leave! Get rid of your cousin. Rape her and, if she resists, kill her!'

Bazilio, who had sat down in another armchair, gave a prolonged stretch of his arms, and said:

'She's mine for the taking!'

'Well, hurry up and take her then!'

With agonising slowness, he picked up his copy of *The Times*, yawned and ordered some soda water, English soda water!

There was none, the waiter told him. Reinaldo stared at Bazilio with mingled horror and alarm, then muttered grimly:

'What a vile country!'


When Luiza got home, Juliana, still in her street clothes, announced to her as soon as she came in through the door:

'Senhor Sebastião is in the drawing room. He's been waiting for ages. He was here when I got back.'

He had, in fact, arrived half an hour before. When Joana, red-faced and looking as if she had just woken up, had opened the door to him, mumbling something about her mistress being out, Sebastião had turned and started back down the stairs, filled with the delicious relief of a difficulty postponed. But he had stopped himself in time, stiffened his resolve and gone back in to sit down and wait. The previous evening, he had decided to talk to her, to warn her that these repeated, ostentatious visits from her cousin, in a gossip-ridden street such as hers, could easily compromise her. It was awful having to tell her, but it was his duty! His duty to her, to her husband and to the good name of the household! He had to forewarn her. And he did not feel shy about doing so. Confronted by the claims of duty, he was filled with decisive energy. His heart was beating a little faster than usual, and he was slightly pale, but, damn it, he had to tell her!

And as he paced about the room, with his hands in his pockets, he was composing phrases, trying to put things in as delicate and friendly a way as possible.

But then the doorbell rang, the corridor was filled by the rustle of a dress, and his courage shrivelled like a punctured balloon. He went and sat down at the piano and started pounding away at the keys. When Luiza came in, without her hat on and removing her gloves, he got up and blurted out:

'I was just knocking out a bit of a tune . . . I've been waiting. Where have you been?'

She sat down wearily. She had been at the dressmaker's, she said. And it was so hot! Why had he not come in when he had called before? She hadn't been entertaining any formal visitors. It was a member of her family, her cousin, who had just returned from abroad.

'And how is your cousin?'

'Fine. He's been here quite often. He's terribly bored in Lisbon, poor thing. Well, of course, for someone accustomed to living abroad . . .'

Sebastião sat, slowly rubbing his knees and repeated:

'Yes, of course, for someone accustomed to living abroad . . .'

'Has Jorge written to you?' asked Luiza.

'Yes, I got a letter from him yesterday.'

So had she. They talked about Jorge, about the longueurs of his trip, about what he had told them about Sebastião's eccentric relative, about his probably delayed return.

'We need him here with us, the rascal!' said Sebastião.

Luiza coughed. She was looking rather pale now. She occasionally ran a hand over her forehead, closing her eyes.

Then, suddenly, Sebastião decided to speak:

'My dear friend,' he began, 'I have come . . .'

But he saw her sitting at the other end of the sofa with her head bowed, one hand covering her eyes.

'What's wrong? Are you ill?'

'I've got a migraine, it's just come on. I thought I was getting one as I was on my way home just now. It's really bad.'

Sebastião immediately snatched up his hat:

'And here am I bothering you! Do you need anything? Do you want me to call a doctor?'

'No, no! I'll go and lie down for a few moments. It will soon pass.'

She must avoid draughts, he advised her. Perhaps a poultice might help, or slices of lemon placed on the temples. Anyway, if she didn't feel better, she must call him at once.

'It will pass! But do drop by, Sebastião. Don't hide yourself away.'

Sebastião went down the stairs, uttering a long sigh; he was thinking: 'I simply cannot do it!' But at the front door, he glanced up and saw, in the dark interior of the coal shop, the vast bulk of the coal merchant's wife in her white peignoir, craning her neck to see; up above, from behind the faded cotton curtains, three of the Azevedo girls had their curly little heads pressed together in some malign confabulation; behind her window, the doctor's maid was sewing, constantly darting hungry glances out at the street; and from next door, in the furniture shop, came the hawking and spitting of 'the patriot'.

'A cat couldn't walk past here without them noticing!' thought Sebastião. 'And such vicious tongues! I have to do it, even if I die in the attempt. If she's feeling better tomorrow, I'll tell her everything!'

She was, in fact, feeling much better by nine o'clock the next morning, when Juliana came to wake her with 'a note from Senhora Dona Leopoldina'.

Leopoldina's maid, Justina, a very dark, thin little woman

with a moustache and a squint, was waiting in the dining room. She was a friend of Juliana's; they always kissed each other fondly on the cheek and exchanged compliments. And having put Luiza's note of reply away in the little basket she carried on her arm, she adjusted her shawl over her chest and said, smiling:

'So, Senhora Juliana, any news to report?'

'Only old news, Senhora Justina.'

And lowering her voice, she added:

'Madam's cousin comes here every day now. He's a handsome fellow too!'

They both quietly and maliciously cleared their throats.

'And who's your current visitor, Senhora Justina, how are things over there?'

Justina made a dismissive gesture.

'A mere boy, a student. Certainly nothing to write home about!'

'Is he as tight-fisted as ever, then?' said Juliana with a giggle. Justina exclaimed:

'The miser! He never gives me a thing!'

And rolling her eyes nostalgically, she added:

'Oh, he's not like Gama. Now when *he* was around, he never left without giving me ten *tostões*, sometimes as much as half a *libra*. He was the one who helped me buy my silk dress, I'll have you know. But this fellow! He's barely out of nappies. I don't know why my mistress puts up with him! He's so thin and unhealthy-looking too! I shouldn't think he's up to much!'

Juliana said:

'You know, Senhora Justina, I've been thinking lately that the best houses to work in are precisely the ones where there are the most goings-on! I ran into Agostinha yesterday; she's working at the Comendador's house, in Largo do Rato. Well, you just can't imagine! She has everything! Everything! She's got the ring, the silk dress, the sunshade, the hat! And according to her, she's got enough underwear for a trousseau! And all because of Couceiro, who's with the mistress of the house. And he always slips her a bit extra on feast days too. He's a very generous man, she says. Mind you, it's a lot of work: she

145

has to let him in through the garden and then hang around to let him out again.'

'Oh, it's not like that where I am!' said Justina. 'He just uses the stairs.'

They tittered, enjoying the scandal of it all.

'Well, it takes all sorts!' said Juliana.

'Oh, the master of the house is made of sterner stuff,' said Justina. 'He passes them on the stairs and doesn't turn a hair.'

Then, readjusting her shawl again, she said affectionately:

'Anyway, I'd better be off, Senhora Juliana, it's getting late. My mistress is coming here to supper tonight. I've spent all morning starching her petticoats; since seven o'clock I've been at it!'

'So have I,' said Juliana. 'That's the problem with these women; when they've got a lover, there's always so much starching and ironing to do.'

'Yes, they certainly get through more underwear,' said Justina.

'Always assuming they bother to change their underwear!' exclaimed Juliana scornfully.

Just then, Luiza rang the bell.

'Goodbye, Senhora Juliana,' said Justina, adjusting her hat.

'Goodbye, Senhora Justina.'

Juliana went out with her to the landing. They once again exchanged fond kisses. Juliana hurried back to Luiza's room. Luiza was already up and in high spirits, singing to herself as she dressed.

The note had said in Leopoldina's sloping hand:

'My husband is going to the country today, so I'm inviting myself over to dinner, but I can't come before six o'clock. Is that all right?'

Luiza was thrilled. She hadn't seen Leopoldina for weeks. How they would laugh and talk! And Bazilio should be there at two. It looked set to be a full and entertaining day . . .

She went straight up to the kitchen to give her orders for supper. When she came back down, Sebastião's little errand boy was ringing the bell, bringing a bouquet of roses for her and asking if she was feeling better.

'Yes, absolutely!' cried Luiza. And to reassure Sebastião and to discourage him from visiting, she added that she was fine and might even be going out.

The roses, though, were most timely. Bright-eyed and still singing, she arranged them in the vases, pleased with herself and with her life, which had suddenly become so interesting and full of incident.

And at two o'clock, she dressed, went into the drawing room and sat down at the piano to practise Gounod's 'Medjé', which Bazilio had brought for her, and whose warm, sighing notes delighted her.

At half past two, however, she began to feel impatient; her fingers fumbled over the keys. 'You should be here by now, Bazilio!' she was thinking.

She went over to the windows, opened them and leaned out; but the doctor's maid, who was sewing at her window, immediately looked up at her with such searching eyes that Luiza rapidly closed the windows again. She went back to her playing, but she was on edge now.

A carriage came down the street. She stood up, flustered, her heart pounding. The carriage passed by.

Three o'clock! The heat seemed to have intensified, to have become unbearable; she felt as if her cheeks were burning and went to apply more powder. What if Bazilio were ill! Alone in a hotel room, tended only by neglectful servants! But, no, in that case, he would have written to her. He had not come, he did not care! How rude, how selfish!

She was a fool to worry. It was better like this. But she was so very hot! She went to look for a fan, and her frantic hands wrestled with the drawer which, slightly stiff, did not immediately open. She would not receive him again. It was all over.

And her great love suddenly disappeared, like smoke swept away by a gust of wind! She felt a sense of relief and a great desire for peace. With a husband like Jorge, it really was absurd even to consider another man, let alone a frivolous libertine!

The clock struck four. On a despairing impulse, she ran into Jorge's study, snatched up a piece of paper and hurriedly wrote:

Dear Bazilio,

Why haven't you come? Are you ill? If you only knew the torments you were putting me through . . .

The doorbell rang. It was him! She crumpled up the note, thrust it into the pocket of her dress and stood waiting, her heart beating fast. A man's footsteps crossed the drawing room carpet. She went in, her eyes shining. It was Sebastião.

Sebastião, looking slightly pale, clasped both her hands. Was she feeling better? Had she slept well?

Yes, thank you, she was much better. She sat down on the sofa, her face very red. She hardly knew what to say.

She said again, with a vague smile: 'Yes, I'm much better!' And she was thinking: 'I'll never get this bore out of my house now!'

'So you didn't go out, then?' asked Sebastião, sitting down in the armchair, holding his hat in his hands.

No, she was still a little tired.

Sebastião slowly smoothed his hair with his hand and then, in a voice hoarse with embarrassment, said:

'And, of course, you have company in the afternoons.'

'Yes, my cousin Bazilio has been visiting me. We haven't seen each other for years! We were practically brought up together. I've seen him nearly every day.'

Sebastião moved the armchair a little closer, then, leaning forward and lowering his voice, said:

'Actually that's what I wanted to speak to you about.'

Luiza opened surprised eyes.

'About what?'

'People have begun to notice. The neighbours here are frankly terrible, my dear friend. They don't miss a thing. There has already been talk. The teacher's maid and Senhor Paula . . . Someone has even mentioned it to Tia Joana. And since Jorge is not at home . . . Neto has noticed too. They don't know he's a relative of yours. And what with these daily visits . . .'

Luiza leaped to her feet, a look of fury on her face:

'Can I not even receive visits from my own relatives without being insulted?' she exclaimed.

Sebastião had got up too. Such sudden anger in this normally docile creature shook him like a clap of thunder out of a clear blue summer sky.

He started saying, almost pleadingly:

'My dear lady, please, it's not me who is saying this, it's the neighbours . . .'

'But what can they possibly have to say?'

There was a sharp edge to her voice. And clapping her hands together, she went on passionately:

'This really is most odd! I have one relative, with whom I was brought up, whom I haven't seen for some years, who has visited me briefly on three or four occasions, and already they're spreading malicious rumours.'

She spoke with utter conviction, entirely forgetting Bazilio's words, his kisses, the coupé . . .

Sebastião was shamefacedly turning his hat round and round in his trembling hands. And in subdued tones, he said:

'I thought it best to warn you; Julião thought so too . . .'

'Julião!' she exclaimed. 'But what has Julião to do with this? What right have you to interfere in what happens inside my house? Julião, indeed!'

Julião's intervention and opinions seemed to her even more of an affront. She fell back into a chair, her hands pressed to her chest, her eyes staring up at the ceiling.

'Oh, if only Jorge were here! Oh, dear God, if only he were here!'

Sebastião stammered weakly:

'It . . . it was for your own good.'

'But what evil could possibly befall me?'

And standing up and walking back and forth amongst the furniture, greatly agitated, she said:

'He's my only relative. We were brought up together, we played together. He was always there in mama's house in Rua da Madalena. He dined there every day. We're like brother and sister. When I was little, he looked after me.'

And in describing this fraternal relationship, she piled detail

149

upon detail, exaggerating some and randomly inventing others, improvising them out of her anger.

'He comes here,' she went on, 'he stays for a while, we play music together, because he plays beautifully, he smokes a cigar and then he leaves.'

She was, instinctively, finding reasons to justify her position.

Sebastião simply stood there without an idea or a decision in his head. She seemed to him to be another, different, rather frightening Luiza; and he almost bowed his shoulders beneath the strident tones of her voice, which he had never known to be so loud or so clumsily voluble.

At last, he said with melancholy dignity:

'I felt it was my duty, madam.'

A grave silence fell. That sober, almost severe tone made her blush a little at her extravagances; she looked down and said awkwardly:

'Forgive me, Sebastião! Please, really, I swear it, I'm truly grateful to you for warning me. You were quite right!'

To which he responded warmly:

'All I wanted was to stop these wicked tongues spreading any further calumnies! I was right to do so, wasn't I?'

He then justified his intervention as the act of a friend; sometimes one word is all it takes to start a rumour, but if a person is forewarned . . .

'Of course, Sebastião!' she said. 'You were absolutely right to warn me. Absolutely.'

She had sat down again; there was a feverish light in her eyes, and she kept dabbing with her handkerchief at the dry corners of her mouth.

'But what should I do, Sebastião? Tell me!'

He was touched now to see her submit and seek his advice; he almost regretted having come to trouble the joys of her private life with the grave nature of his remarks. He said:

'Obviously you must see your cousin and receive him, but, in this neighbourhood, a certain reserve is always a good thing. If I were you, I would talk to him . . . explain the situation.'

'But what are these people actually saying, Sebastião?'

'They've noticed his visits. They want to know who he is and what he's doing here!'

Luiza started impetuously to her feet:

'I've always said as much to Jorge! I've told him again and again! This street is just impossible! You can't move a finger without someone spying on you, whispering about you!'

'They have nothing else to do.'

There was a silence. Luiza was pacing about the room, her head down, her brow furrowed; then, stopping and looking almost eagerly at Sebastião:

'If Jorge found out, he would be so angry! Oh, dear God!'

'There's no reason why he should ever know!' cried Sebastião. 'This is between you and me!'

'It's just that I don't want to upset him,' added Luiza.

'Of course! As I say, this is between you and me.'

Then Sebastião held out his hand to her and said almost humbly:

'You're not angry with me, are you?'

'Me? Angry with you, Sebastião? What nonsense!'

'Good. Believe me,' and he clapped one hand to his breast, 'I felt it to be my duty. Because, of course, you, my dear friend, would know nothing about what was going on.'

'I had no idea!'

'Of course. Well, I'll say goodbye, then. I don't want to trouble you any further.' And he added quietly, but with great feeling: 'I'm always here if you need me.'

'Goodbye, Sebastião. They're such awful people! And all because they've seen the poor lad visit me a few times!'

'A rabble, a complete rabble!' said Sebastião, casting his eyes heavenwards.

And with that he left.

As soon as he had closed the door, Luiza exclaimed:

'The impudence of the man! Oh, this could only happen to me!'

Sebastião's intervention had actually irritated her more than the neighbourhood gossip! Her life, her visitors and her home were, it seemed, problems to be discussed and resolved by Sebastião, by Julião, by *tutti quanti*! She was twenty-five years old and yet, it seemed, she was still in need of guides and counsellors! Really! And why, dear God? All because her cousin, her sole relative, came to see her!

Then, suddenly, she fell quiet inside. She remembered how Bazilio looked at her, his exalted words, those kisses, that trip to Lumiar. Her soul silently blushed, but her resentment continued raging loudly: True, there were feelings between them, but they were honest, ideal, entirely platonic! They would never be anything else! She might harbour a certain weakness inside her, deep down, but she would always be a good, faithful wife, true to her husband!

And that certainty made her turn her ire instead on the street gossips. Was it really possible that after seeing Bazilio visit her house a mere four or five times, at two o'clock in the afternoon, they had immediately begun to murmur against her and to speak ill of her? Sebastião was an old stick-in-the-mud, with the timid sensibility of a hermit. And fancy consulting Julião! Julião of all people! It was doubtless his idea for Sebastião to come and preach at her, frighten her, humiliate her! Why? Out of bitterness and envy! Because Bazilio had good looks, fine clothes, manners, money . . . oh, that he did!

Bazilio's qualities seemed to her then as magnificent and abundant as the attributes of a god. And he was in love with her! And wanted to live by her side! The love of that man who had drained so many sensations to the last drop and had doubtless abandoned many other women seemed to her a glorious affirmation of her beauty and of her own irresistible charm.

The joy she derived from his worship of her brought with it the fear that she might one day lose it. She did not want those feelings to diminish; she wanted them to be always there, undimmed, lulling her with the languid murmur of tender words! How could she ever part from Bazilio! But if the neighbours and their friends began to talk, to whisper, Jorge might find out! Her heart went cold at the thought. Sebastião was obviously right!

To the inhabitants of a small street of twelve houses, the daily visits of that handsome, elegant young man in the absence of her husband, well, it must look awful! Dear God, what was she to do?

The doorbell rang loudly; Leopoldina came in.

She was furious with the coachman. What did Luiza think of this? She had stopped off at the post office on the way, and the man had wanted to charge her for two journeys! The scoundrel!

'And it's so hot!' She threw down her sunshade and her gloves; she shook her hands in the air to drive down the blood and restore them to their normal pallor; and pink-cheeked, tightly corseted, looking admirable in her stiff bodice, she stood at the dressing table, delicately composing the curls of her hair.

'But what's wrong with you, my dear? You seem distracted!'

Oh, it was nothing. She had lost her temper with the maids.

'Oh, aren't they unbearable!' She recounted Justina's demands and failings. 'But I suppose I should be grateful she doesn't simply leave. One depends on them so!' And dabbing on some face powder, she said slowly: 'Anyway, my lord and master has gone off to Campo Grande. I was going to have supper out with . . .' She paused and smiled, then, turning to Luiza, said in a quieter voice and in a happy, earnest tone: 'But you know, to be perfectly honest, I didn't know where to go and I had no money. The poor love has barely enough to live on with his allowance. So I said to myself: "Right, I'll go and see Luiza." And men always bore one so in the end. What's for supper? You didn't go to a lot of trouble, did you?'

Then an idea suddenly struck her:

'Have you got any salt cod?'

'Probably, possibly. But what a strange thing to ask. Why?'

'Oh!' Leopoldina exclaimed. 'Have them make me a little bit of baked cod! My husband loathes it, the beast! I adore it! With oil and garlic!' Then she stopped talking, as if annoyed. 'Oh, damn!'

'What?'

'I can't have garlic tonight.'

And she walked into the drawing room, laughing. She plucked a rose from the bouquet Sebastião had sent and put it in her buttonhole. She would like to have a drawing room like this, she was thinking, looking around. She would have blue upholstery, two large mirrors, a gas chandelier and a full-length portrait of herself in a low-cut dress, posing beside a beautiful vase of flowers. She sat down at the piano, and pounded out a few melodies from *Bluebeard*.

Seeing Luiza come back in, she asked:

'Did you order the salt cod?'

'I did.'

'Baked?'

'Yes'

'*Gracias*!' And in her provocative voice, she launched into her favourite song from *The Grand Duchess of Gérolstein*:

> I've heard it said that my grandpapa
> Loved his wine so very very much . . .

But Luiza found the song too noisy; she wanted something sad and sweet. The *fado*! Yes, she should play that *fado* of hers!

Leopoldina immediately said:

'Oh, there's a new *fado*! Haven't you heard it? It's lovely! The words are just divine!'

She played the opening notes and began singing, languidly swaying her head back and forth and staring into space, her eyes dark:

> The young man I saw yesterday
> Was dark and oh so handsome . . .

'Don't you know this one, Luiza? Oh, my dear, it's the very latest! And it's so sad, it will make you weep!'

She began again, in a voluptuous voice. It was the story in rhyme of an unhappy love affair. It spoke of 'jealous rages, the rocks at Cascais, of moonlit nights and wistful sighs', the usual morbid, sentimental, Lisbon prattle. Leopoldina sang on in mournful tones, rolling back her eyes; there was one verse that

154

she found particularly moving and she repeated it in impassioned tones:

> I see him in the clouds in the sky,
> In the waves of the endless sea,
> But however far away he is,
> He is always close to me.

'How lovely!' sighed Luiza.

And Leopoldina finished on a few long, sighing notes, slightly off-key.

Standing beside the piano, Luiza could smell Leopoldina's cheap cologne; the words of the *fado* made her feel rather sad; and she followed with yearning eyes Leopoldina's thin, agile fingers as they danced over the keys, fingers that glittered with the bejewelled rings given to her by Gama.

Then Juliana came in, wearing her best dress and her new false hair. Supper was on the table!

Leopoldina declared that she was almost faint with hunger! And she felt cheered by the dining room, with its open windows, the green of the empty lots opposite and the blue horizon on which small, white, cottony clouds were gathering; her own dining room, which opened onto the hall, was gloomy enough to take your appetite away!

She began picking at the grapes, nibbling a few conserves and then, noticing the portrait of Jorge's father as she was unfolding her napkin, remarked:

'He must have been most amusing your father-in-law! He looks like a man who enjoyed himself!'

How long had it been since the two of them last had supper together? When was it?

'It was during my first year of married life,' said Luiza.

Leopoldina blushed slightly. They used to see a great deal of each other; Jorge let them go to the shops together, to the patisserie, to the church in Graça . . . The memory of that period of camaraderie led Leopoldina to more distant recollections of schooldays. Some days ago, she had seen Rita Pessoa out walking with her nephew. 'Do you remember him?'

'Not "Weed"?'

They may have called him 'Weed', but at school he was their ideal man, their hero; they all used to write little notes to him, draw him hearts with flames pouring out of them, stick garlands of paper flowers in his distinctly grimy cap . . . And what about the time Micaela was caught in the attic where all the trunks were kept, devouring him with kisses!

Luiza said:

'How dreadful!'

'No, Micaela was just bolder than the rest of us!'

Poor thing! She had married a second lieutenant who beat her. And she now had masses of children.

'What a vale of tears this is,' said Leopoldina, leaning back.

She was in a loquacious mood. She greedily piled food on her plate, speared a forkful, tasted it, then put it down and started eating crusts of bread thickly spread with butter. And she continued to wallow in those schoolday memories! What good times they had been!

'Do you remember when we fell out?'

Luiza did not.

'It was because you kissed Teresa, on whom I had a crush,' said Leopoldina.

They started talking about their 'crushes'. Leopoldina had had four, the prettiest of whom was Joaninha Freitas. What eyes! And a lovely figure too! She had courted her for a whole month.

'It was all so silly,' said Luiza, colouring slightly.

'Silly? Why?'

She always spoke nostalgically of her girlhood 'crushes'. Those had been her first and her most intense experiences of love. The agonies of jealousy she went through! The delirium of reconciliation! The stolen kisses and the furtive glances! And those love notes and the way her heart beat wildly, and all for the first time in her life.

'Never,' she declared, 'never, as a woman, have I felt for a man what I felt for Joaninha! I mean it . . .'

A look from Luiza silenced her. Juliana was there! Damn! She had forgotten. Her presence constrained them, as did her crooked little smile, her flat-chested figure, the metallic tick-tack of her heels.

'Whatever became of Joaninha?' asked Luiza.

She died of tuberculosis, and Leopoldina's voice grew sad with longing. An awful illness. Not that she was afraid of catching it herself. And she patted her own shapely bosom.

'I'm strong and healthy!'

Juliana left the room, and Luiza immediately said:

'Watch what you say, my dear! Be careful!'

Leopoldina bowed.

'Ah, yes, the respectability of the house! You're quite right!' she murmured.

And when Juliana came in bearing the baked cod, Leopoldina applauded:

'Bravo! It looks superb!'

She poked at it hungrily with the tip of one finger; it was golden brown, slightly burned, and breaking into flakes.

'See?' she said. 'Aren't you tempted? You don't know what you're missing!'

Then with a brave, decisive gesture, she said:

'Bring me some garlic, Senhora Juliana! Bring me a good clove of garlic!'

And as soon as she had gone:

'I'm meeting Fernando afterwards, but I don't care! Ah, thank you, Senhora Juliana! There's nothing like garlic!'

She crushed the clove and distributed it around the plate, then solemnly drizzled the cod flakes with a little oil. 'Gorgeous!' she exclaimed. She refilled her glass; this, she said, was 'a veritable feast'.

'But what's wrong?'

Luiza did indeed seem preoccupied. She kept sighing softly. Twice, sitting up in her chair, she had said to Juliana anxiously:

'I thought I heard the doorbell. Go and see, will you?'

It was no one.

Who could it possibly be, asked Leopoldina. She wasn't expecting her husband, was she?

'No!'

Then, while apparently concentrating on her plate, as she

slowly and carefully separated out the small flakes of fish, Leopoldina asked:

'Did your cousin come to see you?'

Luiza blushed.

'Yes, he did. He's been several times.'

'Ah!'

And after a silence:

'Is he still as handsome?'

'Well, he's certainly not ugly.'

'Ah!'

Luiza hurriedly asked her if she had ordered that check dress. No, she hadn't. And they started discussing clothes, fabrics, shops, prices, then moved on to various acquaintances, other women, rumours, immersing themselves in the kind of conversation in which women on their own tend to indulge, delicate and endlessly digressive, rather like the whispering of leaves.

The roast meat was served. Leopoldina was already quite flushed. She asked Juliana to fetch her fan, then leaning back, fanning herself, she declared that she felt like a prince. And she continued taking sips of wine. What a good idea it had been to have supper together!

As soon as Juliana had set out the fruit plates, Luiza told her that she could leave the room and that she would call her when they needed coffee. She herself went and closed the door and drew the cretonne door curtain.

'Now we can relax! It makes me feel old just looking at the creature! I can't wait to see the back of her!'

'But why don't you just put her out in the street?'

Jorge did not want her to, otherwise . . .

Leopoldina protested. Husbands should have no say in domestic matters. Honestly!

'But what about yours?' said Luiza, laughing.

'Touché!' exclaimed Leopoldina. 'He even has his own separate bedroom!'

Besides, she couldn't stand men who worried about maids, shopping lists, oils and vinegars . . .

'My gentleman even weighs the meat!' She gave a smile full

of loathing. 'Mind you, that's all he's good for! Frankly, it makes me feel sick even to go into the kitchen.'

She went to pour herself more wine, but the bottle was empty.

Luiza said:

'Would you like some champagne?'

She had some very good champagne which a Spanish mine-owner had sent to Jorge.

She herself went to get the bottle and unwrapped the blue paper, and then, laughing, half-frightened, they removed the cork. The foam delighted them; they gazed silently at their glasses, with a sense of happy well-being. Leopoldina boasted of her abilities as an opener of champagne bottles; she spoke vaguely of other suppers she had enjoyed.

'On Shrove Tuesday, two years ago!'

And reclining in her chair, a warm smile on her lips, her nostrils flared, her eyes shining, she watched with sensual pleasure as the bright little bubbles rose unceasingly in the slender glass.

'If I were rich, I would drink nothing but champagne,' she said.

Luiza disagreed: she wanted a coupé; she wanted to travel: to Paris, Seville, Rome . . . But Leopoldina's desires were more ambitious: she yearned for a larger life, with carriages, a box at the theatre, a house in Sintra, suppers, balls, clothes, gambling. Because she loved playing monte, she said, it made her heart beat faster. And she was convinced that she would just adore roulette.

'Oh!' she exclaimed. 'Men are so much more fortunate than we are! I was born to be a man! The things I would do!'

She got up and went over to the wing chair by the window where she sat down languidly. The tranquil evening was coming on; gathering behind the houses, beyond the empty lots, were round, yellowish clouds, edged with blood-red or orange.

And returning to the idea of action and independence, she said:

'A man can do anything! Nothing is barred to him! He can travel, have adventures . . . You know, I would love a cigarette.'

The trouble was Juliana would smell it, and it would look bad.

'It's like a convent in here!' muttered Leopoldina. 'Though, I must say, you do have a very comfortable prison!'

Luiza did not respond; leaning her head on her hand and staring into space, she said, as if taking up some earlier remark:

'But all that business about going out and about and travelling is just so much nonsense really! The best thing for a woman in our world is to stay at home with her husband and one or two children . . .'

Leopoldina sat up in her chair. Children! Don't even talk about such a thing! She gave thanks to God every day that she did not have any!

'It would be absolutely ghastly!' she declared with conviction. 'One would be so constrained . . . And then there's the expense and the work and the illnesses! No, thank you! That really *is* a prison! And then, when they grow up, they notice everything you do and they tell on you too. A woman with children can do nothing, she's bound hand and foot. There's no pleasure in life! She just has to put up with them! Heavens! God forgive me, but if I ever had that misfortune, I think I would pay a visit to the old woman in Travessa da Palha!'

'What old woman?' asked Luiza.

Leopoldina explained. Luiza thought it 'utterly vile'. Leopoldina shrugged and added:

'And then, my dear, it ruins a woman's figure; no body, however beautiful, can withstand it. Even the best is ruined. If you look like your friend, Dona Felicidade, that's one thing, but when everything is in its proper place, oh no, life's hard enough!'

Down below, in the street, the local hurdy-gurdy man, on his evening round, was playing the final aria from *La Traviata*; it was growing dark; the green of the gardens was now a uniform grey, and the houses beyond had dissolved into the shadows.

*La Traviata* reminded Luiza of *The Lady of the Camellias*; they talked about the novel, recalling certain episodes.

'I was madly in love with Armand when I was a girl!' Leopoldina said.

'And I was in love with D'Artagnan,' exclaimed Luiza ingenuously.

They both giggled.

'We started young,' remarked Leopoldina. 'Give me another drop of champagne.'

She took a sip, then put down her glass, and with a shrug of her shoulders said:

'But were we so very young? Now, everyone begins young! By the age of thirteen, they're already on to their fourth grand passion. That's women for you, we all feel the same!' And keeping time with her foot, she sang:

> Love is a sickness that lives in the air;
> just stand at your window,
> you'll catch love's fever right there.

'I seem to be able to talk of nothing else today!' And stretching languidly, she went on: 'But then it's the best thing life has to offer; everything else is so insipid by comparison. Don't you agree? Tell me. Don't you agree?'

Luiza murmured:

'Hm, yes,' then added: 'Absolutely!'

Leopoldina got up and repeated mockingly:

'Absolutely! The poor little innocent! The little angel!'

She went and stood by the window, watching the coming of the twilight through the panes; then, very slowly, she began:

'Is it really worth being some humble little person who spends her life always slaving away and putting her family first, just so that one day, along comes a fever, a chill wind or too much sun, and it's goodnight and off to the cemetery with you? No, thank you!'

It was quite dark in the room now.

'Don't you agree?' she asked.

The conversation was making Luiza uncomfortable: she

could feel herself blushing; but the twilight hour and Leopoldina's words had the softening effect on her of a temptation. She nevertheless declared such an idea 'immoral'.

'Immoral? Why?'

Luiza spoke vaguely of 'duty', of 'religion'. But the word 'duty' irritated Leopoldina. If there was one thing, she said, guaranteed to make her angry it was people talking about duty!

'Duty? To whom? To a scoundrel like my husband?'

She fell silent, pacing the room, then went on in animated tones:

'And as for religion, huh! Father Estevão, the one with the pince-nez and the nice teeth, he said he would absolve me as many times as I wanted if I'd go to Carriche with him!'

'Ah, but that's just priests,' murmured Luiza.

'What do you mean "just priests"? Priests and religion are one and the same! God, my dear, is somewhere far away and doesn't concern himself with what we women get up to.'

Luiza thought 'that way of thinking' horrible. True happiness, according to her, lay in being honest and decent.

'And having a nice game of cards with the family!' snorted Leopoldina bitterly.

Luiza said firmly:

'Besides, your affairs, one after the other . . .'

Leopoldina interrupted:

'What about them?'

'They don't make you happy!'

'Of course they don't!' exclaimed Leopoldina. 'But . . .' She searched for the right word and presumably chose not to use it; she merely retorted abruptly: 'They amuse me!'

They lapsed into silence. Luiza ordered the coffee.

Juliana came in with the tray and some candles; shortly after that, they moved to the drawing room.

'Do you know who mentioned you to me yesterday?' said Leopoldina, lying down on the divan.

'Who?'

'Castro.'

'Which Castro?'

'The one who wears spectacles, the banker.'

'Oh, him.'

'He's still madly in love with you, you know.'

Luiza laughed.

'No, really, he's mad about you,' Leopoldina said.

The room was in darkness, with the windows open; the street had dissolved into a grey twilight, and a breeze, languid and sweet, softened the night.

Leopoldina sat for a moment saying nothing; but the champagne, the near darkness, soon bred in her the need for whispered confidences. She stretched out still more on the divan, in an attitude of complete abandon; she started talking about 'him'. This was still Fernando, the poet. She adored him.

'If you only knew!' she murmured in an ecstatic voice. 'He's such a love!'

And there was a warm, tender note in her husky voice. Luiza – almost lying down too and in an enervated state – could feel her breath and the warmth of her body; sometimes, on an out-breath, she seemed almost to sigh; and in response to certain of the more piquant details proffered by Leopoldina, she would give a brief, heartfelt chuckle, as if she were being tickled. But the heavy sound of hobnail boots could be heard coming up the street, and then the gas leaped into life in the streetlamp opposite. A pale, gentle light filled the room.

Leopoldina sat up. She must leave at once; they were lighting the lamps! The poor boy would be waiting for her! She went into the bedroom, despite the darkness there, to put on her hat and fetch her sunshade. She had promised him, poor lad, and she couldn't let him down. But she really didn't like to go alone. It was so far! Perhaps Juliana could go with her . . .

'Of course, she will, my dear!' Luiza said.

Sighing loudly, she got lazily to her feet and went to open the door, where she came face to face with Juliana, who was standing in the shadows in the corridor.

'Heavens, woman, you gave me such a fright!'

'I was just coming to ask if you needed more candles.'

'No, we don't! Go and put on your shawl so that you can accompany Senhora Dona Leopoldina. Quickly!'

Juliana raced off.

'So when will I see you again, Leopoldina?' asked Luiza.

As soon as she could manage it. She was thinking of going to Oporto next week to see her Aunt Figueiredo and spend a fortnight at Foz.

The door opened.

'Whenever you're ready, madam,' said Juliana.

Luiza and Leopoldina said goodbye fondly and kissed each other warmly. Luiza whispered in Leopoldina's ear, laughing: 'Enjoy yourself!'

Then she was alone again. She closed the windows, lit the candles and began walking up and down the room, slowly rubbing her hands together. And, despite herself, she could not stop thinking about Leopoldina on her way now to see her lover. Her lover!

She followed her in her mind: she was doubtless walking along, talking to Juliana; she arrived; she went up the stairs, feeling greatly agitated; she flung open the door and how delicious, how eager, how deep was that first kiss! She sighed. She too loved someone, someone far more handsome, far more fascinating. Why had he not come?

She sat indolently down at the piano and began softly, sadly singing the fado Leopoldina had taught her:

> But however far away he is,
> He is always close to me!

Then that sense of loneliness and abandonment aroused in her feelings of irritation. It was so dull being there all alone! The lovely, hot, sweet night was drawing her on, calling to her from outside, to go for romantic strolls, or to sit on a bench in the garden, holding hands, gazing up at the stars. Her life seemed so stupid! And it was all Jorge's fault! Fancy going off to the Alentejo!

Leopoldina's words and the thought of her happiness kept coming back to her; a little champagne spark stirred in her blood. The clock in her bedroom began slowly striking nine o'clock, and suddenly the doorbell rang.

She jumped; it couldn't be Juliana back already! She listened, frightened. She could hear voices talking at the door.

Joana came into the room and said softly:

'Madam, it's your cousin; he's come to say goodbye.'

Luiza smothered a cry and stammered:

'Tell him to come in!'

She fixed wide, feverish eyes on the door. The curtain was drawn back, and Bazilio entered, looking pale, and with a stiff smile on his face.

'You're leaving?' she cried softly, throwing herself into his arms.

'No, no, I'm not!' And he held her close. 'No, I just used that as an excuse. I thought you probably wouldn't receive me at this hour.'

He clasped her to him and kissed her; she allowed him to kiss her, abandoned herself to his arms; her lips met his. Bazilio glanced quickly around and, still holding her, led her across the room, murmuring: 'My love! My sweet!' He even tripped on the tiger-skin rug by the divan.

'I adore you!'

'You frightened me so!' sighed Luiza.

'Did I?'

She did not reply; she was losing any clear perception of things; she felt as if she were falling asleep. She muttered: Dear God, no! no!' Her eyes closed.

When the doorbell rang loudly at ten o'clock, Luiza had been sitting for some moments on the edge of the divan. She barely had the strength to say to Bazilio:

'It must be Juliana, she had to go out . . .'

Bazilio smoothed his moustache, walked twice around the room and lit a cigar. To break the silence, he sat down at the piano, played a few notes at random and then, quite loudly, began to sing the aria from the third act of *Faust*:

> Let me gaze upon your face
> Beneath the pale beams of the moon . . .

With her nerves still jangled, Luiza was gradually returning to reality; her knees were trembling. Then, when she
heard that melody, a memory started taking shape in her
barely awakened mind. It was one night, years ago, in a box
at the Teatro de São Carlos with Jorge; the spotlight shining
onto the stage garden lent it the livid tones of mythical
moonlight; and the tenor, in an attitude of ecstatic longing,
was invoking the moon; Jorge had turned to her and said:
'Wonderful, isn't it?' And his eyes devoured her. It was the
second month of their marriage. She was wearing a dark
blue dress. And when they rode back home in the carriage,
Jorge had put his arm around her waist and repeated the
words of the aria:

> Let me gaze upon your face
> Beneath the pale beams of the moon . . .

And he had clasped her to him.

She sat motionless on the divan, so near the edge, she was
almost slipping off, her arms limp, her eyes fixed, her face
suddenly older, her hair coming loose. Bazilio came and gently sat down beside her.

'What are you thinking about?'

'Oh, nothing.'

He put his arm around her waist and started talking about
how they should find a little place where they could see each
other more freely, where they could feel more at ease; it really
wasn't a good idea to continue meeting at her house . . .

And as he spoke, he kept turning his face away to exhale the
smoke from his cigar.

'My coming here every day might be noticed.'

Luiza got abruptly to her feet; his words had suddenly
reminded her of Sebastião's visit! And in a slightly distraught
voice, she said:

'It's so late!'

'Yes, you're right.'

He tiptoed over to pick up his hat, then gave her a long kiss
and left.

Luiza heard him strike a match, then gingerly close the front door.

She was alone; she looked foolishly around her. The silence in the room seemed to her enormous. The candles were burning with a reddish flame. She blinked; her mouth was dry. One of the cushions on the divan had fallen off and she picked it up.

And then she walked dazedly into her bedroom. Juliana came to give her the various lists for the next day. She was just going to sort out the nightlight now, she would be down with it soon.

Juliana had taken off her false hair; she almost ran up to the kitchen. Joana, who was dozing, stretched and yawned widely.

Juliana started trimming the wick on the lamp; her fingers were trembling; her eyes glinted; clearing her throat, she said to Joana with a smile:

'So what time did madam's cousin arrive, then?'

'Shortly after you went out, the clock was just striking nine.'

'Ah!'

She went downstairs with the lamp and hearing Luiza getting undressed in her room, she asked eagerly:

'Do you not want any tea, madam?'

'No.'

She went into the drawing room and closed the piano lid. There was a strong smell of cigar smoke. She looked carefully, furtively around. Then she crouched down eagerly: just by the divan, something gleamed. It was a tortoiseshell comb with a gold top, belonging to Luiza. She tiptoed back into the room and placed it on the dressing table amongst the curls of false hair.

'Who's there?' asked Luiza's sleepy voice from the bedroom.

'It's only me, madam, I was just closing the drawing-room door. Goodnight, madam!'

At that same moment, Bazilio was going into his club. He walked through all the rooms. They were almost deserted. Two men, face cupped in hands, were bent glumly over their newspapers; here and there, next to the small round tables, men in white trousers were placidly, contentedly eating toast; the closed windows, the hot night, the listless heat from the gaslights all made for a suffocating atmosphere. He was about to go downstairs, when, from a gaming room, came the abrupt sounds of an altercation; insults were exchanged; someone shouted: 'You're lying! *You're* the one who's an ass!'

Bazilio stood still, listening. Then suddenly a great silence fell; one of the voices said meekly:

'Clubs!'

The other responded condescendingly:

'That's what you should have done in the first place.'

And the quarrel started up all over again, more stridently this time. They swore and cursed.

Bazilio went into the billiards room. Viscount Reinaldo was standing, leaning on his cue, gravely following his partner's game; but as soon as he saw Bazilio, he went straight over to him and asked eagerly:

'Well?'

'It's done,' said Bazilio, chewing on his cigar.

'At last, eh?' exclaimed Reinaldo, opening his eyes wide with satisfaction.

'At last!'

'Glad to hear it, my boy, glad to hear it!'

He patted him warmly on the shoulder.

But it was his turn to play; and stretched out over the table, one leg in the air, in order to gain the precise effect he wanted, he said in a voice constrained by his pose:

'This whole business really was beginning to drag on a bit.'

Tac! He missed the red.

'Useless!' he muttered bitterly.

He rejoined Bazilio and as he chalked his cue, began:

'I say . . .'

Then he whispered something in Bazilio's ear.

'Like an angel, old chap!' sighed Bazilio.

# VI

It was Juliana who woke Luiza the next morning, standing at the bedroom door and saying in a low, confidential voice:

'Madam! Madam! It's a messenger with a letter, he says he's from the hotel.'

She tiptoed over and opened a window, then going back into the bedroom, said with an air of mysterious caution:

'He's waiting at the front door for an answer.'

Luiza, barely awake, opened the large blue envelope stamped with a monogram – two Bs, one purple, the other gold, beneath the crown of a count.

'It's all right, there's no reply.'

'There's no reply,' Juliana told the messenger, who was waiting in the corridor, leaning against the banister, smoking a big cigar and stroking his dark side whiskers.

'No reply? Right, good day to you then.' And he briefly touched his bowler hat and swaggered off down the stairs.

'Handsome devil!' thought Juliana on her way up to the kitchen.

'Who was that, Senhora Juliana?' Joana the cook asked her.

Juliana muttered:

'Oh, no one, just a note from the dressmaker.'

It seemed to Joana that Juliana had been behaving oddly all morning. She had heard her moving about the house since seven o'clock, sweeping, dusting, shaking rugs, cleaning the windows in the dining room, sorting out the china in the sideboard. And with such zeal too! She had heard her singing 'O beloved letter', accompanied by the loud warbling of the canaries in their cages out on the open, sunny balconies. When she came into the kitchen to have her coffee, she was unusually silent; she seemed absent and preoccupied.

Joana even asked her:

'Are you feeling bad again, Senhora Juliana?'

'Me? No, I've never felt so well in my life, thank God!'

'It's just that you seem so quiet.'

'I'm just thinking my own thoughts. People don't always feel like chattering, you know.'

It was nine o'clock, but she preferred not to wake her mistress just yet. 'Let her rest, poor thing,' she said. She filled the large bathtub in the room as slowly as she could; in order not to make any noise, she went into the corridor to shake out the petticoats and dress that Luiza had worn the previous night: and there was an avid gleam in her eyes when she heard the rustle of crumpled paper in the pocket! It was the note that Luiza had written to Bazilio: 'Why have you not come? . . . If you knew the torments you were putting me through! . . .' She held it in her hand for a moment, biting her lip, her eyes fixed on one point as she made shrewd calculations; in the end, she put it back in the pocket, folded up the dress and laid it very carefully down on the chaise longue.

Later, when she heard the cuckoo clock chime, she called Luiza in the sweetest of voices:

'It's half past ten, madam!'

Luiza, in bed, had read and re-read Bazilio's note. He could not, he wrote, wait a moment longer to tell her that he adored her. He had barely slept! He had risen very early that morning in order to swear his love to her, and to tell her that he placed his life at her feet. This piece of prose had, in fact, been written the night before, at the club, at three o'clock in the morning, after a few rubbers of whist, a steak, a couple of glasses of beer and a leisurely read of a magazine. And he closed by exclaiming: 'Others may want fortune, glory, honours, but I want only you. Yes, only you, my dove, because you are the one thing that binds me to life, and if, tomorrow, I were to lose your love, I swear that I would put an end, with a single trusty bullet, to this pointless existence!' He had then ordered another beer and taken the letter back to the hotel with him, so that he could put it in a monogrammed envelope, because that 'always made a better impression'.

And Luiza had sighed and devoutly kissed the paper! It was the first time that anyone had written to her in such romantic terms, and her pride relaxed into the amorous warmth of these words, like a desiccated body sinking into a warm bath;

she felt her self-esteem grow, and it seemed to her that she was finally entering a superior and more interesting existence, where each hour had a different charm, each step led to some new ecstasy, and in which her soul was clothed in a splendour radiant with sensations!

She jumped out of bed, slipped on a peignoir and raised the blinds on the window. What a beautiful morning! It was one of those late-August days when summer seems to pause; there is about the heat and the light a kind of premature autumnal peace; the sun still falls abundantly, brilliantly, but it alights delicately; the air has lost its dog-day dullness, and the high blue sky shines with a new-washed clarity; one breathes more easily; and there is no sign in passers-by of the lethargy brought on by the debilitating midsummer heat. She was filled with a feeling of joy: she felt light, she had enjoyed a deep, unbroken sleep, and all the anxiety and impatience of the last few days seemed to have vanished. She went to look at herself in the mirror; her skin seemed clearer, fresher, and there was a tender gleam in her eyes. Was Leopoldina right when she said that there was nothing like a little mischief to make one prettier? She had a lover!

And standing in the middle of the room, staring into space, her arms folded, she said again: 'I have a lover!' She was remembering the previous night, the drawing room, the pointed flames of the candles, and certain extraordinary silences when it seemed to her that life had stopped, while in the portrait of Jorge's mother's, dark eyes in a pale face watched from the wall with their fixed, painted gaze. Just at that moment, Juliana came in carrying a basket of ironed clothes. It was time to get dressed.

Nothing seemed too much trouble to Luiza that morning! She added perfume from Lubin's to the bath water; she chose a chemise trimmed with the very finest lace. Ah, how she longed to be rich! She wanted the most expensive cottons and linens, the most luxurious furnishings, heavy English jewellery, a coupé upholstered in satin . . . For those of a susceptible nature, the joys of the heart tend to seek confirmation in the sensuality of luxury: the first slip committed by a hitherto

invulnerable soul immediately admits others by more tortuous routes; just like a thief who sneaks into a house and opens
all the doors to his starving horde.

She went up to breakfast, looking very fresh in a white
robe, her hair in two plaits. Juliana hurriedly closed the windows, 'because although it's not particularly hot, it's always
cooler with the shutters closed!' And noticing that Luiza had
forgotten her handkerchief, she bustled off to find her one,
which she scented with a few drops of eau-de-cologne. She
served her tenderly. When she saw that Luiza was eating a lot
of figs, she exclaimed almost tearfully:

'Are you sure they won't upset you, madam?'

She prowled around her noiselessly, a servile smile on her
lips; or else, standing by the table, her arms folded, she
appeared to be admiring her proudly, as if Luiza were a
precious, beloved being, who was all hers, *her mistress*! Her
bulging eyes gazed upon her possessively.

And all the time she was saying to herself:

'Slut! Whore!'

After breakfast, Luiza went to her room and sat down on
the chaise longue with the newspaper. Not that she could
concentrate enough to read.

Thoughts of last night kept whirling up inside her soul, like
leaves caught up now and then from the quiet earth by the
autumn wind: certain words he had spoken, certain impulsive
movements, his whole way of loving . . . And she sat still, her
eyes moist, feeling these recollections vibrate long and gently
along the nerves of her memory. Thoughts of Jorge had still
not left her; he had been constantly in her mind since the
previous night; this did not frighten or torment her; he was
there, unmoving, but present, filling her neither with fear nor
remorse; it was as if he had died or had gone far away, never to
return, or as if he had abandoned her! She herself was frightened at her own calmness. And yet she felt annoyed too at his
constant, impassive presence inside her head, obstinate and
spectral; she instinctively began to heap up excuses. It hadn't
been her fault! She had not voluntarily opened her arms to
Bazilio! It had been 'fate'; it had been the heat of the moment,

the twilight, perhaps a little too much wine . . . She must be mad. And she repeated to herself the traditional excuses: she wasn't the first woman to deceive her husband; and many did so out of mere lust, not out of passion, as she had done . . . How many famous, much-admired women had had adulterous affairs! Even queens had had lovers. And he loved her so very much! He would be so faithful, so discreet! His words were so captivating and his kisses so intoxicating! And, besides, there was nothing she could do about it now! Nothing!

And she resolved to reply to his note. She went into the study. As soon as she did so, she caught sight of Jorge's photograph – a life-size image of his head – in its black varnished frame. Her heart contracted; she stood as if paralysed – like a person hot from running who suddenly enters a cold underground chamber; and she studied his curly hair, his dark beard, his cravat, and the two crossed swords glinting on the wall above. If he found out, he would kill her! She turned very pale. She looked vaguely around – at the velvet jacket hanging from a hook, the blanket he wrapped around his feet, all neatly folded up, the large sheets of drawing paper on the other table at the far end, the jar for his tobacco, and the box of pistols! Yes, he would kill her!

The room was so imbued with Jorge's personality that it seemed to her he was about to walk into the room at any moment . . . What if he did suddenly return? She had not had a letter for three days – and he, the *other man*, might catch her there red-handed, as she was sitting writing to her lover! No, this was nonsense, she thought. The steamship from Barreiro didn't get in until five o'clock; and, besides, in his last letter, he had said that he would be away for another month, possibly longer . . .

She sat down, picked up a sheet of paper and began, in her rather large handwriting:

My darling Bazilio . . .

But a sudden fear paralysed her; she felt a kind of premonition that Jorge had come back, that he was about to walk in

. . . Perhaps it would be better not to write the letter . . . She got up and wandered into the drawing room, where she sat down on the divan; and as if contact with that broad sofa and, with it, ardent memories of the night before had given her the courage to commit guilty, loving acts, she marched straight back into the study and wrote rapidly:

You cannot imagine how happy I was to get your letter this morning . . .

The old pen wrote badly; she dipped it in the ink again and when she shook it, her hand trembled slightly, and a black blot fell onto the paper. This upset her, it seemed to her a 'bad omen'. She hesitated for a moment and as she sat, scratching her head, her elbows resting on the desk, she could hear Juliana sweeping the landing outside, humming 'O beloved letter'. In the end, she impatiently tore the paper up into tiny pieces and threw them into the varnished wooden chest with two metal handles which stood next to the desk and where Jorge deposited his old drafts and waste paper; they used to call it the 'sarcophagus', and Juliana had obviously not bothered to empty it, because it was overflowing with paper.

She took another sheet and began again:

My darling Bazilio,
You cannot imagine how I felt on receiving your letter this morning when I woke up. I covered it with kisses . . .

Just then, the door curtain drew back very slightly, forming soft folds, and Juliana's voice said discreetly:

'The seamstress is here, madam.'

Startled, Luiza had quickly covered the paper with her hand.

'Ask her to wait.'

And she went on writing:

What a shame that it was only your letter and not you in person! I am astonished at myself, at how, in such a brief time, you have taken possession of my heart, but the truth is I never stopped loving you. Don't think me fickle because of this, don't think badly of me, because I want you to respect me, but the fact is I have never stopped loving you and when I saw you again, after the futile journey that carried you so far away, I could not control the feelings that impelled me towards you, my darling Bazilio. I could not help myself, Bazilio. Yesterday, when that wretched maid said that you had come to say goodbye, Bazilio, I almost died; but when I saw it was not true, oh, I can't explain it, but I just adored you! And if you had asked me for my life, I would have given it to you, because I myself am amazed at how much I love you . . . But why did you lie and why did you come? It was very naughty of you! I had wanted to say goodbye to you for ever, but, my darling Bazilio, I simply cannot! There's nothing I can do. I have always loved you and now I am yours, I belong to you body and soul, I feel, were that possible, as if I loved you even more . . .

'Where is she? Where is she?' said a voice in the drawing room.

Luiza leaped to her feet, deathly pale. It was Jorge! She frantically screwed up the piece of paper and tried to stuff it into her pocket, but the robe she was wearing had no pockets! Desperate, unthinking, she threw it into the 'sarcophagus'. She stood waiting, resting her two hands on the desk, as if life itself had stopped.

The door curtain was drawn back, and she saw Dona Felicidade's blue velvet hat appear.

'Ah, there you are, you minx! What are you up to? But what's wrong, my dear, you're as white as chalk.'

Luiza, very pale and cold, fell back into the armchair and said with a weary smile.

'I was writing something and I suddenly felt terribly dizzy . . .'

'Oh, don't talk to me about dizzy spells,' said Dona Felicidade. 'Mine are so bad sometimes that I have to cling on to the furniture for support; I'm even afraid of going out walking on my own. What you and I both need is a good purgative!'

'Let's go into my room,' said Luiza. 'We'll be more comfortable there.'

As she got to her feet, her legs were shaking.

They walked through the drawing room; Juliana was just beginning to tidy up. Luiza, in passing, noticed some ash on the marble top of the console table, underneath the oval mirror: it was from the previous night, from *his* cigar! She brushed it off and, when she looked up, was shocked to see how pale her face was.

The seamstress, all in black, and wearing a hat adorned with purple ribbons, was waiting, perched on the chaise longue, with a package on her lap and a despondent look on her face; she had come to let Luiza try on the bodice of a two-piece outfit; as she fitted and pinned and tacked, she spoke softly, with an air of sad humility, occasionally uttering a dry little cough; as soon as she had left, with a light, ghostly step, her dark shawl wrapped tightly about her bony shoulder blades, Dona Felicidade began talking about *him*, about the Councillor. She had met him in Moinho de Vento. And do you know, he did not even speak to her! He gave her the briefest of bows and off he went; why, anyone would think he was running away! What do you make of that? His indifference was killing her! She did not understand it, she really did not understand it!

'After all,' she cried, 'I may be no spring chicken, but I'm no old crock either! Isn't that so?'

'Absolutely,' said Luiza distractedly. She had suddenly remembered the letter.

'I may be in my forties, but I can still carry off a low-cut gown! My shoulders and neck are my best feature!'

Luiza was about to get up, but Dona Felicidade said again:

'Yes, my best feature! They would be the envy of many women far younger than myself!'

'I'm sure,' agreed Luiza, smiling vaguely.

'And he's not a young man himself.'

'No.'

'Though very well preserved,' she added, her eyes shining. 'He could still make a woman very happy!'

'Very.'

'He's such an attractive man!' sighed Dona Felicidade.

Then Luiza said:

'Would you excuse me just a moment. I'll be back in a second.'

'Off you go, my dear, off you go.'

Luiza ran into the study, straight to the 'sarcophagus'. It was empty! And what about her letter?

Terrified, she summoned Juliana.

'Did you empty the wastepaper bin?'

'I did, madam,' Juliana replied serenely.

Then she enquired with interest:

'Why? Have you lost some papers?'

Luiza turned pale.

'It was a piece of paper that I threw in the bin. Where did you empty it?'

'In the rubbish bin, as usual, madam. I assumed it wasn't needed . . .'

'Let me see!'

She ran up to the kitchen.

Behind her, Juliana was saying.

'It was only five minutes ago! The bin was really full. I was just tidying the study. Heavens, if madam had told me . . .'

But the rubbish bin was empty. Joana had just that minute taken it downstairs; seeing Luiza's distress, she asked:

'Why? Have you lost something, madam?'

'A piece of paper,' said Luiza, terribly pale, looking around her on the floor.

'There was quite a lot of paper, madam,' said the girl, 'I threw it all in the bin.'

'Some of it might have fallen out, Senhora Joana,' Juliana suggested timidly.

'Go and see, Joana, go and see,' urged Luiza, suddenly gripped by hope.

Juliana seemed genuinely upset.

'Dear Lord! How was I to know? Why didn't you tell me, madam?'

'It's all right. It's not your fault, woman.'

'Oh dear, I feel quite sick. Was it something important, madam?'

'No, it was just a bill.'

'Oh, my goodness!'

Joana returned, waving a piece of grubby paper. Luiza snatched it from her and read: 'the diameter of the first exploratory shaft . . .'

'No, no, that's not it!' she cried angrily.

'Then it's gone down the chute, madam, there's nothing else.'

'Did you have a good look?'

'I searched everywhere.'

And Juliana continued to wail:

'Oh, this is dreadful, madam, I would rather have lost ten *tostões*! Oh, madam, how was I to know . . .'

'All right, all right,' muttered Luiza, going downstairs.

But she was uneasy, she felt a kind of ill-defined suspicion. She remembered the note she had written to Bazilio the night before and which she had crumpled up and put in the pocket of her dress. She went back into the room, in a state of some agitation.

Dona Felicidade had taken off her hat and settled herself on the chaise longue.

'I'm so sorry about that,' said Luiza.

'Oh, don't worry, my dear. What's the problem?'

'Oh, it's a bill I seem to have lost,' she replied.

She went over to her wardrobe and found the note in her pocket. This calmed her. The letter must have been thrown out with the rubbish. But what a foolish thing to have done!

'Oh well, that's that!' she said, sitting down resignedly.

And Dona Felicidade immediately lowered her voice confidentially:

'I've come to talk to you about something – a secret!'

Luiza immediately looked concerned.

'As you know,' Dona Felicidade continued slowly, pausing now and then, 'my maid, Josefa, is going to be married to a Galician fellow. He's from a village near Tui, and he says that

178

there's a woman in his village who can make an amazing charm for bringing two people together in matrimony. He says it's the best charm there is. She puts a spell on a particular man, and the man is filled with such passion that he arranges the marriage right there and then, and everyone lives happily ever after.'

Luiza, calm now, smiled.

'Now,' said Dona Felicidade, 'don't start in with your ifs and buts . . .'

There was a tone of superstitious respect in her voice.

'They say she's worked miracles. Men who have abandoned young women to their fate or merely neglected them, husbands who take mistresses, in short, every possible kind of male ingratitude . . . As soon as the woman casts the spell, the men begin to soften, to be filled with remorse, to fall in love, and, before you know it, they're head over heels . . . it was Josefa who told me about her. So it occurred to me . . .'

'To put a spell on the Councillor!' cried Luiza.

'What do you think?'

Luiza laughed out loud, and Dona Felicidade was positively shocked. She recounted other case histories: a nobleman who had dishonoured a washerwoman; a man who had abandoned his wife and children to run away with a slut . . . In every case, the spell had had a dramatic effect, inducing in the men a sudden, passionate love for the scorned woman. If they lived nearby, they would surrender at once; if they lived farther off, they would return urgently, on foot, by horse, by stagecoach, as fast as they could, aflame with love . . . And they would give themselves up, as docile and humble as chained slaves.

'But the Galician,' she went on, very excited now, 'says that for him to go back to his village, talk to the woman, taking with him a picture of the Councillor, because she needs his picture and mine, for mine is necessary too, to go there, to talk to her and come back, would cost seven *moedas*!'

'Dona Felicidade!' said Luiza reprovingly.

'Now, no ifs and buts. I know of cases . . .'

Then getting to her feet, she added:

'But seven *moedas*! Seven *moedas*!' she cried, opening her eyes wide.

Juliana appeared at the door and very softly, and with a smile on her face, said:

'Excuse me, madam.'

She beckoned her into the corridor:

'There's a letter for you. It's from the hotel.'

Luiza blushed scarlet.

'For heaven's sake, woman, there's no need to make such a mystery of it!'

But she did not go back into the room, she opened the letter there in the corridor; it was hurriedly written in pencil:

'My love,' wrote Bazilio, 'by a happy coincidence I have discovered precisely what we need, a discreet little nest where we can meet.' And he indicated the street, the number of the house, important landmarks on the way, the quickest route. 'When will you come, my love? Come tomorrow. I have christened the house "Paradise", because for me, my darling, it is Paradise. I'll be there from midday onwards: as soon as I see you, I'll come down.'

Such amorous haste to find a 'nest' – proof of his impatient passion, of his concern for her alone – aroused in her a delicious welling up of pride; at the same time, that secret 'Paradise', like something out of a novel, filled her with the hope of exceptional joys; and all her anxieties and fears about the lost letter vanished before that warm feeling, like vaporous mists before the rising sun.

She went back into her room, her eyes bright.

'So what do you think, then?' asked Dona Felicidade, whose idea had taken a tyrannical hold on her.

'About what?'

'Do you think I should send the man to Tui?'

Luiza shrugged; she felt suddenly bored by these machinations with witchcraft, by such obsessive love. Proud of her own romantic intrigue, she found such senile sentimentality repugnant.

'Certainly not!' she said with great disdain.

'Oh, my dear, don't say that, don't!' cried Dona Felicidade forlornly.

'All right, then, send him!' said Luiza impatiently.

'But it costs seven *moedas*!' exclaimed Dona Felicidade, close to tears.

Luiza burst out laughing.

'That strikes me as quite cheap for a husband.'

'And if the charm fails?'

'Then it's expensive!'

Dona Felicidade gave a heavy sigh. She was so unhappy, caught between her concupiscent impulses and her financial caution. Luiza took pity on her and, selecting a dress from her wardrobe, said:

'Don't worry, my dear, you don't need charms or witchcraft!'

Dona Felicidade raised her eyes to heaven.

'Are you going out?' she asked gloomily.

'No.'

Dona Felicidade suggested that she come with her to the convent hospital of the Incarnation. They could visit Senhora Dona Ana Silveira; the poor woman had a boil! And they could see the festival decorations in the church; there was a brand-new frontal cloth, which was absolutely gorgeous!

'And I'd rather like to say a prayer or two, to find some relief for my insides,' she added with a sigh.

Luiza agreed. She was in the mood to see brightly lit altars and hear whispered prayers in the choir, as if such devotional refinements were suited to her sentimental inclinations. She hurriedly got dressed.

'How you've filled out, my dear!' exclaimed Dona Felicidade in surprise, when she saw her shoulders, neck and throat.

Luiza, standing in front of the mirror looking at herself, pleased with her own figure, smiled her sensual smile and very slowly and voluptuously stroked her smooth, white skin.

'Nicely rounded!' she said, admiring herself.

'Nicely rounded! Why, you're round as a ball!'

And she added sadly:

'Of course, with the life you lead and with a husband like yours, with everything you could possibly want, with no children, no worries . . .'

181

'But, my dear,' said Luiza, 'your misfortunes have hardly made you thin.'

'Too true, too true! But . . .' and she seemed suddenly quite inconsolable, as if poring over the ruins of her own self, 'my insides, my stomach, my liver . . . are in a disastrous state!'

'If the woman in Tui can perform miracles, she'll make everything good as new!'

Dona Felicidade gave a doubtful, disconsolate smile.

'Have you seen my new hat?' cried Luiza suddenly. 'You haven't? Oh, it's lovely!'

She fetched it from the wardrobe. It was made of fine straw and decorated with forget-me-nots.

'What do you think?'

'Oh, it's gorgeous!'

Luiza was looking at it, flicking the little blue flowers with her fingertips.

'So fresh,' said Dona Felicidade.

'It is, isn't it?'

She carefully put it on, her face serious. It really suited her! If Bazilio were to see her wearing it, he was bound to like it, she thought. And, who knows, they might bump into him.

She was suddenly filled, for no reason, by a feeling of exuberant joy: she found it so delicious to be alive, to be going to visit the convent church, to be thinking about her lover! And, head in the clouds, she searched the room for the keys to the dressing table.

Where had she left them? In the dining room perhaps! She would go and look. She ran giddily out of the room, singing softly:

*Amici, la notte è bella . . .*
*La ra la la . . .*

She almost collided with Juliana, who was sweeping the corridor.

'Don't forget to starch that embroidered petticoat for tomorrow, Juliana!'

'I won't, madam. It's in the starch now!'

182

And following her with fierce eyes, she muttered:

'Sing, little dumpling, little whore, little slut!'

And she herself, filled by a sudden intense joy, briskly continued her sweeping and sang out in her cracked voice:

> Soon, soon, the end of war is nigh,
> That is what they've told me
> and I hope it is no lie . . .

And she concluded with heavy emphasis:

> For, O, how happy I shall be!

The next day, at two o'clock in the afternoon, Sebastião and Julião were walking in the gardens of São Pedro de Alcântara.

Sebastião had been describing his encounter with Luiza and how much his respect for her had grown since. At first, she had, indeed, seemed angry.

'But she was quite right. After all, hearing something like that out of the blue . . . And I didn't broach the subject delicately enough, I was far too brutal.'

Then, poor thing, she had concurred at once, she had revealed how distressed she was, how fearful for her reputation, she had asked his advice. She had even had tears in her eyes.

'I told her that the best thing would be to talk to her cousin and tell him what was happening. What do you think?'

'Hm,' said Julião vaguely.

He had listened to Sebastião distractedly, drawing on his cigarette, sucking in the cheeks of his bilious, lacklustre face.

'So do you think I did the right thing?'

And after a pause:

'She's a thoroughly decent woman, Julião, thoroughly decent!'

They continued in silence. The day was muggy and overcast, with thunder in the air: fat, heavy, grey clouds were piling up, growing black over towards Graça, behind the hills; a light wind stirred now and again and set the leaves on the trees shivering.

'Anyway, I feel much happier now,' said Sebastião in conclusion. 'What do you think?'

Julião shrugged and gave a sad smile.

'I wish I had your problems, old man!' he said.

And then he spoke bitterly about his own anxieties. A week ago, the post of substitute teacher at the School of Medicine had been advertised, and he was preparing for it. It would be his salvation, he said; if he got the post, he would immediately gain reputation, clients and money. It certainly couldn't hurt to be inside the system! But his confidence in his superiority did not reassure him, because this was, after all, Portugal! Here such matters as knowledge, education and talent count for nothing, what matters are one's sponsors. He had none, but his rival, an insipid fellow, was the nephew of the director-general and had relatives in high places, which made him, therefore, a colossus! That was why he was working so hard, but it seemed to him vital that he should have his own champions! But who?

'Do you know anyone, Sebastião?'

Sebastião remembered a cousin of his, a deputy in the Alentejo, a fat fellow with a nasal voice, who belonged to the majority party. If Julião wanted, he could talk to him. But he had always heard that the School of Medicine did not go in for intermediaries and for intrigues. Otherwise, there was always Councillor Acácio . . .

'A fool!' snorted Julião. 'An impostor! Who would take any notice of him? Your cousin, though, he seems a possibility. Someone will have to talk to him, to work on him.' For he had great belief in the influence of intermediaries and 'important people', and in the docile nature of fortune when directed by skilled intriguers. And with a pride that was mingled with menace, he said: 'I'll show them what knowledge means, Sebastião!'

He was about to explain the subject of the thesis he intended to present, when Sebastião interrupted him:

'There she is.'

'Who?'

'Luiza.'

She was walking along past the Passeio Público, all in black, and alone. Blushing slightly, she responded to the bows of the two men with a smile and a little wave of the hand.

And Sebastião stood utterly still, following her devotedly with her eyes:

'She positively breathes honesty! The dear girl's off to the shops!'

She was going to meet Bazilio in 'Paradise' for the first time. And she was very nervous: she had been unable to master the fear she had felt all morning, an ill-defined fear that had prompted her to put on a very thick veil and that made her heart beat faster when she saw Sebastião. At the same time, though, an intense, multifaceted curiosity was driving her on, affording her a little shiver of pleasure. She was, at last, going to have the kind of adventure she had read about so often in romantic novels! She was going to experience a new variety of love, all sorts of extraordinary sensations! All the necessary ingredients were there: the mysterious little house, the illicit secret, the heart-pounding turmoil of danger! For she was more impressed by the arrangements than by the sentiment behind them; indeed, she found the house more interesting and alluring than Bazilio! What would it be like? It was near Arroios, opposite the Largo de Santa Bárbara: she had a vague memory of a row of old houses . . . She wished it could be in the country, in a villa, with murmuring trees and soft grass; they would go for strolls, in poetic silence, hands entwined; and, later, the sound of water falling in the stone basins of fountains would lend a languid rhythm to their amorous dreams. But it was on the third floor; Heaven knows what it would be like inside. She remembered a novel by Paul Féval in which the hero, a poet and a duke, lines the walls and floors of a humble cottage with satins and tapestries; there he meets his lover; passers-by, seeing that ramshackle house, think pityingly of the poverty that doubtless inhabits it, while inside, in utter secrecy, flowers in Sèvres vases drop their petals and bare feet tread venerable Gobelin tapestries! She knew Bazilio's tastes; their 'Paradise' was sure to be just like the one in Paul Féval's novel.

But in Largo de Camões she noticed that the man with the long goatee beard, the one she had seen in the Passeio Público, was pacing after her like a cockerel; she immediately hailed a carriage. And as she drove down the Chiado, she savoured the delicious sensation of being carried swiftly towards her lover, and even looked rather scornfully at the people she passed, caught up in life at its most trivial, while she was heading for a romantic hour of life at its most amorous! Yet as they came nearer, she was assailed by shyness, by a pang of reticence, like a plebeian who has to climb the steps of a palace, past ranks of solemn halberdiers. She imagined Bazilio waiting for her, reclining on a silk divan, and she was almost afraid that her inexperienced, bourgeois simplicity would prove incapable of finding sufficiently lofty words or suitably exalted caresses. He must have known such beautiful, wealthy women, educated in the ways of love! She wished she could arrive in her own coupé, wearing lace worth hundreds of *mil-réis*, and ready with witty sayings straight out of a book . . .

The carriage stopped outside a yellowish house with a tiny front door. As soon as she went in, she was overwhelmed by a bland, salty, sickening smell. The stairs, with their worn steps, rose steeply between narrow, flaking, damp-stained walls. On the landing of the mezzanine, the grimy light from the central courtyard filtered in through a window covered by a small wire grille, grey with accumulated dust and covered in cobwebs. And behind a narrow door to one side, she could hear a cradle creaking and the anguished crying of a child.

Just then, Bazilio came down the stairs, cigar in mouth, saying softly:

'You're late! Come up! I thought you weren't coming. What happened?'

The stairs were too narrow for them to be able to walk up them side by side. And going ahead of her, Bazilio half-turned to say:

'I've been here for an hour, my dear! I thought you must have got the wrong street!'

He pushed open the door and ushered her into a small room, lined with blue-and-white striped paper.

At the far end, Luiza caught sight of an iron bed with a yellowish bedspread made from a motley patchwork of different fabrics, and thick, grey, ill-washed sheets that lay immodestly open.

She flushed scarlet and sat down, silent and embarrassed. Her wide eyes gradually took in the ignoble scratches left on the walls near the bed by people striking matches; the fraying, threadbare mat, with an inkstain on it; the window blind made from a piece of much-darned red cloth; the lithograph in which a figure, wearing a diaphanous blue tunic floated about, scattering flowers . . . Her eye was particularly drawn to a large photograph on display above the wicker settee: it showed a short, stout individual, with a cheerful, foolish expression on his face and a narrow beard, and who looked, for all the world, like a ship's pilot in his Sunday best; he was wearing white trousers and was seated, legs splayed, with one hand on his knee and the other outstretched and resting on a truncated column; and beneath the frame, as if on a gravestone, a wreath of everlasting flowers hung from the yellow head of a nail.

'It's all I could find,' Bazilio said. 'And it was pure luck really; it's very out of the way, very discreet . . . Admittedly, it's not exactly luxurious . . .'

'No,' she said quietly. She got up and went to the window, where she lifted one corner of the cotton blind; opposite was a row of poor houses: a grizzled cobbler was sitting in a doorway, hammering away at the sole of a shoe; at the entrance to a small shop a bundle of kindling and a packet of cigarettes dangled from a piece of string; and at a window, a dishevelled young woman was sadly rocking a sickly child in her arms, its small, yellowish head covered in large scabs.

Luiza bit her lip and felt herself grow sad. Then someone rapped discreetly at the door. Startled, Luiza hastily lowered her veil. Bazilio opened the door. A mellifluous, sibilant voice whispered something. Luiza thought she heard: 'So sorry to disturb you, here's your keys . . .'

'Fine, fine,' said Bazilio hurriedly and slammed the door.

'Who was that?'

'The landlady.'

The sky was growing black; at intervals, heavy drops of rain splashed down onto the cobbles in the street below; the crepuscular light made the room seem even more melancholy.

'How did you find this place?' asked Luiza bleakly.

'Someone recommended it to me.'

So other people had come there, had 'loved' there, she thought. And the bed seemed to her utterly repugnant.

'Take off your hat,' said Bazilio almost impatiently. 'It bothers me seeing you with that hat on your head.'

She slowly unfastened the elastic that held it in place and laid it down disconsolately on the wicker settee.

Bazilio took her hands in his and led her over to the bed, where they sat down.

'You look so lovely!' He kissed her throat and rested his head on her breast. Then he looked at her voluptuously and said:

'I dreamed about you all night!'

A sudden flurry of rain beat against the windows. There was immediate rapid knocking on the door.

'What is it?' yelled Bazilio angrily.

The sibilant voice explained that she had left a blanket out on the balcony to dry. If it got wet, it would be ruined!

'I'll pay you for the blanket, now go away!' bawled Bazilio.

'You can keep the blanket if you like.'

'To hell with the blanket!'

And Luiza, feeling the chill air on her bare shoulders, sank back beneath Bazilio with an air of vague resignation, conscious all the time of the pilot's foolish face turned to look at her.

It was as if a yacht, magnificently fitted out for a romantic voyage, had run aground in the mudflats of the river as it set sail, and its adventurous captain, who had dreamed of the incenses and musks of aromatic forests, now stood motionless

on the deck, covering his nose against the stench of the
sewers.

As soon as Luiza began going out every day, Juliana
thought: 'She's going to meet that man!'

And she became even more servile. When Luiza returned
at five o'clock, Juliana would rush excitedly to open the front
door, an obsequious smile on her lips. And what zeal! What
attention to detail! A missing button, a ribbon coming loose,
and it was: 'a thousand apologies, madam', 'do forgive me, just
this once', and many other such humble lamentations. She
took a devoted interest in Luiza's health, in her clothes, in
what there was for supper . . .

And this despite the fact that, ever since the visits to 'Paradise' had begun, her workload had increased; she had starching and ironing to do every day; often she was up until eleven
o'clock at night soaping collars, lace or cuffs in a brass bowl.
At six o'clock in the morning, or even earlier, she was already
hard at work with the iron. And all this without a word of
complaint. She even said to Joana:

'It's a real treat to see a lady so well turned out! Because I
can tell you, some ladies . . . well! And I'm not just saying
that, it gives me real pleasure. And now that I have my
health back, thank God, I'm not afraid of hard work any
more!'

She no longer grumbled about 'the mistress'. She even said
to Joana over and over:

'Our mistress is a saint! And so easy to get on with . . .
There's none better!'

Her face had lost its bilious hue, its look of sour tightness.
Sometimes, over supper or at night, as she sat silently sewing
beside Joana, by the light of the oil lamp, a sudden smile would
cross her face, or else her eyes would shine with expansive
pleasure.

'You look like you're thinking about something nice,
Senhora Juliana.'

'Oh, just thinking my own thoughts, Senhora Joana!' she
would reply smugly.

She seemed to have lost her envy; she even listened calmly to a description of the new silk dress that Gertrudes, the mathematics teacher's housekeeper, had sported on a public holiday in September. She said only:

'One day, I'll have new dresses as well and good ones too! Made by a dressmaker!'

Similarly ambiguous words spoken on other occasions seemed to reveal the hope of some period of imminent abundance. Joana had even asked her:

'Are you expecting to come into money, Senhora Juliana?'

'Possibly!' came the tart response.

Juliana, in fact, loathed Luiza more with each day that passed. In the mornings, when she watched Luiza getting all dressed up and perfuming herself with eau-de-cologne, admiring her reflection in the dressing table mirror and singing to herself, she sometimes had to leave the room because she was gripped by such a spasm of hatred that she was afraid she might explode! She hated Luiza for her dresses, her happiness, her underwear, for the man she was going to see, for all the pleasures she enjoyed as mistress of the house. 'Hussy!' When Luiza left the house, she would peer out of the window after her and watch her walking up the street, and then, as she closed the window, she would give a rancorous giggle and say to herself:

'Have fun, my little dumpling, have fun, because my day will come! Oh, it will!'

Luiza was, indeed, having fun. She left the house at two o'clock each day. In the street, people were already saying that 'the Engineer's wife was up to something'.

As soon as she rounded the corner, the 'council' would gather to exchange views. They were sure she was going off to meet 'the dandy'. But where? That was what the coal merchant's wife burned to know.

'At his hotel,' muttered Senhor Paula. 'It's scandalous what goes on in hotels these days! Or perhaps,' he would add dully, 'in one of those disgusting houses in the Baixa!'

The tobacconist's widow thought it a great shame, for Luiza seemed such a sensible woman.

'You know what they say: a stray cow will graze anywhere,' snorted Senhor Paula. 'Women are all the same.'

'*I'm* not!' protested Senhora Helena. 'I've always been a decent woman!'

And so had she, declared the coal merchant's wife. No one could say anything against her!

'I'm talking about high society, about noblewomen, the sort who dress all in silk. Scum, the lot of them! I should know!' Then he added solemnly: 'Ordinary people have far more morality! Ordinary people are a different race entirely!' And legs akimbo, hands plunged in his pockets, he would stand absorbed, head down, eyes fixed on the ground. 'Oh, yes!' he would mutter. 'Oh, yes!' As if he found the stones in the street less numerous than the many virtues of 'the people'!

Sebastião, who had spent nearly two weeks at his villa in Almada, was appalled when, on his return, Tia Joana gave him the 'big news', that Luiza now left her house everyday at two o'clock prompt and that the cousin had not been back; Gertrudes had told her; in the street, they spoke of little else . . .

'Can the poor woman not even go to the shops, about her own business?' exclaimed Sebastião. 'Gertrudes is a shameless gossip; I don't know why you even allow her to set foot in this house. Coming here with such tittle-tattle!'

'There's no need to get so hoity-toity about it!' retorted Tia Joana, greatly put out. 'Really, Master Sebastião!' The poor woman was merely repeating what she had heard in the street. In fact, she had stood up for Luiza! She had actually been complaining about all the gossip! And with that, Tia Joana left the room, muttering: 'Honestly, fancy getting so hoity-toity!'

Sebastião called her back and calmed her down:

'But who is it who's saying these things, Tia Joana?'

'Who?' Then emphatically: 'The whole street! The whole street!'

Sebastião was lost for words. The whole street! Of course! There she was going out every day, a woman who, normally, when Jorge was at home, never left the house! The neighbours who had gossiped about her cousin's visits would naturally begin to comment on her daily outings! She was ruining her reputation! And he could do nothing about it! Warn her again? Endure another scene like the last one? He simply couldn't.

He went to visit her. He had no wish to touch on any of this, he merely wanted to see her. She was out. He returned two days later. Juliana came to the door and said with her pallid smile: 'She just went out, a moment ago. You might still catch her in Rua da Patriarcal.' He did finally meet her at the bottom of Rua de São Roque. Luiza seemed very pleased to see him. Why had he spent so long in Almada? How could he desert her like that!

He had some carpenters working there and had to keep an eye on them. What about her?

'Oh, not too bad. A bit bored. Jorge says he'll be away for some time yet. I've been awfully lonely. Julião hasn't been to see me, nor has the Councillor; in fact, Dona Felicidade is the only one who has occasionally dropped in. She's very involved with the convent church of the Incarnation at the moment. You know what these devout people are like!' And she laughed.

So where was she off to?

To buy a few things and then to the dressmaker's. 'But do come and see me, Sebastião.'

'I will.'

'In the evening. I'm so alone then! I've been playing the piano a lot. I'd be lost without my piano!'

That same afternoon, Sebastião received a letter from Jorge: 'Have you seen Luiza? I've been quite worried because I haven't had a letter from her for more than five days. Besides, she's so lazy that, when she does write, she only manages to scribble me about four lines because the post is always about to leave. Why can't she tell the post to wait, damn it! She complains of being bored, of being all alone, that everyone has abandoned her, that it's like living in a desert. Go and see if you can keep the poor thing company.'

The following evening, he went to her house. She received him red-faced and sleepy-eyed, wearing a white peignoir. She had felt exhausted when she came in, and had fallen asleep on the chaise longue after supper. Did he have any news, she asked, yawning.

They talked about the work being done at Almada, about the Councillor, about Julião, then they fell silent. There was an awkwardness between them.

Luiza lit the candles on the piano and showed him the new music she was studying, Gounod's 'Medjé'; but there was one passage where she always got muddled up; she asked Sebastião to play it while she stood by the piano, keeping time with her foot, softly singing the melody, to which Sebastião's playing lent a penetrating charm. Then she wanted to try, but when she went wrong again, she got angry, threw the sheet music down beside her and flounced over to the sofa, saying:

'I hardly ever play now. My fingers are getting rusty!'

Sebastião did not dare to ask after cousin Bazilio. Luiza did not even mention his name. And seeing in that reserve a diminution of trust and a lingering remnant of resentment on her part, Sebastião announced that he had to pay a visit to the General Association of Agriculture and left, in a mood of great dejection.

Each day that followed brought with it its own disquieting news. Sometimes it was Tia Joana saying to him in the evening: 'Luiza went out again today. In this heat, she might catch something!' At other times, it was the council of neighbours, whom he spotted from afar, and who were doubtless 'picking holes in the poor lady'.

It reminded him strongly of the 'Slander aria' in *The Barber of Seville*: the slander was at first as light as the fluttering wings of a bird, rising to a terrifying crescendo, until it burst forth like thunder!

He now went the long way around in order to avoid having to pass Senhor Paula and the tobacconist's: he felt so ashamed! He had met Teixeira Azevedo who had asked him:

'When is Jorge coming back? Is he going to stay away for ever?'

This trivial remark terrified him.

One day, when he was feeling even more preoccupied than usual, he went in search of Julião. He found him working away in his fourth-floor room, in shirtsleeves and slippers, grimy and dishevelled, surrounded by papers, with a small coffee pot at his elbow. The black floor was littered with cigarette butts; in one corner was a pile of dirty clothes; books lay open on the unmade bed; and the whole place gave off a fetid odour of neglect. The window looked out onto the central courtyard whence came the strident singing of a housemaid and the clatter of pots being scrubbed.

As soon as Sebastião went in, Julião got up, stretched, rolled himself a cigarette and announced that he had been working since seven o'clock! Good, eh? Just so that Senhor Sebastião knew!

'Besides, you've arrived at a very opportune moment. I was about to send a message to your house. I was supposed to receive some money and it hasn't come. Lend me a *libra*, will you?'

And he immediately started discussing his thesis. It was going really well now!

With paternal delight, he read out whole paragraphs from the prologue and, greatly pleased and brimming with the confidence that comes from the stimulus of work, he strode about the room, saying:

'I'll show them that there are still real Portuguese men in Portugal, Sebastião! They'll be astonished! Just you wait!'

He sat down and began whistling as he set to, numbering the sheets. Sebastião, almost ashamed to disrupt this scientific train of thought with his domestic concerns, said timidly:

'Actually I came to talk to you about our friends . . .'

Just then, however, the door was flung open, and a young man with a wild beard and slightly crazed eyes entered; he was a student from the School of Medicine and a friend of Julião's; the two immediately resumed the discussion they had begun that morning and which had been interrupted at eleven o'clock when the young man with the crazed eyes had left to have lunch at the Áurea restaurant.

'No, my friend!' declared the student, much excited. 'I still stick to my view! Medicine is a half-science, physiology is another half-science! They are both conjectural sciences because we lack the very basis, the vital principle!'

And standing, arms folded, before Sebastião, he roared:

'What do we know of the vital principle?'

Sebastião humbly lowered his eyes.

But Julião responded indignantly:

'You poor wretch, you've been corrupted by the vitalist doctrine!' He fulminated against vitalism, which, he declared, went 'counter to the scientific spirit'. 'Any theory that proposes that the laws governing inanimate bodies are not the same as those governing animate ones is a grotesque heresy!' he exclaimed. 'And Bichat, who proclaims it, is a fool!'

The student, beside himself with rage, thundered that only a nincumpoop would call Bichat a fool.

Julião, however, scorned the insult and went on, intoxicated by his own ideas:

'What does the vital principle matter to us? It's about as important to me as the first shirt I ever wore! The vital principle is like any other principle: a secret! We will live in eternal ignorance of it! We cannot know any principle. Life, death, origins, ends, all are mysteries! They are primary causes with which we have nothing to do, nothing! We can battle for centuries and not advance an inch. The physiologist, the chemist, have nothing to do with the principles of things: what they care about are phenomena! Now phenomena and their immediate causes, my dear friend, can be determined with as much rigour in the inanimate as they can in the animate, in a stone and in a judge! And physiology and medicine are just as much exact sciences as chemistry! Descartes says so!'

They then engaged in a shouting match about Descartes, and immediately, without the astonished Sebastião noticing any transition, launched into a bitter argument about the idea of God.

The student appeared to need God in order to explain the universe, but Julião angrily attacked God, describing him as 'a hackneyed hypothesis', 'a relic of the Miguelista party'! Then they began attacking each other on the social question, like two fighting cocks.

The student, eyes bulging, thumped the desk with his fist and upheld the principle of authority! Julião propounded 'individual anarchy'! And having furiously quoted Proudhon, Bastiat and Jouffroy, they were reduced to making personal remarks. Julião, who dominated because he had the louder voice, violently censured the student for his six per cent bonds, for the absurdity of being the son of a stockbroker and for the large steak he had just eaten at the Áurea!

They exchanged hostile looks.

But moments later, the student uttered a few scornful remarks about Claude Bernard, and the whole furious debate began again.

Sebastião picked up his hat.

'Goodbye,' he said softly.

'Oh, goodbye, Sebastião,' said Julião promptly.

He accompanied him out to the landing.

'And if you want me to speak to my cousin . . .' murmured Sebastião.

'Hm, yes, we'll see, I'll think about it,' said Julião coolly, as if his pride in his work had dissipated his terror of injustice.

Sebastião went down the stairs, thinking: 'It's impossible to talk to him about anything now!'

Suddenly, an idea came to him: what if he went to see Dona Felicidade and told her everything! Dona Felicidade was an extremely loud, rather silly person, but she was, nevertheless, a woman of a certain age and a close friend of Luiza's; she had more authority than he, perhaps more ability too.

He did not hesitate and took a carriage to Rua de São Bento.

Dona Felicidade's maid appeared, looking tearful and near inconsolable:

'Haven't you heard?'

'No.'

'Really?'

'What's happened?'

'My mistress! It was so unfortunate. She sprained her foot while visiting the convent of the Incarnation; she had a fall. She's been very ill, very ill indeed.'

'Is she here?'

'No, she's still at the convent hospital. She can't move. She's with Senhora Dona Ana Silveira. It was just awful! She's in a terrible state!'

'But when did this happen?'

'The day before yesterday in the evening.'

Sebastião got back into his carriage and ordered the driver to go straight to Luiza's house.

Dona Felicidade, ill, and at the convent hospital of the Incarnation! That was why Luiza went out every day. She was going to see her, to keep her company, to look after her.

The neighbours had no basis for their mutterings! She was going to visit a poor sick friend!

It was two o'clock when the carriage stopped outside Luiza's door. He met her coming down the steps, all dressed in black, with pearl-grey gloves and a black veil.

'Oh, come in, Sebastião, come in! Would you like to come upstairs?'

She hovered on the steps, blushing slightly, somewhat embarrassed.

'No, thank you. I came to tell you . . . Didn't you know? Dona Felicidade . . .'

'What?'

'She's sprained her foot. She's not at all well.

'What?!'

Sebastião gave her the details.

'I'll go at once.'

'Yes, you should. I can't because they don't allow male visitors. Poor lady, she's not at all well.' He accompanied her to the corner of the street, even offered her his carriage. 'And give her my best regards and say how sorry I am that I can't come and see her myself! Poor lady! She's in a terrible state apparently!'

He watched her walking towards Rua da Patriarcal,

admiring her graceful figure, then he rubbed his hands together in satisfaction.

Those daily outings were now justified, even sanctified. She was going to be poor Dona Felicidade's nurse! He must ensure that everyone knew: Senhor Paula, the tobacconist, Gertrudes, the Azevedos, everyone, so that when they saw her the next day walking up the street, they would say: 'Off she goes to keep the poor patient company! What a saint!'

Senhor Paula was standing at the door of his shop, and Sebastião took it into his head to go over and talk to him. He felt proud of his own skill, of his fecund resourcefulness.

Pushing his hat slightly back on his head, he pointed with his parasol at the panel representing Dom João VI:

'How much do you want for this, Senhor Paula?'

Senhor Paula was taken aback:

'Are you joking, Senhor Sebastião?'

'Joking?' Sebastião said.

No, he was deadly serious! He needed a few paintings for the hallway in Almada, old ones, without frames, that would go well with the dark wallpaper. 'Like this one. Joking, indeed! Really!

'Forgive me, Senhor Sebastião . . . Well, in that case, there are a few paintings over there that might suit . . .'

'No, I like this portrait of Dom João VI. How much is it?'

Senhor Paula said without hesitation:

'Seven thousand two hundred. But it's a real masterpiece.'

It was a faded, somewhat blackened canvas in which one could just make out, against a sombre background, a few fragments of a ruddy face and ringleted hair. A splash of dull vermilion indicated the velvet of a courtly tailcoat, while a magnificent, protuberant belly filled a greenish waistcoat. The best-preserved part was the royal crown on the cushion beside him, which the artist had worked on with enthusiastic diligence, either out of an idiot's sense of perfectionism or a courtier's reverence.

Sebastião thought it expensive, but Senhor Paula showed him the price written on the back on a strip of paper; he lovingly dusted the painting; he emphasised its beauties, spoke of his own honesty; he found other sellers of second-hand goods so depressing, for 'they had no scruples at all'; he swore that the portrait had belonged to the Palace of Queluz, and he was just about to set to with an attack on matters public, when Sebastião cut things short by saying:

'Right, I'll have it. Send it to me straight away. And send me the bill too.'

'You've got yourself a lovely painting there!'

Sebastião was looking around him. He wanted to mention 'Dona Felicidade's twisted foot', and was searching for a way into the subject. He examined a few Indian vases and a pier glass, then, spotting an invalid chair, cried:

'That's just what Dona Felicidade needs, that chair! It's a good quality one too!'

Senhor Paula opened his eyes wide.

'Dona Felicidade Noronha,' Sebastião repeated. 'So that she could sit comfortably. Didn't you know, man? She's broken her foot, she's been very ill.'

'Dona Felicidade, their friend over there?' And he jerked his thumb in the direction of the Engineer's house.

'Yes. She broke her foot in the church of the Incarnation! And there she has stayed. Dona Luiza goes to see her every day in the convent hospital to keep her company. She was just on her way there now.'

'Ah,' said Senhor Paula slowly. And then, after a pause: 'But I saw Dona Felicidade going into the house about eight days ago.'

'It only happened the day before yesterday.' Sebastião coughed and added, looking away and studying some engravings with exaggerated attention. 'Dona Luiza has been going to the hospital every day anyway to visit Dona Ana Silveira, who has been ill. Poor thing, she's been playing nurse for three weeks now. She spends all her time there. And now it's Dona Felicidade's turn. It never rains but it pours!'

'Well, I had no idea,' murmured Senhor Paula, his hands deep in his pockets.

'Anyway, send me that Dom João VI, will you?'

'Of course, Senhor Sebastião.'

Sebastião went home. He went up to the drawing room, and throwing his hat down on the sofa, said to himself: 'Right, at least appearances have been saved!' He paced up and down for a while with his head down; he felt sad; the fact that he had, by pure chance, succeeded in justifying her outings to the neighbours only made the idea that he could not justify them to himself even crueller. The neighbours' malicious comments would stop for a while, but what about his own thoughts? He wanted to believe them to be false, puerile, unjust, but, despite himself, his good sense and his rectitude were always quietly pondering them. He had, nevertheless, done his duty! And with a sad gesture, he said out loud to the silence in the room:

'Now it rests with her conscience!'

By the afternoon, everyone in the street knew that Dona Felicidade Noronha had sprained her foot while visiting the church of the Incarnation (others said she had broken her leg) and that Dona Luiza barely left her bedside. Senhor Paula declared authoritatively:

'She's a fine young woman, a fine young woman!'

That evening, Gertrudes, the mathematics teacher's housekeeper, went straight to see Tia Joana, to find out 'if it was true about the broken leg'. Tia Joana corrected her: it was her foot, she had twisted her foot. And Gertrudes informed her employer over tea that Dona Felicidade had had the most terrible fall. 'It happened in the church of the Incarnation,' she added. 'Such a commotion! Dona Luiza has even spent the night there apparently.'

'A lot of devout nonsense!' grumbled the teacher in a bored voice.

But everyone else in the street praised her. A few days later, even Teixeira Azevedo (who normally barely acknowledged her) stopped and gave a low bow when he met her in Rua de São Roque.

'Forgive me, madam, but how is your patient getting along?'

'Much better, thank you.'

'Well, madam, it has been most charitable on your part, going to the hospital every day in this heat.'

200

Luiza blushed.

'Poor thing! She doesn't lack for company, but . . .'

'Most charitable, madam,' he declared emphatically. 'I've said so to everyone who cares to listen. Most charitable! Your servant, madam.'

And he departed, feeling greatly moved.

Luiza had, indeed, gone directly to visit Dona Felicidade. She had suffered a simple sprain, but, reclining in Dona Ana da Silveira's rooms, her foot swathed in arnica compresses, terrified that she might 'lose her leg', she spent the day surrounded by friends, feeling sorry for herself, savouring the hospital gossip and nibbling titbits.

As soon as anyone came in to see her, she would redouble her exclamations and complaints; she would launch into the story of 'the accident' in minute, prolix, exhaustive detail: she had been just about to go down the stairs, had placed her foot on the step and had slipped; she had felt herself falling, but had managed to keep her balance and cry out to Our Lady of Good Health! It had not hurt very much at first; but, really, it was a miracle she hadn't died!

All the other ladies agreed that 'it was indeed a miracle'. They gazed at her, much affected, and took it in turns to go up to the chancel to prostrate themselves and ask their particular saints to bring relief to Dona Felicidade!

Luiza's first visit was a great consolation to Dona Felicidade; 'it made her feel so much better', largely because it distressed her greatly to be there in bed and have no news of *him*, to be unable to speak of *him*!

And during the days that followed, as soon as she was alone in the room with Luiza, she would call her over to the bed and ask in a mysterious murmur: 'Have you seen him? Have you any news of him?' She was much concerned that the Councillor might not know that she was unwell and would therefore be unable to bestow on her foot the compassionate thoughts which were its due and which would be such a salve to her heart! But Luiza had not seen him, and so Dona Felicidade would stir her tea, uttering long, painful sighs.

At two o'clock, Luiza would leave the convent hospital and take a carriage to the Rossio; in order not to stop directly outside the door to 'Paradise', with all the noise that a cab would make, she would get out at Largo de Santa Barbara and, making herself as small as possible, shrinking into the shadows cast by the houses, she would hurry along, eyes downcast and a faint smile of pleasure on her lips.

Bazilio would be lying on the bed in his shirtsleeves, waiting for her: so as not to get too bored on his own, he had brought with him to 'Paradise' a bottle of cognac and some sugar and lemons; and with the door ajar, he would smoke his cigars and make himself the occasional glass of cold grog. Time dragged, he kept looking at his watch and could not help but hear all the intimate noises made by the landlady's family, who inhabited the interior rooms: the fretful crying of a child, an angry adenoidal voice, and a puppy breaking into sudden furious barking. Bazilio, finding all this utterly vulgar and despicable, would grow impatient. But then he would hear the rustle of a dress coming up the stairs, and all his boredom, and all Luiza's fears, would vanish in the warmth of their first kisses. However, she was always in a hurry and anxious to be back home by five o'clock, 'and it was absolutely miles away'! She would arrive feeling hot and bothered, and Bazilio enjoyed the warm sheen of sweat on her bare shoulders.

'And what about your husband?' he would ask. 'When is he coming back?'

'He doesn't say.' Or: 'I haven't had a letter, I don't know.'

In the selfish joy of recent possession, this seemed to be Bazilio's main preoccupation. He would then caress her ecstatically, kneel before her and say in a childish voice:

'Lili doesn't love her Bibi.'

She, half-undressed, would laugh an earthy, musical laugh:

'Lili adores her Bibi. She's mad about Bibi!'

And she would ask him if he had thought about her and what he had done the previous night. He had been to the club, played a few rubbers of whist, gone home early and dreamed of her.

'I live only for you, my love, believe me!'

And he would rest his head on her lap, as if overwhelmed by an excess of happiness.

At other times, he would wax more serious and advise her on certain matters of taste, on her clothes; he asked her not to wear false hair and not to use bootees with elastic sides.

Luiza greatly admired his experience of the life of ostentation; she obeyed him and moulded herself to his ideas, even going so far as to affect, without actually feeling it, a disdain for virtuous people, purely in order to imitate his libertine views.

And gradually, seeing her docility, Bazilio no longer bothered to constrain himself; he used her, *as if he were paying her*! One morning, he scribbled her a pencilled note saying bluntly that he was unable to meet her at 'Paradise' that day, and offering no further explanation. On one occasion, he had simply, without warning, failed to turn up, and Luiza had found the door locked. She had knocked timidly, peered through the keyhole, waited with pounding heart, then returned sadly home, exhausted by the heat, eyes pricking with dust, and feeling a strong desire to cry.

He would not go out of his way to do anything, even if it would please her. Luiza had asked him to come and spend the occasional Sunday evening at her house; Sebastião would be there, the Councillor, and Dona Felicidade when she was better; she would like that, and it would give their relationship a more familial, more legitimate air.

Bazilio had recoiled:

'What! Spend an evening nodding off with four first-class bores! Certainly not!'

'But we would talk, play music . . .'

'Oh, no, I know what the music at Lisbon soirées is like: the "Waltz of the Kiss" and "The Troubador". No, thank you!'

Then, on two or three occasions, he had spoken scornfully of Jorge. This had offended her.

And lately, when she arrived, he no longer showed the delicacy of a lover by leaping to his feet, he merely sat on the bed, languidly took his cigar out of his mouth and said:

'Ah, there you are, my flower!'

And the superior air he adopted when he spoke to her! His way of shrugging his shoulders and exclaiming: 'Oh, you understand nothing about these things'. He had even used crude language, brutal gestures. And Luiza began to suspect that Bazilio did not respect her, he merely desired her.

At first, she wept. She resolved to have it out with him and, if necessary, to break off their relationship. But she kept postponing the moment, she did not dare: the figure of Bazilio, his voice, his eyes, all prevailed over her, and, by inflaming her passion, deprived her of the courage required to disrupt that passion with words of complaint. For she was convinced then that she adored him: what else could provoke such exalted desire if not the grandeur of her feelings? The only reason she experienced such pleasure was because she loved him so! And her natural honesty and modesty found refuge in this subtle reasoning.

True, he was sometimes harsh and abrupt with her; yes, he occasionally treated her with indifference, but at other times, what sweetness, what wild caresses, what passionate, trembling words! He loved her too, there was no doubt about it. And that certainty was her justification. And because love was the cause, she felt no shame at the sense of voluptuous anticipation with which she made her way to 'Paradise' each day.

On a few occasions, on her return, she had met Juliana, bustling along Rua do Moinho do Vento. Back at the house, she had asked her:

'Where have you been?'

'To the doctor's, madam.'

She complained of chest pains, palpitations, breathlessness.

'Oh, and fainting fits too!'

Juliana did all her work in the morning now; at around one o'clock, as soon as Luiza had disappeared around the corner of the street, Juliana would go upstairs and get changed, then, tightly corseted into her merino dress, with her hat on and carrying her parasol, she would announce to Joana:

'Bye now, I'm off to see the doctor.'

'Goodbye, Senhora Juliana,' the cook would reply glee-fully, and immediately send a signal to her carpenter.

Juliana walked down São Pedro de Alcântara, turned off in the direction of Largo do Carmo and down the little street opposite the barracks. There, on the third floor, lived her close friend, Tia Vitória.

She was an old lady who used to act as a kind of employment agency for domestic servants. She still had a metal plaque on the door which said in black letters: VICTORIA SOARES, DOMESTIC EMPLOYMENT AGENCY. But in recent years, her work had become more complicated, more tortuous.

She carried out this work in a small room with rugs on the floor and fly papers dangling from the filthy ceiling, all dimly lit by two mean little windows. A vast sofa occupied most of the back wall; it had clearly once been upholstered in green, but beneath the many large stains covering it, the worn, frayed, patched material was now of a greyish hue; the broken springs uttered sudden melancholy twangs; in one corner of the sofa, in a hollow carved out by use, a cat spent all day sleeping; one side of the wooden frame was charred, revealing that it had once been saved from a fire. Above the sofa hung a lithograph of Senhor Dom Pedro IV. Between the two windows stood a tall dresser and, on it, flanked by a statue of St Anthony and a box made of shells, was a small stuffed monkey with glass eyes, balanced on the branch of a tree. On entering, the first thing one saw, next to the window by the door, at a table covered with an oilcloth, was a thin, bent back and a silk cap complete with an upturned tassel. This was Senhor Gouveia, the scrivener!

The stuffy air in the room had a complex, indefinable smell, a mixture of the stable, boot blacking and fried tomatoes and onions. There were always people there: stout matrons in cape and shawl, with fleshy cheeks and faint moustaches; coachmen in striped jackets and with gleaming hair slicked down with oil; sullen, chalk-faced errand boys with heavy footsteps and a doltish appearance; little pale-skinned, hollow-eyed house-maids carrying bone-handled parasols and wearing kid gloves darned at the fingertips.

Opposite this room was another which gave onto the central courtyard; the respectable backs of wealthy men or the rustling trains of suspicious dresses would occasionally disappear through its small green door.

At certain times, on Saturdays, five or six people would be gathered there; old ladies spoke in low voices and gestured mysteriously; a muffled altercation rumbled outside on the landing; young girls would suddenly burst into tears; and Senhor Gouveia would scribble impassively in his registers, occasionally leaning to one side to spit melancholy gobs of saliva.

Tia Vitória, meanwhile, in her black lace cap and purple dress, would come and go, whispering, gesticulating, jingling coins and gobbling down cough drops which she took from her pocket.

Tia Vitória was a great utility, she had become a centre. Ordinary maidservants and even the classier maidservants had their office there. She lent money to the unemployed; she looked after the savings of the prudent; she had Senhor Gouveia write the amorous or domestic letters of those who had never been to school; she sold second-hand dresses; she loaned out tailcoats; she gave advice on jobs, received confidences, fomented intrigues, offered expert knowledge about childbirth. She did not actually recommend people for jobs, but both the employed and the recently dismissed came and went, up and down Tia Vitória's stairs. She knew everyone and did a great many favours: mature bachelors would consult her when seeking the consoling presence of a plump, young kitchen maid; it was she who found servants for married women with overly vigilant husbands; she knew where to find the most discreet moneylenders. And it was said of her: 'Tia Vitória knows more dodges than she's got hairs on her head!'

But lately, despite all her many occupations, as soon as Juliana came in, she would carry her off to the room at the back, close the door and they would be in there 'for a good half hour'!

And Juliana always emerged, red-faced, eyes shining and

happy! She would hurry home and as soon as she got in would ask:

'Is the mistress not back yet, Senhora Joana?'

'Not yet, no.'

'She must still be at the hospital, poor thing! It's quite a cross to bear, putting up with the old lady! And then, of course, she'll need to go for a walk. Quite right too! She deserves a bit of fun!'

Joana was doubtless dense and obtuse; moreover, her animal passion for her young man had a stupefying effect on her; however, even she had noticed that Senhora Juliana had gone 'very soft' on their mistress. One day, she said as much:

'You know, Senhora Juliana, lately you seem to be more on the mistress's side somehow.'

'On her side?'

'Yes, I mean, more, more . . .'

'More attached to her, you mean?'

'Yes, more attached.'

'I always was. But we all say things in the heat of the moment. The truth is that you and I couldn't hope for a better post than this one, Senhora Joana. A good-tempered mistress, no eccentricities to put up with, no ties . . . We should give thanks to Heaven that we've found this nice peaceful place.'

'Not half.'

The house was indeed now filled by a cheerful atmosphere of tranquil contentment: Luiza went out every day and was pleased with everything; she never got annoyed; and her antipathy towards Juliana seemed to have vanished; she considered her merely a poor unfortunate! Juliana enjoyed her bowls of broth, went on her walks and ruminated. Joana, meanwhile, with plenty of free time and often left with the run of the house, made merry with her carpenter. There were never any visitors. Dona Felicidade, in hospital, was smearing herself with arnica. Sebastião had gone to Almada to supervise the work being carried out there. The Councillor had left for Sintra, 'to give his soul a holiday,' as he had said to Luiza, 'and to revel in the marvels of that Eden'. Senhor Julião, 'the doctor', as Joana called him, was working on his thesis. The hours were very regular, and a peaceful silence reigned. One day in the kitchen, Juliana, impressed by the air of quiet comfort in the house, suddenly exclaimed to Joana:

'Things couldn't be better! It's as if the ship were sailing on a sea of roses!'

And then she added with a giggle:

'With me at the helm!'

# VII

At around this time, one afternoon when Luiza was on her way to 'Paradise', she suddenly saw emerging from a doorway, just beyond the Largo de Santa Bárbara, the harassed figure of Ernestinho.

'What are you doing here, cousin Luiza!' he said, greatly surprised. 'What are you doing in this part of town? How extraordinary! Who would have thought it!'

He was very red-faced, his alpaca jacket flapped open and he was excitedly brandishing a thick roll of papers.

Luiza was slightly embarrassed; she said she had come to visit a friend. No, he wouldn't know her, she had just arrived from Oporto.

'Ah, I see. And what have you been up to? When is Jorge coming back?' He immediately apologised for not having come to see her, but he had not had a moment free! In the mornings, he worked at the Customs office and in the evenings, he had rehearsals.

'So that's still going on?' asked Luiza.

'Indeed it is.'

And he added enthusiastically:

'Oh, yes, indeed it is! It's going wonderfully well! But it's such a lot of work!' He had just been to visit the actor Pinto, who was playing the role of the lover, the Count of Monte Redondo; he had heard him recite the final words of the third act: 'Accursed be this cruel fate crushing me! So be it, then, I will fight hand to hand with fate itself. Let battle commence!' Absolutely wonderful. He had also come to tell him that he had changed the monologue in the second act. The impresario thought it too long.

'So he's still interfering, is he, the impresario?'

Ernestinho looked slightly hesitant.

'Just a touch . . .' Then, his face radiant: 'But he's thrilled with the play itself! They all are! Yesterday he said to me: "Pipsqueak . . ." That's what they call me, just for fun, you understand. It's amusing, don't you think? Anyway, he said to me: "Pipsqueak, the whole of Lisbon will be there for the first night! It'll be a sensation!" He's a good fellow really! Now I'm off to see Bastos, the columnist from *The Truth*. Do you know him?'

Luiza couldn't quite remember.

'You know Bastos!' he insisted.

And seeing that Luiza knew neither the name nor the man, he exclaimed:

'But everyone knows him!' And he was on the point of describing him in detail and listing his works, when Luiza, impatient to be done, said:

'Oh, yes, I remember him now! Of course . . . I know who you mean!'

'Well, anyway, I'm going to his house,' he said smugly. 'We're great friends, you know, he's an excellent fellow, and he's got the sweetest little baby boy!' Then squeezing her hand tightly, he went on: 'Goodbye, then, cousin Luiza, I can't stop. Do you want me to walk with you?'

'No, thank you, it's only around the corner.'

'Goodbye, then, and give my regards to Jorge.'

He was just about to bustle off, when he turned suddenly and ran back to her:

'I forgot to tell you: all will be forgiven in the end!'

Luiza opened her eyes very wide.

'At the end of my play, I mean!' exclaimed Ernestinho.

'Ah!'

'Yes, her husband forgives her, he's given the post of ambassador and they go and live abroad. It's more realistic that way.'

'Of course,' said Luiza vaguely.

'The plays ends with her lover, the Count of Monte Redondo saying: "I will go into the wilderness where I will die of this ill-starred passion!" It works really well!' He stood looking at her for a moment, then said brusquely: 'Goodbye, cousin Luiza. Regards to Jorge!'

And he scurried off.

Luiza entered 'Paradise' feeling most upset. She told Bazilio about the encounter. Ernestinho was such a silly creature! He might talk about it later, mention the time of day, and she might be asked about this 'friend from Oporto'.

Taking off her hat and veil, she added:

'It really isn't sensible to meet so often. It would be best if we didn't. Someone might find out.'

Bazilio gave an irritable shrug and said:

'If you don't want to come, then don't.'

Luiza looked at him for a moment, then bowed deeply:

'Thank you very much!'

She was about to put on her hat again, but he came over to her, clasped her hands and embraced her, murmuring:

'You were the one who talked about not coming! What would happen to me, though? You're the only reason I'm in Lisbon.'

'It's just that sometimes you say things . . . you behave as if . . .'

Bazilio smothered her words with kisses.

'Now, now, no quarrels. Forgive me. You look so lovely.'

When Luiza went home, she went over that scene in her mind. No, she thought, it was not the first time he had been short with her and shown himself to be utterly indifferent towards her, her reputation and her well-being! He simply and selfishly wanted her to be there every day! Let the gossips talk, let the noonday sun burn her, what did he care? But why was that? It was patently obvious that he loved her less now. His words and his kisses were growing cooler by the day. He was never gripped now by a desire that caught her up in one trembling caress, nor by a superabundance of feeling that made him fall to his knees, his hands trembling like those of an old man! He no longer hurled himself upon her as soon as she appeared at the door, as if upon a frightened prey. They no longer had those silly, meandering, childish conversations, full of laughter, into which they would blithely plunge after the ardent, physical hour was past, when she would lie in sweet lassitude, her blood cool, resting her head on her bare arms! Now, once they had exchanged a last kiss, he would light a cigar, as if he had just finished supper in a restaurant! And he would go straight over to a small mirror that hung above the washbasin to comb his hair with a little pocket comb. (Oh, how she hated that comb!) Sometimes, he would even look at his watch! And while she was getting dressed, he no longer came over to her, as he used to at first, to help her put on her collar, pricking himself on the pins, laughing as he did so, and bestowing farewell kisses on her bare shoulders before her dress closed about them. Instead he went and drummed his fingers on the windowpanes or else sat morosely, jiggling one leg up and down!

And he showed her no respect, no consideration. He looked down his nose at her, as if she were an under-educated bourgeois woman of limited experience who knew only her own small neighbourhood. And he had a way of walking up and down, head held high, smoking and talking of 'Madame so-and-so's wit' or 'Countess so-and-so's clothes!' As if she were stupid and her dresses mere rags! It really was too much! Indeed, it was as if he were doing her a great honour by possessing her. She immediately thought of Jorge, Jorge who was so respectful in his love for her! Jorge, for whom she was, without a doubt, the prettiest, most elegant, most intelligent and most captivating of women! And the idea began to grow in her that perhaps she had sacrificed her blissful, tranquil life for a most uncertain love!

One day, when he seemed even more than usually cold and distracted, she spoke to him openly about this. Sitting up very straight on the wicker sofa, she spoke sensibly and slowly, with a calm, dignified air. She said that she could see he was bored, that his great love for her had died, that it was therefore humiliating to her that they should continue seeing each other in these conditions, and that she felt it would be more dignified if they finished.

Bazilio was looking at her, surprised at her solemnity; her words seemed so studied and affected; he smiled and said serenely:

'You learned that little speech off by heart!'

Luiza got brusquely to her feet and confronted him, a sneer on her lips.

'Are you mad, Luiza?'

212

'I've had enough! I make all kinds of sacrifices for you, I come here every day, I compromise myself, and for what? To see you utterly indifferent, utterly bored.'

'But my love . . .'

She gave a scornful laugh.

'*My love*! Oh, don't pretend, it's too ridiculous!'

Bazilio got angry:

'That's all I needed, a scene like this!' he said vehemently. And standing before her, arms folded, he went on: 'What do you want? Do you want me to love you the way they do in the theatre, in the Teatro de São Carlos? You women are all the same! When a poor wretch loves a woman naturally, like everyone else, with his heart, but with no fancy, leading-man gestures, they say he's cold, that he's bored and ungrateful, but what do you expect? Do you want me to throw myself at your feet, to declaim and roll my eyes, to make vows and other such nonsense?'

'You used to do all that "nonsense".'

'Yes, at the beginning,' he replied brutally. 'But we've known each other far too long for that now, my dear.'

It had only been five weeks!

'Goodbye,' said Luiza.

'I see. Are you angry with me?'

Eyes downcast, nervously pulling on her gloves, she replied: 'No.'

Bazilio stood, barring the door and holding out his arms:

'Be reasonable, my love. A relationship like ours isn't like the duet from Gounod's *Faust*. I love you; you, I think, care for me; we make the necessary sacrifices, we meet, we're happy. What more do you want? What are you complaining about?'

She replied with a sad, ironic smile:

'I'm not complaining. You're quite right.'

'So you're not angry, then?'

'No.'

'Word of honour?'

'Yes.'

Bazilio took her hands.

'Give Bibi a little kiss then.'

213

Luiza kissed him lightly on his cheek.

'On the lips, on the lips!' And wagging a threatening finger and looking at her hard, he said: 'What a temper she's got! It's easy to see whose blood you've got running in your veins, that of Senhor António de Brito, our devoted uncle, who used to pull the maids' hair!' He chucked her under the chin. 'Will you be here tomorrow?'

Luiza hesitated for a moment, then said:

'Yes.'

She arrived home feeling exasperated and humiliated. It was six o'clock. Juliana announced angrily that Joana had gone out at four o'clock and had not returned, and supper wasn't ready yet.

'Where did she go?'

Juliana shrugged and gave a little smile.

Luiza understood. She had gone to see some lover, some love. She pulled a face expressive of disdainful pity.

'And much good may it do her, the little fool!' she said.

Juliana looked at her, shocked.

'She's drunk,' she thought.

'Oh well, never mind!' exclaimed Luiza. 'I'll wait.'

And pacing excitedly about her room, she brooded on her anger.

'How selfish, how rude, how base! And a woman ruins herself for a man like that. How stupid!'

How he had pleaded, how small and humble he had made himself at first! But that is what men's love is like – it tires easily!

And she was immediately assailed by thoughts of Jorge! *He* wasn't like that! He had lived with her for three years, and his love was always the same – intense, tender, devoted. But this other man. How despicable. They had known each other far too long, he had said! It was clear to her now that he had never loved her. He had wanted her out of vanity, on a whim, out of boredom, merely in order to have a woman in Lisbon! That was all it was, but love? Huh!

And what about her? Did she love him? She thought hard, questioning herself. She imagined situations, circumstances: if

214

he wanted to carry her far away, say, to France, would she go? No! If, by some misfortune, she were widowed, could she foresee being happily married to him? No!

So what, then? And like someone removing the stopper from a long treasured bottle and, to her amazement, finding that the perfume has evaporated, she stood, astonished, to find that her heart was empty. What had drawn her to him, then? She did not even know: having too little to do; the romantic, morbid curiosity attached to having a lover; a thousand small, inflamed vanities; a degree of physical desire. But had she ever perchance felt the happiness brought by the illicit love so common in novels and in operas, that make one capable of forgetting all else in life, of facing death, of almost longing for death? Never! All the pleasure she had felt at first, and which she had mistaken for love, came from the novelty of it all, from the delicious thrill of eating the forbidden fruit, from their meetings in 'Paradise' all cloaked in secrecy, possibly from other things which she did not even want to admit to herself, which made her blush inside!

But did she feel anything very extraordinary now? Good grief, she was beginning to feel less excited to be with her lover than to be with her husband! She found the thought of a kiss from Jorge more arousing, and they had lived together for three years! She had never felt bored with Jorge, never! And she felt deeply bored with Bazilio. What had Bazilio become for her? He was like a husband of whom she was not particularly fond and with whom she had secret meetings outside the house! Was it really worth it?

What had gone wrong? Did the defect lie in love itself? After all, the necessary conditions for her and Bazilio to achieve great happiness were there: they were young, their affair was shrouded in secrecy, they found the sheer difficulties they had to surmount exciting ... Why then were they almost yawning with boredom? Because love was highly perishable, and the moment it is born, it starts to die. Only the beginnings are good. Then there is ecstasy, enthusiasm, a little bit of heaven. But afterwards ... In order to be always able to *feel*, was it necessary to be constantly beginning all over again?

That was what Leopoldina did. And she suddenly understood Leopoldina's faithless existence with utter clarity, taking a lover, keeping him for a week, and then throwing him away like a squeezed lemon, and thereby constantly renewing the flower of sensation! And by the tortuous logic of illicit love affairs, her first lover made her think vaguely about the second!

The next day, she said to herself that 'Paradise' really was awfully far away. What a nuisance, in that heat, to have to get dressed and go out! She sent Juliana to find out how Dona Felicidade was and she stayed at home, wearing a white peignoir, savouring her idleness.

That afternoon, she received a letter from Jorge, saying that he would be away for some time yet, but that his widowhood was beginning to weigh upon him. When would he ever see his own little house and his own sweet bedroom again?

She was very touched. She was filled to the very depths of her being by a feeling of shame and remorse, by a tender compassion for poor, good Jorge, by a vague desire to see him and to kiss him, by the memory of past happinesses. She replied at once, assuring him that she too had had enough of being alone, telling him to come home, that such a separation was sheer nonsense. And at the time, she meant it.

She had just sealed the envelope when Juliana brought her 'a letter from the hotel'. Bazilio was in despair: 'You did not come to see me, and so I assume you must be angry; but it is doubtless your pride and not your love that holds you in its sway: you cannot imagine my feelings when I realised that you would not be there today. I waited until five o'clock; what torment! Maybe I *was* cold towards you, but you were no more pleasant to me. We should forgive each other, kneel down before each other and forget all our anger in our love. Come tomorrow. I adore you! What further proof do you need than that I abandon all my interests, my friendships, my pleasures and bury myself here in Lisbon.'

She grew agitated, not knowing what she should do or what she should want. It was true. Why else was he in Lisbon? Because of her. But she recognised now that she did not love him, or only very slightly! And it was terrible to betray Jorge, who was so good, so loving and who lived so entirely for her. But if Bazilio really was so very much in love with her . . . Her ideas whirled about like autumn leaves, buffeted this way and that by contradictory winds. She wanted to be left in peace, to be left alone. Why had that man come back? Heavens, what was she to do? Her thoughts and feelings were painfully confused.

The following morning, she was in the same state of uncertainty. Should she go or shouldn't she? The heat and the dust outside in the street made her want to stay at home! But how disappointed the poor boy would be! She flipped a five *tostão* coin in the air. It came down heads. She should go. She got dressed reluctantly, irritably, albeit filled by a certain desire for the refined pleasures that always accompany loving reconciliations!

What a surprise, though! She expected to find him humbled and on his knees, but instead he wore a look of frowning severity.

'Honestly, Luiza, why weren't you here yesterday?'

The night before, when he realised she would not be coming, Bazilio felt angry, but more than that, he felt afraid; his concupiscence feared losing that lovely, youthful body, and his pride was appalled to see his docile little slave reclaiming her freedom. He had resolved, therefore, 'to bring her to book'. He wrote to her, feigning submission in order to draw her back, but determined to be severe in order to punish her. And so he went on:

'Really, such childishness! Why didn't you come?'

His manner enraged her.

'Because I didn't want to.'

Then she added:

'Besides, I couldn't.'

'Is this any way to reply to my letter, Luiza?'

'And is this any way to greet me?'

They looked at each other for a moment, in mutual detestation.

'So you want an argument, do you? You're just like all the others.'

'What others?'

Then, outraged, she said:

'Oh, really, this is too much. Goodbye!'

She was about to leave.

'Are you going, Luiza?'

'I am. It's best that we finish this once and for all.'

He quickly locked the door.

'Are you serious, Luiza?'

'Of course. I've had enough.'

'All right, then. Goodbye.'

He opened the door to allow her past and bowed silently.

She took a step forward, then Bazilio, in a slightly tremulous voice, said:

'Is this goodbye for ever?'

Luiza stopped, her face white. Those sad words 'for ever' aroused a flurry of emotions. She burst into tears.

Tears had always made her look even prettier. She seemed so wounded, so fragile, so helpless . . .

Bazilio knelt before her; his eyes were full of tears too.

'If you leave me, I'll die!'

Their lips met in one long, deep, penetrating kiss. Their overwrought state momentarily lent both of them the sincerity of passion; and they spent a delicious afternoon.

Pale as wax, she held him in her arms, murmuring:

'Say you'll never leave me!'

'I swear it! Never, my love!'

But it was getting late, she had to go! And they were both doubtless gripped by the same idea, because they looked at each other avidly, and Bazilio said softly:

'If only you could spend the night here!'

She said in a terrified, supplicant tone:

'Oh, don't tempt me, don't tempt me!'

Bazilio sighed and said:

'No, you're right, it's nonsense. Go.'

Luiza began hurriedly getting dressed. Then suddenly she stopped and smiled:

'Do you know something?'

'What, my love?'

'I'm absolutely dying of hunger! I didn't have any lunch and I'm starving hungry!'

He said forlornly:

'Oh my poor love! If only I'd known.'

'What time is it, my dear?'

Bazilio looked at the clock and said, almost shamefacedly:

'Seven o'clock!'

'Good heavens!'

She hastily put on her hat and veil.

'It's so late, oh dear Lord, it's so late!'

'And what about tomorrow? What time will you be here?'

'One o'clock.'

'Are you sure?'

'Yes, I'm sure.'

The following day she was very punctual. Bazilio was waiting for her at the bottom of the stairs, and as soon as they went into the room, he devoured her with kisses, crying:

'What have you done to me? I've been like a madman since yesterday.'

But Luiza was intrigued by the basket sitting on the bed.

'What's that?'

He smiled and led her by the hand to the iron bedstead, where he opened the basket and said with a grave bow:

'Provisions, banquets, bacchanalia! Now you won't be able to complain afterwards that you're hungry!'

It was their lunch. There were sandwiches, pâté de foie gras, fruit, a bottle of champagne and ice wrapped in a piece of flannel.

'It's wonderful!' she said with a voluptuous smile, her cheeks pink with pleasure.

'It was all I could manage, my dear cousin! You see how I think of you!'

He put the basket down on the floor and approached her with open arms:

'And did you think of me, my love?'

Her eyes and the way her arms folded passionately about him gave her answer.

219

They lunched at three o'clock. It was delightful; they spread a napkin on the bed; the china bore the mark of the Hotel Central; it all seemed to Luiza so very bohemian and so terribly sweet; and she gave a throaty laugh as she clinked the little bits of ice in her champagne glass. She was filled with an exuberant happiness that overflowed in little shrieks and kisses and all kinds of spontaneous gestures. She ate greedily; and her bare arms, as she reached out for the different plates, were simply adorable.

She had never found Bazilio so handsome; even the room seemed cosy and utterly perfect for such romantic intimacies; she thought it would be almost possible to live with him for years in that gloomy room, in a permanent state of love, with lunch every day at three o'clock. They did all the usual foolish things: fed each other titbits, which made her laugh, revealing her small, white teeth; they both drank from the same cup, then devoured each other with kisses; then he wanted to show her the correct way to drink champagne. Did she not know about it?

'What is it?' asked Luiza, raising her glass.

'No, not with the glass, please! No self-respecting person drinks champagne from a glass. A glass is fine for white wine, but . . .'

He took a sip of champagne, then passed the champagne into her mouth with a kiss. Luiza roared with laughter and found it 'divine' and wanted to drink more. Her face was growing flushed, her eyes were shining.

They had removed the plates from the bed; and as she sat there on the edge of the bed, with her little pink-stockinged feet dangling, her elbows resting on her knees, her head on one side, she had all the languid grace of a weary dove.

Bazilio found her irresistible: who would think that a little bourgeois woman could have such chic, such style! He knelt down and, taking her feet in his hands, he kissed them; then, criticising her garters, 'those metal fastenings are so ugly', he respectfully kissed her knees; and then he murmured a request. She blushed and smiled and said: 'No! No!' And when she emerged from her ecstasy, she covered her scarlet face with her hands, muttering reprovingly:

'Oh, Bazilio!'

He twirled his moustaches, very pleased with himself. He had taught her a new sensation; he had her in the palm of his hand!

Only at six o'clock did she leave his arms. Luiza made him promise to think of her all night. She did not want him to go out; she was jealous of the club, of the air, of everything! And when she was on the landing, she turned and kissed him passionately, saying:

'Let's get here earlier tomorrow, shall we? So that we can spend the whole day together.'

'Aren't you going to see Dona Felicidade?'

'Oh, who cares about Dona Felicidade! I don't care about anyone else. I want you, only you!'

'At midday, then?'

'At midday!'


How the solitude of her room weighed on her that night! She was in the grip of an impatience that drove her to prolong the excitement of that afternoon, to maintain herself in a state of agitation. She tried to read, but soon threw the book down; the two candles burning on the dressing table gave off such a gloomy light; she peered outside at the night; it was warm and calm. She summoned Juliana:

'Go and put a shawl on, we're going to Dona Leopoldina's house.'

When they got there, after a long delay, a dishevelled Justina dressed in a white peignoir opened the door to them. She looked quite shocked:

'My mistress has gone to Oporto!'

'To Oporto!'

Yes, she would be away for a fortnight.

Luiza was much put out. She did not want to go back home, her solitary room terrified her.

'Let's go for a little walk, Juliana. It's such a lovely night.'

'It is, madam!'

They walked down Rua de São Roque. And as if guided by

the two lines of gaslights lining Rua do Alecrim, her thoughts and her desires went straight to the Hotel Central.

Would he be there? Would he be thinking about her? If only she could surprise him, throw herself into his arms, see his unpacked luggage . . . The idea made her breathe more heavily. They reached the Praça de Camões. People were strolling about; in the deepest shadows cast by the trees, they sat chatting on benches; there was cool water to be drunk; the harsh lights from the windows and doorways of shops stood out against the surrounding dark of night; and the shrill voices of newspaper vendors rose up above the slow murmur of the streets.

Then a man wearing a straw hat passed so close to her, so deliberately, that Luiza felt afraid.

'We'd better go back,' she said.

In the middle of Rua de São Roque, however, the straw hat reappeared and almost brushed Luiza's shoulder; two puffy eyes leered at her.

Luiza walked desperately along, the tick-tack of her boots loud on the paving stones; suddenly, near São Pedro de Alcân-tara, a lilting Brazilian voice emerged from beneath the straw hat and said, very close to her ear:

'Where do you live, sweetheart?'

Terrified, Luiza gripped Juliana's arm.

The voice said again:

'Don't be angry, sweetheart, where do you live?'

'You scoundrel!' roared Juliana.

The straw hat immediately disappeared amongst the trees.

They were out of breath by the time they reached home. Luiza felt like crying; she fell onto the chaise longue, exhausted and miserable. What folly to go out walking the streets at night, with only a maidservant for company! She must be mad, what had happened to her? What a day that had been! She remembered it all: the lunch, the champagne she had drunk from Bazilio's kisses, her lewd excesses, how shameful! And then going to Leopoldina's house at night, and being mistaken in the street for a woman of easy virtue! She suddenly remembered Jorge slaving away in the Alentejo, thinking only of her . . . She hid her face in her hands, she hated herself, and her eyes grew wet with tears.

The following morning, however, she woke feeling very happy. She did, it is true, feel slightly ashamed of her 'foolishness' the night before, and had a vague feeling, an instinct or a premonition, that she should not go to 'Paradise' that day. Her desire, though, which was strongly urging her to go, immediately furnished her with reasons: Bazilio would be disappointed; if she did not go today, then she should never go again, and that would mean breaking off their relationship . . . Besides, the lovely morning was calling to her from the street; it had rained in the night, and the heat had abated; there was a sweet, washed-clean coolness about the light and the blue sky.

At half past eleven, she was walking down Rua do Moinho do Vento when she saw the dignified figure of Councillor Acácio coming slowly up Rua da Rosa, his sunshade furled, his head erect.

As soon as he saw her, he made haste to join her and bowed deeply:

'What a very fortunate encounter!'

'How are you, Councillor! How nice to see you!'

'And how are you, madam? You look extremely well!'

He moved solemnly over to her left and began walking along beside her.

'You will, of course, permit me to accompany you on your excursion.'

'Of course, with the greatest pleasure. But what have you been up to? I should be very angry with you really!'

'I have been in Sintra, my dear lady.' Then, stopping, he said: 'Didn't you know? It was in the newspaper!'

'Yes, but *since* your visit to Sintra.'

'Ah,' he said. 'I've been extremely busy! Extremely busy! I have been entirely absorbed in the collation of certain documents which are indispensable for my book.' Then after a pause: 'A book whose title, I believe, is not unfamiliar to you.'

Luiza could not quite remember the title. The Councillor then provided her not only with the title, but with the aims of the book and a few chapter headings, assuring her of the great utility of the work: it was entitled *A Picturesque Description of the Principal Cities of Portugal and Their Most Famous Establishments.*

'It's a guide, a scientific guide. Let me illustrate this for you with an example: let us say that you, dear lady, wish to go to Bragança; without my book it is quite possible (nay, I would say, inevitable) that you would return without having sampled the local curiosities; with my book you would have visited the most notable buildings and received both a solid grounding of facts and a great deal of enjoyment.'

Luiza was barely listening to him, smiling vaguely beneath her white veil.

'It's a lovely day today, isn't it?' she said.

'Exquisite. A positively fecund day!'

'It's so deliciously cool here!'

They had reached the garden of São Pedro de Alcântara; a gentle breeze was blowing amongst the greenest of the trees; the ground was still damp and, despite the bright sun, the blue sky seemed pale and remote.

The Councillor then spoke about the summer; it had been positively torrid! In his own dining room, it had been forty-eight degrees in the shade! Forty-eight degrees! Then in a foolish impulse to exonerate his dining room of all blame for such excessive heat: 'But then, of course, it does face south. Let us be fair now. It does face due south. Today, though, is most restoring.'

He even invited her to take a turn about the garden. Luiza hesitated. And the Councillor, taking out his watch and holding it some way from his eyes, declared that it was not yet midday. It was correct according to the Arsenal clock; it was an English watch. 'Far superior to the Swiss!' he added solemnly.

Out of sheer cowardice and inertia, and wearied by the Councillor's pompous voice, Luiza grudgingly descended the steps into the park. Besides, she was thinking, she still had time, she could always get a carriage.

They went and stood by the railings. Through the gaps they

could see, falling away below them, dark rooftops, spaces formed by courtyards, fragments of wall revealing the occasional sparse green of a parched garden; then, down below in the valley, lay the Passeio Público, its large oblong of dense foliage broken here and there by white, sandy paths. On this side, there rose up the inexpressive façades of Rua Oriental, windows glittering in the full brunt of the sunlight; behind that, though on the same plane, were plots of faded green surrounded by strong, sombre walls, the sad, yellow stonework of the convent church of the Incarnation, and other disparate buildings, up as far as Graça, which was crammed with ecclesiastical edifices, narrow convent windows and church towers, very white against the blue; and beyond, the Penha da França set off bright whitewashed walls, against which stood out a dark green strip of trees. To the right, on the bare hill, sat the castle, squat and squalid; and the fractured line of rooftops and houses in the Mouraria and the Alfama formed a series of abrupt angles, all the way down to the two heavy towers of the portly, ancient cathedral. Beyond, they saw a stretch of river, glinting in the sun; two white sails passed slowly by; and on the farther shore, at the bottom of a low hill, made blue by the distant air, stood a row of gleaming, white, terraced houses belonging to a small village. From the city below came a low, slow murmur, in which was mingled the growl of carriages, the heavy rumble of ox carts, the metallic jingle of carts transporting ironwork, and the occasional shrill cry of some street seller.

'A magnificent panorama!' said the Councillor emphatically. And he launched at once into a paean of praise for the city. It was definitely one of the most beautiful in Europe and the approach to the city was comparable only to that of Constantinople! Indeed, it was the envy of many foreigners! Once a great centre of international commerce, it was only a shame that the drains were so poor and the city fathers so negligent!

'This should really be in the hands of the English, dear lady!' he exclaimed.

However, he immediately regretted such unpatriotic

sentiments. He swore that this was 'just a manner of speaking'. He wanted his country's continued independence; he would die for it if necessary; he, of course, wanted neither the English nor the Spanish! 'Only ourselves, dear lady, the Portuguese!' And in a respectful voice, he added: 'And God!'

'Doesn't the river look pretty!' said Luiza.

Acácio agreed and murmured in a cavernous voice:

'Ah, yes, the Tagus!'

He then wanted to take a stroll about the garden. Above the flowerbeds fluttered white and yellow butterflies; the rhythmic dripping of water in the pool was reminiscent of a modest, bourgeois garden; a strong smell of vanilla hung in the air; birds alighted on the heads of the marble busts that rose up amongst the bushes and the dahlias.

Luiza liked this little garden, but hated the tall railings.

'They're there because of the suicides!' said the Councillor. In his opinion, however, the number of suicides in Lisbon had fallen considerably, and he attributed this to the harsh, but highly praiseworthy way in which the press had condemned them.

'Because believe me, dear lady, here in Portugal, the press is a force to be reckoned with!'

'Shall we move on?' suggested Luiza.

The Councillor bowed, but seeing that she was about to pick a flower, he quickly grabbed her arm:

'Ah, dear lady, please! The regulations are most explicit! Let us not infringe them!' And he added: 'The example must always come from above.'

They climbed back up the steps, and Luiza was thinking: 'Please, go home and leave me in Largo do Loreto.'

In Rua de São Roque, she glanced at the clock outside a cakeshop: it was half past twelve! Bazilio would be waiting!

She hurried on and stopped in Loreto. The Councillor looked at her, smiling expectantly.

'Oh, I thought you were going home, Councillor!'

'I would rather accompany you, if I may. Are you sure I'm not being a nuisance?'

'No, no, of course not.'

A hired carriage passed by, followed, at a gallop, by a post chaise.

The Councillor hurriedly and ostentatiously doffed his hat.

'It was the Prime Minister. Did you see? He waved to me.' He immediately began singing his praises. He was our finest parliamentarian, a man of enormous talent, and such a way with words! Acácio was just about to make a speech about public affairs, when Luiza crossed over to the church of the Martyrs, lifting the hem of her dress slightly to avoid some mud. She stopped at the door of the church and said, smiling:

'I'm just going to say a prayer or two. I don't want to keep you waiting. Goodbye, Councillor. Now be sure to visit.' She furled her parasol and held out her hand.

'My dear lady, I will, of course, wait for you, as long as you do not take too long over your prayers. No, no, I'll wait, I'm in no hurry.' And he added respectfully: 'Such zeal is most praiseworthy!'

Luiza entered the church in a state of despair. She stood beneath the choir, thinking: 'If I stay here for long enough, he'll get tired of waiting and leave!' Up above glinted the pendants on the glass chandeliers. The light inside was veiled, uniform, slightly muted. And the whitewashed walls, the scrubbed floorboards and the stone balustrades created a pale, bright backdrop for the gold of the chapel, the purple frontals on the pulpits, the darker purple of the drapery beyond, and the golden throne beneath the violet-coloured dossel. A cool, lofty silence reigned. Before the baptistry, a boy on his knees, with a zinc bucket beside him, was discreetly washing the floor with a rag; here and there the backs of devotees, wearing hoods or black shawls over their heads, could be seen genuflecting before the various altars; and an old man in a dark woollen jacket, kneeling in the central aisle, was mumbling prayers in a doleful, sing-song voice; he kept bowing and desperately beating his chest, and one could see his bald head and the enormous hobnails on the soles of his shoes.

Luiza walked up to the high altar. Bazilio would be getting impatient, poor love. She shyly asked the time of a passing sacristan. The man raised his sallow face to a window in the cupola, gave Luiza a sideways glance and said:

'It must be getting on for two o'clock.'

Two o'clock! Bazilio might not wait. She was suddenly filled by a fear of missing her afternoon of love, by an urgent desire to be once more in 'Paradise', in his arms! And, full of voluptuous haste, seeing once more the room, the iron bedstead, Bazilio's trim moustache, she looked vaguely round at the saints, at the virgins pierced by swords, at the wounded Christs. But still she lingered, hoping to 'wear the Councillor down and make him go away'. When she judged that he would have gone, she crept out. She saw him at the door, an erect figure, his hands behind his back, reading the list of church appointments.

He began at once to praise her devotion. He had not gone in himself, not wishing to disturb her meditations, but he heartily approved! It was a lack of religion that lay behind the general spread of immorality.

'And, besides, it shows good breeding. You will doubtless have observed that all the nobility attend regularly.'

He fell silent; he drew himself up, proud to be walking down the Chiado with a lovely, much-admired lady. When they passed a group of men, he even bent towards her mysteriously and whispered in her ear with a smile:

'What a perfect day!'

And when they came to Baltreschi's, he offered to buy her cakes. Luiza declined.

'Quite right. I myself believe in the importance of keeping regular mealtimes.'

His voice seemed now to Luiza like an importunate whine; and even though the day was not, in fact, particularly hot, she felt as if she were suffocating; her blood was prickling in her veins; she wished she could simply run away, and yet still she walked slowly and wretchedly along, like a sleepwalker, only just suppressing a strong desire to cry.

For no reason, completely at random, she wandered into Valente's. It was half past two! After a moment's hesitation, she

228

asked a jovial, fair-haired assistant if she could see some foulard cravats.

'White? Coloured? Stripes? With spots?'

'Yes, an assortment.'

She did not like them. She unfolded them, shook them out and put them to one side; and she glanced about her vaguely, looking very pale. The assistant asked if she was feeling unwell; he offered her a glass of water or perhaps she would prefer something else . . .

No, it was all right; she just needed some fresh air. She would come back. She left. The Councillor was all solicitude, he volunteered to accompany her to an excellent pharmacy he knew in order to buy some orange-flower water. They walked down Rua Nova do Carmo, and the Councillor went on at length about the assistant's excellent manners; not that he was at all surprised, for he knew that the assistants at Valente's were often the sons of excellent families, and he went on to give examples.

Then, getting no response, he asked:

'Are you still feeling unwell?'

'No, no, I'm fine.'

'Well, we're certainly having a delightful walk!'

They walked the whole length of the Rossio. Then they turned and walked diagonally back across. They walked along past Arco do Bandeira towards Rua do Ouro. Luiza kept frantically looking about her, in search of an idea, an opportunity, an incident; meanwhile, the Councillor, walking gravely by her side, continued to discourse. The sight of the Teatro de Dona Maria led him onto the subject of dramatic art; he had found Ernestinho's play a little too intense. Besides, he only really liked comedies. Not that he was immune to the beauties of a *Brother Luís de Sousa*, but his health did not permit exposure to many strong emotions. For example . . .

But Luiza had had an idea:

'Oh, I forgot! I have to go to Vitry's. I have to have a tooth filled.'

The Councillor, cut off in mid-stream, stared at her. And Luiza, holding out her hand, said hurriedly:

'Goodbye, Councillor. Do come and visit.' And she almost flew to Vitry's.

Catching up her dress, she raced up the stairs to the first floor, where she stopped, panting, and waited; then, very slowly, she went back down and peered out. The erect, dignified figure of the Councillor was moving off towards the government offices.

She hailed a carriage.

'As fast as you can!' she exclaimed.

The carriage almost galloped into the street where they had their 'Paradise'. Startled faces appeared at the window. She went up the stairs, heart pounding. The door was locked; the next door along immediately opened and the landlady's sweet voice whispered:

'He's gone. He left half an hour ago.'

Luiza went down the stairs. She gave her address to the coachman, hurled herself into the depths of the carriage and burst into hysterical crying. She drew the blinds in order not to be seen; filled by unexpected feelings of violence, she tore off her veil and ripped one of her gloves. She felt an urgent desire to see Bazilio. She rapped desperately on the windows and shouted:

'To the Hotel Central!'

For she was in one of those moods when susceptible temperaments give way to uncontrollable impulses; there is a mad delight in demolishing duty and propriety; and the soul, with a sensual tremor, sets off eagerly in search of all that is wrong.

The horses skidded to a halt outside the hotel. Senhor Bazilio de Brito was not in, although Viscount Reinaldo was.

'Take me home, then, to the address I gave you before.'

The coachman raced off again. And Luiza, gripped by a febrile rage, rained down insults on the Councillor, the dullard, the imbecile, and cursed the life that had brought her into contact with him and with all their other friends! She was filled by a violent desire to send marriage to the devil and to do whatever took her fancy!

When they reached the house, she had no change to give

the coachman. 'Wait!' she said, flouncing up the stairs. 'I'll send the money out!'

'What a tartar!' thought the coachman.

Joana opened the door and almost recoiled when confronted by a red-faced Luiza who was clearly in a highly agitated state.

Luiza went straight to her room; the cuckoo clock sang out three o'clock. Everything was in a mess; there were potplants on the floor, the cloth on the dressing table had not been changed, there was dirty laundry draped over the chairs. And Juliana, a scarf tied around her head, was calmly sweeping and singing to herself.

'Haven't you cleaned this room yet?' bawled Luiza.

Juliana shuddered at this unexpected burst of anger.

'I was just doing it now, madam.'

'Oh, I can see that!' roared Luiza. 'It's three o'clock in the afternoon, and look at the state this room is in!'

She had thrown down her hat and her parasol.

'Well, since madam has been coming home later recently . . .' began Juliana.

And her lips turned white.

'What has it got to do with you when I come home? What's that to you? Your duty is to tidy my room as soon as I get up. And if you don't like it, you can pack your bags and leave!'

Juliana turned scarlet and, fixing Luiza with bloodshot eyes, she said.

'I'm not putting up with this!'

And she flung down the broom.

'Out!' roared Luiza. 'Out this instant! I don't want you in this house a moment longer!'

Juliana planted herself in front of her and, repeatedly striking her own breast, said in a hoarse voice:

'I'll leave when I want to, when I want to, do you hear?'

'Joana!' screamed Luiza.

She wanted to summon the cook, a man, a policeman, anyone! But Juliana, beside herself with rage, was trembling all over and brandishing her fist:

'Don't push me too far, madam! Don't make me do something I'll regret!' And in a thread of a voice, through gritted teeth, she said: 'Not all the papers were thrown out with the rubbish!'

Luiza drew back and cried:

'What did you say?'

'Those letters you wrote to your lover, I've got them here!' And she patted her pocket fiercely.

Luiza stared at her for a moment, wild-eyed, then fell to the floor in a faint, beside the chaise longue.

# VIII

Luiza's first impression when she began to come round was of two figures bending over her, neither of whom she knew. The burlier of the two moved away; she was woken by the cold, hard sound of a glass bottle being set down on the marble top of the dressing table. Then she heard a muffled voice say:

'She's much better now. Did she faint, Senhora Juliana?'

'Yes, just like that.'

''She looked awfully flushed when she got home.'

Cautious steps crossed the carpet, and with her face close to Luiza's, Joana asked:

'Are you feeling better, madam?'

Luiza opened her eyes, and the things around her gradually came back into focus; she was lying on the chaise longue, they had loosened her clothes, and there was a strong smell of vinegar in the room. She raised herself up on one elbow and looked vaguely about her:

'Where is she?'

'Senhora Juliana? She's gone to lie down. She wasn't feeling well either. It was seeing madam so ill, poor thing. Are you better now?'

Luiza lay back again. Her whole body felt tired; everything in the room seemed to be shaking slightly.

'You can go now, Joana,' she said.

'Are you sure you don't need anything, madam? Perhaps a bit of broth . . .'

When she was alone, Luiza looked about her in horror. Everything was tidy now, the windows closed. A glove lay fallen on the floor; she got unsteadily to her feet and went to pick it up, mechanically tugging at its fingers, like a sleep-walker, before putting it away in the dressing-table drawer. She smoothed her hair; it seemed to her that her face had changed, that it had a quite different expression, as if she were a different person; and the silence in the room seemed to her extraordinary.

'Madam,' said Joana's shy voice.

'What is it?'

'It's the coachman.'

Luiza turned round, uncomprehending.

'What coachman?'

'A coachman; he says that you had no change and that you told him to wait.'

'Ah!'

And as happens in the theatre, when the lights suddenly go up on stage, she was suddenly and acutely aware once more of her 'misfortune'.

She was trembling so much that she could barely open the drawer of the bureau.

'I'd forgotten all about him,' she stammered.

She gave Joana the money, then lay back down on the chaise longue.

'I'm lost!' she murmured, clutching her hands to her head.

All was discovered! And in her mind's eye, as stark as drawings done in black paint on a white wall, she saw Jorge's rage, their friends' horror, the indignation of some, the mockery of others; and these images, which fell, crackling, down into her soul, like so much fuel on a bonfire, only increased and inflamed her terror and desperation.

What was left for her but to run away with Bazilio?

That idea, her first and only idea, took immediate hold, overwhelmed her, just as flood waters rapidly fill a field.

He had told her so often how happy they would be in Paris, in his apartment in Rue Saint-Florentin! All right, she would go! She would take no luggage, she would merely pack some underwear and mama's jewels in her little morocco leather bag. But what about the servants? The house? She would write a letter to Sebastião telling him to come and close everything up! On the journey she would wear her blue-striped dress, or possibly her black dress. She would take nothing else. She would buy anything she needed later, far away, in other cities . . .

'Supper is ready, madam,' said Joana from the bedroom door.

She had put on a white apron. She added:

'Senhora Juliana is lying down, she's says she's in too much pain to serve at table.'

'I'm just coming.'

She took only a spoonful of soup and a large sip of water; then, getting up, she asked:

'What's wrong with her?'

'She says she's got a really bad pain in her heart.'

If only she would die! Then she would be safe! Then she could stay! Filled by a perverse hope, she said:

'Go and see how she is, Joana!'

She had heard of so many people dying of a pain like that! She would go straight up to the woman's room and search through her trunk and get that letter back! And she wouldn't be afraid of the silence of death or of the corpse's pallor.

'She's feeling more rested, madam,' Joana reported when she returned. 'She says she'll soon be up and about. Heavens, madam, is that all you're having to eat?'

'Yes.'

And Luiza went back into her room, thinking: 'What's the point of imagining possible scenarios? All that's left for me now is to run away.'

She decided to write at once to Sebastião, but she could get no further than 'My dear friend!' written at the top of the page in a tremulous hand.

Why write to him? When she did not come back the following day, in the evening or at night, the maids, including that vile woman, would go straight to Sebastião. He was the family's closest friend. He would be sick with worry! He would imagine some accident, he would rush to the hospital, then to the police station, and would wait anxiously until dawn! The whole of the following day would be filled with new hopes that she would come home, but each hope would be cruelly shattered; then he would telegraph Jorge! And at that same hour, she would be sitting hunched in a train carriage, heading for some entirely new destination, accompanied by the huff and hiss of the train's engine!

235

Why was she so upset? Many other women would envy her plight! What was so unfortunate about having to leave this narrow life spent between four walls, studying household lists and doing crochet, and to set off with a new lover for Paris! Paris! To live with all the consolations of luxury, in silk-lined bedrooms, with a box at the Opera! She was a fool to be upset! This so-called 'disaster' was almost a source of joy! Without it, she would never have had the courage to slough off her bourgeois life; however urgent the desire to do so, a far greater timidity would always have kept her there!

And by fleeing, her love would gain in dignity! She would belong to only one man; she would not have to love both at home and away from home!

She even considered going straight to Bazilio 'to sort it out once and for all'. But it was too late to go to the hotel; she feared the dark streets, the night and the drunks.

She went to pack her bag. She put in scarves and hand-kerchiefs, some underwear, her manicure case, the rosary that Bazilio had given her, some face powder, a few jewels that had belonged to her mother. She wanted to take Bazilio's letters too. She had stored them away in a sandalwood box in the wardrobe drawer. She spread them out on her lap; she opened one and a dried flower fell out; another contained the photograph of Bazilio. It suddenly occurred to her that they were not all there! She had received seven: five short notes and two letters, the first, very sweet, letter that he had written to her and the last one after they had had that argument! She counted them. The first was missing, as were two notes! They had obviously been stolen! She got to her feet, ashen-faced. How base! Enraged, she felt like going up to the attic room and wrestling with the woman, wrenching the letters from her and strangling her! After all, what did it matter now!

Instead, overcome, she fell back on the chaise longue. It was equally disastrous whether the woman had one, two or all the letters.

In a state of great nervous excitement, she went to prepare the black dress she would wear, her hat, her travelling shawl.

The cuckoo sang out ten o'clock. She went into the

bedroom; she placed the candlestick on the bedside table and stood staring at the large bed with its white dimity curtains. This was the last time she would sleep there! She herself had crocheted that blanket during the first year of marriage; every stitch was filled with joy. Jorge had sometimes come to watch her working and had silently, smilingly observed her, or else he had spoken to her softly, twining the thick woollen thread about his fingers. She had slept with him in that bed for three years: her place was there, by the wall. It was in this bed that she had been ill with pneumonia. He had hardly slept for weeks, watching over her, smoothing her bedclothes, feeding broth to her, administering medicine and murmuring tender, restoring words! He used to talk to her as if she were a little child, saying: 'It won't last long, you'll be better tomorrow and then we can go away somewhere together.' But his anxious eyes were full of tears! Or else he would say pleadingly: 'You will get better, won't you? Please get better, my love, please!' And she so wanted to get better that she felt the gentle wave of life returning and cooling her blood!

During the first few days of her convalescence, he was the one who dressed her; he would kneel down to put on her shoes, he would make sure she was well wrapped up in her peignoir and would help her to lie down on the chaise longue, then sit at her side and read novels to her, draw landscapes for her or cut out paper soldiers. And she was entirely dependent on him, she had no one else in the world to look after her, to suffer and weep for her, only him! She always fell asleep with her hands in his because the illness had left her with a slight fear of feverish nightmares; and poor Jorge, in order not to wake her, would sit for hours, not moving, his hand between hers. He would sleep, fully clothed, on a little mattress placed on the floor beside her. Often, when she woke in the night, she had seen him wiping away his tears; doubtless tears of joy because she was saved. The doctor, kindly Dr Caminha, had told him: 'She's out of danger, now all she has to do is to get strong again.' And Jorge, poor Jorge, had said nothing, he had simply taken the old man's hands in his and covered them with kisses!

And now, when he found out, when he came back . . . When he came into their bedroom and found their two pillows still there, side by side! She would be somewhere far away with another man, travelling strange roads and hearing another language. How awful! And there he would be, alone in the house, weeping and clinging to Sebastião! And all those memories of her would be left behind to torture him! Her clothes, her slippers, her combs, the whole house! What a sad life his would be! He would sleep there alone! He would have no one to wake him in the morning with a kiss, no one to put her arms about his neck and say: 'It's late, Jorge!' It was all over for both of them. For ever! She lay face down on the bed and burst into tears.

Then she heard Juliana's voice in the corridor talking loudly to Joana. She sat up, terrified. Was that vile creature coming to speak to her? The slippered footsteps moved slowly off, and Joana came in bearing the household list and the nightlight.

'Senhora Juliana got up for a moment,' she said, 'but she's still not well, poor thing. She's gone to lie down. Do you need anything else, madam?'

'No,' Luiza said from the bedroom.

She got undressed and fell into a deep, exhausted sleep.

Upstairs, Juliana could not sleep. The pain had gone, but she lay tossing and turning on the straw mattress, as she had on so many other nights in recent weeks, 'dogged by insomnia'. She had been in a fever of excitement ever since she had taken that letter from the 'sarcophagus'; she had been sustained and uplifted, though, by a feeling of intense joy and great hope. God had finally remembered her! Ever since Bazilio had started coming to the house, she had had a feeling, a sense that her turn had come at last! She had got her first real clue that this was so when Bazilio had left the house at ten o'clock at night, and she had found Luiza's hair comb beside the sofa. But what an explosion of joy when, after all that spying, all that effort, she had plucked that letter out of the 'sarcophagus'! She had run to the attic, had read the letter avidly and, when she realised its significance, her eyes had filled with tears, and she had lifted her perverse soul to heaven, crying out triumphantly to herself:

'Praise be to God!'

Then her one concern was what to do with 'it'. At first, she had thought of selling it to Luiza for a large sum, but where could Luiza get the money? No, it would be best to wait for Jorge to come back and then threaten to make the letter public and extract a great deal of cash from him. Through a third party, of course, thus keeping her own identity concealed. However, there were days when Luiza's appearance, her clothes and her outings all irritated her beyond endurance, and then she felt like running into the street, assembling all the neighbours and reading the letter to them out loud, thus muddying Luiza's name and having her revenge on the 'hussy'!

Tia Vitória calmed her down and counselled her. She saw at once that 'for the trap to be complete they needed a letter from the dandy too'. And Juliana had begun the slow work of getting that letter! This had required great delicacy, much trying of locks, two keys made from wax moulds, the patience of a cat and the skills of a petty thief! But she had got it, and what a letter it turned out to be! She had read it with Tia Vitória, who had laughed and laughed! Especially the part in which Bazilio had said: 'I can't come today, but I will expect you tomorrow at two; I send you this rose and ask you to do as you did with the other rose, and wear it between your breasts, so that I can smell your sweet, perfumed bosom!' Tia Vitória, fighting for breath, simply had to show it to her old friend, Pedra, Fat Pedra, who was in the next room.

Pedra was bent double with laughter. Her enormous breasts, which hung down like half-empty udders, shuddered furiously with laughter. Red-faced, hands on hips, she roared out with her trombone of a voice:

'That's priceless, Tia Vitória! Brilliant! It ought to be printed in the papers, that one! The dirty rascals!'

Tia Vitória had then turned very seriously to Juliana and said:

'Right, now you have both the knife and the cheese! Now you definitely have the upper hand! You just have to wait for the right opportunity. Be very polite, wear your happiest face, be all smiles, so that she suspects nothing, but keep your eyes peeled. You've caught the rat, now let it squirm!'

And from that day on, Juliana had greedily, secretly savoured the delight, the sheer pleasure of having Luiza, the mistress, the boss, 'the dumpling', in her hand! She watched Luiza getting all dressed up to go and see that man, watched her singing to herself and enjoying her food, and all the time Juliana was thinking with a kind of feline voluptuousness: 'Go on, make hay while you can because I've set a trap for you!' This thought filled her with perverse pride. She felt in some sense that she was the real mistress of the house. Held fast in her hand, she had her employers' happiness, good name, honour and peace of mind! What sweet revenge!

And the future was certain. It meant money and bread for her old age. Ah, her time had finally come! Every day she said a Hail Mary to give thanks to Our Lady, Mother of all men!

But now, after that scene with Luiza, with those letters in her pocket, she could not simply sit there and do nothing. She had to get out of the house, she had to act, she had to do something. But what? Tia Vitória would be able to advise her.

The next morning, at seven o'clock, without drinking her usual cup of coffee or speaking to Joana, she went slowly down the stairs and out of the house.

Tia Vitória was not at home. There were people in the small room, waiting. Senhor Gouveia, the tassel on his silk cap at a more than usually jaunty angle, was bent over his desk, scribbling and spitting. Juliana said a general 'Good morning' to everyone and sat down, very erect, in one corner, her parasol on her lap.

People were chatting to each other. Sitting on the sofa was a woman in her thirties with pock-marked skin who smiled at Juliana and then continued her conversation with a plump little woman in a red-checked shawl:

'Oh, Senhora Ana, you've no idea! It's disgraceful! He creates such a racket! Sometimes he even wakes me up with the noise he makes talking to himself or stumbling on the stairs . . . But what really worries me is him dropping off to sleep with the candle still burning and causing a fire. He's just impossible!'

'Who's that?' asked a handsome young man in a footman's tunic, who was standing talking to a tall manservant with long sideburns and a grubby white cravat.

'Cunha, my boss's son. It's shameful, really!'

'Likes his drink, does he?' said the young man, rolling a cigarette.

'I should say! His room smells so bad in the mornings I can't bring myself to go in there. His mother, poor thing, cries and frets, and he's already lost his job. I've just about had enough!'

'Well, there's all kinds of ructions where I am too,' said the woman in the checked shawl, lowering her voice.

The two men joined them.

'The master of the house,' she said with a look of horror on her face, 'can't keep his hands off his sister-in-law! The mistress knows, of course, and they bicker about it day and night. And she and her sister are at it hammer and tongs as well. The husband takes the sister's side, and the wife raises the roof. It's all going to end in tears.'

'But then, of course, if *we* do the slightest thing wrong,' said the man in the white cravat indignantly, 'all hell breaks loose.'

'Yes, but your people are nice, quiet folk, Senhor João,' said the woman with the pock-marked face.

'Yes, they're good people, but the girls are terrible flirts . . . and the maids make the most of it, of course, and get paid for their services in clothes and hard cash. But the old folk are absolute saints. And the food's good too!'

Then turning to the footman and clapping him on the shoulder, he said in half-admiring, half-envious tones:

'Now this fellow here has really fallen on his feet!'

The young man gave a smug smile.

'A lot of it's just talk.'

'Go on, show them,' said the man in the white cravat, nudging him with his elbow. 'Show them!'

The young man resisted at first, but then, wriggling his hips, he pulled up his tunic and took a gold watch from the pocket of his striped waistcoat.

'Oh, I say,' said the two women, 'isn't that lovely!'

'Gained with the sweat of my brow,' said the young man, stroking his chin.

The man in the white cravat retorted in mock indignation: 'You young rascal!' And then addressing the two women: 'Sweat of his brow, indeed! Pay no attention to him, it's that angel of a mistress of his, a high society lady all dressed in silks, who gives him all these presents, expensive watches like that – gorgeous woman she is, getting on a bit, but still gorgeous!'

The young man plunged his hands in his pockets.

'If I like, she'll give me a watch chain next!'

'She can certainly afford it!' exclaimed the man in the white cravat. 'She owns whole rows of houses in the Baixa, as well as half of Rua dos Retroseiros!'

'She's very tight with money, though!' said the young man, swaying his body, a cigarette dangling from one corner of his mouth. 'I mean I've been with her for two months now, and all I've got out of her is this watch and three gold *libras*! One of these days, I'll give her the boot! 'And smoothing his hair, he added: 'There are plenty of other women around, women with a real talent for it as well!'

Tia Vitória came bustling in at that point, her shawl over her arm. Seeing Juliana, she cried:

'What are you doing here? I had a few errands to run, I've been up and about since six o'clock. Good morning, Senhora Teodósia; good morning, Ana. Ah, and the young dandy's here, is he? Come straight in, Juliana! I'll be with you in a moment, my doves!'

She led Juliana into the room overlooking the courtyard:

'So, what news?'

Juliana began to describe at length what had happened the previous evening, about the fainting fit . . .

'Well, my dear,' said Tia Vitória, 'what's done is done; there's no time to lose; it's all hands to the pump! You must go straight to Brito at the hotel and make a deal with him.'

Juliana refused outright; she wouldn't dare, she was too afraid.

Tia Vitória sat thinking for a while, scratching her ear; she left the room, had a muttered conversation with Senhor Gouveia, then returned, closing the door behind her.

'We can get someone else to go. Have you got the letters?'

Juliana took an old scarlet morocco leather purse from her pocket, but then hesitated for a moment, eyeing Tia Vitória distrustfully.

'You're not afraid of letting them go, are you, woman?' Tia Vitória cried in wounded tones. 'Well, sort it out yourself, then!'

Juliana immediately handed the letters over. But Tia Vitória would be sure to keep them in a safe place, wouldn't she, she'd be very careful!

'The person,' said Tia Vitória, 'will go and speak to Brito tomorrow night and ask him for one *conto de réis*!'

Juliana was taken aback. One *conto de réis*! Tia Vitória was joking, surely!

'Certainly not! There's a woman who rides up and down the Chiado in a carriage – I saw her only yesterday with her little baby – who paid three hundred *mil réis* recently for a far less damaging letter. And in notes too. It was the man who paid, you understand. If it was anyone else, it might be different, but Brito . . . He's rich and a spendthrift, he'll pay up at once.'

Juliana, ashen-faced, tremulously grasped Tia Vitória's arm:

'Oh, Tia Vitória, I'll buy you a length of silk.'

'I'll even tell you the colour I want! Blue!'

'But Brito's a strong chap, Tia Vitória, what if he grabs the letters, what if he gets violent?'

Tia Vitória gave her a scornful look:

'Don't be so simpleminded! You don't think I'd send a fool there, do you? I won't even send the letters, just a copy! I'll send my brightest man!'

Then after pondering for a moment:

'Now off you go back to the house.'

'No, I can't.'

'No, you're right. Until we see how the land lies, you'd better sleep here. Come and have supper with me tonight. I've got a lovely bit of fish in.'

'But isn't there a danger, Tia Vitória, that Brito will go to the police?'

Tia Vitória gave an impatient shrug:

'Be off with you now, you're beginning to get on my nerves! The police, indeed! What police? People don't take such matters to the police. Leave it with me. Now, off you go, and I'll see you at four for dinner, all right?'

Juliana left the room as if walking on air. One *conto de réis*! It was the *conto de réis* that was coming back to her, the one she had glimpsed before, but which had eluded her, and was now about to fall into her hands with a clink of *libras* and a rustle of notes! And her mind filled up with a whole array of possibilities, all of them marvellous: a shop selling trinkets; a husband by her side at dinner time; chic, good-quality pairs of boots. Where would she put the money? In the bank? No, at the bottom of the chest, where it would be safer and handier.

In order to pass the morning, she bought a bag of sweets and went and sat down in the Passeio Público, with her parasol up, savouring and pondering her new life of wealth, as if she were already a lady; she even made eyes at a placid, rubicund man of property, who scurried away, scandalised.

At that hour, Luiza was only just waking up. She sat bolt upright in bed and her first thought was: 'It's today!' Her heart contracted with fear and with a horrible sense of sadness. She began to get dressed, dreading the idea of seeing Juliana. She was even considering locking herself in her room and foregoing breakfast, then creeping out at eleven o'clock to go and find Bazilio at his hotel, when Joana's voice at the bedroom door said:

'Excuse me, madam . . .'

Joana, greatly alarmed, immediately launched into an account of how Senhora Juliana had gone out early that morning and had not come back, and how no housework had been done and . . .

'All right, make me some breakfast. I'll be there shortly.'

What a relief!

She realised at once that Juliana had left the house. But why? Doubtless in order to set some trap for her! It was best if she went out at once. She could wait for Bazilio in 'Paradise'.

She went into the dining room and took a hasty sip of tea, standing up.

'Do you think anything's happened to Senhora Juliana?' an alarmed Joana came in to ask.

Luiza shrugged and replied vaguely:

'I'm sure we'll find out eventually.'

It was half past the hour, she went and put on her hat. Her heart was beating fast, but despite her fear of seeing Juliana arrive back, she could not get herself to move; she even sat down with her morocco leather bag on her knees. 'Come on!' she told herself. At last, she got up; but it was as if some strong, subtle force were holding her fast, ensnaring her. She went slowly into the bedroom; her peignoir lay at the foot of the bed, her slippers were there on the soft carpet. 'Oh, dear God, this is awful!' she said out loud. She went over to the dressing table, fiddled with her combs and opened some drawers; suddenly she went into the living room, found the album, removed the photograph of Jorge and placed it tremulously in her bag, then she glanced around her as if disoriented, and left, slamming the door, and ran down the stairs.

A hire carriage was passing in Rua da Patriarcal. She got in and asked to be taken to the Hotel Central.

Senhor Brito had left the hotel early, said the harassed porter. A steamship had obviously just arrived, for luggage was being carried in, heavy suitcases covered in oilskin, and iron-bound wooden boxes; passengers with the startled look of the newly arrived, still unsteady after the motion of the waves, were talking and calling to each other. The hustle and bustle cheered her; she was filled by a desire for travel, for the night-time clamour of gas-lit stations, for the joyful commotion of departures in the early cool of morning, standing on the deck of a ship!

She gave the coachman the address of 'Paradise'. And as they drove along, it seemed to her that the whole of her past

245

life, Juliana and the house, were fading and dissolving into a horizon she was leaving behind her. At the door of a bookshop she thought she saw Julião; she leaned out of the window, but couldn't be sure it was him and she felt sorry to be leaving without seeing a single one of her and Jorge's mutual friends! All of them now, Julião, Ernestinho, the Councillor, Dona Felicidade, seemed to her adorable, endowed, every one of them, with noble qualities she had never before perceived and which were suddenly imbued with great charm. And poor, kind Sebastião! She would never again hear him play the *malagueña*.

At the end of Rua do Ouro, the carriage got caught up amongst some carts, and on the pavement Luiza noticed Castro, the bespectacled banker, who 'was madly in love with her', according to Leopoldina; a ragged boy was offering to sell him some lottery tickets; and the oily-complexioned Castro, his thumbs hooked in the pockets of his white waistcoat, was joking with the boy in the scornful way the very rich do, all the while ogling Luiza through his gold-rimmed spectacles. She was watching him out of the corner of her eye: that man was in love with her, what a ghastly thought! She found him hideous, with his paunch and his little short legs. She was assailed by the memory of Bazilio's fine figure. And in her haste to see him, she impatiently banged on the window to urge the driver on.

The carriage finally moved off. The main square, the Rossio, glittered in the sunlight: people in white trousers and light dresses, arriving from Belém or Pedrouços, were hurriedly clambering down from the horsedrawn tram that had stopped on the corner; street vendors cried their wares. They were all coming to stay with their families, with their sundry happinesses; she alone was leaving!

In Rua Ocidental, she saw Dona Camila walking along: she was married to a much older man and was famous for her many lovers. She appeared to be pregnant and, with her smug, white face and her look of round, corporeal lassitude, she was advancing slowly along the pavement, accompanied by a boy in a waist-length, beige jacket, a girl in stiff petticoats and,

246

ahead of them, a nursemaid, dressed like a peasant, who was pushing a pram in which a baby dribbled and drooled. And the happy Camila strolled calmly down the street, displaying her adulterous fecundity for all to see! She was much admired and no one had a bad word to say about her; she was rich and gave soirées . . . 'What a world!' thought Luiza.

The carriage stopped outside 'Paradise'. It was midday. The upstairs door was closed, and the landlady immediately appeared, whispering that she was most terribly sorry, the gentleman had the only key, but if the lady simply wanted to rest . . . At that moment, another carriage arrived, and Bazilio came bounding up the stairs.

'At last!' he cried, unlocking the door. 'Why didn't you come yesterday?'

'Oh, if only you knew . . .'

And grabbing both his arms and looking him straight in the eye, she said:

'Bazilio, I'm lost!'

'What's happened?'

Luiza threw the morocco leather bag down on the sofa and, in one breath, told him the story of her letter plucked from amongst the discarded papers, his letters stolen from her, the scene in her room . . . 'All that remains for me now is to run away. Here I am. Take me with you. You said you could, you've often told me so. I'm ready. I've brought that one bag with just the essentials, handkerchiefs, gloves . . . What do you say?'

Bazilio, hands in his pockets, jingling his change and his keys, followed her every gesture and word in astonishment.

'This could only happen to you!' he exclaimed. 'You're mad, woman!' Then he went on, very excitedly: 'This isn't a question of running away! Why on earth are you talking about running away? It's a question of money. What she wants is money. You just have to find out how much she wants and pay her off!'

'No, no!' cried Luiza. 'I can't stay!' There was real distress in her voice. The woman might sell her back the letters, but she would still have the secret; at any moment, she might talk and then Jorge would find out; she was lost, she hadn't the courage to go home! 'I simply can't rest as long as I remain in Lisbon. We'll leave today, won't we? If you can't leave today, then tomorrow. I'll go to some hotel, where no one knows me, I'll hide myself away tonight. But tomorrow we'll leave. If he finds out, Bazilio, he'll kill me! Say yes!'

She clung to him, eagerly searching his eyes for some sign of agreement.

Bazilio gently disentangled himself.

'You're mad, Luiza, you're not yourself! How can we possibly think of running away? It would cause a terrible scandal, and we would be bound to be caught, by the police, by the telegraph offices! It's impossible! Running away is the stuff of novels! Besides, my dear, it's not necessary. It's a simple question of money.'

Luiza turned pale as she listened to him.

'And anyway,' Bazilio went on, nervously pacing the room, 'I'm not prepared, nor are you. You can't just run off like that. You would be dishonoured for the rest of your life, for ever, Luiza. A woman who runs away ceases to be Senhora Dona So-and-so and becomes plain So-and-so, that woman who ran away, that hussy, someone or other's mistress! I'll probably have to go back to Brazil at some point, and what will you do then? Would you want to go with me and spend a month in a narrow berth and risk catching yellow fever? And what if your husband pursues us, what if we're arrested at the frontier? How would you like to be brought back by two policemen and spend a year in Limoeiro prison? It's perfectly simple. You come to an agreement with the woman, give her a couple of *libras*, which is what she wants, and you continue living quietly in your house, as respected as you've always been, only much wiser! And that's that!'

These words fell on Luiza's plans like axe blows felling trees. Sometimes the truth they contained cut irresistibly through her, bright as a lightning flash, cruel as a cold blade. But she saw in his refusal only ingratitude and rejection. Having, in her imagination, installed herself in happy safety, far away in Paris, it seemed to her unbearable to have to go back home, head bowed, to put up with Juliana and await death; and now that the contentments she had glimpsed in that other destiny were slipping through her fingers, they seemed to her marvellous and almost essential! And what was the point of buying back the letter? The woman would still know her secret! And having that danger constantly prowling around her would sour her whole life!

She had fallen silent, as if lost in vague reflections; then, suddenly looking up, her eyes flashing:

'What should I do?'

'I've already told you what I think you should do.'

'You don't want to run away, then?'

'No!' said Bazilio forcefully. 'You may be mad, but I'm not!'

'Oh, what am I going to do?'

She fell back onto the sofa and covered her face with her hands. Her body was shaken by muffled sobs.

Bazilio sat down next to her. Her tears tormented and exasperated him.

'For heaven's sake, listen to me!'

She turned to him, her eyes bright with tears:

'Why then did you say to me, over and over, that we would be happy, that if I wanted to . . .'

Bazilio got abruptly to his feet:

'You mean you really wanted to run away with me, get on a train, go to Paris and live with me and be my mistress?'

'I've left home for ever, that's what I've done!'

'Well, you're going straight back!' he exclaimed almost angrily. 'Why should you run away? Out of love? If so, we should have left a month ago, but there's no reason now for us to leave. Why? To avoid a scandal by creating an even bigger one? A terrible, irreparable scandal! I'm talking to you as a friend, Luiza!' Very tenderly he took her hands in his. 'Of course I would be happy to live with you in Paris, but I've seen the results, I have more experience than you. Besides, the whole scandal can be avoided with a few *libras*. Do you really imagine the woman is going to talk? It's in her interests to leave, to disappear; she knows what she did, that she robbed you and made copies of your keys. It's just a matter of paying her off.'

Luiza spoke very deliberately:

'And where am I going to get the money?'

'I've got the money!' Then after a pause: 'Well, I haven't got much, actually, because I don't have that much cash at the moment, but anyway . . .' He hesitated, then said: 'If the woman wants two hundred *mil réis*, give it to her!'

'And what if she doesn't?

'What else could she possibly want? She stole the letter in order to sell it, not because she wanted your autograph!'

His mind filled up with harsh words, he paced angrily about the room. What presumption wanting to come to Paris with him and complicate his life for ever! And what unnecessary expense, giving so much money to a thief! The whole incident, the love letter snatched from amongst the waste paper, the servant, the copy made of the key to the wardrobe drawer, all struck him as supremely bourgeois, even rather shameful. He stopped pacing and made his final offer:

'All right, then, offer her three hundred *mil réis*, if you like, but for God's sake, don't do it again. I can't afford to pay for your mistakes at three hundred *mil réis* a go!'

Luiza turned as white as if he had spat in her face!

'If it's just a matter of money, then I'll pay, Bazilio!'

She didn't know how. What did it matter? She would borrow it, she would work, she would pawn something . . . She would not accept his money!

Bazilio shrugged:

'Now you're giving yourself airs; where exactly will you get the money?'

'What does it matter to you?' she exclaimed.

Bazilio scratched his head in desperation. Then, taking her hands in his again, this time with barely suppressed irritation, he said:

'This is all pure nonsense, my dear, we're both of us getting annoyed. The fact is, you don't have any money.'

She interrupted him, violently grabbing his arm:

'All right, then, you talk to the woman, you talk to her and arrange everything. I never want to see her again. If I do, I'll die, I mean it. You talk to her!'

Bazilio drew back and stamped hard on the floor:

'You're mad, woman! If I talk to her, she'll ask for even more money, she'll have the shirt off my back! This is your business. I'll give you the money and you sort yourself out!'

'You won't even do that for me?'

Bazilio could not contain himself:

'No, damnation, I won't!'

'Goodbye, then!'

'You're not thinking clearly, Luiza!'

'No, you're right. It's all my fault,' she said, lowering her veil with tremulous hands, 'it's up to me to sort things out.'

And with that she opened the door. Bazilio ran over to her and caught her by the arm.

'Luiza! Luiza! What are you going to do? We can't just break off like this! Listen . . .'

'Let's run away together, then; save me from all this!' she cried, clinging to him.

'For God's sake, I've told you already that simply isn't possible!

She slammed the door and ran down the stairs. The carriage was waiting for her.

'To the Rossio,' she said.

And hurling herself into a corner of the carriage, she broke into convulsive sobs.

Bazilio left 'Paradise' feeling deeply troubled. He was so irritated by Luiza's presumptuous ideas, by her bourgeois fears and by the ghastly triviality of the whole business, that he was almost inclined never to go back there, but simply to lie low and let things take their course, but he felt sorry for her, poor girl! And although he did not love her, he certainly desired her: she was so sweet and had such a lovely body, and the licentious ways he had taught her provoked in her the most adorable ecstasies. She had been a source of such piquant pleasure during his stay in Lisbon! Damn these complications! As he went into the hotel, he said to his servant:

'When the Viscount returns, tell him to come to my room.'

He was staying on the second floor, with a view over the river. He drank a glass of cognac and lay down on the sofa. On the low table next to him lay his blotter embossed in silver with his monogram and the crown of a Count, as well as his boxes of cigars and his books: *Mademoiselle Giraud: My Wife*, *The Virgin of Mabille*, *Those Rogues! The Secret Memoirs of a Chambermaid*, *Pointers*, *The Hunter's Handbook*, some back numbers of *Le Figaro*, a photograph of Luiza and a photograph of a horse.

Exhaling the smoke from his cigar, he began to ponder, with some horror, the 'situation'! That was all he needed, going off back to Paris with that particular millstone tied around his neck! He had had his life nicely sorted out for the last seven years, and then, bang, he's supposed to ruin it all simply because someone has stolen Miss Luiza's love letter and she's afraid of what her husband will do. The nerve of the woman! The whole adventure had been a mistake from the start. Seducing his cousin was an idea worthy of some over-excited bourgeois gentleman. He had come to Lisbon intending to sort out his business affairs, put up with the heat and the Hotel Central's *boeuf à la mode* for a while, then catch the steamboat back and bid a fond farewell to the homeland! But not he, the fool! He had finished his business there, but, like an idiot, had stayed on, roasting in Lisbon, spending a fortune on carriages to Largo de Santa Bárbara, and for what? To find himself in a situation like this! He would have done better to have brought Alphonsine with him!

The fact was that, while in Lisbon, the romance had been pleasant, indeed, exciting, because it was so perfect, involving as it did both adultery and just a hint of incest. This latest episode spoiled everything though. The only sensible thing to do now was to disappear!

He had made his fortune from a rubber plantation in Paraguay: the magnitude of the deal had necessitated forming a company using Brazilian capital; but Bazilio and a few French engineers had wanted to buy up the Brazilian shares, which were proving 'an impediment', and to form another company in Paris, thus giving the business a whole new impetus. Bazilio had come to Lisbon in order to hold talks with some of the Brazilians and had managed to buy the shares from them at a good price. The prolongation of his amorous entanglement was beginning to get in the way of his practical life . . . And now that the affair had taken this annoying turn, it really would be best to move on!

The door opened, and Viscount Reinaldo burst in, wearing blue-tinted spectacles and a furious expression on his face, which was scarlet with the heat.

He had been to Benfica! He had nearly died in that positively African sun! He had had the ridiculous idea of going to visit an aunt, who had promptly made him a member of some association or other that provided nursery care for poor families and then had the gall to preach morality at him! What a puerile idea to go and visit his aunt in the first place! If there was one thing he hated more than anything else it was being in the bosom of one's family!

'Anyway, what did you want? I'm going to sit in the bath until supper time!'

'Guess what happened,' said Bazilio, getting up.

'What?'

'No, guess. It's the most stupid thing.'

'Her husband has found out.'

'No, the maid!'

'Disgraceful!' exclaimed Reinaldo in disgust.

Bazilio told him all the details, then standing before him, arms folded, said:

'So now what do I do?'

'You disappear!'

And he got up from his chair.

'Where are you off to?'

'I'm going to have my bath.'

Bazílio asked him to wait, he needed to talk to him.

'I can't, I'm afraid,' cried Reinaldo in a frenzy of selfishness. 'Come downstairs! I can talk perfectly well while immersed in water!'

He left, bellowing for William, his English manservant.

When Bazilio went down to the baths, Reinaldo was already reclining voluptuously in waters heavily scented with Lubin cologne, and relishing his own comfort.

'So, the letter was found in the waste paper, eh?'

'Look, Reinaldo, I'm in a real predicament here; what do you think I should do?'

'Pack your bags, my boy!'

And sitting there in the tub, slowly soaping his thin body, he added:

'That's what comes of making love to cousins who live in insalubrious neighbourhoods!'

'Oh, really!' snorted Bazilio impatiently.

'What do you mean "Oh, really"?' And, covered in foam, resting his hands on the marble edge of the tub, he went on: 'Do you think it decent for a woman to treat her cook as a confidante, to allow herself to fall into her clutches, to leave such a letter amongst the waste paper, to weep and ask you for two hundred *mil réis*, to declare that she wants to run away with you — that is not how a lover should behave! This is a woman who, as you yourself told me, wears woollen stockings!'

'Yes, my friend, but she *is* gorgeous!'

The Viscount gave a sceptical shrug.

Bazilio provided evidence: he described the particular beauties of Luiza's body and cited certain libidinous episodes.

The ceiling and the white partition walls reflected the soft, milky light; the steam from the water added to the tepid warmth of the air; and the atmosphere was fragrant with the fresh smell of soap and Lubin cologne.

'You're obviously besotted,' Reinaldo concluded dully, stretching out in the bath.

Bazilio made a movement with his shoulders as if to shrug off such a grotesque supposition.

'All right, then, do you want to stay clinging to her skirts or do you want to get rid of her? The truth now.'

'Well,' Bazilio began softly, drawing closer to the tub, 'if there were some decent way in which I could get rid of her . . .'

'You poor fool! You've got the perfect opportunity! According to you, she stormed off. Fine, then, you write her a letter saying that since she clearly wishes to break off the relationship, you have no desire to stand in her way and are leaving Lisbon. You've finished your business here, haven't you? Don't deny it, Lapierre told me so. Fine, do the decent thing, then: pack your bags and get rid of the wretched woman!'

He picked up a sponge and squeezed great spurts of water over his head and shoulders, blowing out as he did so, revelling in the aromatic coolness.

'But then again,' said Bazilio, 'I can't just leave her in that bind with her maid! After all, she is my cousin.'

Reinaldo waved his arms about in great hilarity.

'Such family feeling is truly admirable! Go on, you fool, just tell her you've got to leave, business calls and all that, and stuff a few notes into her hand.'

'It's awfully brutal.'

'It's awfully expensive!'

Bazilio said:

'But it really is a damnably awkward situation, the poor girl caught out by her maid like that . . .'

Reinaldo stretched still more and said gleefully:

'They're probably tearing each other's hair out at this very moment!'

He leaned blissfully back; he asked the time; he declared that he was comfortable, that he was happy! As long as William had remembered to chill the champagne.

Bazilio twirled his moustaches and said nothing. He was imagining Luiza's green-upholstered drawing room and the hideous figure of Juliana with her vast pile of false hair. Would they really be fighting and arguing? How undignified it all was. He really should leave.

'But what excuse can I give for having to leave Lisbon?'

'A telegram! There's nothing like a telegram! Telegraph your man in Paris, Labachardie or Labachardette, or whatever his name is, and tell him to send you this message at once: "Return Paris immediately, business bad, etc." That's the best way!'

'I'll do it now,' said Bazilio, getting resolutely to his feet.

'And we leave tomorrow?' cried Reinaldo.

'Tomorrow.'

'Via Madrid?'

'Via Madrid.'

'*Salero*!' In his enthusiasm, he stood up, dripping with water, and with the gangling movements of the very thin, jumped out of the tub and wrapped himself in a Turkish robe. His servant William glided noiselessly in, knelt down, took one foot between his hands and carefully dried it, before respectfully slipping onto it a black silk sock embroidered with tiny horseshoes.

The following day, shortly before noon, Joana knocked discreetly on Luiza's bedroom door and announced in a low voice – since Luiza's fainting fit, she always spoke to her softly, as if to a convalescent:

'Your cousin's here, madam.'

Luiza was taken by surprise. She was still in her peignoir, and her eyes were red from crying; she quickly dabbed on some powder, smoothed her hair and went into the drawing room.

Bazilio, wearing a pale-coloured suit, was sitting dejectedly on the piano stool. He was looking very grave and, without further ado, he began by saying that, despite her anger of the previous day, he still considered that everything was 'exactly as it had been'. He had come because he did not feel they could part just like that, without some words of explanation, and, in particular, without resolving the matter of the letter. He put on a sad face, as if he were holding back his tears:

'I'm afraid I have to leave Lisbon, my love!'

Without even looking at him, Luiza gave a silent, scornful smile. Bazilio added:

'Only for a short time, of course, three or four weeks. But I do have to go. If only my own interests were at stake . . .' He gave a dismissive shrug. 'But other people are involved, you see. Here, I received this telegram this morning.'

He gave her the telegram. She held onto it for a moment, without opening it; it trembled in her hand.

'Read it, I beg you!'

'Why?' she said.

Then she read out loud: 'Come at once, grave complications. Your presence here vital. Leave immediately.'

She folded it up and handed it back to him.

'So you're leaving, then?'

'I must.'

'When?'

'Tonight.'

Luiza suddenly got to her feet and, holding out her hand, said:

'Goodbye, then.'

Bazilio murmured:

'You're cruel, Luiza! Not that it matters. However, there is still some unfinished business. Did you speak to the woman?'

'It's all arranged,' she replied, frowning.

Bazilio took her hand and said almost solemnly:

'My dear, I know how proud you are, but I beg you, please, tell me the truth. I don't want to leave you in difficulties. Did you speak to her?'

She withdrew her hand and with growing impatience insisted:

'I told you, it's all arranged.'

Bazilio seemed extremely embarrassed; he had even turned rather pale. Then, removing a wallet from his pocket, he began:

'Whatever happens, it is possible, indeed, natural (we don't know who we're dealing with here), it is only natural that she might make other demands.' He opened the wallet and took out a small, fat envelope.

Luiza, growing redder by the minute, was following his every movement.

'That is why I feel it only right to leave you some money, so that you can sort things out with her more easily.'

'Are you mad?' she cried.

'But . . .'

'You want to give me money?' There was a tremor in her voice.

'But after all . . .'

'Goodbye!' And she made to leave the room in great indignation.

'For God's sake, Luiza! You misunderstand me . . .'

She stopped and said briskly, as if impatient to be done:

'Thank you, Bazilio, I understand perfectly. But it won't be necessary. I'm just a little upset, that's all. Let's not prolong this meeting any further. Goodbye.'

'But I'll be back, in three weeks or so.'

'Fine, we'll see each other then.'

He drew her to him and kissed her on the mouth, only to find her lips passive and inert.

This coldness wounded his vanity. He pressed her to him and said softly, passionately:

'Won't you even give me a kiss?'

There was the slightest glimmer in Luiza's eyes; she kissed him briefly, then pulled away:

'Goodbye.'

Bazilio stood for a moment looking at her and said with a little sigh:

'Goodbye!' And turning at the door, he added sadly: 'At least write to me. You know my address: Rue Saint-Florentin, 22.'

Luiza went over to the window. Out in the street, she saw him light a cigar, talk to the coachman, then jump into the carriage and slam the door, without even a glance up at the windows!

The carriage moved off. She noticed the number on it – 10 . . . She would never see him again. They had pulsated with the same love, they had committed the same sin. He, however, was leaving gaily, carrying with him romantic memories of their affair; she was staying, caught in the permanent bitterness of error. That was the way of the world!

She was filled by a poignant sense of solitude and

abandonment. She was all alone, and life seemed to her like a vast, unfamiliar plain, plunged in dark night and bristling with dangers.

She went slowly back into her room and sat down heavily on the sofa; she saw the morocco leather bag beside it, the bag she had prepared the night before in order to flee; she opened it and slowly started taking out the handkerchiefs, the embroidered chemise, then she found Jorge's photograph! She sat with it in her hand, studying his loyal gaze, his kindly smile. No, she wasn't all alone in the world! She had him! He loved her and would never betray or abandon her! She pressed her lips to the photograph, making it wet with her violent kisses, then she threw herself down on the sofa, her face bathed in tears, saying: 'Forgive me, Jorge, dear Jorge, my beloved Jorge, my own dear Jorge!'

After supper, Joana came to ask Luiza timidly:

'Don't you think, madam, that we should try and find out what has happened to Senhora Juliana?'

'But where would you go to ask?' said Luiza.

'She sometimes used to go to the house of a friend who lives near Carmo. She might have fallen ill, she might be unwell. But it is very odd her not sending any word since yesterday morning. I could go and ask.'

'All right, then, go.'

Juliana's abrupt disappearance was worrying Luiza too. Where was she, what was she doing? It seemed to her that somewhere far from her something was being concocted in secret, something that would suddenly and terribly burst over her head . . .

It grew dark. She lit the candles. She was slightly afraid of being alone in the house like that; and as she walked up and down the room, she was thinking of how, at that hour, Bazilio would be at Santa Apolónia station happily buying his ticket, installing himself in his carriage, lighting a cigar and how, shortly afterwards, the train would puff out of the station, carrying him away for ever. For she did not believe in his 'three or four weeks'! He was going for good, he was running away! And however much she detested him, she nevertheless felt that, with his departure, something inside her was breaking and painfully bleeding!

It was nearly nine o'clock when the bell rang urgently. She assumed it must be Joana and went to the door carrying a candle; when she saw before her a terribly pale, distraught Juliana, she drew back:

'May I speak to you for a moment, madam?'

She followed Luiza into her room and immediately began shouting angrily:

'You surely don't imagine that things can go on like this! You surely don't imagine that just because your lover has gone away, things will simply carry on as they were!'

'Whatever's the matter, woman?' asked Luiza, petrified.

'If you think that because your lover has run off, nothing's going to happen . . .' Juliana roared.

'For God's sake, woman!'

And there was such pain in her voice that Juliana fell silent. After a moment, though, she said, more softly:

'You know perfectly well I was keeping those letters for a reason. I was going to ask your cousin to help me! I'm tired of working, I need a rest. I wasn't going to cause a scandal or anything, I just wanted him to help me out. I sent someone to the hotel this evening, but your cousin had already upped sticks and left! He's gone off to Olivais or somewhere! And his servant will be following tonight with the luggage! Don't think you're going to get the better of me, though!' Once more in the grip of rage, she was thumping the table hard: 'May God strike me down if this house isn't overtaken by a scandal that will have all Portugal talking!'

'How much do you want for the letters, you thief?' said Luiza, drawing herself up.

For a moment, Juliana did not know what to say.

'I won't give them to you for less than six hundred *mil réis*!' she replied haughtily.

'Six hundred *mil réis*! Where do you think I'm going to get that sort of money?'

'In hell, for all I care!' bawled Juliana. 'You either give me

260

the six hundred *mil réis*, or, as sure as I'm standing here, your husband will read those letters!'

Luiza fell helplessly back into a chair.

'What did I do to deserve this, dear God, what did I do to deserve this?'

Juliana planted herself insolently in front of her.

'You're quite right, it's true, I am a thief; I stole that letter from the rubbish and took the other two from the wardrobe drawer. It's true! But the only reason I did it was to get some money!' In a frenzy of excitement, she kept wrapping and unwrapping her shawl about her shoulders. 'It was about time my luck changed. After all I've suffered, I've had enough! Just find the money! But I won't accept five *réis* less! I've spent years and years slaving, and all to earn half a *moeda* a month. I work myself silly from dawn to dusk, while you laze around doing nothing! I get up every day at six o'clock in the morning and then it's one long round of polishing, sweeping, tidying, toiling away, while you're tucked up in bed, without a care in the world and with nothing to do. For a whole month now, I've been getting up at daybreak to do the starching and ironing! All you do is get through mounds of laundry and go swanning off in your nice underwear to see whoever you like, and here's me, your slave, with pains in my heart, killing myself to get the ironing done! For you, life is all outings, carriages, fine silks, anything you fancy, but what about me, your slave? Your slave is busily working herself to death!'

Luiza was too exhausted to reply and cowered beneath Juliana's rage like a bird in a rainstorm. Juliana was getting more and more agitated, ranting on and on in the same violent tone of voice. The thought of the drudgery and the humiliations she had endured only added fuel to her rage, like wood thrown onto a bonfire.

'Do you see how it is?' she went on. 'I eat the leftovers and you have all the titbits! If I fancy a drop of wine after working all day, who's going to give it to me? I have to buy it! Have you ever actually been into my room? It's like a prison cell! There are so many bedbugs I have to sleep with most of my clothes on! But if madam gets so much as a bite, your slave here has to dismantle your whole bed and search it inch by inch. A maid? Huh! A maid is just an animal. Work if you can, but if you can't then it's out in the street with you, to the hospital. But now my time has come.' And she beat her breast, aflame with vengeance. 'I give the orders now.'

Luiza was sobbing softly.

'Oh, so you're crying, are you? Well, I've cried plenty of tears in my time! Oh, I don't wish you ill, madam, really I don't. Have fun, enjoy yourself! All I want is my money, here in my hand, otherwise I'll have to make those letters public! May the roof fall in on me if I don't show the letters to your husband, your friends, to the whole neighbourhood, and see your reputation in ruins!'

She fell silent, suddenly drained; and in a weary, broken voice, she went on:

'But give me my money, my beloved money, and you can have your letters, and what's done is done. I'll even deliver them for you. But I want my money now! And I'll tell you this too, may lightning strike me dead this instant, if, when I've got my money, I say a word to anyone!' And she covered her mouth with her hand.

Luiza had got slowly to her feet, looking very pale.

'All right,' she said, almost in a murmur, 'I'll get you your money. You'll just have to wait a few days.'

There was a silence, which seemed all the deeper for the preceding clamour, and the whole room seemed to grow even stiller. Only the clock continued its tick-tock, while the two candles on the dressing table burned slowly down, giving off a clear, reddish light.

Juliana picked up her parasol, wrapped her shawl around her and after looking at Luiza hard for a moment, said sharply:

'Right then, madam.'

And she turned and left.

Luiza heard the front door slam.

'Oh dear God, how I am punished!' she cried, falling into a chair, her face once more bathed in tears.

It was almost ten o'clock by the time Joana returned.

'I didn't find out anything, madam, no one at Tia Vitória's has had any news of her.'

'All right, bring me my nightlight.'

As Joana was getting undressed in her room, she was mumbling to herself:

'She's got herself a man, she's holed up somewhere with some good-for-nothing!'

What a night Luiza spent! She kept starting awake, opening her eyes to the darkness in the room, and then the same painful questions would plunge into her soul like a knife: What should she do? How was she going to find the money? Six hundred *mil réis*! Her jewellery was worth maybe two hundred *mil réis*. But then what would Jorge say when he found out? There was the silver, but the problem would be the same.

It was a hot night and, in her restlessness, the bedclothes had slipped off and she was covered only by the sheet. Sometimes, out of sheer exhaustion, she fell into a superficial sleep, interspersed with vivid dreams. She saw piles of *libras* dimly gleaming, bundles of notes falling gently through the air. She would get to her feet and jump up to try and catch them, but the coins would start to roll away across the smooth floor like infinite tiny wheels, and the notes would disappear, flitting lightly off with a rustle of ironic wings. Or else someone would come into the room, bow respectfully and, doffing his hat, drop into her lap *libras*, five-*mil-réis* coins, and a profusion of other coins; she did not know the man, but he was wearing a red wig and an impudent goatee. Could it be the Devil? What did it matter? She was rich, she was saved! She called out, shouting for Juliana, running after her along a never-ending corridor that began to grow narrower and narrower, until it was no more than a crack along which she had to squeeze sideways, barely able to breathe, clutching to her the pile of coins that left the cold touch of metal on her bare chest. She woke feeling frightened, and the contrast between her real poverty and that dream wealth was an added source of bitterness. Who could help her? Sebastião! Sebastião was both rich and kind. But how could she, Luiza, Jorge's wife, send for him and say: 'Lend me six hundred *mil-réis*.' 'What for, my dear lady?' Could she then reply: 'So that I can buy back some letters that I wrote to my lover'? It was impossible. No, she was ruined. All that remained for her was to enter a convent.

She kept turning over the pillow, which scalded her cheek; she took off her nightcap, and when her long hair fell loose, she caught it up again with a clip; and lying on her back, her head resting on her bare arms, she thought bitterly about the complicated story of that summer: Bazilio's arrival, the trip out to Campo Grande, the first visit to 'Paradise' . . .

Where would he be now, the scoundrel? Sleeping peacefully on the cushioned seats of the train!

And there she was in torment!

She threw off the sheet, feeling as if she were suffocating. And thus, uncovered, barely distinguishable from the white bed linen, she slept until daybreak.

She woke late, feeling utterly downcast, but the beauty of the glorious morning flooding into the dining room revived her spirits. The sun poured abundantly and radiantly in through the open window; the canaries were putting on a concert; from the forge nearby came the sound of jovial hammering; and the broad, vigorous blue of the sky was rousing the city's inhabitants. The joy imbuing everything around her filled her with unexpected courage. She could not succumb to inert despair. Heavens, no, she must fight!

New hopes arose within her. Sebastião was so kind and Leopoldina so resourceful, and there were other possibilities too, even chance itself; all of that, added together, could well amount to six hundred *mil-réis* and save her! Juliana would disappear; Jorge would come back! Excited, she saw prospects of possible joys glinting deliciously in the future!

At midday, Sebastião's young servant called: his master had arrived back from Almada and wanted to know how Senhora Luiza was.

She herself went to the door and asked him to tell Senhor Sebastião to come as soon as he could!

That was that! She had reached a decision, she would speak to Sebastião. There was nothing else she could do: either she told Sebastião everything, or that woman would tell her husband everything. She could not risk further delay! She could diminish the importance of the letters, saying that the correspondence had been purely platonic ... And Bazilio's departure relegated her mistake firmly to the past, converting it almost into ancient history. And Sebastião was such a good friend!

He arrived at one o'clock. Luiza, who was in her room, heard him come in, and even the sound of his heavy footsteps on the carpet in the drawing room made her feel shy and slightly frightened. It seemed to her now very difficult, almost terrible to tell him. She prepared phrases, explanations, a tale of courtship and letters exchanged; and she stood with her hand on the doorknob, trembling. She was afraid of him! She heard him pacing up and down the drawing room and, fearing that impatience might put him in a bad mood, she went in.

He seemed to her to cut a taller, more dignified figure than usual; never had his gaze seemed to her more honest, his beard more serious!

'What's wrong? Do you need something?' he asked after a few preliminary words about Almada and the weather.

Luiza, filled by invincible cowardice, said:

'It's Jorge!'

'I bet he hasn't written to you!'

'No, he hasn't.'

'He didn't write to me for ages either.' Then, laughing, he added: 'But today I received two letters together.'

He looked for them amongst some other papers that he removed from his pocket. Luiza had gone to sit on the sofa; she was watching him with her heart pounding, slowly scratching at the upholstery with impatient nails.

'Yes,' said Sebastião, going through the sheaf of papers, 'I got two letters from him, he's talking of coming home, says he's had enough.' And holding out a letter to Luiza, he said: 'Here you are.'

Luiza unfolded it and began to read, but Sebastião suddenly reached out to grab it back:

'Oh, I'm sorry, that's the wrong one!'

'No, let me see.'

'There's nothing of interest, just business.'

'No, no, I want to see!'

Sebastião sat on the edge of his chair, agitatedly stroking his beard, watching her. Luiza frowned.

'What's this?' As she read, a look of irritated surprise appeared on her face. 'Oh, really!'

'It's just nonsense, pure nonsense!' muttered Sebastião, red-faced.

Luiza started reading the letter out loud, very slowly:

' "I'll have you know, friend Sebastião, that I've made a conquest here. She's not what one might describe as a princess, for she is none other than the tobacconist's wife. She seems to be afire with the most impure passion for yours truly here. God forgive me, but I fear she even undercharges me for my cigars, thus ruining not only her husband, the good Carlos's happiness, but likewise his business!" Oh, very funny,' said Luiza angrily. ' "I very much fear a repeat of that biblical episode with Potiphar's wife. I deserve some credit for resisting too because the woman, tobacconist's wife or no, is very pretty indeed. I fear my poor virtue may succumb . . ." '

Luiza stopped reading and gave Sebastião a baleful look.

'It's just a joke!' he spluttered.

She continued reading: ' "I hate to think what would happen if Luiza found out! And my success doesn't stop there: the delegate's wife keeps making eyes at me too! She's from Lisbon, her family name is Gamacho; they live near Belém apparently, do you know them? Anyway, she pretends to be dying of boredom in the provincial melancholy of the place. She gave a soirée in my honour and wore a very decolleté dress, also, I believe, in my honour. Damn fine throat and neck . . ." ' Luiza blushed scarlet, ' "and she has a wicked way with her." '

'Honestly!' she exclaimed. ' "From your friend turned Don Juan of the Alentejo, leaving a trail of romantic flames throughout the province! Pimentel sends his regards . . ." '

Luiza read a few more lines softly to herself, then, getting abruptly to her feet, handed the letter back to Sebastião.

'Well, I'm glad he's having fun!' she said rather shrilly.

'There's really no need to take what he says seriously!'

'Of course not,' she exclaimed. 'To be honest, it strikes me as perfectly natural!'

She sat down again and began talking volubly about other things, about Dona Felicidade, about Julião . . .

'He's working hard for that competitive exam at the moment,' said Sebastião. 'The person I haven't seen is the Councillor.'

'Who are these Gamacho people in Belém?'

Sebastião shrugged and said almost chidingly:

'So you did take it seriously.'

Luiza broke in:

'Oh, by the way, my cousin Bazilio has left.'

Sebastião felt a thrill of joy.

'Oh, really?'

'Yes, he's gone back to Paris, and I don't think he'll return.' Then, after a pause, as if she had forgotten all about Jorge and the letter: 'He's only really happy in Paris . . . He's been dying to get back there.' And she added, lightly patting the folds of her dress. 'He needs to get married, that young man.'

'And settle down,' said Sebastião.

But Luiza did not think that a man with such a love of travelling and horses and adventure could ever make a good husband.

Sebastião was of the opinion that sometimes such men do quieten down and make excellent family men.

'They're more experienced,' he said.

'But basically fickle,' she observed.

And after those few vague words, they both fell into an embarrassed silence.

'To tell the truth,' Luiza said then, 'I'm glad my cousin has left. There has been so much foolish talk in the neighbourhood . . . though I've hardly seen him at all lately. He was here yesterday, he came to say goodbye. I was quite surprised actually.'

The whole story about a platonic courtship and an exchange of letters was becoming impossible, but something stronger than her was urging her to minimise the importance of her relationship with Bazilio and to distance herself from him. She even added:

'We're friends, but we're very different. Bazilio is a selfish fellow, and rather cold. Not that we were ever close . . .'

She stopped talking, sensing that she was 'getting in too deep'.

Sebastião seemed to remember her telling him once that they had been brought up together as children; but he felt that her way of talking about her cousin was the best possible proof that there had been nothing between them. He felt almost guilty about his earlier unjustified doubts!

'And will he be back?' he asked.

'He didn't say, but I shouldn't think so. Not once he's in Paris again!'

Then returning to the subject of the letter, she said suddenly:

'So you're Jorge's confidant, are you?'

He laughed.

'Now, really, my dear lady . . .'

'When he writes to me, it's all about how bored and lonely he is, how he can't abide the Alentejo.' But seeing Sebastião glancing at his watch: 'Must you leave already? It's still early.'

He had to be in the Baixa by three o'clock, he said.

Luiza tried to detain him. She didn't know why, for with each minute that passed she could feel her resolve shrinking and disappearing like water in a parched river bed. She started asking him about the work being carried out in Almada.

Sebastião had begun the work thinking that two hundred or three hundred *mil-réis* would be enough for the restoration work, but then one thing led to another. 'It's becoming a real drain on my resources!'

Luiza gave a forced laugh.

'But when the owner is rich!'

'Ah, yes! You wouldn't think it would cost much, but having a door painted, a new window fitted, a room papered and a new floor put down, it all adds up, and before you know it, you've spent eight hundred *mil-réis* . . . Anyway . . .'

He stood up, saying:

'Well, I hope our truant doesn't stay away very much longer.'

'Always assuming that the tobacconist's wife will let him go.'

She started pacing nervously about the room, consumed by that idea. Fancy flirting with the tobacconist's wife, and the wife of the delegate too, *and* all the others! She trusted him, but really, men! She suddenly imagined the tobacconist's wife taking him in her arms behind the counter or imagined Jorge, during some night-time rendezvous, kissing the pretty throat of the delegate's wife! And all the reasons that provided irrefutable proof of Jorge's treachery crowded in on her: he had been away for two months; he had grown weary of his widowhood; he had met a pretty woman; he had accepted it as a passing pleasure, of no importance! How base! She decided to write him a dignified but wounded letter telling him to come home at once, otherwise she would come and fetch him! She went into her room, feeling greatly agitated. The photograph of Jorge, which, the day before, she had removed from the morocco leather bag, was on the dressing table. She stood looking at it; she wasn't surprised that women should fall in love with him, he was so handsome, so sweet . . . A wave of jealousy swept over her, obscuring her vision: if he was deceiving her, if she found out anything, anything at all, had happened, she would leave him, retreat to a convent, where she would doubtless die; she would kill him!

Then Joana appeared:

'Excuse me, madam, but there's a man come with this letter. He's waiting for a reply.'

Oh, no, how awful! It was from Juliana!

Written on lined paper in appalling handwriting and a rambling style, it read:

Dear madam,

I know I was imprudent, which you must attribute both to my unfortunate circumstances and to my general lack of health, which does sometimes cause us to behave strangely.

But if you would like me to come back and do the same work as I did before, which I do not think you could be averse to, I would be very pleased and agreeable to this and be assured that I will never again speak about that matter until you so desire and do as you have promised. I promise to carry out my duties and I hope you are in favour because it is for the good of us all. It was bad temper on my part but then we all have our moods, and, not to trouble you further, I sign myself

Your most obedient servant

Juliana Couceiro Tavira

She sat with the letter in her hand, uncertain what to do. Her first impulse was to say 'No!' What, have her in the house again and have to see her horrible face and that vast false hairpiece of hers! Knowing that she had her letter and her dishonour in her pocket, and having to ring for her, ask for water, for the nightlight, and be served by her! No! But one thing frightened her; if she refused, she risked angering the woman, and God knows what she would do then! She was in her hands, and she had to put up with it. It was her punishment. She hesitated a moment longer.

'Tell her, yes, she should come, that's the reply.'

Juliana arrived promptly at eight o'clock. She tiptoed up to the attic, put on her house dress and her slippers and went straight down to the ironing and starching room, where Joana was sitting on a rug sewing by the light of an oil lamp.

Joana, burning with curiosity, bombarded her with questions. Where had she been? What had happened? Why had she not sent word? Juliana told her that she had visited a friend, in Calçada Marquês de Abrantes, and that she had suffered one of her attacks there and had that pain in her heart again. She hadn't sent word because she thought she would soon be better. But, as it happened, she had had to spend a day and a half in bed.

Then she, in turn, wanted to know what the mistress had been up to, if she had been out, what visitors there had been.

'The mistress hasn't been feeling well,' said Joana.

'It's the weather,' remarked Juliana. She had brought her sewing down with her and they sat on together in silence.

At ten o'clock, Luiza heard someone knocking softly at her bedroom door. It was bound to be *her*!

'Come in.'

Juliana's voice announced perfectly naturally:

'Tea is on the table, madam.'

But Luiza could not bring herself to go into the drawing room, out of fear or, rather, horror, of seeing her! She paced about her room, killing time; at last, she went in, trembling. Juliana was just coming along the corridor; she shrank back against the wall and said respectfully:

'Shall I bring the nightlight, madam?'

Luiza nodded without looking at her.

When she returned to her bedroom, Juliana was filling the water jug; then, once she had drawn back the covers on the bed and closed the shutters, almost tiptoeing about the room, she asked:

'Do you need anything else, madam?'

'No.'

'Goodnight then, madam.'

And not another word was spoken.

'It's like a dream!' Luiza was thinking as she gloomily got undressed. 'That creature, with my letters, installed in my house to torment and rob me!' How had she, Luiza, got herself into that situation? She couldn't explain it. Things had happened so suddenly, with the furious haste of a breaking storm! She had not had time to think clearly, to defend herself; she had been confused; and there she was, almost without realising it, living in her own house under the rule of her maid. If only she had spoken to Sebastião! She would probably have the money by now, in notes and coins. How gladly she would hurl that money at her, then drive her, her wooden chest, her clothes and her false hair out of the house! She promised herself that she would talk to Sebastião and tell him everything! She would even go to his house, to impress on him the importance of the matter!

Shortly afterwards, worn out from the day's excitements,

she fell asleep and dreamed that a strange black bird had come into her room, creating a breeze with its black, bat-like wings; it was Juliana! Luiza had run into the study, terrified and screaming: Jorge! But she found neither books, nor shelves, nor desk: instead there were the vulgar trappings of a tobacconist's shop, and Jorge was ensconced behind the counter, fondling a beautiful, amply endowed woman, who was sitting on his knees and asking in a voice faint with desire, her eyes ablaze with passion: 'Do you want Brejeiro cigars or Xabregas?' Luiza stormed indignantly back into the house and, after a series of confusing incidents, found herself by Bazilio's side, in an endless street, lined with palaces that had the façades of cathedrals, and along which opulent carriages rolled with all the pomp of a cortège. Sobbing, she told Bazilio of Jorge's betrayal. And Bazilio, jigging clownishly around her, strummed a guitar and sang:

> I sent off a letter to Cupid
> to find out if he knew
> if a heart howe'er sore wounded
> should still its love pursue!

'No, it shouldn't!' squawked Ernestinho, triumphantly brandishing a roll of paper. And then, suddenly, everything went dark again beneath Juliana's bat-like wings as she circled and swooped about the room.

# IX

Juliana had returned to Luiza's house on the advice of Tia Vitória.

'Look, my dear,' she had said, 'there's nothing else you can do, the bird has flown. Sigh all you like, but the really big money has gone! How were we to know the man would run off like that? No, you won't get any joy out of him! And you won't get a penny out of her either.'

'I could still send the letter to her husband, Tia Vitória!'

The old woman shrugged:

'You'll gain nothing by that. They'll either go their separate ways, or he'll break every bone in her body or else send her to a convent, and you'll end up with nothing. And if they come to some agreement, you'll be even worse off, because you won't even have the consolation of being able to make any mischief. And that's if things turn out well, because you might find yourself in real trouble and get beaten for your pains.' And seeing Juliana's look of horror. 'It wouldn't be the first time, my dear, it wouldn't be the first time. Lots of things happen in Lisbon that never get into the newspapers!'

No, she would have to go back to the house. After all, what remained of this whole business? Dona Luiza's fear, the fear that was always there churning away in her stomach, and Juliana must take advantage of that fear.

'You go back,' Tia Vitória said, 'in the hope that she will keep her promise. If she gives you the money, fine, if she doesn't, you still have a hold over her, you're on the inside, you know what's going on, you can wheedle all kinds of things out of her . . .'

Juliana was unsure. It would be difficult to live under the same roof without them falling out over some trivial matter.

'She won't say a word to you, you'll see.'

'But I'm afraid.'

'Afraid of what?' exclaimed Tia Vitória. Luiza was not the kind of woman who would try and poison her, was she? Well, then. Nothing ventured, nothing gained. 'It's up to you,' she added. 'Otherwise, all that's left for you is to get work some-where else if you can and hide those letters away at the bot-tom of your trunk. What does it matter? You'll see: if you can't stand it, you can leave.'

Juliana decided to give it a try.

And she saw at once that 'sly old Tia Vitória' was abso-lutely right.

Luiza did, indeed, appear resigned to the situation. Sebas-tião had gone back to his house in Almada, and since Luiza had resolved, as soon as he returned, to go to his house one morning, throw herself at his feet and tell him *everything*, she put up with Juliana, thinking: 'It's only a matter of days'; and that is why she did not say a word to her. What was the point? All she had to do was pay her off and get rid of her. Until she was able to do that, it was a case of enduring in silence. Until Sebastião's return . . .

In the meantime, she avoided seeing Juliana. She never called her. She did not leave her bedroom in the morning until she had heard her filling the bath with water and shaking out her dresses. She would go into the dining room with a book and would sit reading, without once looking up. During the day, she stayed in her room with the door closed, reading, sewing, thinking about Jorge, and sometimes, with loathing, about Bazilio, longing for Sebastião to return and preparing her story.

One morning, Juliana came across Luiza in the corridor carrying the watering can, full of water, to her room.

'Why didn't you call me, madam?' she exclaimed, almost scandalised.

'It's all right,' said Luiza.

But Juliana followed her into her room and, closing the door, said in deeply offended tones:

'Madam, things can't go on like this! Good heavens, it's as if you were afraid of the sight of me! I came back in order to carry out my duties as before. True, I still hope, as is only natural, that you will keep your promise, because I won't let go of the letters until I've secured enough for my old age.

What happened earlier was just a fit of bad temper and I've already asked your forgiveness for that. I want to be able to do my job properly. Now, if you don't want me to, then I'll leave, but that,' she added with a hard edge to her voice, 'might be worse for all of us!'

Luiza, greatly distressed, stammered:

'B-but . . .'

'No, madam,' Juliana interrupted her sternly, 'I'm the servant here.'

And she left the room, holding herself very erect.

Such boldness terrified Luiza. This thief was capable of anything!

Thereafter, in order not to anger her, she began calling for her and saying: 'Bring me this, bring me that', but without ever once looking at her.

Juliana, however, made herself so useful and was so silent, that, little by little, Luiza, with her mutable, inconsistent, *laisser-faire* nature, began to forget the painful dilemma she was in. And when three weeks had passed, 'things' as Juliana put it, 'were back to normal'.

Luiza used to shout for her from her room and send her off on errands; Juliana even had occasional brief conversations with her: 'It's sweltering out there' or 'The laundress is late again'. One day, she risked a more personal comment: 'I met Senhora Dona Leopoldina's maid today.'

Luiza asked:

'Is Dona Leopoldina still in Oporto?'

'She'll be away another month yet, madam.'

Apart from that, a great calm reigned in the house, and Luiza, after so much agitation, abandoned herself gladly to the pleasures of that peace. She occasionally went to the convent hospital of the Incarnation to visit Dona Felicidade, who was up and about now. And she waited for Sebastião to return, though without impatience, almost glad to be able to postpone the terrible moment when she would have to say to him: 'Sebastião, I wrote a letter to a man.'

So the days passed; it was nearly the end of September.

One evening, Luiza had lingered longer than usual at the

dining room window; her book lay on her lap, and she was smiling as she watched a flock of pigeons that had flown in from some neighbouring garden to alight on the fence surrounding the empty plot. She was thinking vaguely about Bazilio, about their 'Paradise' . . . She heard footsteps; it was Juliana.

'What is it?'

The woman had closed the door and, coming over to her, she said in a low voice:

'You haven't come to any decision then, madam?'

Luiza felt her stomach turn over.

'No, I haven't been able to sort anything out yet.'

Juliana stood staring at the floor for a moment.

'I see,' she murmured at last.

And Luiza heard her say out loud in the corridor:

'Well, we'll have to settle up when the master comes home.'

When Jorge came home! In her heart, which, of late, had gradually grown calm, all her fears and anxieties were set trembling again, the way a sudden gust of wind can convulse a tree. She would have to do something before Jorge came back! He had just written to her saying that he would not be away much longer and would advise her by telegram. Now she wished that the Ministry would send him off on a longer journey, to Spain or Africa, that some catastrophe, while leaving him quite unscathed, would nevertheless delay him for several months more.

What would he do if he found out? Would he kill her? She remembered his grave words on the night when Ernestinho had described to them the ending of his play. Would he put her in a carriage and send her off to a convent? She could see the great convent door closing behind her with the funereal sound of bolts sliding shut, and doleful, inquisitive eyes studying her.

Her irrational terror made her lose any clear idea of her husband; she imagined *another* Jorge, bloodthirsty and vengeful, forgetting his kind, unmelodramatic nature. One day, she went into his study, took the box of pistols, locked it in a trunk full of old clothes and hid the key away!

She took comfort in one idea: that as soon as Sebastião returned from Almada, she would be safe; and yet despite the tiny agony of each passing moment, she nevertheless also dreaded hearing of his arrival home – for having to confess the truth seemed to her a still greater agony! It was around this time that it suddenly occurred to her to write to Bazilio. Her permanent state of terror had softened her pride, the way the slow infiltration of water weakens a wall; and every day she found yet another reason to write to that 'cad': he had been her lover, he knew all about the letters, he was her only relative . . . And then she might not have to speak to Sebastião! It had sometimes occurred to her that refusing Bazilio's money had been 'a foolish piece of vainglory'. And one day, she did write to him. It was a long, rambling letter in which she asked him for six hundred *mil-réis*. She herself took it to the post office, putting far too many stamps on it.

By chance, Sebastião had arrived back from Almada that afternoon and he came to see her. She received him with joy, glad that *she no longer had to tell him*. She talked about Jorge's return; she even alluded to Bazilio and to the 'shameless neighbourhood' she lived in.

'That,' she said, 'will be the first thing I tell Jorge about.'

For she considered herself safe now! And day by day, she followed her letter on its way to France as if her own life were inside that envelope abandoned to the random nature of trains and to the confusions of journeys! It had reached Madrid, then Bayonne and, finally, Paris! A postman ran to deliver it to Rue Saint-Florentin. Bazilio would open it, trembling, then stuff an envelope with notes, lots of notes, which he would cover with kisses, and the envelope, bearing with it her salvation and her peace of mind, would begin its journey southwards, through France and through Navarre, a huffing, puffing monster, hastening on its way like a messenger.

On the day when the reply *should* have arrived, she got up earlier than usual, in a state of great agitation, and sat, ears pricked, listening for the postman to call. She could already

277

see herself driving Juliana out and weeping tears of joy! But at half past ten, she began to feel anxious; at eleven, she called Joana to ask if the postman had called.

'Yes, madam, he's already been.'

'The scoundrel!' she muttered, meaning Bazilio.

Perhaps he had not replied by return of post! She resumed her waiting, but she did so disconsolately, with little faith. Nothing came. Not the next day, or on any of the days that followed. The villain!

Then she thought of the lottery, because, imperceptibly, hope had become entirely necessary to her. The first time she went out, she bought a few tickets. Although she was neither religious nor superstitious, she placed them under the pedestal of a statue of St Vincent de Paul which she kept on the chest of drawers in her bedroom. It was worth a try! She studied them every day, adding up the numbers, to see if they came to lucky seven, or else some even number, which is always a good omen! And during that daily contact with the saint's image, which doubtless made her think of the unexpected protection of heaven, she promised to pay for fifty masses if her tickets won!

They did not, and then she fell into utter despair; abandoning herself to inaction with something bordering on the voluptuous, spending whole days doing nothing, not even getting dressed, hoping to die, devouring every news item in the newspaper about suicides, deaths and misfortunes, consoling herself with the idea that she was not the only one who was suffering, and that life around her in the city was teeming with afflictions.

Sometimes, she would feel a sudden pang of fear. She would decide again to confide in Sebastião; then she thought that it would be best to write to him; but she could not find the words, could not come up with a rational story; and she succumbed to cowardice and fell back into her inertia, thinking: 'Tomorrow, tomorrow . . .'

Alone in her room, when she happened to look out of the window, she set to imagining 'what the neighbours would say when they found out'! Would they condemn her? Would they feel sorry for her? Would they say: 'Shameless hussy!' or would they say: 'Poor thing!'? And from behind the window, she followed, with something akin to horror, Senhor Paula's visits up and down the street, the coal merchant wife's look of obese stupefaction, the Azevedo girls behind their cotton curtains! They would all cry: 'We told you so! We told you so!' Oh, it was too awful! Or she would suddenly see the terrifying figure of Jorge, beside himself with rage, the letters in his hand; and she shrank back then as if beneath the wrath of his clenched fists.

But what tormented her still more was Juliana's tranquillity – dusting, singing, serving supper in her white apron. What was she up to? What was she plotting? Sometimes, she felt a wave of anger; if she were strong or brave, she would grab her by the throat, strangle her and take the letters from her! But, alas, she was such a weakling!

One morning, Juliana came into the room, carrying a black silk dress over her arm. She spread it out on the chaise longue and showed Luiza a long tear on the skirt, near the bottommost frill, apparently made by a nail; she had come to ask if Luiza wanted to have it sent to the seamstress.

Luiza clearly remembered tearing it one day in 'Paradise' when she and Bazilio were 'playing'.

'It's easy enough to mend,' Juliana was saying, stroking the silk with the tender slowness of a caress.

Luiza was examining it, then, hesitantly, she said:

'It's quite an old dress. Look, why don't you have it!'

A shiver ran through Juliana, and she turned bright scarlet:

'Oh, madam!' she cried. 'Thank you so much! It's a wonderful present. Thank you so much, madam. Really . . .' And her voice almost broke with emotion.

She gathered it carefully in her arms and ran straight up to the kitchen. And Luiza, who had slowly followed behind her, heard her saying excitedly:

'It's a wonderful present, just wonderful! And it's new too. Such fine silk!' She held the dress so that the train brushed over the floor, with a frou-frou of silk. She had always wanted it and now it was hers, it was *her* silk dress! 'She's such a kind mistress, Senhora Joana, an absolute angel!'

Luiza went back to her room in a state of high excitement; she was like a person lost in the night, in the open countryside, who, suddenly, far off, sees the glimmer of light in a window. She was saved! All she had to do was to load her with presents! She immediately began to think about what else she could give her, little by little: her purple dress, some underwear, her old peignoir, a bracelet!

Two days later – on a Sunday – she received a telegram from Jorge: 'Leave from Carregado tomorrow. Arrive Oporto train 6 a.m.' What a surprise! He was finally coming home!

She had a young woman's loving impulses, and, initially, all her fears and anxieties disappeared beneath the feelings of love and desire flooding through her. He would arrive in the early morning, when she would still be in bed; already she was thinking of that first delicious kiss!

She went to look at herself in the mirror; she had grown rather thin, and she looked rather tired. And Jorge's image appeared to her then so clearly, burned by the sun, a tender look in his eyes, his curly hair . . . It was very odd, but she had never before so longed to see him. She immediately set about arranging things to his liking: Was the study tidy? He would want a warm bath, so they would have to heat the water in the big tub! And she came and went, singing to herself, a gleam of excitement in her eyes.

But the sound of Juliana's voice in the corridor made her shudder. What would *she* do? Surely she would allow her, at least for those first few days, to enjoy Jorge's return in peace! Emboldened, she called for Juliana.

Juliana came in, wearing her new silk dress, moving with great care.

'Did you want something, madam?'

'Senhor Jorge is coming home tomorrow,' said Luiza.

And she paused, her heart pounding.

'Oh!' said Juliana. 'Very well, madam.'

And she made to leave.

'Juliana!' said Luiza, a note of distress in her voice.

Juliana turned, surprised.

And Luiza put her hands together in a supplicant gesture:

'For the first few days at least, you won't . . . I will sort things out, I promise . . .'

Juliana broke in:

'Please, madam, I don't want to upset anyone. All I want is a little bread for my old age. But I wouldn't open my mouth to harm anyone. All I ask of you, madam, if you would be so kind and are still willing to help me . . .'

'Oh, of course . . . anything you like . . .'

'You can be sure that my lips are sealed.' And she closed her lips with her fingers.

What a relief for Luiza! She would have a few untormented days, a few weeks even, with *her* Jorge! She abandoned herself then entirely to her feelings of delicious impatience to see him again. It was strange, but it seemed to her that she loved him even more! Later, she would think about what else she could give Juliana and would gradually prepare the ground with Sebastião. She felt almost happy!

In the afternoon, Juliana came in, all smiles, to say:

'It's Senhora Joana's day off, so she's gone out, but I really need to go out too. If you wouldn't mind very much being on your own, madam . . .'

'No, not at all. Off you go!'

Shortly afterwards, Juliana's heels came click-clacking down the corridor and Luiza heard the front door slam.

Then a dazzling idea flashed across her mind like lightning: to go to Juliana's room, to search through the chest and steal back the letters!

From the window, she saw Juliana turn the corner. She went slowly up to the attic, listening for the slightest sound, heart beating fast. The door to Juliana's bedroom stood open; from it came a sickening, musty smell of mice and dirty clothes; the melancholy light of a dark afternoon came in through the window; and below it, against the wall, was the chest, doubtless locked! She ran downstairs to fetch her bunch of keys. She felt ashamed, but if she found those letters . . . This hope filled her with as much courage as a draught of strong wine. She began trying the keys; her hand shook; suddenly the latch gave with a click! She lifted the lid, the letters might be in there! And then cautiously, in very feminine fashion, she began taking the things out one by one and placing them on the bedspread: the merino wool dress; a fan with a gold design on it, wrapped in tissue paper; old purple and blue ribbons, carefully ironed; a pin-cushion made out of pink satin, with a matching embroidered heart; two unopened bottles of perfume, with little bunches of paper roses stuck to the glass; three pairs of boots wrapped in newspaper; underwear that smelled of wood and apple leaves. Between two chemises there was a bundle of letters tied with cotton thread . . . None of them was hers. None of them was from Bazilio! They were written in some unintelligible, yellowing, rustic hand. How maddening! And she stood gazing into the empty chest, her arms hanging sadly by her sides.

A shadow suddenly crossed the window. She shuddered, terrified. It was a cat wandering the rooftops with stealthy step. She replaced everything exactly as she had found it, closed the chest and was about to leave, when it occurred to her to look in the drawer in the table and beneath the pillow. Nothing. She grew impatient then; she did not want to leave before she had exhausted all hope; she unmade the bed, rummaged in the softened straw inside the mattress, shook out Juliana's old boots, scrutinised every corner . . . Nothing, absolutely nothing!

Suddenly the doorbell rang. She ran downstairs. What a surprise! It was Dona Felicidade.

'It's you! How are you? Come in.'

She was much better, she told Luiza as they walked along the corridor. She had left the convent hospital the day before: her foot still hurt her occasionally, but, thank God, she was out of danger! Luiza should feel honoured, this was the very first call she had made!

They went into the drawing room. It was getting dark and so Luiza lit the candles.

'How do I look?' asked Dona Felicidade, standing before her.

'A little paler.'

Well, she had suffered greatly! She lifted her skirt to reveal the injured foot shod in a broad-fitting shoe, which she made Luiza touch. Her one consolation, though, was that all of Lisbon had been to see her, thank God! The whole of Lisbon, the very cream of Lisbon!

'But you,' she added, 'didn't come and see me once this week! The knives were out for you, you know.'

'I couldn't, my dear. Didn't you know, Jorge is coming home tomorrow.'

'The rascal! I bet that little heart of yours is leaping!' And she whispered something in her ear.

They both laughed loudly.

'Well,' went on Dona Felicidade, sitting down, 'I've organised a little party for you tonight. This morning I met the Councillor, who told me that he would be coming. I met him at the Church of the Martyrs! It must have been fate, meeting him like that on my first day out! And a little further on, I ran into Julião: he says he's coming too!' Then in a faint voice, she said: 'You know I really could do with a spoonful of something sweet . . .'

It was Luiza who opened the door to the Councillor and to Julião, who had met on the stairs, and she said to them, laughing:

'I'm the doorman today!'

In the drawing room, Dona Felicidade, in order to disguise the agitation provoked in her by the beloved spectacle of Acácio, began talking volubly, censuring Luiza for allowing both her maids to go out on the same day.

'What if you felt unwell, my dear, what if you fainted?'

Luiza laughed. She didn't suffer from fainting fits.

Nevertheless, they all thought she looked distinctly tired. And the Councillor enquired with interest:

'Are you still suffering with your teeth, Dona Luiza?'

Her teeth? That was the first she had heard of it, exclaimed Dona Felicidade. Julião declared that he had rarely seen such a perfect set.

The Councillor hurriedly quoted:

Between lips of coral, the finest pearls . . .

adding:

'Quite true, quite true, but the last time I had the honour of Dona Luiza's company, she was so badly afflicted with tooth-ache that she had to rush off to Vitry's to have it filled!'

Luiza blushed scarlet. Fortunately, the doorbell rang. It must be Joana, she would go and see.

'It's quite true,' the Councillor went on, 'we were having the most delightful stroll, when, suddenly, Dona Luiza turned quite pale, and the pain was so appalling that she had to rush up the stairs to the dentist like a mad thing.'

Speaking of pain, Dona Felicidade, who was anxious to catch the Councillor's interest and to touch his heart, launched into the story of her foot: she described the fall, said what a miracle it was she had not died, spoke of the assiduous visits of countesses and viscountesses, of the general distress of everyone at the convent, of good Dr Caminha's ministerings . . .

'How I suffered!' she sighed, her eyes fixed on the Council-lor, hoping to elicit some words of sympathy.

Acácio merely said authoritatively:

'It is always a mistake, when descending a steep staircase, not to hold on to the banister.'

'But I might have died!' she exclaimed. And appealing to Julião, she said: 'Isn't that so?'

'In this world, one can die of almost anything,' said Julião, sitting back in his armchair, smoking voluptuously. He him-self had nearly been knocked down by a carriage that very afternoon: he had decided to give himself a holiday and had gone for a long stroll on the outskirts of the city. 'I've been shut up in my little room for a month now, like a Benedictine monk in the monastery library!' he added, laughing, casually dropping the ash from his cigarette onto the carpet.

The Councillor immediately wanted to know the doubt-less momentous subject of his thesis! And as soon as Julião said: 'Physiology, Councillor', Acácio observed in a grave voice:

'Ah, physiology! It must then be a work of great magnitude! And it lends itself well to a more colloquial style.'

He himself complained of being 'bowed beneath the weight of my literary tasks', adding:

'Let us hope that our sleepless nights do not prove fruitless!'

'Yours, at least, I am sure will not, Councillor!' said Julião, adding earnestly: 'When are you going to give us your new work? People are impatient to read it!'

'There is, it is true, a certain degree of impatience,' agreed the Councillor gravely. 'A few days ago, that most robust of talents, the Minister of Justice, did me the honour of saying: "Let us have your new book soon, Acácio, for we are much in need of illumination!" That's how he put it. Naturally, I bowed and replied: "Minister, I would not wish to deny my country illumination in time of need!"'

'Oh, very good, Councillor, very good!'

'And just between ourselves,' the Councillor went on, 'the Minister gave me to understand that, in the not too distant future, I might receive the Order of Santiago!'

'Why, they should have given it to you already, Councillor!' exclaimed Julião, enjoying himself. 'But what can one expect in a wretched country like this . . . You should already have it pinned to your chest, Councillor.'

'Oh, yes, years since!' cried Dona Felicidade warmly.

'Thank you, thank you!' muttered the Councillor, his cheeks flushed. And caught up in the enthusiasm of his own joyful feelings, he offered Julião his snuff box with grateful familiarity.

'I'll take some just to clear my head,' Julião said.

He was in benevolent mood that evening; his work and the high hopes he had placed in it had doubtless diminished his bitterness; he seemed to have forgotten the humiliation he had suffered when he had met cousin Bazilio in that same room, for as soon as Luiza returned, he asked after him.

'Oh, didn't you know, he left for Paris ages ago!'

Dona Felicidade and the Councillor both praised Bazilio.

285

He had left visiting cards with both of them, which had enchanted Dona Felicidade and swelled the Councillor's pride. 'A real gentleman!' exclaimed Dona Felicidade. And Acácio said with great authority:

'And a baritone voice worthy of the Teatro de São Carlos.'

'And so elegant!' said Dona Felicidade.

'Oh, yes, a gentleman through and through!' concluded the Councillor.

Julião said nothing, but sat joggling one leg. His resentment was undergoing a resurgence in the light of these words of praise; he remembered how abruptly Luiza had spoken to him that day, and the poses struck by Bazilio. He blurted out:

'I felt he rather overdid the jewels and the embroidered socks myself, although that is, I believe, the fashion in Brazil.'

Luiza blushed; she hated Julião and felt a vague nostalgia for Bazilio.

Dona Felicidade then asked after Sebastião; it had been an age since she had seen him, and she regretted this, for he was someone whose mere presence made one feel better.

'A great man,' said the Councillor emphatically. He did, however, reproach him slightly for not working and making himself useful to his country. 'After all,' he declared, 'it's all very well being able to play the piano, but it does not give one a position in society.' He cited Ernestinho, who, although devoted now to the dramatic arts, was, according to all accounts, nevertheless (and here his voice grew graver) an excellent customs official.

'What is Ernestinho up to?' everyone asked.

Julião had seen him. *Honour and Passion* was due to open in a couple of weeks' time, the posters were being printed now, and in Rua dos Condes people were already referring to him as the Portuguese Dumas *fils*! And poor Ernestinho believed them!

'I'm afraid that is an author unknown to me,' said the Councillor sternly, 'although, to judge by his name, I assume him to be the son of the writer who achieved fame with *The Three Musketeers* and other works of the imagination. Our Ernestinho, on the other hand, is an accomplished cultivator of the art of the Corneille brothers! Don't you agree, Dona Luiza?'

'Hm,' she said with a vague smile.

She seemed preoccupied. She had gone into her room twice to look at the clock; it was nearly ten, and Juliana was still not back! Who would serve the tea? She herself had set out the cups on the tray and filled the toothpick holder. When she went back into the drawing room, she noticed a bored silence. 'Would you like me to play something?' she asked.

Dona Felicidade was standing over Julião, looking at the edition of Dante illustrated with Doré's engravings that Julião was leafing through. Suddenly she exclaimed:

'Oh, how pretty! What is that? Very pretty, indeed! Have you seen it, Luiza?'

Luiza went closer.

'It's a tale of unhappy love, Senhora Dona Felicidade,' said Julião. 'It's the sad story of Paulo and Francesca da Rimini.' Then explaining the illustration: 'That lady sitting there is Francesca; this young man with the wild hair, kneeling at her feet and embracing her, is her brother-in-law, and, I regret to say, her lover. And that great bearded chap lifting the curtain at the back and getting out his sword is her husband who is coming to . . .' And he made a stabbing gesture.

'Oh dear!' said Dona Felicidade, shuddering. 'And that book fallen on the ground, what's that? Were they reading?'

Julião said discreetly:

'Yes . . . they started reading, but then . . .

*quel giorno più non vi leggemmo avante*

which means: "That day we read no further!"'

'Oh, so they started flirting with each other,' said Dona Felicidade with a smile.

'Worse than that, my dear lady, much worse! For Francesca herself says of this young man, the one with all the hair, the brother-in-law:

which means: "He kissed my mouth and trembled as he did . . ." '

'Oh!' said Dona Felicidade, shooting a rapid glance at the Councillor. 'Is it a novel?'

'It's Dante, Dona Felicidade,' the Councillor said sternly, 'an epic poem considered to be amongst the finest, but far inferior to our own Camões, albeit a worthy rival to the great Milton!'

'The husbands always end up killing their wives in these foreign stories!' she exclaimed. Then turning to the Councillor: 'It's true, isn't it?'

'Yes, Dona Felicidade, such domestic tragedies are commonplace elsewhere. Unbridled passion is rife. But I think we can say with pride that amongst ourselves, there is more respect for the home. For example, amongst my many acquaintances in Lisbon, I, thank God, know only model wives.' And with a courtly smile, he added: 'Of whom the lady of this house is definitely the flower.'

Dona Felicidade turned her eyes to Luiza, who was leaning on her chair, and patted her arm:

'This one's a jewel!' she said fondly.

'Besides,' said the Councillor, 'our Jorge deserves such a wife. For, as the poet says:

> Noble of heart, his lofty brow
> Reveals the very essence of his soul.'

This conversation was making Luiza uneasy. She was about to sit down at the piano, when Dona Felicidade said: 'Is there no tea to be had in this house today?'

Luiza returned to the kitchen. She told Joana to bring in the tea herself. And shortly afterwards, a flustered, red-faced Joana, in a white apron, came in with the tray.

'Where's Juliana?' Dona Felicidade immediately asked.

'She had to go out, poor thing,' explained Luiza. 'She's not been well.'

'And you let her stay out as late as this? Really! It's enough to give a house a bad name.'

The Councillor also thought it imprudent.

'After all, the city is full of temptations, my dear lady!'

Julião burst out laughing:

'If that woman gets tempted, then I will lose any faith I had in my contemporaries!'

'Senhor Zuzarte!' said the Councillor almost severely. 'I was referring to other temptations, for example, visiting some drinking establishment or the circus, not to mention general neglect of one's duties.'

Dona Felicidade, however, could not bear Juliana; she thought she had the face of a Judas, definitely not a person to be trusted.

Luiza defended her; she was hardworking, excellent at starching and ironing, very honest . . .

'And she stays out at night until eleven o'clock! Goodness. If it were me . . .'

'And I believe,' remarked the Councillor, 'that she has a fatal illness. Isn't that so, Senhor Zuzarte?'

'Yes, indeed. An aneurism,' replied Julião, without looking up from his Dante.

'Well, then!' cried Dona Felicidade. And lowering her voice, she added: 'You should get rid of her! A maid with an illness like that! Heavens, she might die when she was bringing you a glass of water!'

The Councillor agreed.

'And there can be terrible complications with the police!'

Julião closed his edition of Dante and said:

'Yes, I meant to warn Jorge; one day, she'll drop down dead on you.' And he took a sip of tea.

Luiza was beside herself. It seemed to her that yet another complication had arisen to torment her. She started saying how difficult it was to find servants.

Oh, yes, everyone agreed, it most certainly was.

They talked about servants and their demands. They got bolder every day. Give them an inch. . . . And the immorality . . .

'The fault often lies with the mistresses themselves,' said Dona Felicidade. 'They make their maids their confidantes, and as soon as the maids get hold of some secret, then they become mistress of the house.'

Luiza's trembling hands made her cup rattle on its saucer. In an affectedly jovial voice, she said:

'And what are your servants like, Councillor?'

Acácio coughed:

'Well, I have a most respectable person in my employ, an excellent cook and scrupulously honest when it comes to money.'

'And not bad-looking either,' said Julião. 'At least so I thought on my one visit to Rua do Ferregial.'

A rosy blush was spreading over the Councillor's bald pate. Dona Felicidade was watching him anxiously, her eyes flashing. Acácio, however, remarked sternly:

'I never pay the slightest attention to the physiognomy of my inferiors, Senhor Zuzarte.'

Julião sat up and, thrusting his hands into his pockets, said cheerily:

'It was a great mistake abolishing slavery!'

'But what about the principle of liberty?' said the Councillor. 'What about that? The blacks were fine cooks, I grant you, but liberty is a greater good.'

He warmed to his theme: he fulminated against the horrors of the slave trade, he cast aspersions on the so-called philanthropy of the English, he severely criticised the plantation owners in New Orleans and recounted the case of the French slave ship, the *Charles et George*; he addressed these remarks solely to Julião, who sat smoking despondently.

Dona Felicidade sat down next to Luiza and whispered anxiously in her ear:

'Have you ever met the Councillor's maid?'

'No, I haven't.'

'Do you think she's likely to be pretty?'

Luiza shrugged.

'Oh, my poor heart, Luiza! I can barely breathe!'

And while Acácio continued his peroration to Julião, Dona Felicidade confided to Luiza her passionate woes.

What a relief for Luiza when they left! The secret suffering she had had to endure all night! The bores, the idiots! And that woman had still not come back! What a life!

She went into the kitchen to speak to Joana.

'Be patient, will you, and wait up for Juliana. She can't be much longer; for all we know, she might have taken a turn for the worse.'

But it was gone midnight and Luiza was already in bed when the doorbell rang softly, then more loudly and, finally, impatiently.

'The girl's fallen asleep,' thought Luiza. She leaped out of bed and went up to the kitchen in her bare feet. Joana, sprawled on the table, was snoring beside the fetid, smoking oil lamp. Luiza shook Joana hard and hauled her to her feet, still barely awake, then ran back to bed; shortly afterwards, she heard Juliana's voice in the corridor, saying smugly:

'Everything sorted out here? I've been to the theatre. It was lovely, just wonderful, Senhora Joana, really wonderful!'

It took a while for Luiza to fall asleep and, during the night, she was troubled by a distressing dream. She was in a vast theatre, gilded like a church. It was a gala night; jewels glittered upon soft bosoms and medals glinted on courtly uniforms. In the royal box sat a sad, young king, frozen in a stiff, hieratic pose, holding an armillary sphere in his hand, and with his dark velvet mantle, starred with precious stones like the heavens and arranged about him in sculptural folds, over which stumbled a multitude of courtiers dressed as knaves of spades.

She was on the stage; she was an actress; it was her first performance in Ernestinho's play; feeling very nervous, she saw before her, in the vast whispering audience, rows of dark, burning eyes fixed furiously on her; in the middle, the snowy, noble roundness of the Councillor's bald head stood out, sur-rounded, like a flower, by an amorous flight of bees. On stage, the vast backcloth of a forest swayed; she noticed to the left, an ancient oak tree, almost heroic in its arrogance, whose trunk formed the vague shape of a face, which bore a strong resemblance to Sebastião.

The stage manager clapped his hands; he was tall and thin, like Don Quixote, wore round, wire-framed spectacles, and was brandishing a rolled-up copy of a newspaper and wailing: 'On with the love scene! On with that marvellous scene!' Then, in the orchestra pit, the eyes of the musicians glowed like pomegranates and their hair stood on end like handfuls of tow, as, with melancholy slowness, they began playing Leopoldina's fado; and a harsh, cracked, falsetto voice sang:

> I see him in the clouds in the sky,
> In the waves of the endless sea,
> But however far away he is,
> He is always close to me.

Luiza found herself in Bazilio's entwining, scalding embrace: she went limp, felt herself disappearing, melting into something warm as the sun and sweet as honey: she experienced prodigious pleasure; but even as she groaned and sighed, she felt ashamed, for Bazilio was brazenly repeating on stage the libidinous excesses of the 'Paradise'! How could she possibly allow him to do so?

The theatre gave them an enormous ovation, roaring: Bravo! Encore! Encore! Thousands of handkerchiefs fluttered like white butterflies in a field of clover; with a rippling gesture of their bare arms, women hurled bouquets of double violets; the spectral figure of the king rose to his feet and he limply hurled his armillary sphere as if that too were a bouquet; and the Councillor, in a frenzied desire to follow His Majesty's example, deftly unscrewed his bald head and threw it onto the stage with a howl of pain and triumph! The stage manager bleated: 'Take a bow! Take a bow!' She bowed and her long, Magdalene-like locks brushed the stage, and, by her side, Bazilio, bright-eyed, watched for the cigars being thrown to him and picked them up with the grace of a bullfighter and the agility of a clown!

Suddenly, though, the whole audience gave a horrified

gasp. There was a fearful, tragic silence; and all eyes, thousands of astonished eyes, were fixed on the backcloth, where a pergola stood, all studded with small white roses. She too turned round, as if hypnotized, and saw Jorge approaching, dressed entirely in black, with a dagger in his black gloved hand; and the blade glittered, although not as fiercely as his eyes! He came down the stage and, bowing, said graciously:

'Your Royal Highness, Prince, Civil Governor, ladies and gentlemen, now it is my turn! Observe my technique!'

He came towards her with marmoreal steps that made the whole stage tremble; he grabbed her hair, as if it were a clump of grass he wanted to uproot; he bent her head back; he raised his dagger in the classical manner; he took aim at her left breast; and swaying slightly, narrowing his eyes, he plunged the steel into her!

'Oh, very nice!' said a voice. 'Excellent technique!'

It was Bazilio who was making his entrance on stage in his phaeton. Sitting upright in the driver's seat, his hat at a jaunty angle, a rose in his buttonhole, he controlled with one negligent hand his proud, jittery English horses; and beside him, like a footman, rode the Patriarch of Jerusalem in his priestly robes! But Jorge had pulled out the dagger all scarlet; the drops of blood dripped from the point, coagulated, then fell to the floor with a crystalline sound and began to roll across the stage like tiny red glass beads. She lay down to die beneath the oak tree that looked like Sebastião; and, because the ground was hard, the tree arranged its roots beneath her, soft as feather pillows; and because the sun was burning her, the tree unfurled its branches above her, like a tent, and dripped Madeira wine down its leaves onto her lips! Then she noticed with horror that her strong, red blood was flowing out of the wound, running and spreading, creating pools here, tortuous little streams there. And she heard the audience roar:

'Author! Author!'

Ernestinho came onto the stage, pale-faced and with his hair tightly curled; he tearfully thanked the audience and, bowing, skipped hither and thither in order not to stain his patent leather shoes with cousin Luiza's blood.

She felt as if she were about to die . . . A voice said vaguely: 'Hello, how are things?' It sounded like Jorge's voice. Where was it coming from? From heaven? From the stage? From the corridor? She was woken by a loud noise, like the sound of someone putting down a suitcase. She sat up in bed.

'That's all right, leave it there,' said Jorge's voice.

She leaped out of bed in her nightdress. He came in. And they flung their arms about each other in a long embrace and their lips met in a wordless kiss. The clock in the room struck seven.

# X

That same day, at around one o'clock, as on the eve of his departure, Jorge and Luiza had just finished lunch. Now, however, the glittering, pitiless midsummer heat no longer weighed on them, and the windows stood open to the pleasant October sun; there was already a hint of autumnal coolness in the air, a tender paleness about the light; in the evenings, it felt good to don an overcoat; and the green leaves were becoming tinged with yellow.

'How good to be back in our own little nest again!' said Jorge, sprawling comfortably in his wing chair.

He had been telling Luiza about his trip. He had worked like a black and made money too! He had the makings of an excellent report and had made friends amongst the good people of Alentejo; but from now on, there would be no more hot sun, no more rides through scrublands, no more rooms at inns; he was, at last, back in his own home. And, just as on the eve of his departure, he exhaled the smoke from his cigarette and contentedly smoothed his moustaches – for he had shaved off his beard! Luiza could not get over her surprise when she saw him. He had explained, humbly and sadly, that he had had a boil on his chin, from the heat.

'But the moustache really suits you!' she had said. 'It really does!'

Jorge had brought her a present of six very old China plates painted with plump mandarins in enamelled tunics, poised majestically in the blue air: a treasure he had discovered in the house of some old followers of Dom Miguel, in Mértola. Luiza was placing them very decoratively on the shelves of the dresser; and as she stood there, on tiptoe, with the long train of her robe trailing out behind her, her mass of heavy, fair hair coming slightly unpinned at the back, she appeared to Jorge even slimmer, even more irresistible and he had never longed so much to put his arms about her slender waist.

'It was a Sunday last time I had lunch here, just before leaving, do you remember?'

'I do,' said Luiza, without turning around, and very delicately putting another plate in position.

'Oh, by the way,' said Jorge suddenly, 'what happened with your cousin? Did you see him? Did he come and visit you?'

The plate slipped, and there was a tinkle of glasses.

'Yes, he did,' said Luiza, after a silence. 'He came here a few times. He didn't stay long.'

She bent down to open the main drawer in the dresser and fiddled around with the silver spoons; at last, she stood up and turned, smiling and brushing off her hands, her face all red.

'There we are!'

And she went and sat on Jorge's lap.

'It really does suit you!' she said, playing with his moustache. She admired him now, ardently. When she had fallen into his arms that morning, she had felt her heart open and an impulsive love stir deliciously within; she had been filled by a desire to adore him for ever, to serve him, to hold him so tightly in her arms that she bruised him, and to obey him humbly; it was a complicated feeling of infinite sweetness, which had penetrated down into the deepest part of her being. And putting an arm about his neck, she said in a tone of almost lascivious adulation:

'Tell me, are you content? Are you happy? Tell me!'

He had never seemed to her so handsome, so good; after that separation, his body filled her with all the wonder and ecstasy of a new passion.

'It's Senhor Sebastião,' Juliana announced to Jorge, beaming.

Jorge leaped to his feet, brusquely pushing Luiza aside, and raced down the corridor, shouting:

'Let me embrace you, you rascal!'

A few days later, one morning when Jorge had left to go to the Ministry, Juliana came into Luiza's room and, closing the door slowly behind her, said in a pleasant voice:

'May I talk to you about something, madam.'

And she began explaining how her room in the attic was worse than a prison cell; that she couldn't possibly stay there; the heat, the stench, the bed bugs, the lack of air, and, in the winter, the damp, were all killing her! She would like to move downstairs to the box room.

The box room had a window that gave onto the back of the house; it had high ceilings and was very spacious; they kept Jorge's oilskins in there and his suitcases, as well as the ancient overcoats and venerable, red leather trunks with gold studs that dated back to his grandmother's days.

'I would be in heaven there, madam!'

But where would they put the trunks?

'In my room, upstairs.' And with a little laugh: 'Trunks aren't people, madam, they don't suffer.'

Somewhat embarrassed, Luiza said:

'I'll see. I'll talk to Senhor Jorge about it.'

'I know I can rely on you, madam.'

But when, later that day, Luiza explained to Jorge 'the poor woman's wishes', he burst out:

'What? Move the trunks? Are you mad?'

Luiza insisted; it had been the poor creature's dream, ever since she came to the house. She played on his feelings. He couldn't possibly imagine, no one could, just what the poor woman's present room was like. It stank to high heaven, the mice literally ran over her body, the ceiling had holes through which the rain came in; she had been up there a few days ago, and had nearly fainted.

'Good heavens! That's exactly how my grandmother used to describe the cells in Almeida! Move her then, my dear, move her at once! I'll put my beloved trunks up in the attic.'

When Juliana learned of this 'favour', she said:

'Oh, madam, you're giving me new life! May God reward you! In my state of health, I just can't live in pokey rooms like that any more.'

She had been complaining more about her health lately: she looked pale and her lips had a purplish tinge to them; on some days, she was prey to a black melancholy or to a morbid irritability; her feet were never warm. What she needed was comfort, lots of it!

That is why, two days later, she went to ask Luiza if she would be so kind as to accompany her up to the box room. She showed her the old, worm-eaten floor.

'It can't possibly stay like this, madam, it needs a carpet, otherwise there's no point in moving. If I had any money of my own, I wouldn't bother you, but . . .'

'All right, I'll sort it out,' said Luiza patiently.

And she bought a carpet, without saying anything to Jorge. But on the morning when the carpet-layers were nailing the carpet down, Jorge came, in some astonishment, to ask Luiza what the rolls of carpet were doing in the corridor.

She burst out laughing and placed her hands on his shoulders:

'Poor Juliana asked for some carpet because the floor was rotten. She even offered to pay and to have the cost taken out of her wages. But it's such a tiny amount of money . . .' And with a look of compassion on her face: 'After all, servants are God's creatures too, they're not slaves, my dear.'

'Oh, wonderful! I suppose next it will be mirrors and bronze statues! I must say you've changed your tune; you couldn't stand the sight of her before.'

'Poor woman,' said Luiza. 'I've come to realise that she's a good soul really. And being so alone, I've got to know her better. I had no one to talk to, and she kept me company. Even when I was ill . . .'

'You were ill?' exclaimed Jorge, horrified.

'Oh, only for three days,' she said, 'it was just a cold. But she didn't leave my side day or night.'

Luiza was then afraid that Jorge would mention her 'illness' to Juliana and that Juliana, caught unawares, would deny it, which is why, that evening, as it was growing dark, she called Juliana into her room:

'I told Senhor Jorge that you kept me company during an illness . . .' And her face blazed red with shame.

Juliana smiled, pleased at their complicity.

'I understand, madam. Don't worry!'

The next day, after coffee, Jorge did indeed turn to Juliana and say kindly:

'It seems you've been a good companion to Senhora Dona Luiza.'

'I was just doing my duty,' she cried, bowing, one hand pressed to her breast.

'Very good, very good,' said Jorge, rummaging in his pocket. And as he left the room, he pressed a half-*libra* coin into her hand.

'Fool!' she muttered.

That same week she began to complain to Luiza that her clothes were getting all creased up inside her trunk. She hated to spoil them. If she had money herself, she wouldn't ask madam, but . . . Then one morning, she declared straight out that she needed a chest of drawers.

Luiza felt anger burning in her blood, and without looking up from her embroidery, she asked:

'A half-size one?'

'If you would be so kind, madam, I'd prefer a full-size one . . .'

'But you have so few clothes,' said Luiza. She was beginning to grow accustomed to humiliation and she now haggled over these favours.

'True, madam,' replied Juliana, 'but I'm hoping to remedy that situation!'

The chest of drawers was bought in secret and introduced into the house by stealth. What a joyous day that was for Juliana! She could not get enough of the smell of new wood! With the tremor of a caress, she passed her hand over the shiny, polished surface! She lined the drawers with tissue paper and began 'to remedy the situation'.

These were bitter weeks for Luiza.

Juliana used to come into her room every morning, greet her very courteously and start to tidy, then, suddenly, in a mournful voice, she would say:

'You know, madam, I have hardly any chemises, if you could possibly help me out . . .'

Luiza would go to her packed, perfumed drawers of under-wear and sadly begin setting aside the older items. She adored her underwear; she had a dozen of everything, all beautifully embroidered with her initials, all carefully stored away with scented sachets; and these gifts felt like lacerating mutilations! In the end, Juliana would ask for things abruptly, outright.

'What a lovely chemise!' she would say. 'You don't want it, do you, madam?'

'No, take it, take it!' Luiza would reply, smiling, out of pride, in order not to show how it upset her.

And every night, Juliana, cloistered in her room, sitting cross-legged on the carpet, puffed up with joy, the oil lamp on a chair, would carefully unpick Luiza's two initials and replace them, in red thread, with her own three enormous initials: J.C.T. – Juliana Couceiro Tavira.

In the end, though, that stopped, because as she herself said, she was 'up to her eyes in underwear'.

'Now, if you could help me out with some clothes to wear to go out in . . .'

And Luiza began to 'dress' her.

She gave her a purple silk dress and a black woollen jacket with herring-bone braiding. And fearing that Jorge would find such generosity strange, she altered them so that he would not recognise them: she had the dress dyed brown and she herself added a velvet trim to the jacket. Now *she* was working for *her*! Good God, where would it end?

One Sunday, Jorge even said laughingly over supper:

'Juliana is looking very smart these days. She's obviously prospering.'

That night, Dona Felicidade remarked:

'She dresses better than a servant at the Palace!'

'Poor thing! They're just some of my old cast-offs.'

Juliana was indeed prospering! She now only ever used linen sheets. She had demanded new mattresses and a soft rug to put at the bottom of the bed. The sachets that used to perfume Luiza's underwear had found their way into Juliana's neatly folded knickers. She had cotton curtains at the window, tied back with old blue silk ribbons; and on the chest of drawers stood two gilt Vista Alegre vases! One day, she appeared wearing a chignon made of real hair!

Joana was astonished at this ostentation! She attributed it to madam's kindness and resented being 'forgotten'. One day, when Juliana was sporting a new parasol, Joana commented sourly in Luiza's presence:

'Some get everything and others get nothing!'

Luiza laughed and said:

'Nonsense! I treat everyone the same.'

But it gave her pause for thought; Joana might have her suspicions too, she might have heard something from Juliana . . . The next day, in order to keep Joana happy and well-disposed towards her, she gave her two silk handkerchiefs, then, later, two *mil-réis* to buy a dress, and thenceforward, she never refused her permission to go out in the evening 'to visit her aunt's house'.

Joana went around telling everyone that her mistress was 'an angel'. Even in the street, Juliana's new prosperity had not gone unnoticed. They knew about the 'new room', which, it was murmured, even had carpets! Senhor Paula declared indignantly that 'there was something going on'. But one afternoon, Juliana, in order to calm suspicions, said to Senhor Paula and the tobacconist's wife:

'Everyone's saying that I've got this and I've got that, but I don't really have that much. I have my comforts, true, but then just think of the way I looked after that aunt of theirs, day and night, never stinting . . . It ruined my health and they could never repay me for that!'

Thus was Juliana's sudden prosperity explained. It was proof of their gratitude, they said; they were treating her like one of the family!

And gradually, the Engineer's house acquired the vague allure of a paradise for the other servants in the neighbourhood; it was said that the wages were enormous, that there was unlimited wine, that they received presents every week and dined each night on chicken soup! Everyone envied that 'plum job'! Through Tia Vitória, the fame of the 'Engineer's house' spread. A kind of legend grew up.

Jorge was astonished to receive letters every day from

people offering their services as housemaids, lady's maids, cooks, valets, governesses, coachmen, doormen, kitchen assistants . . . They listed the noble houses in which they had worked; they begged an audience; suspecting that certain other duties were required, a particularly pretty lady's maid enclosed her photograph; a cook brought a letter of recommendation from the director general of a Ministry.

'How very odd!' said Jorge, amazed. 'They're all clamouring for the honour of serving me! Do they think I've won the lottery?'

But he paid little attention to this strange situation. He was busy writing his report; he left every day at noon and returned at six, tired but radiant, bearing rolls of paper, maps and pamphlets and calling for his supper.

However, he did jokingly mention it one Sunday night. The Councillor remarked:

'Given Dona Luiza's good humour and yours, Jorge, given the salubrious neighbourhood in which you live and the fact that yours is a virtuous household free of scandal or family disputes, it is only natural that those less favoured servants should aspire to such an agreeable position.'

'We're the ideal employers!' said Jorge, blithely patting Luiza's shoulder.

The house had, in fact, become 'most agreeable'. Juliana had demanded that supper should be a more lavish affair (so that she could have her part of it, and not just the leftovers) and since she was a good cook, she took charge of the ovens, tasted the food and taught Joana some new dishes.

'Our Joana is a revelation!' said Jorge. 'She gets more talented by the day!'

Juliana, well-lodged, well-fed and with fine clothes on her back and soft mattresses to lie on, was enjoying life: her temperament had grown sweeter amongst such abundance; on the sound advice of Tia Vitória, she did her work with careful, scrupulous zeal. Luiza's dresses were cared for like relics. Jorge's shirtfronts gleamed as never before. The October sun gladdened the spotless house, which was as peaceful as an abbey. Even the cat was getting fatter.

★

In the midst of this prosperity, only Luiza languished. How far would Juliana's tyranny go? That was the question that haunted her now. And how she hated her! She would sometimes fix her with such a fiercely malevolent gaze that she feared Juliana might suddenly turn round, as if she had been stabbed in the back. She saw how pleased she was, singing her favourite song 'O beloved letter', sleeping on mattresses as good as her own, strutting around in *her* clothes, ruling the roost in *her* house! Was this fair?

Sometimes she would rebel and would flail her arms about and blaspheme and rail against her misfortunes, as if caught in a net; unable to find any solution, though, she would fall back once more into the harsh mood of melancholy that was distorting her true nature. She gloatingly watched Juliana's increasingly sallow features; she had high hopes of that aneurism: surely, one day, she would die.

To Jorge, of course, she had to sing her praises.

Life weighed heavily on her. As soon as Jorge left in the morning, closing the door, her sadness and her fears would fall upon her soul like great, thick, dark veils; she did not bother to get dressed until four or five o'clock, and in her loose peignoir and her slippers, her hair uncombed, she would trail her misery about the room with her. She would be suddenly gripped by a desire to run away or to enter a convent! Her overwrought feelings would have impelled her unerringly towards some melodramatic solution, were she not constrained – with all the force of an enduring enchantment – by her love for Jorge. For she loved him now immensely! She loved him with all the doting care of a mother, with all the impetuous passion of a concubine. She was jealous of everything, even of the Ministry, even of the report he was writing! She would keep interrupting him, plucking the pen from his hand, demanding that he look at her, speak to her; and the sound of his footsteps in the corridor filled her with all the excitement of an illicit love.

And she did her best to fuel that passion, finding in it an ineffable compensation for all her humiliations. How had this happened to her? For she had always loved him, she knew that now, but never so much, never so exclusively! Not even she understood the reasons. She even felt ashamed of herself, sensing vaguely that such amorous violence was not dignified in a married woman; she was afraid it might be a mere capricious fancy, and for her own husband! It did not seem quite chaste somehow. But then what did it matter? It made her happy, prodigiously happy. Whatever it was, it was delightful!

At first, the idea of 'the other man' hovered constantly over her love, leaving a bitter taste in every kiss, a sense of remorse in every night. Eventually, though, she had so completely forgotten him that when she did happen to think of him, his memory lent as much bitterness to this new passion as a lump of salt might to the waters of a torrent. How happy she would be, were it not for 'that vile woman'!

'That vile woman', on the other hand, was very happy indeed! Sometimes, alone in her room, she would look around her with a miserly smile on her lips; she would unfold and shake out her silk dresses; she would line up her boots and stand contemplating them ecstatically from afar; and, poring over the open drawers, she would count and recount her underwear, caressing them with a gaze of smug ownership. 'Just like "the dumpling's"!' she would murmur, blushing out of sheer glee.

'I'm in seventh heaven!' she told Tia Vitória.

'I don't doubt you are! The letter didn't get you any money, but it's brought you a fair few presents. It's proving to be a nice little business: a bit of fine linen, the odd piece of jewellery, a few fat tips now and then, and she's grateful to boot! Fleece her, my dear, fleece her!'

But there was not much left to fleece. Juliana began to think that what she should do now was simply enjoy it. She had good mattresses, so why get up early? She had lovely dresses, so why not go out and flaunt them in the street? It was time to take advantage.

On one particularly cold morning, she stayed in bed until nine o'clock, with the windows half-open, and the sunshine pouring in onto the carpet. Afterwards, she said tartly that she had had a pain in her heart. Two days later, at ten o'clock, Joana came to tell Luiza softly:

'Senhora Juliana is still in bed and none of the housework has been done.'

Luiza was terrified. Was she now going to have to endure her laziness just as, previously, she had put up with her every demand?

She went to Juliana's room:

'What sort of time is this to be getting up?'

'It's what the doctor recommended,' replied Juliana insolently.

And from that day on, Juliana rarely got up before it was time to serve lunch. Luiza asked Joana to do Juliana's work for her: it wouldn't be for long and the poor creature was so unwell. To mollify the cook, she gave her half a *moeda* towards a dress.

Then, without bothering to ask permission, Juliana began going out. When she arrived back late for supper, she didn't even apologise.

One day, seeing Juliana walking down the corridor, drawing on her black gloves, Luiza could contain herself no longer.

'Are you going out?'

Juliana retorted boldly.

'What does it look like? I've done my work for the day.' And off she went, with a click–clack of heels.

She certainly wasn't going to rein herself in because of 'the dumpling'!

Joana started grumbling: 'Senhora Juliana spends all her time out of the house, and I have to do her work.'

'If you were ill, no one would want to upset you either,' said Luiza, herself upset, when she noticed that Joana was growing restive. And she gave her more presents. She even allowed her wine and dessert.

There was now an air of neglect about the house. The household lists grew longer. Luiza was utterly dejected. How would it all end?

Juliana's laxness was becoming serious.

In order to leave the house as early as possible, she did only the bare minimum. Luiza ended up filling the water jugs, clearing the table after lunch, and carrying up to the attic the dirty clothes that lay discarded in various corners . . .

One day, Jorge came back at four o'clock and happened to notice that the bed was still unmade. Luiza hastened to assure him that Juliana was out, she had sent her to the dressmaker's.

Days later, Juliana failed to return by six o'clock in time to serve the supper. 'She's gone to the dressmaker's again,' Luiza explained.

'Well, if all Juliana's time is taken up with going to the dressmaker's, perhaps we'd better take on another servant to do the housework,' he said.

At these sharp comments, Luiza turned pale and two tears rolled down her cheeks.

Jorge was astonished. What was it? What was wrong? Luiza could control herself no longer and burst into nervous, hysterical crying.

'But what is it, my love, what's wrong? Are you angry with me?'

She could not respond, tears overwhelmed her. Jorge made her inhale some smelling salts and covered her in kisses.

Only when she had stopped crying was she able to say in a tearful voice:

'You spoke to me so sharply, and I've been so nervy lately . . .'

He laughed and told her not to be so silly and wiped away her tears, but he was, nevertheless, worried.

He had already noticed occasional inexplicable bouts of sadness and depression, a certain nervous irritability. What could it be?

In order to prevent Jorge from stumbling upon further evidence of Juliana's negligence, Luiza herself began to finish off the housework every morning. Juliana saw this and calmly decided 'to leave her more and more things to keep her busy'. First, she stopped sweeping, then she neglected to make the bed; then, one morning, she failed to empty out the chamber pots. Luiza peered out into the corridor to make sure that Joana would not come down the stairs and see her, then she herself emptied them. When she came back and washed her hands with soap, the tears were running down her cheeks. She wanted to die! To what depths had she sunk?

One day, Dona Felicidade arrived unexpectedly and found her sweeping out the dining room.

'I can understand me doing it,' she exclaimed, 'because I have only the one maid, but you!'

Juliana had so much starching and ironing to do.

'Oh, don't lighten her workload, she won't thank you for it, in fact, she'll laugh at you. You'll get her into bad habits! She'll just have to put up with it!'

Luiza smiled and said:

'It's only this once.'


Her sadness grew with each day that passed.

She took refuge in Jorge's love as her one consolation. With the night came her revenge; Juliana was sleeping at that hour; she would not have to see her hideous face; she did not have to fear her; she did not have to sing her praises or do her work! She could be herself, the Luiza she used to be! She was safe in her bedroom with her husband, she was free! She could live, laugh, talk, even feel hungry! Indeed sometimes she brought bread and jam into the bedroom in order to have a midnight feast!

Jorge was bemused. 'You know, you're a different person at night,' he said. He called her 'his nightbird'. She would wander, laughing, about the room, dressed only in her white petticoats, with her arms, throat and neck bare, and her hair loosely caught up; she idled about, sang, talked, until Jorge would say to her:

'It's gone one o'clock, my love!'

Then she would quickly get undressed and fall into his arms.

But what an awakening! However bright the morning, everything seemed to her somehow grey. Life tasted sour to her. She would get dressed slowly, reluctantly, entering the day as if it were a prison.

She had lost all hope now of setting herself free. Sometimes the desire 'to talk to Sebastião and tell him everything' still came to her like a flash of lightning. But when she saw his honest eyes, saw him embrace Jorge, when she saw them laughing together and smoking their pipes, and saw how full of admiration he was for her, it seemed to her that it would be easier to go out into the street and ask for the money from the first man she met than to go to Sebastião, Jorge's closest friend, their best friend, and say to him: 'I wrote a letter to a man; my maid stole it from me!' No, she would rather endure that daily agony and have to get down on her knees and scrub the steps herself! Sometimes she would stop and think: 'What am I hoping for?' She didn't know. For some chance event, for Juliana's death . . . And she drifted on, enjoying each day that came as if it were a favour, sensing vaguely, in the distance, something dark and indefinite into which she would eventually plunge!

Around that time, Jorge began to complain that his shirts were not being properly starched. Juliana really was 'losing her touch'. One day, he got so angry that he called her in and threw the crumpled shirt at her.

'I can't possibly wear this, it's dreadful!'

Juliana turned deathly pale and shot Luiza a burning glance; she apologised, though, with trembling lips: 'The starch is no good, I'll change it . . .'

As soon as Jorge had left for work, she burst into Luiza's room, closed the door and started berating her, saying that the mistress dirtied so many clothes and the master dirtied so many shirts that if she didn't get someone in to help her then she wouldn't be able to cope. If they wanted slaves, they should bring some over from Brazil!

'And I'm not putting up with your husband's bad temper, either, do you understand? You'll just have to get someone in to help me.'

Luiza said simply:

'I'll help you.'

She had entered a state of dumb, sombre resignation, and she would accept anything!

By the end of the week, there was a large bundle of clothes, and Juliana announced that if Luiza would iron, she would starch. Otherwise, she wouldn't do it at all.

It was a beautiful day, and Luiza had been intending to go out. Instead, she put on a peignoir and, without a word, went to fetch the iron.

Joana was astonished.

'Are you going to do the ironing, madam?'

'There's an awful lot of it, and Juliana can't manage it all on her own, poor thing!'

She went into the ironing room and was laboriously ironing Jorge's underwear, when Juliana appeared, with her hat on.

'Are you going out?' exclaimed Luiza.

'That's what I came to tell you. I'm afraid I have to.' And she buttoned up her black gloves.

'But what about the shirts, who's going to starch them?'

'I'm going out,' Juliana replied tartly.

'But who, in heaven's name, is going to starch the shirts?'

'Why, you, of course! Who do you think?'

'You vile woman!' screamed Luiza, and she flung the iron down on the floor and ran from the room.

Juliana heard her running, sobbing, down the corridor.

Frightened, she quickly took off her hat and gloves. A moment later, she heard the street door slam. She went into Luiza's room and saw the peignoir lying in a heap, the hat box fallen on its side. Where could she have gone? To complain to the police? To get her husband? Heavens! It was that stupid temper of hers! She quickly tidied the room and went to do the starching, one ear cocked, thoroughly repentant. Where could she have gone? She really should be more careful. If she drove her to do something foolish, then who would be the loser? She would. Dear God, she would have to leave the house, leave her room, her many presents and her job!

Luiza had run out of the house like a madwoman. In Rua da Escola, an empty carriage passed her; she leaped in and gave the coachman Leopoldina's address. Leopoldina must be back from Oporto by now; she wanted to see her, she needed her, quite why she did not know . . . Perhaps in order to unburden herself! To ask if she had some idea of how she might avenge herself! For the wish to free herself from that tyranny was now less urgent than the desire to avenge herself for all those humiliations. She was assailed by the most ludicrous ideas. What if she poisoned her! It would, she thought, afford her exquisite pleasure to see Juliana writhing about, seized by violent retching, howling in agony, and dying!

She raced up the stairs to Leopoldina's house; a frantic tug with her feverish hand set the bell ringing for several seconds.

Justina opened the door and, as soon as she saw her, she shouted down the corridor:

'It's Senhora Dona Luiza, madam, it's Senhora Dona Luiza!'

And Leopoldina, hair all dishevelled, in a scarlet robe with a long train, ran towards her, arms outstretched.

'It's you! What miracle is this? I've just this minute got up! Come into my room. Everything's in a mess, but it doesn't matter. What is it? What's wrong?'

She opened the windows, which were still closed. There was a strong smell of toilet water; Justina hurriedly took away a brass bowl containing soapy water; dirty towels lay around on the floor; on a small table, from the night before, there were still bits of false hair, a corset and a cup with a little tea in it, full of cigarette ends. Leopoldina was drawing the blinds, saying:

'How good of you to honour my house, my lady!'

But seeing the distraught expression on Luiza's face, seeing her eyes red with tears, she said:

'But what is it? What's wrong? What's happened?'

'Oh, it's awful, Leopoldina!' Luiza exclaimed, clutching her hands.

Leopoldina ran to close the door.

'What is it?'

Luiza was weeping, unable to respond. Leopoldina gazed at her in astonishment.

'Juliana stole some letters from me!' Luiza finally managed to say between sobs. 'She wants six hundred *mil-réis*. I'm lost . . . She's been tormenting me . . . I want you to tell me what to do, think of something . . . I'm going mad. I do all the work around the house now . . . I'll die, I just can't go on like this!' And her tears redoubled.

'What about your jewels?'

'They're only worth two hundred *mil-réis*, and how could I explain their absence to Jorge?'

Leopoldina stood for a moment in silence, then, looking around her and opening wide her arms, she said:

'Everything I have, my dear, is in the pawnshop and is worth, at most, twenty *libras*!'

Luiza was wiping her eyes and murmuring:

'What a penance, dear God, what a penance!'

'What did the letters say?'

'Terrible things! I wasn't in my right mind . . . She has one of mine and two letters from him.'

'From your cousin?'

Luiza nodded slowly.

'And what about him?'

'I don't know. He's in France, he never answered my letter.'

'The scoundrel! How did the woman get hold of them?'

Luiza rapidly told her the story of the 'sarcophagus' and the sandalwood box.

'But really, Luiza, fancy throwing away a letter like that! That's sheer madness, woman!'

Leopoldina began pacing about the room, dragging behind her the long train of her scarlet robe; her large, dark eyes seemed to be frantically searching out some means, some expedient . . . She was muttering to herself:

'It's all a question of money.'

Luiza, lying prostrate on the sofa, repeated:

'It's all a question of money.'

Then Leopoldina stopped pacing and stood stockstill in front of her:

'I know who would give you the money!'

'Who?'

'A man.'

Luiza sat up, startled:

'Who?'

'Castro.'

'The one with the spectacles?'

'The one with the spectacles.'

Luiza blushed crimson.

'Oh, Leopoldina!' she murmured. And then, after a silence, she added quickly: 'Who told you?'

'I just know. He told Mendonça. They used to be bosom pals, you see. He said he'd give you anything you asked for! He said it more than once.'

'That's disgusting!' exclaimed Luiza, suddenly indignant. 'And you're actually proposing that I should do such a thing?' Her eyes flashed angrily from beneath her frowning brows. Go with a man for money! She snatched off her hat and with shaking hands, threw it down on a table, then paced rapidly up and down the room: 'I'd rather run away, enter a convent, be a maid, sweep the streets!'

'Don't get so excited, child! Who said anything about that? He might lend you the money . . . out of sheer altruism.'

'Do you really think so?'

Leopoldina did not reply; head bowed, she was turning the rings on her fingers round and round.

'But what if he did want something else?' she cried suddenly. 'It would mean one *conto de réis*, maybe two, and you would be saved, you would be happy!'

Luiza shuddered with indignation at these words, or perhaps at her own thoughts.

'It's indecent! It's disgusting!' she said.

They fell silent.

'If I were you . . .' said Leopoldina.

'What would you do?'

'I would write to Castro and tell him to come here and bring the money with him!'

'Oh, yes, no doubt you would!' exclaimed Luiza, not thinking what she was saying.

Beneath her layer of face powder, Leopoldina turned scarlet.

Luiza flung her arms about her neck:

312

'Oh, forgive me, forgive me! I'm out of mind, I don't know what I'm saying!'

They both began to cry out of sheer nerves.

'The idea makes you angry, I know,' Leopoldina was saying, between sobs, 'but it's for your own good. I think it's the best idea. If I could, I would give you the money myself . . . I would do anything, really I would!'

And opening her arms, and displaying her body with a sublime lack of modesty, she said:

'Six hundred *mil-réis*! If I were worth that much money, I would have it tomorrow!'

Someone knocked at the door.

'Who is it?'

'It's me,' said a hoarse voice.

'It's my husband. The beast hasn't left the house yet.' She shouted to him: 'I can't open the door right now. I'll be with you in a moment.'

Luiza was hastily wiping her eyes and had put on her hat.

'When will you come again?' asked Leopoldina.

'When I can, if not, I'll write to you.'

'All right. I'll think about it. I'll look into other possibilities.'

Luiza grabbed her arm:

'Not a word of this to anyone.'

'Of course not!'

She left. She walked slowly up to Largo de São Roque. The door of the church, the Misericórdia, was open, its broad red door curtain, embroidered with coats of arms, fluttered gently in the wind. She felt a desire to go in. She did not know why, but it seemed to her that in her current state of passionate excitement, the cool silence of the church might calm her down. She felt so unhappy that her thoughts turned to God! She needed some higher, stronger force to help her. She knelt down near the altar, made the sign of the cross, then said an Our Father and a Hail Mary. But these prayers, which she used to recite as a girl, failed to console her; she felt that they were empty sounds that got no further along the road to heaven than her own breathing; she did not really understand them and they hardly applied to her situation; God would never understand what she wanted, kneeling there, racked by anxiety. She wanted to speak to God, to open herself entirely to Him, but what language should she use? Should she address Him in the trivial words she would use to speak to Leopoldina! Would her confidences reach up far enough for Him to hear them? Was he near enough to hear them? And she remained on her knees, arms limp, hands folded in her lap, looking at the sad wax candles, the faded embroidery on the frontal cloth, the round, rosy face of a Baby Jesus!

She gradually became lost in thoughts over which she had no control, which formed and stirred inside her brain like a sinuous pillar of smoke. She was thinking of that distant time when, out of melancholy and sentiment, she used to go more often to church. Her mother was still alive then; and she, her heart broken by that letter from Bazilio ending their relationship, had tried to dissipate her sadness through the consolation of religious devotion. A friend of hers, Joana Silveira, had entered a convent in France, and she had sometimes thought of following her, of becoming a sister of charity, carrying the wounded from battlefields or living in the peace of a mystic's cell. How different her life would have been from this life now, so shaken by anger, so laden with sin! Where would she be? Far away in some ancient monastery, amongst dark groves of trees, in a solitary, contemplative valley; in Scotland, perhaps, a country she had loved ever since she first read the novels of Walter Scott. She might be living in the dark green lands of Lammermoor or Glencoe, in an old Saxon abbey. The encircling mountains, thick with fir trees, lost in the mists, enfold those retreats in a funereal peace; the clouds pass slowly, meditatively across a mournful sky; no joyful sound breaks the tender, all-pervading silence; crows cross the air at eventide in v-shaped flocks. There she would live alongside tall, Celtic-eyed nuns, daughters of Norman dukes or of clan leaders who had converted to Rome; she would read gentle

314

books about Heavenly things; sitting at the narrow window of her cell, she would see the tall antlers of deer passing through the bracken, or, on misty afternoons, she would hear the sad, distant sound of bagpipes, played by the shepherd from the vale of Callendar; and the air would be filled by the tearful, dripping murmur of threads of water falling from rock to rock amongst the dark grasses!

Or else she would have another, easier existence, in a peaceful convent in some pleasant Portuguese province. There the roofs are low; the whitewashed walls with their little barred windows glitter in the sun; the bells ring out in the bright, blue air; round about, in the olive groves that provide the convent with its oil, girls sing as they shake the olive trees; in the cobbled courtyard, the mules flick away the flies with their tails and stamp their hooves; old women gossip by the turn-box provided for foundlings; a cart creaks along the white, dusty road; glossy cockerels, shining in the sun, sing out their cockadoodledos; and plump sisters, with dark eyes, chatter in the cool corridors.

There she would live and grow fat, now and then falling asleep in the choir, drinking little glasses of pink liqueur in the scribe's room, copying out in a large hand recipes for cakes; she would die at a great old age, listening to the swallows twittering outside the barred window of her cell; and when the bishop visited, he would listen, smiling, with a pinch of snuff poised between his white fingers, as the abbess recounted the edifying tale of her holy death.

A sacristan walked past, loudly clearing his throat, and, like a flock of birds that fall silent at a sudden noise, all her dreams fled. She sighed, got slowly to her feet and walked sadly homewards.

Juliana opened the door to her and, there in the corridor, in a low, supplicant voice, she said:

'Please, madam, forgive me, I wasn't myself! I wasn't thinking straight, I hadn't slept all night. I was so worried . . .'

Luiza did not respond; she went into the drawing room. Sebastião, who had come to supper, was playing the 'Serenata' from *Don Giovanni*, and as soon as she appeared, he cried:

'Why so pale? Where have you been?'

'I'm just feeling a little tired, Sebastião, I've come from church . . .'

Jorge came in with some papers in his hand.

'From church!' he exclaimed. 'How frightful!'

# XI

On a Saturday around this time, the *Government Gazette* announced the nomination of Councillor Acácio to the rank of Knight of the Order of Santiago, in recognition of his great literary merits, of his many useful published works, etc.

The following night, when he arrived at Jorge's house, everyone gathered round, loudly congratulating him; the Councillor, after enfolding each and every one of them in a vigorous and emotional embrace, collapsed, exhausted, onto the sofa and murmured:

'I never expected to receive such royal munificence so early! No, I certainly did not!' And he added, pressing his hand to his heart: 'In the words of the philosopher: receiving this honour is the best day of my life!'

And he invited Jorge, Sebastião and Julião to have dinner with him at his 'humble abode' the following Thursday, 'a modest repast for the boys', to celebrate this royal largesse.

'At half past five, my dear friends!'

The next Thursday, the three friends, who had rendez-voused at the Casa Havanesa, were shown into the Council-lor's drawing room by a grimy, squint-eyed maid. A vast sofa upholstered in yellow damask occupied the whole of the back wall, and at its feet was a rug on which a purple Chilean was trying to lasso a chocolate-coloured buffalo; above the sofa, a painting, rendered almost entirely in flesh tones and full of naked men in helmets, depicted the valiant Achilles dragging Hector's dead body round the walls of Troy. A grand piano, silent and sad beneath its green baize cover, occupied the space between the two windows. On a card table, flanked by two silver candlesticks, bounded a greyhound made of glass; but the object that seemed to have seen most use was a music box that could play eighteen tunes.

The Councillor received his guests, wearing the insignia of the order of Santiago on the lapel of his black tail coat. There was another man in the room, Senhor Alves Coutinho. He had a pockmarked face, and his head was sunk between his shoulders; whenever his foolish, startled gaze fell on other people, his sparse moustache would immediately, out of sheer habit, stretch into an idiotic grin that revealed a hideous mouth crammed with rotten teeth; he spoke little, was constantly rubbing his hands, and agreed with everything; he had about him an air of banal debauchery and long years of stultifying existence. He was a clerk in the Ministry of Information and Administration, and was renowned for his beautiful handwriting.

Shortly afterwards, a familiar figure joined them, Savedra, the editor of *The Century*. His white face seemed even flabbier than usual; his very black moustache was shiny with brilliantine; his gold-rimmed spectacles emphasised his official demeanour; he still bore on his chin the powder applied only moments before by the barber; and the hand that had written so many banalities and so many lies was sheathed in a brand-new, egg-yolk yellow glove!

'Here we all are!' said the Councillor gleefully. And bowing, he said: 'Welcome, my friends! We would perhaps be more comfortable in my study. Through here. Mind that step, now! This is my *sanctum sanctorum*!'

In a small, spotless room, to which the cotton curtains, the light from two windows and the pale wallpaper lent a general impression of whiteness, was a large desk on which stood a silver inkwell, several carefully sharpened pencils and neat rows of rulers. There was also the Councillor's personal seal, resting on a lavishly bound edition of the Constitution. Framed on the wall hung the royal charter appointing him Councillor; opposite was a lithograph of the King; and positioned prominently on a table was a plaster bust of the politician and orator, Rodrigo da Fonseca Magalhães, his head wreathed with immortelles which simultaneously glorified and mourned him.

Julião immediately began perusing the bookshelves.

'I pride myself on having all the most illustrious authors, Senhor Zuzarte,' said the Councillor smugly.

He showed him *The History of the Consulate and the Empire*, the works of Delille, *The Dictionary of Conversation*, a tiny, plump edition of the *Encyclopaedia Roret*, and *The Portuguese Parnassus*. He spoke of his own works and added that, since he had, gathered there around him, people of such high learning, he would very much like to read to them from his latest book: *A Description of the Principal Cities of the Realm and its Establishments*, the proofs of which he was currently revising, and he wanted their frank, nay, brutal opinions!

'If you wouldn't find it too much of a bore, of course.'

'It would be a pleasure, Councillor, a pleasure!'

He chose, 'in order to give them an idea of the importance of the work', a page about Coimbra. He blew his nose, stood in the middle of the room, with the proof pages in his hand, and in a loud, clear voice, accompanied by stately gestures, he began:

'Reclining indolently on her verdant hills, like an odalisque in her boudoir, lies wise Coimbra, the Athens of Portugal. The ardent Mondego river kisses her feet and whispers to her of love. And in her woods, in her celebrated willow grove, the nightingale and other songbirds give voice to their melancholy trills. As you approach along the Lisbon road, where once an efficient post chaise performed the service now charged by progress to the smoky locomotive, regard her, white and gleaming, crowned by the imposing edifice of the university, wisdom's refuge. There stands the tower and the bell to which the studious young refer, in their playful way, as "the nanny-goat". Beyond that, your eye will be drawn to a leafy tree: it is the celebrated "Tree of the Dórias", which spreads its centuries-old branches in the garden owned by one of the members of that honourable family. And you will see, sitting on the walls of the ancient bridge, busy at their innocent pastimes, the bold young men, the hope of our nation, perhaps flirting with the tender country maids who pass by, brimming with youth and freshness, or perhaps turning over in their minds the more arduous problems contained in their excellently produced textbooks . . .'

'Soup's served,' announced a plump maid in a white apron.

'Very fine, Councillor, very fine!' said Savedra of the *The Century*, getting up. 'Admirable!'

He declared authoritatively to those around him that 'the style was worthy of a Rebelo or a Latino, and that Portugal really was crying out for work of such calibre . . .', all the while thinking to himself: 'Stuff and nonsense!', which was his general reaction to all contemporary work, apart, of course, from the articles he himself wrote for *The Century*.

'What do you think, my good friend?' the Councillor asked Julião softly, placing his hand on his shoulder. 'I want your honest opinion, Zuzarte!'

'Councillor,' said Julião in a deep voice, 'I envy you!' And his dark glasses fixed with growing interest on the large grey shawl neatly covering what, to judge by the jutting shapes, appeared to be tall piles of books. Whatever could they be? 'I envy you!' he said again. 'One other thing, Councillor, I wonder if I could just wash my hands.'

Acácio immediately showed him into his own bedroom and withdrew discreetly. The ever curious Julião noticed with surprise two large lithographs on either side of the bed: an 'Ecce Homo' and a 'Virgin of the Seven Sorrows'. The room was carpeted, the bed low and wide. He opened the small drawer in the bedside table and was taken aback to find a lady's nightcap and a bound edition of Bocage's obscene poems! He peered through the curtains around the bed and was pleased to discover two pillows lying closely, side by side, in tender, conjugal fashion!

As soon as Julião emerged from the bedroom, wiping his hands on his handkerchief, the Councillor led everyone into the dining room, saying jovially:

'Do not expect a Lucullan banquet; it is merely the modest repast of a humble philosopher!'

But Alves Coutinho went into ecstasies over the abundance of desserts set out on trays; there was crème brulée, custard tarts and milk pudding with the Councillor's initials written on it in cinnamon.

'It's a great day for Sebastião!' said Jorge.

Alves Coutinho immediately turned to Sebastião, rubbing his hands, a smile on his sallow face.

'So, you're like me, are you? You like sweet things too! I love 'em!'

There was a silence. Silver spoons, slowly stirring the scalding soup, disturbed the long, soft, white tubes of macaroni.

The Councillor said:

'I don't know if you like soup. I adore macaroni!'

'Oh, you like macaroni, do you?' asked Alves.

'Very much, my dear Alves. It makes me think of Italy!' the Councillor said, adding: 'It's a country I have always wanted to visit. They say it has some first-rate ruins. You can bring in the stew now, Senhora Filomena . . .' Then he stopped her with a grave gesture and addressed his guests: 'Tell me frankly, though, which would you prefer stew or fish? The fish is bream.'

There was a moment's hesitation, then Jorge said:

'Perhaps stew.'

And the Councillor said fondly:

'Our Jorge here favours the stew.'

'I'm with him!' exclaimed Alves Coutinho, turning to Jorge, his eyes ablaze with gratitude: 'Bring on the stew!'

And the Councillor, in the belief that it was his duty to lend nobility and interest to the conversation, said, slowly wiping from his moustaches the grease from the soup:

'They tell me that the Italian Constitution is very liberal!'

Liberal! According to Julião, if Italy was truly liberal, then the Italians would have driven out with the butts of their rifles the Pope, the Holy College and the Society of Jesus!

The Councillor pleaded gently with Zuzarte to show a little benevolence to the 'Head of the Church'.

'Not,' he explained, 'that I am a proselyte for the Syllabus of Errors. Nor do I wish to see the Jesuits enthroned in the bosom of the family! But,' his voice grew graver, 'the respected prisoner of the Vatican is, nonetheless, the vicar of Christ! Sebastião, pass the rice, will you?'

The Councillor's opinions did not surprise him, remarked Julião, given that he had two holy images hanging on either side of his bed.

Acácio's bald head turned scarlet. Savedra of *The Century* exclaimed, his mouth full of food:

'I had no idea you were so devout, Councillor!'

An embarrassed Acácio, his knife poised over a piece of bright red sausage, replied:

'I would ask my friend Savedra not to draw erroneous conclusions from that fact. My principles are well known. I am no great supporter of the Pope, nor do I long for the restoration of religious persecution. I am a liberal. I believe in God. And I recognise that religion acts as a brake . . .'

'For those of us who need one,' broke in Julião.

They all burst out laughing; Alves Coutinho positively writhed about with laughter. The Councillor hesitated, then replied slowly, arranging the slices of sausage on the platter:

'We, the enlightened classes, do not require it. But the masses do, Senhor Zuzarte. We would otherwise see a vast increase in the crime statistics.'

Savedra of *The Century* raised his eyebrows, a look of great seriousness on his face, and remarked:

'You have spoken a great truth.' He repeated the maxim with one slight modification: 'Religion acts as a curb!' And he mimed the action of reining in a particularly recalcitrant mule. Then he asked for more rice, which he promptly devoured.

The Councillor continued his explanation:

'I am, as I was saying, a liberal, but I feel that certain lithographs or engravings, alluding to the mystery of the Passion, have their place in the bedroom and, in a way, inspire Christian sentiments. Isn't that so, Jorge?'

But Savedra burst in noisily, his face aflame with voluptuous glee:

'The only paintings I'd allow in a bedroom would be a lovely naked nymph and a bacchante in the throes of unbridled passion!'

'Absolutely!' bawled Alves Coutinho. 'Absolutely!' His mouth spread wide in sensual admiration. 'That Savedra!' Adding in hushed tones to Sebastião: 'He's so clever!'

The Councillor turned to Julião, arranging his napkin on his stomach.

'I hope no such immoral images can be found in your study.'

Julião corrected him:

'In my monk's cell, you mean. Oh no, Councillor! I have only two lithographs, one is of a man with all his skin removed in order to reveal the arterial system, the other is of the same individual, equally devoid of skin, showing the nervous system.'

The Councillor put one white hand to his mouth in a vague gesture of disgust and expressed the view that the great science of medicine certainly had its repellent aspects. For example, he had heard tell of anatomy students with progressive ideas who carried their scorn for morality so far that they found amusement in hurling body parts at each other – feet, thighs, noses . . .

'But it's just like someone digging around in the earth, Councillor!' said Julião, filling his glass. 'It's inert matter!'

'And what about the soul, Senhor Zuzarte?' exclaimed the Councillor. He made a gesture as if about to say more, then, judging that he had crushed Julião with that one supreme word, he turned and bestowed upon Sebastião a polite, protective smile:

'And what does our good Sebastião have to say?'

'Oh, I'm just listening, Councillor.'

'Don't pay any heed to doctrines such as his!' And Acácio indicated with his fork Julião's irascible presence. 'Keep your soul pure. Such doctrines are pernicious. Even our Jorge here (and this is most regrettable in a man of business and a civil servant) tends slightly towards these exaggerated forms of materialism!'

Jorge laughed and agreed that he did indeed have that honour.

'Do you really expect me, an engineer, a student of mathematics, to believe that there are souls living in heaven, wearing little white wings and blue tunics, and playing musical instruments?'

The Councillor was quick to reply:

'No, not musical instruments, no!' And addressing

everyone: 'I don't believe I mentioned instruments of any kind. The musical instruments are an exaggeration. They are, shall we say, the tactics of a reactionary party . . .'

He was about to fulminate against those wishing to invest all power and authority in the Pope, when Senhora Filomena placed before him a platter containing a leg of roast veal. Filled at once by a sense of duty, he solemnly sharpened the carving knife and began cutting fine slices of meat, his brow furrowed as if he were engaged in carrying out the gravest of tasks. Julião, with his elbows on the table and delving around in his teeth with one fingernail, asked:

'So, is the government going to fall or not?'

Sebastião had heard someone say on the afternoon steamship from Almada that 'the situation had stabilised'.

Savedra, on the other hand, emptied his glass, wiped his lips and declared that within two weeks, the whole thing would have collapsed. The situation couldn't possibly go on like this; it was a scandal! They had not the slightest idea of how to govern. Not the remotest idea! He, for example, he . . . And he thrust his hands in his pockets, leaning back in his chair . . . He had supported them, had he not? And loyally too, because he was a loyal fellow and always had been when it came to politics! But they had sacked his cousin, the tax collector in Aljustrel, without so much as a word of explanation, when they had explicitly promised him the post. That was no way to do politics! They were a bunch of idiots!

Jorge would welcome a change; he might get back his post in the Ministry; all he wanted was a quiet life.

Alves Coutinho kept a prudent silence, swallowing down lumps of bread.

'As far as I'm concerned, whether they go or stay,' said Julião, 'whether this lot come in or another lot go out . . . Thank you, Councillor,' and he took his plate of veal, 'is a matter of complete indifference to me. They're all as corrupt as each other!' The whole country filled him with despair; the whole place was riddled with corruption; he only hoped that, very soon, the logical thing would happen, and a revolution would simply sweep away all the rubbish.

324

'A revolution!' cried Alves Coutinho, startled, looking anxiously about him and nervously scratching his chin.

The Councillor sat down and said:

'I do not wish to enter into political arguments, they serve only to divide the most united families, but I would remind you, Senhor Zuzarte, of one thing: the excesses of the Commune.'

Julião leaned back and replied in the calmest of voices:

'But Councillor, where's the harm in shooting a few bankers, priests, overweight landowners and decrepit marquises! It would be no more than a bit of spring-cleaning!' And he made a gesture as if sharpening his knife.

The Councillor smiled politely; he took this bloodthirsty outburst as a joke.

Savedra intoned authoritatively:

'Basically, I'm a republican.'

'Me too,' said Jorge.

'Me too,' piped up Alves Coutinho uneasily. 'Count me in!'

'However,' Savedra went on, 'I am a republican only in principle. For the principle is beautiful, the principle is ideal. But the practice? Yes, what about the practice?'

He turned his flabby face to everyone in the company.

'Yes, what about the practice?' echoed Alves Coutinho admiringly.

'In practice, it's impossible!' declared Savedra, shovelling slices of veal into his mouth.

The Councillor summed up:

'The truth is this, the country is genuinely attached to the royal family. Don't you agree, my dear Sebastião?' He addressed him as a landowner and as an owner of government bonds.

Cornered, Sebastião blushed and said that he understood nothing about politics; there were, however, certain facts he found troubling; it seemed to him that the working classes were very badly paid; poverty was on the increase; the workers in cigarette factories, for example, earned between nine and eleven *vinténs* a day, and that was a pittance if one had a family to raise . . .

'Disgraceful,' said Julião, shrugging.

'And there are far too few schools,' remarked Sebastião timidly.

'Shameful,' insisted Julião.

Savedra said nothing, busy with his food; he had undone the back buckle on his waistcoat; his fat face was flushed with wine, and he sat in his chair, a bloated figure with a vague smile hovering on his lips.

'And what about those idiots in São Bento?' exclaimed Julião.

But the Councillor interrupted him:

'My dear friends, let us talk of other things, things worthier of us as Portuguese citizens and loyal subjects.'

Turning at once to Jorge, he enquired after the delightful Dona Luiza.

She had been slightly off-colour for some days now, said Jorge. But it was nothing serious, just the change of season, a touch of anaemia . . .

Savedra set down his glass and, bowing, said:

'I had the honour of seeing her pass by my house this summer almost every afternoon,' he said. 'She was heading in the direction of Arroios. Sometimes in a carriage and sometimes on foot.'

Jorge seemed somewhat surprised, but the Councillor was saying how deeply he regretted not having the pleasure of seeing her here, sharing this modest repast; as a bachelor, however, having no wife to do the honours . . .

'That's what I can't understand, Councillor,' remarked Julião, 'here you are living in a comfortable house and yet you have never married, never sought the consolation of a wife.'

Everyone agreed. It was true! The Councillor should have married.

'The responsibilities of a head of the family, both before God and before society, are grave indeed,' he said ponderously.

It is, nevertheless, the most natural state, they all said. And surely, sometimes, he must feel lonely. And what if he were ill? Not to mention the joy of having children!

The Councillor offered as an excuse: 'My years, my snow-white hair . . .'

No one was saying he should marry a girl of fifteen! No, that was too risky. But a modest woman of a certain age, still attractive . . . It was the moral thing to do.

'After all, Councillor, Nature is Nature!' said Julião mischievously.

'Ah, my friend, the flames of passion long ago burned out in me.'

Now, really! That was one fire that never burned out! Was it possible that the Councillor, despite his fifty-five years, could be indifferent to a pair of lovely, dark eyes and a nicely rounded figure . . .

The Councillor blushed. Resorting to a prim circumlocution, Savedra declared that none of the ages of man was exempt from Venus's influence. 'It's all a question of taste,' he said. 'At fifteen, one is drawn to a plump, older woman, at fifty, one yearns for a tender young fruit. Isn't that so, friend Alves?'

Alves rolled concupiscent eyes and clicked his tongue.

Savedra went on:

'My first love was a neighbour of ours, the wife of a sea captain and a mother of six, who wouldn't even have fitted through that door. But, gentlemen, I wrote her verses, and the excellent creature taught me a few very agreeable things. It's best to start early, don't you agree?' And he turned to Sebastião.

Everyone wanted to know the views of Sebastião, who blushed bright scarlet.

At last, when pressed, he said shyly:

'I think that one should marry a decent girl and cherish her all one's life.'

These simple words provoked a brief silence. But Savedra, reclining in his chair, categorised such an opinion as 'bourgeois'; marriage was a burden; there was nothing like variety.

And Julião announced dogmatically:

'Marriage is a mere administrative formula which will, one day, simply die out.' Besides, according to him, the female was an inferior being; the man should only approach her at certain seasons of the year (as do animals, who understand these things better than we do), and should mate with her and then crawl away.

This view shocked everyone, especially the Councillor, who found it typical of 'the most vile materialism'.

'These females about whom you speak so disparagingly, Senhor Zuzarte,' he exclaimed, 'these females are our mothers, our loving sisters, the wife of the Head of State, the illustrious ladies of our nobility.'

'They are the sweetest morsel to be had in this vale of tears,' broke in Savedra fatuously, patting his stomach. He then discoursed at length on women. Most important of all was a pretty foot; there was nothing like a small, well-turned foot! And Spanish women were his particular favourites!

Alves' vote went to French women; he named a number of performers in *cafés-concerts* who were enough to turn a man's head! And his eyes grew even more bloodshot.

Savedra made a dismissive gesture and said:

'Yes, they're all right for a bit of cancan . . . oh, yes, there's no one like Frenchwomen when it comes to that . . . but they're real bloodsuckers!'

The Councillor, adjusted his glasses and affirmed:

'Knowledgeable travellers have assured me that Englishwomen make excellent mothers.'

'Yes, but they're as cold and unfeeling as this piece of wood,' said Savedra, striking the table. 'Made of ice, they are!' It was Spanish women for him! He wanted fire, he wanted brio! His eyes had a vinous gleam to them; the food had inflamed his feelings!

'A beautiful *señorita* from Cádiz, that's what we want, eh, friend Alves?'

But in the presence of the desserts that Senhora Filomena had now placed on the table, Alves Coutinho had forgotten all about women and, turning to Sebastião, he was now discussing sweetmeats. He told Sebastião which were the best places to buy certain specialities: for puff pastry, Cocó's; for custard tarts, Baltreschi; for jellies, Largo de Santo Domingos! He proffered recipes and recounted, with much eye-rolling, various feats of sweet-toothed gluttony.

For, he said, cakes and women were the only two things that really touched his heart!

This was quite true: he scrupulously divided any time not spent working in the service of the State between cakeshops and brothels.

Savedra and Julião were discussing the press. The editor of *The Century* praised the profession of journalist, as long, of course, as one had a private income to tide one over; later, one always finds a little niche for oneself, isn't that so? And then, of course, there were the free theatre tickets, the cachet it gave one amongst singers . . . They were always slightly in awe of one.

And the Councillor, cutting into his custard tart, and revelling in the joys of company, was saying to Jorge:

'What greater pleasure, my dear Jorge, than to pass the hours with cultivated friends discussing the truly important matters of the day and engaging in erudite conversation. This cake's awfully good.'

Then Senhora Filomena solemnly placed a bottle of champagne before him.

Savedra immediately asked to be allowed to open it, because he did it with such panache. And no sooner had the cork popped and, in the ensuing ceremonial silence, their glasses been filled, than Savedra, who had remained standing, said:

'To the Councillor!'

Acácio, looking pale, bowed.

'Councillor, it is with the greatest pleasure that I drink, that we all drink, to the health of a man who,' and, throwing out one arm, he gave an eloquent tug at his shirt cuff, 'is one of this country's great figures, renowned for his respectability, his social position and his vast knowledge! Your health, Councillor!'

'To the Councillor! To our friend, the Councillor!'

They drank noisily. Acácio dabbed at his lips, stroked his bald head with one tremulous hand and got to his feet, much moved.

'My good friends! I was not prepared for this circumstance. Had I known about it beforehand, I would have made a few notes. I lack the fluency of a Rodrigo or a Garrett, and I fear I may not be able to speak for tears . . .'

Then he spoke modestly about himself: he recognised, when he saw in the capital such illustrious parliamentarians, sublime orators, consummate stylists, he recognised that he was a zero! And raising his hand, he formed in the air, with his thumb and forefinger, an O: a zero! He proclaimed his love for his country; if, tomorrow, the public institutions or the royal family needed him, he would gladly give them his body, his pen and his modest savings! He would spill his blood for the Throne! Waxing prolix, he cited Herculano's *Eurico*, the public institutions of Belgium, Bocage and selected passages from his prologues. He was honoured to be a member of the First of December Society . . . 'On that memorable day,' he exclaimed, 'marking the restoration of the Portuguese monarchy, I myself illuminate my windows, not with the bright lights of the great establishments in the Chiado, but with an honest soul!'

And he ended by saying: 'Let us not forget, my friends, as good Portuguese, to pray for our illustrious monarch, who bestowed on my white locks, before they go down into the tomb, the consolation of being able to wear the honourable insignia of Santiago! My friends, to the royal family!' And he raised his glass. 'To that model family, who, seated at the helm of the State, surrounded by the great figures of our political life, steer . . .' he fumbled for a closing phrase; there was an anxious silence, '. . . steer . . .' from behind his smoked lenses, his eyes, in search of inspiration, fixed on the tray containing the milk pudding, '. . . steer . . .' he fretfully scratched his bald pate; but at last, a smile lit up his face; he had found the phrase; and reaching out his arm, he said: 'who, to the envy of all our neighbouring nations, steer the ship of public governance!'

'To the royal family!' everyone cried respectfully.

Coffee was served in the drawing room. The tallow candles lent a sad light to that cold room; the Councillor wound up the music box; and to the wedding chorus from *Lucia di Lammermoor*, he offered round the cigars.

'Tell Senhora Adelaide she can bring in the liqueurs now,' he said to Filomena.

There then appeared a beautiful woman in her thirties, with very white skin, dark eyes and an ample figure, wearing a dress of blue merino wool and carrying a silver tray tinkling with small liqueur glasses, a bottle of cognac and a flask of curação.

'What a woman!' growled Alves Coucinho, his face ablaze.

Julião almost covered his mouth with his hand. And whispering into Alves' ear, while looking straight at the Councillor, he recited:

'Do not dare to raise bold eyes
to gaze on Caesar's wife!'

And as the curação was being drunk, Julião crept into the study and lifted one corner of the grey shawl that had so fascinated him; underneath were piles of bound books tied up with string – uncut copies of the Councillor's own books!

It was eleven o'clock by the time Jorge got home, and Luiza was already in bed, reading, waiting for him.

She wanted to hear all about the Councillor's supper.

Excellent, said Jorge, starting to get undressed. He praised the wines highly. There had even been speeches . . . Then suddenly:

'By the way, what were you doing going to Arroios?'

Luiza slowly drew her hands across her face to disguise her discomfiture. Yawning slightly, she said:

'Arroios?'

'Yes. Savedra, who was at the Councillor's house, says that he saw you pass by every day, in a carriage or on foot, heading in that direction.'

'Oh,' said Luiza, after clearing her throat. 'I was going to see Guedes' wife, a girl I went to school with, who had just arrived from Oporto. Her husband is Silva Guedes!'

'Silva Guedes,' said Jorge thoughtfully. 'I thought he was secretary-general in Cape Verde!'

'I don't know. They were here for a month this summer. They were staying in Arroios. She was ill, poor thing, and so I went to see her a few times. She sent for me. Put that light out, will you, it's hurting my eyes.'

She complained that she had been feeling odd all evening. She felt weak, with a touch of fever.

And in the days that followed, she felt no better. She still complained vaguely of a weight on her head, a general malaise. One morning, she even stayed in bed. Jorge, worried, did not go out and even wanted to call in Julião. But Luiza insisted that 'it was nothing', she was just feeling a little weak.

Upstairs in the kitchen, this was Juliana's opinion too.

'She's not strong, that lady. It'll be her chest,' she said authoritatively.

Joana, who was leaning over the oven, said:

'She's a saint, our mistress!'

Juliana fixed Joana's back with a rancorous look. Then, with a little laugh, she added:

'You say that as if other people were positively evil.'

'What other people?'

'Me, you, everyone else . . .'

Still stirring the pots and without turning round, Joana said:

'You won't find another like her, Senhora Juliana! A mistress who lets you do what you like and even does the work herself. The other day, I caught her emptying the chamber pots! She's a saint I tell you!'

Joana's hostile tone exasperated Juliana, but she did not respond, for, despite her 'position' in the house, she was still dependent on Joana for soups, steaks and other occasional culinary treats; in her presence, she experienced the vague, respectful shyness that people with frail constitutions feel for the physically robust. In an ambiguous, insinuating tone, she said:

'It's all a question of temperament. She likes tidying. She's a very orderly person, it must be said, and she enjoys working. Sometimes, all it takes is for her to spot the tiniest speck of dust and she grabs the duster. It's a question of temperament.

I've known women like her before.' And she cocked her head on one side, pursing her lips.

'She's a saint,' repeated Joana.

'It's just her temperament. She's always working. I don't leave the house until everything's clean as a new pin, but she's never satisfied. Only the other day, she was downstairs ironing. I was just about to go out, but I immediately took off my hat and insisted on doing it myself. Do you know what I think? She hasn't got enough to do, no children. I mean it's not as if she lacks for anything.'

She fell silent and examined her foot, then said with satisfaction:

'But then neither do I.'

Joana started singing. She did not want to get into an argument with Juliana, but lately, she had felt that things in the house 'were not as they should be', with Juliana always off somewhere or stuck in her room, doing her own work, not bothering about the house, leaving everything higgledy-piggledy, and the poor mistress sweeping and ironing and growing thinner and thinner! No, something was going on! But her Pedro, whom she had consulted on the matter, told her slyly, twirling his moustache: 'Oh, let them get on with it! You just make the most of it and don't worry about anyone else. It's a good house, enjoy it.'

But 'inside her' Joana felt a growing antipathy towards Senhora Juliana. She was fed up with Juliana's fine clothes, long walks and hoity-toity ways; she didn't refuse to do Juliana's work because, if she did the work, she received presents from the mistress, but she had, nevertheless, taken against her! She was consoled by the knowledge that the slightest thing could bring about the death of that old bag of bones, and so she too would take what she could from the house. Pedro was quite right.

Juliana did not bother to moderate her behaviour now. After the 'ironing episode', she had taken fright, because, after all, the scandal could mean the loss of her 'position'; for some days she did not go out and rigorously performed all her duties; but when she saw that Luiza was resigned to the situation, she immediately abandoned herself, almost fervently, to the pleasures of idleness and the joys of revenge. She went out for walks, she sat in her room sewing, and 'the dumpling' could do as she liked! She was still careful in front of Jorge, for she was afraid of him, but as soon as he went out, that was that! She could be in the middle of sweeping or tidying, but, as soon as she heard the front door close, she would throw down the iron or the broom and do whatever took her fancy. 'The dumpling' was there to finish things off.

Luiza, meanwhile, was growing worse; she suffered sudden, brief, inexplicable fevers; she was losing weight, and her general air of gloom was a torment to Jorge.

She blamed it all on her nerves.

'What can it be, Sebastião?' Jorge was constantly asking. He remembered with terror that Luiza's mother had died of a heart complaint.

In the street, through the cook and through Tia Joana, it was known that the Engineer's wife was unwell. Tia Joana swore that it must be a tapeworm. After all, why else would a person who lacked for nothing, had an angel of a husband, a good house and all her comforts be wasting away like that? It must be a tapeworm! It couldn't be anything else! And every day she reminded Sebastião to call in the man from Vila Nova de Famalicão who knew a cure.

Senhor Paula had another explanation.

'It's some mental problem,' he would say, frowning and looking very deep. 'You know what her problem is, Senhora Helena, her head's too stuffed with novels. I bet you she's there morning to night with a book in her hand. She sits reading novels and more novels . . . And the result? She's a nervous wreck!'

One day, suddenly and for no reason, Luiza fainted, and when she came round, she was very weak, with the faintest of pulses and great, hollow eyes. Jorge immediately went in search of Julião, whom he found in a state of considerable agitation because the competition was the next day and he had 'the shakes'.

All the way back to Jorge's house, he jabbered on about his thesis, about the scandal of patronage, about the fuss he would make if the result was unfair, regretting now that he hadn't made more use of 'contacts'!

Having examined Luiza, he said to Jorge angrily:

'There's nothing wrong with her at all! Fancy dragging me out for something so trivial! She's a bit anaemic, but then aren't we all. She needs to go out more, to have fun. Plenty of distraction and plenty of iron, lots of iron. And you could try splashing cold water on her spine!'

Since it was five o'clock, he invited himself to supper, ranting on all evening about the state of the country, cursing the medical profession, insulting his rival for the post, and furiously smoking Jorge's cigars.

Luiza did take more iron, but she refused any offers of distraction; it wore her out getting dressed up and she didn't feel like going to the theatre. Then, when she saw how worried Jorge was about her condition, she tried to seem strong, happy, good-humoured; these efforts proved extraordinarily draining.

'What about going to stay in the country for a while?' Jorge said bleakly, seeing her so downhearted.

Fearing possible complications, she declined; she didn't feel well enough, she said; where could she possibly be more comfortable than in her own home? Then there was the expense and the upheaval . . .

One morning, Jorge came home unexpectedly and found her still in her peignoir, with a scarf tied round her head, morosely sweeping.

He stood at the door, astonished:

'What *are* you doing? Why are you doing the sweeping?'

She blushed deeply, immediately threw down the broom and came to embrace him.

'I didn't have anything else to do . . . I just fancied doing some cleaning . . . I was bored; besides, it's good for me, it's exercise.'

That night, Jorge told Sebastião about Luiza's 'nonsensical insistence' on wearing herself out.

'Really, my dear lady, someone in your weak state . . .' scolded Sebastião.

No, she said, she was feeling better. She was much better . . .

And yet she hardly spoke all night, bent over her crochet, looking slightly pale; she would sometimes glance up, looking sad and weary, a disconsolate smile on her lips.

She asked Sebastião to play something from Mozart's *Requiem*. She thought it was so lovely. She would like it to be sung in church when she died.

Jorge got angry. What a ridiculous thing to say!

'Well, I might die, mightn't I?'

'All right, die then and leave us all in peace!' he roared.

'What a good husband!' she said to Sebastião, smiling.

She put her crocheting down in her lap and asked him to play something from *L'Africaine*. She listened, leaning her head on her hand: the notes entered her soul with the sweetness of mystic voices calling to her; she felt as if she were being carried off by them, she let go of everything that was terrestrial and troubling, and found herself on a deserted beach, by a sad sea, beneath a cold moon, and there, pure spirit, free of all fleshly miseries, she gambolled in the undulating air, she trembled in the luminous rays, she stepped across the heather in the salt breezes . . .

Her melancholy pose infuriated Jorge.

'Sebastião, for heaven's sake, play a fandango, will you, or something from *Bluebeard* or *Pirolito*! Otherwise, if you want something really melancholy, I'll start singing plain chant!'

And he sang in funereal tones:

> *Dies irae, dies illa,*
> *Solvet sæculum in favilla!* . . .

Luiza laughed.

'You're mad! Can't people be sad if they want to be?'

'Of course, they can!' exclaimed Jorge. 'But then let's have something beautifully, utterly sad.' And in a terrifying voice, he began intoning the 'Blessing'.

'The neighbours will think we've gone mad, Jorge,' she said.

'Well, we have, haven't we?' And he stormed off into his study, slamming the door.

Sebastião played a few more notes, then turned to her and said softly:

'What are all these strange ideas? Why so melancholy?'

Luiza looked up at him: she saw his kind, friendly face, full of sympathy; she was possibly, in an explosion of pain, about to tell him everything, but Jorge emerged from his study again. She smiled, shrugged and slowly returned to her crochet work.

The following Sunday night, they were talking in the drawing room. Julião was describing his interview. He was pleased with himself; he had talked precisely and lucidly for two hours.

Dr Figueiredo had told him that 'he should have made it easier to understand'.

'These literary fellows!' said Julião with a scornful shrug. 'They can't talk for five minutes about the ankle bone without mentioning "the flowers of the spring" and "the blazing torch of civilisation"!'

'The Portuguese are obsessed with "rhetoric",' said Jorge.

At that moment, Juliana came into the room bearing a letter.

'Oh, it's from the Councillor!'

Everyone was worried. But Acácio was merely apologising for not being able to come, as he had promised, to partake of Dona Luiza's excellent tea; an urgent task kept him tied to the bench of duty; he sent his best wishes to Sebastião and Julião and his 'affectionate respects to the delightful Dona Felicidade'.

The blood rushed to the excellent lady's face. She began breathing heavily, greatly agitated; she changed chairs twice, went over to the piano and picked out the tune of 'The Pearl of Ophir' with one finger, then, at last, unable to control herself any longer, she asked Luiza quietly if they could go into her room, for there was something she wanted to tell her.

As soon as they were alone, Dona Felicidade closed the drawing-room door and asked Luiza:

'What did you think of his note, then?'

'My congratulations!' said Luiza, laughing.

'It's the miracle!' exclaimed Dona Felicidade. 'It's the miracle beginning to happen!' Lowering her voice, she said: 'I sent the man, the one I told you about, the Galician!'

Luiza did not understand.

'I sent the man to see that woman in Tui, the one who makes charms! He took my picture with him and one of the Councillor. He left a week ago; the woman must already have started sticking pins in his heart.'

'What pins?' asked Luiza, astonished.

They were standing by the dressing table. In a mysterious voice, Dona Felicidade said:

'The woman makes a heart out of wax and glues the photograph of the Councillor to it, then every night at midnight, for a week, she dips a pin in this special preparation of hers and sticks it into the wax heart, meanwhile reciting the appropriate prayers . . .'

'And you gave the man money?'

'Eight *moedas.*'

'Oh, Dona Felicidade!'

'I know, I know! But you can see the change already! In a few days' time, he'll be in love! Our Lady of Joy willing, of course! The man is driving me mad. I have such dreams! I'm up to my ears in mortal sin! And I sweat so. I have to change my nightdress three or four times a night!'

She looked at herself in the mirror, trying to convince herself that her personal beauty would help the witch's pins; she smoothed her hair.

'Do you think I'm looking thinner.'

'Not really.'

'But I am, my dear, I am!' And she tugged at her loose bodice.

She was already making plans. They would spend their honeymoon in Sintra . . . Her eyes glazed over lubriciously.

'May our Lady of Joy permit it. I have two candles burning for her, day and night.'

338

Suddenly, Joana yelled down from the kitchen stairs; she sounded frightened:

'Madam, Madam, come quickly!'

Luiza hurried up to her, so did Jorge, who had heard the shout from the drawing room. Juliana was stretched out on the kitchen floor in a dead faint.

'She just came all over, all of a sudden,' said Joana, who was very pale and trembling. 'She just suddenly keeled over.'

Julião calmed them down; it was nothing but a simple fainting fit. They carried her up to her bed. Julião had them rub her extremities hard with a hot flannel, and even before a dazed, hatless Joana had raced to the herbalist's for an antispasmodic, Juliana had come round, although she was still very weak. When they went back down to the drawing room, Julião rolled a cigarette and said:

'It's nothing. These fainting fits are common occurrences with any kind of heart disease. This one was quite straightforward, but sometimes they can be apoplectic in nature and then paralysis can result; it doesn't last, because only a small amount of blood is released into the brain, but it's most unpleasant nevertheless.' And lighting his cigarette, he went on: 'One day, she'll simply drop down dead.'

Jorge was pacing anxiously up and down in the drawing room, his hands in his pockets.

'As I've always said,' said Dona Felicidade in a quiet, frightened voice. 'It's what I've always said. You should get rid of the woman.'

'Besides, the treatment is incompatible with any kind of job,' said Julião. 'Well, she could still do the starching and ironing if she took digitalis or quinine, but the real treatment is complete rest and the avoidance of any tiring activities. She might get angry one day or have a particularly exhausting morning, and she could go, just like that!'

'Is the disease very advanced?' asked Jorge.

'According to her, she already suffers from asthma, breathlessness, intense pain in the cardiac region, flatulence, swollen ankles, the lot!'

'Well, it's a damned nuisance!' muttered Jorge, looking around him.

'You should put her out in the street!' declared Dona Felicidade.

At eleven o'clock, when Jorge and Luiza were alone, Jorge said:

'What do you think, eh? We'll have to get rid of the creature. I don't want her dying here in the house!'

Luiza was sitting at the dressing table, removing her earrings, and, without turning round, she began saying that they couldn't very well send the poor creature to die in the street either. She made vague mention of all she had done for Aunt Virginia . . . She chose her words slowly and carefully, with the caution of someone treading on treacherous ground. Perhaps they could give her some money so that she could go and live somewhere else.

After a silence, Jorge replied:

'I'd be prepared to give her ten or twelve *libras* so that she can just leave and sort herself out!'

'Ten or twelve *libras*', thought Luiza, smiling grimly. And seated at the dressing table, she looked at her own face in the mirror with a kind of nostalgia, as if knowing that her cheeks would soon be gaunt with suffering and her eyes weary with crying.

The crisis had come. If Jorge insisted on dismissing the woman, she could not say to Jorge, at least not without provoking amazement and the need for some explanation: I don't want her to leave, I want her to die here! And if Juliana, desperate and ailing, were dismissed and saw that Luiza made no effort to defend her or demand her return, then she would have her revenge! What should she do?

The next day, she woke in a state of great nervous tension. Juliana was still too tired to get out of bed. And while Joana was laying the table, Luiza, in the wing chair by the dining room window, was mechanically reading the daily newspaper, barely taking in a word of it, when an item of news at the top of the page made her start: 'The day after tomorrow, our friend, the well-known banker, Castro, of Castro, Miranda &

Co., is leaving for France. He is retiring from business and going to settle near Bordeaux, where he has recently bought a valuable piece of property.'

Castro! The man who, according to Leopoldina, would be willing to give her any amount of money, as much as she wanted. And he was leaving Portugal! Although it had seemed to her, from the very first, an utterly shameful thing to do, she nevertheless felt almost saddened to see him go. For Castro would never again return to Portugal! And suddenly an idea pierced her, made her shudder and turn pale and sit up very straight. What if, on the eve of his departure, she were to consent . . . Oh, no, it was too horrible! It did not even bear thinking about.

But she did think about it, and felt herself succumbing to a growing temptation that coiled about her soul with persuasive caresses. Then she would be safe! She would give Juliana the six hundred *mil*-réis, and Juliana would go away and die somewhere far from there!

And he, the man, would leave on the steamship to France. She would never have to blush before him; her secret would sail off to foreign parts, as lost as if it had gone to its tomb. And if Castro really did nurse a passion for her, he might well be prepared to lend her the money with no conditions attached!

Dear God, the next day she could have the notes, or indeed the gold, there in her pocket. Yes, why not? Why not? And she felt an urgent desire to live happily again, to be free of suffering and torments.

She went back into her room. She started moving things around on the dressing table, casting sideways glances at Jorge, as he got dressed. His presence immediately filled her with remorse; going to ask a man for money and consenting to his lascivious looks, his lustful words! How awful! But, she reasoned, it was for Jorge's sake that she was doing it! It was to save him from the pain of finding out! It was in order to be able to love him freely, for the rest of her life, without fears or constraints . . .

She sat silently through breakfast. She was moved by Jorge's kind face; the other man seemed to her hideous, hateful.

When Jorge left for work, she was gripped by anxiety. She went over to the window; the sunshine looked adorable, the street beckoned. Why not? Why not?

She heard Juliana's harsh voice on the kitchen stairs, and that odious sound decided her.

She dressed carefully; she was, after all, a woman and wanted to look pretty. And she arrived, breathlessly, at Leopoldina's house when the church clock was striking noon.

She found Leopoldina dressed and waiting for her lunch. Throwing down her hat and installing herself on the sofa, Luiza laid out her plan to Leopoldina. She wanted the money from Castro. Regardless of whether it was a loan or a gift, she wanted the money. She was in a terrible predicament and desperate measures were called for! Jorge wanted to dismiss the woman. She feared her revenge. She needed money, and it was there to be had!

'Just like that?' said Leopoldina, taken aback by the look of determination in Luiza's eye.

'Castro is leaving tomorrow. He's going to Bordeaux, to the back of beyond! I have to do something now!'

Leopoldina suggested writing to him.

'Whatever you think best . . . I'm ready.'

Leopoldina sat down slowly at the table, took up a sheet of paper and, with her little finger cocked and her head on one side, she began to write.

Luiza paced nervously about the room. She was filled now by a stubborn resolve, which Leopoldina's presence only reinforced. Leopoldina had fun, she went dancing, she went to the countryside, she enjoyed herself, she had a life; unlike Luiza, she had nothing tormenting her and eating away at her, ruining her life! No, she would not go back home until she had her ransom money, her salvation, safely in her pocket! Even if she had to sink as low as those women in the Bairro Alto! She had had enough of humiliations, upsets and nightmares! She wanted to enjoy life, to savour both her love and her dinner, without feeling anxious, with her heart at peace!

'How's this?' said Leopoldina, reading out loud.

My dear friend,

I need to speak to you urgently. It is a matter of the utmost gravity. Come as soon as you can. You may well thank me for it. I will wait for you here until three o'clock at the latest.

With kind regards,

Your friend,

Leopoldina.


'What do you think?'

'Awful! No, really, it's fine. Perhaps it would be best to take out the part that says: "You may well thank me for it."'

Leopoldina copied out the letter again and sent Justina off in a carriage to deliver it.

'And now I'm going to have my lunch. I'm so weak, I can barely stand.'

The dining room opened onto a narrow hallway. The walls were covered by a hideous mural, in which large green stains signified hills and dark blue lines represented lakes. A wardrobe in one corner served as a cupboard. The wicker chairs had red cotton cushions on them, and the table cloth still bore coffee stains from the previous night.

'One thing you can be sure of,' said Leopoldina, gulping down some tea, 'Castro is a good man for a secret. If he does lend you the money, he'll never say a word to anyone about it. He's very reliable in that respect . . . Videira's wife was his mistress for years, but he never said a thing, not even to Mendonça, his best friend, not so much as a hint. He's as silent as the grave.'

'Which Videira is that?'

'The tall woman with a big nose; she rides around in a landau.'

'But she's supposed to be so very proper.'

'You see!' And with a giggle, she went on: 'They're *supposed* to be all kinds of things . . . But once you know their little weaknesses, my dear!'

Spreading butter onto thick slices of bread, she began an account of the scandals of Lisbon, blithely hanging out everyone's dirty linen: she named names and cited particular specialities, she spoke of those women who, having 'done the deed', then pour their guilty feelings into a belated sense of religious devotion; that's where some of them ended up, in sacristies! She spoke of those who, doubtless weary of their monotonously virtuous lives, skilfully prepared for their 'fall' in a resort like Sintra or Cascais. And then there were the young, unmarried women! There were plenty of babies who would have had every right to call them 'mama' but who were farmed out to wetnurses in the outskirts of Lisbon! Other, more prudent women, fearing the results of love, took refuge in the precautions of libertinism. Not to mention the women who, given their husband's rather small salaries, supplemented these by taking on an extra man. She was exaggerating, it was true, but she did so hate them. For they had all, more or less, been able to preserve the outward appearance of decency that she had lost; they were skilled manipulators, whereas she, poor fool, was merely truthful! And while they still had a place in society, received invitations to soirées and the respect of their fellow citizens, she had lost everything and was merely 'that Quebrais woman'!

This conversation was having an enervating effect upon Luiza; in such a landscape of vice, her particular case seemed to grow less stark, to fade, like a building in the mist; and its very insignificance seemed to her almost to justify it.

They fell silent, numbed by that sense of general immorality, in which resistence and pride became as soft and languid as one's muscles in a perfumed hothouse.

'The world is one big lie,' said Leopoldina, getting up and yawning.

'Where's your husband?' asked Luiza as they walked down the corridor.

He had gone to Oporto. They could do as they pleased, they could even commit crimes if they wanted to!

And Leopoldina, in her room, lying down on the sofa, a cigarette in her mouth, began a litany of complaints.

She had been feeling fed up for ages now; she was bored, she found everything so unutterably tedious; she wanted something new, something different! She felt as if every pore in her body were yawning with boredom.

'And what about Fernando?' said Luiza distractedly, going back and forth to the window.

'Oh, that idiot!' retorted Leopoldina with a dismissive, scornful lift of her shoulders.

No, she wanted something else, though quite what she did not know! Sometimes, she even thought of becoming a nun! (And she stretched out her arms in a gesture of dull languor.) All the men she knew were so insipid! All the pleasures she had experienced were so banal! She wanted another life, a vigorous, adventurous, dangerous life, a life that would make her heart beat faster, as the wife of a highwayman or setting out to sea on a pirate ship . . . As for her beloved Fernando, he made her sick! And any other man would be just the same. She had had enough of men! She almost felt like tempting God himself!

Then after opening her mouth wide in a yawn worthy of a caged beast, she said:

'I'm bored, I am so bored!'

They said nothing for a moment.

'What should I say to him, to this man?' asked Luiza suddenly.

Blowing out the smoke from her cigarette, Leopoldina drawled:

'Tell him you need a *conto de réis* or six hundred *mil-réis* . . . What else? And that you'll pay him back.'

'How?'

Leopoldina, lying back, looking up at the ceiling, said:

'With love.'

'Oh, don't be so horrible!' cried Luiza in exasperation. 'You say you're my friend, but you see me here miserable and half-mad, and all you do is laugh and make fun of me . . .' Her voice shook, she was almost in tears.

'But what a stupid question! How else do you think you'll pay him? Do you really not know?'

They looked at each other for a moment.

'I'm going home, Leopoldina!' exclaimed Luiza.

'Don't be such a child!'

A carriage drew up outside in the street. Justina appeared. She had not found Senhor Castro at home, so she had gone to his office; and he had said that he would come immediately.

Luiza, however, looking very pale, already had her hat in her hand.

'Oh, no you don't,' said Leopoldina, quite scandalised, 'you're not going to leave me alone here with that man! Whatever will I say to him?'

'It's too horrible!' murmured Luiza, tears in her eyes, her arms hanging loose by her side, tempted by self-interest, imprisoned by shame, and feeling utterly miserable.

'It's just like taking castor oil,' said Leopoldina cynically. Then, seeing the look of horror on Luiza's face, she added: 'For heaven's sake, what is so dishonourable about borrowing money? Everyone does it.'

At that moment, a carriage came trotting down the street and stopped.

'You go in first! You talk to him first!' begged Luiza, holding her hands up to Leopoldina in a pleading gesture.

The bell rang. Luiza, white and shaking, was glancing around, her eyes wide with fear and anxiety, as if searching for an idea or a solution, or for a corner where she might hide! A man's boots creaked over the carpet in the next room. Leopoldina said to her quietly and slowly, as if to nail each word into her soul, one by one:

'Remember, in an hour's time, you could be safe, happy and free, with your letters in your pocket!'

Luiza stood up, filled with sudden resolve. She dabbed on some face powder, smoothed her hair, then they went into the drawing room together.

Castro started slightly when he saw Luiza. Standing with his little feet together, he bowed his large head with its thinning thatch of fine, fair hair.

An ostentatious gold fob rested on his rounded belly, which the shortness of his legs made more paunch-like. In one hand he carried a walking stick with a silver handle in the form of a Venus, arms entwined. His skin had a prosperous glow; his thick moustache had been waxed to form two sharp points. And there was an authoritarian air about his gold-rimmed spectacles, the air of a banker and a lover of order. He seemed as pleased with life as a plump sparrow.

Well, began Leopoldina, it had certainly come to something when, in order to see him, she had to summon him to her house. And then, after introducing Luiza 'her best friend and schoolmate', she went on:

'What have you been up to? Why haven't you been to see me?'

Castro made himself comfortable in an armchair and, tapping his boots with his walking stick, he blamed his absence on preparations for his imminent departure.

'So you really are leaving us?'

Castro bowed:

'The day after tomorrow. On the *Orinoco*.'

'So the newspapers weren't lying this time. And will you be away for long?'

*'Per omnia sæcula sæculorum.'*

Leopoldina was aghast. Leaving Lisbon! A popular, amusing man like him! 'Isn't that so?' she said, turning to Luiza in order to draw her out of her embarrassed silence.

'Absolutely,' Luiza muttered.

She was sitting on the edge of her chair, as if frightened and ready to flee. She was troubled by the way Castro kept casting her insistent looks, from behind his glinting spectacles.

Leopoldina leaned back on the sofa and wagged a finger at him:

'There's some woman behind this departure of yours to France!'

He shook his head weakly, a fatuous smile on his face.

Leopoldina did not think Frenchwomen at all pretty, but they made up for this by their elegance and their vivacity.

Castro declared them all to be adorable. Especially when it came to pleasure! Oh, he knew them well! He wasn't saying they made good mothers, but there was no one like them if you wanted a nice bit of supper and some cancan ... He declared roundly that, like all the other bourgeois men of his circle, he would rather try his luck with twelve million Frenchwomen than with six *cafés-concerts* prostitutes – he had paid over the odds before now and been heartily bored!

To flatter him, Leopoldina called him 'a libertine'.

He gave a smug smile and twirled his moustache.

'Calumnies,' he murmured, 'mere calumnies.'

Then Leopoldina turned to Luiza:

'He's bought a magnificent estate in Bordeaux, a palace!'

'A mere cottage!'

'And you will of course be throwing lavish parties!'

'The occasional modest tea-party, nothing more,' he said settling back in his chair.

And they both laughed in an affected manner.

Castro then bowed to Luiza.

'I had the pleasure of seeing you some time ago in Rua do Ouro . . .'

'Yes, I remember . . .' she replied.

There was a silence. Leopoldina coughed, shifted nearer to the edge of the sofa, and said with a smile:

'I sent for you because we have something to ask you.'

Castro leaned forward. His eyes never left Luiza; they observed her boldly, probingly.

'Look, I'll come straight to the point, with no preamble.' Leopoldina giggled. 'My friend here finds herself in an extremely difficult situation, and she needs one *conto de réis*.'

In a barely audible voice, Luiza corrected her:

'Six hundred *mil-réis* . . .'

'That doesn't matter,' said Leopoldina with grand indifference, 'we're talking to a millionaire here! The question is this: will you, my friend, do us this favour?'

Castro sat up slowly in his chair and in a drawling, ambiguous voice said:

'Of course, of course . . .'

Leopoldina immediately got to her feet.

'Right. I have my seamstress waiting for me in my room. I'll leave you two to discuss terms.'

And, at the door of her room, she turned to Castro, again wagging her finger, and said in a bright voice:

'And don't you charge too high an interest rate!'

Then she left, laughing.

Castro bowed to Luiza:

'Madam, I . . .'

'Leopoldina was telling you the truth. I am in dire need of money. And I thought of approaching you . . . I need six hundred *mil-réis* . . . I'll try to pay it back as quickly as possible . . .'

'Madam, please!' said Castro, with a generous gesture. He began by saying that he understood perfectly, everyone had their problems. He regretted not having met her before. He had always felt very drawn to her . . . oh, yes, very drawn to her!

Luiza said nothing, her eyes downcast. He placed his walking stick on a table and came and sat on the sofa next to her. Seeing her look of embarrassment, he begged her not to distress herself. It wasn't worth getting upset about money! It would give him great pleasure to serve such a delightful young lady . . . She had been quite right to approach him. He knew of ladies who had gone to moneylenders who had not only exploited them, but were indiscreet to boot. As he talked, he took her hand in his; contact with her longed-for flesh aroused his brute desire, making him breathe loudly; Luiza, rigid with fear, did not even withdraw her hand; and Castro, aflame, was gabbling at her in a slightly hoarse voice, promising her everything, anything she wanted. His small eyes stared ravenously at her very white neck.

'Six hundred *mil réis* . . . whatever you want!'

'But when?' asked Luiza nervously.

He saw her breast rise and fall and, unable to restrain his animal desires any longer, he gasped:

'Now!'

And he seized her round the waist and planted a voracious kiss on her cheek, almost biting her.

Luiza sprang to her feet.

But Castro had slithered down onto the carpet, and was kneeling now, clinging urgently to her skirts.

'I'll give you anything you want, but please sit down! I have nursed a passion for you for years now! Listen to me!' His trembling arms crept upwards, coiling around her, and what he felt of her body only inflamed him still further.

Without a word, Luiza pushed him away with her hands, refusing his advances.

'Anything you want, but j-just listen . . .' he stammered, clutching her violently to him. He was snorting now like a bull, in the grip of sheer bestial lust.

Then, tugging desperately at her skirts, she freed herself and drew back, crying:

'Leave me alone! Leave me alone!'

Castro staggered, panting, to his feet and, teeth gritted, arms wide, lunged at her.

Faced by this display of pure animal concupiscence, Luiza indignantly snatched up the walking stick he had placed on the table and brought it down hard on his hand.

Pain, fury and desire enraged him.

'You little devil!' he growled, grinding his teeth.

He was about to hurl himself upon her, but Luiza, in a frenzy of anger, dealt rapid blows with the walking stick to his arms and shoulders. Deathly pale, deadly serious, a cruel glint in her eyes, she was savouring the pleasure of revenge as she beat that flabby flesh.

An astonished Castro retreated, making only a vague attempt at defending himself by covering his face with his arms; suddenly, he bumped against the table; the porcelain oil lamp toppled over, fell to the floor and shattered, leaving a dark, spreading stain on the mat.

'Now look what you've done!' said Luiza, trembling all over, but still clutching the walking stick.

Hearing the noise, Leopoldina rushed in from her room.

'What's happened? What's happened?'

'Nothing. We were just playing,' said Luiza.

She threw the walking stick down and left the room.

Castro, purple with fury, had snatched up his hat. Fixing Leopoldina with a terrible look, he said:

'Thank you *so* much! If ever you need anything again, do, please, be sure to ask!'

'But what happened?'

'Goodbye!' roared Castro. And picking up his walking stick, which he brandished threateningly in the direction of the room into which Luiza had vanished, he muttered bitterly:

'Lunatic!'

And with that, he left, slamming all the doors.

Still confused, Leopoldina went into her bedroom to find Luiza putting on her hat, her hands still trembling, a satisfied gleam in her eyes.

'Something just came over me, and I hit him round the head with his walking stick,' she said.

Leopoldina stood for a moment petrified, staring at her.

'You *hit* him?' And she burst out in wild laughter. Bespectacled Castro being soundly beaten with his own walking stick! Castro getting a good beating! She flung herself down onto the chaise longue and rolled about, gasping for breath. She was even getting a stitch. Heavens! Poor Castro coming to a friend's house, being asked for a loan of six hundred *mil réis* and then getting beaten for his pains! And with his own walking stick too! Oh dear, it was too funny for words!

'I'm afraid I broke the oil lamp,' said Luiza.

Leopoldina leaped to her feet.

'You spilled the oil? They say that brings bad luck!' She ran into the drawing room. Luiza followed and found her standing, arms folded, pale-faced, staring at the dark stain, as if watching the approach of various catastrophes. 'Oh dear, it's really bad luck to spill oil!'

'Quick, put some salt on it!'

'Does that help?'

'It undoes the bad luck.'

Leopoldina ran off to fetch some salt; as she knelt down, sprinkling it on the stain, she said:

'May Our Lady prevent anything bad from happening! What a thing, though! But what will you do now, my dear?'

Luiza shrugged:

'I've no idea. Suffer, I suppose . . .'

# XII

That same week, Jorge, who had forgotten it was a national holiday, found the Ministry closed and so returned home at midday. Joana was standing at the street door chatting to the old woman who bought any leftover bones from the cooking; the door upstairs was open, and Jorge, entering the bedroom unheard, found Juliana comfortably installed on the chaise longue, calmly reading the newspaper.

She got up, red-faced, as soon as she saw him and stammered:

'I-I'm terribly sorry, but I had such bad palpitations that . . .'

'You just had to sit down and read the newspaper, I suppose,' said Jorge, instinctively tightening his grip on the handle of his walking stick. 'Where is your mistress?'

'She must be in the dining room,' said Juliana, who immediately started sweeping the floor.

Jorge did not find Luiza in the dining room; he found her, still in her peignoir and with her hair all dishevelled, diligently and grimly ironing clothes in the laundry room.

'Why on earth are you doing the ironing?' he exclaimed.

Luiza blushed slightly and put down the iron. Juliana wasn't well and the clothes to be ironed had been piling up . . .

'Tell me something: who is the maid here and who is the mistress?'

He sounded so stern that Luiza turned pale and murmured:

'What do you mean?'

'I mean that I come home to find you doing the ironing and find her downstairs lounging on your chaise longue, reading the newspaper!'

Confused, Luiza bent over the laundry basket and, with trembling hands, began sorting and smoothing and shaking various garments.

'You've no idea how much there is to be done here,' she was saying. 'There's the cleaning, the starching, the ironing, it's a huge task. The poor woman has been ill . . .'

'Well, if she's so ill, she should go to the hospital!'

'No, she can't!'

Her stubborn defence of the woman he had found reclining on the chaise longue downstairs exasperated him:

'Tell me something, are you in some way dependent on her? Anyone would think you were afraid of her!'

'Well, if that's the mood you're in . . .' began Luiza, lips quivering and tears in her eyes.

But Jorge went on, really angry now:

'Look, this behaviour has got to stop once and for all! I'm not having that useless creature with one foot in the grave living a life of ease in my house, lying on my sofas, going out for walks, while you defend her and do all her work for her! This has to stop! You always find an excuse for her! Well, if she can't cope, she'll just have to leave! She can go to the hospital, she can go to hell for all I care!'

Luiza, her face bathed in tears, was blowing her nose and sobbing.

'Now you're crying. What's wrong? Why are you crying?'

She could not reply for weeping.

'Why are you crying, my love?' he asked with urgent concern, going over to her.

'Why do you talk to me that way?' she said between sobs, wiping her eyes. 'You know I'm not well, that my nerves are bad, and yet you're so bad-tempered with me! You only ever say nasty things to me.'

'What do you mean "nasty things"!? My dear, I haven't said anything nasty to you!' And he embraced her tenderly.

But she pulled away from him and, in a voice still broken by sobs, said:

'Is it a crime to be doing the ironing? Why do you get so angry with me because I'm working and taking care of things? Would you rather I simply neglected everything? The woman has been ill! Until we find another maid, the work still has to be done. But you're always going on at me, as if you wanted to upset me!'

'Don't talk nonsense, my dear. You're not yourself. It's just that I don't want you getting overtired!'

'Why did you say, then, that I was afraid of her?' And her tears started flowing again. 'Afraid of what? Why should I be afraid of her? How absurd!'

'All right, I take that back. We won't talk about the woman any more. But don't cry . . . There, there, it's over.' He kissed her. And putting his arm around her waist and leading her gently out of the room, he said: 'Come on, leave the ironing now. Honestly, you're such a child!'

Out of kindness and consideration for Luiza's nerves, Jorge did not mention 'that woman' again for some days. But he thought about her and was exasperated by the idea of that useless creature with one foot in the grave living in his house. Then there was her evident idleness, the many little luxuries in her room which he had seen for the first time on the night that she fainted, and Luiza's absurd generosity towards her! He found it all very strange and very irritating. Since he was out of the house all day and since, in his presence, Juliana was all smiles and affection with Luiza, he imagined that she must have managed to worm her way into Luiza's heart and, through the small intimacies of the mistress–maid relationship, had become both loved and needed. This only increased his feelings of antipathy, and he made no attempt to disguise the fact.

Luiza would occasionally notice him eyeing Juliana malevolently and she would tremble. But what tortured her most was the way Jorge had begun talking about Juliana with mock veneration; he called her, 'my lady and mistress, the illustrious Dona Juliana '. If there was a napkin or a glass missing from the table, he would pretend to be shocked and say: 'How is this possible? Could the perfect Dona Juliana have forgotten?' He made jokes that chilled Luiza's blood.

'What did it taste like that potion she gave you? Was it nice?'

When he was there, Luiza could no longer bring herself to talk to Juliana naturally; she feared his mischievous smiles, his asides: 'Go on, blow her a kiss, I can see from your face that you want to!' And so, in his presence, feeling afraid of his suspicions and wanting to demonstrate her independence, she would address Juliana with a brusqueness that was both harsh and affected. If she asked her for water or for a knife, she would adopt an affectedly petulant tone.

Juliana was intelligent enough to understand the situation and so endured this treatment in silence.

She wanted to avoid any conflict that might disrupt her comfortable life. She felt very ill now and, on nights when her asthmatic attacks kept her from sleeping, she would be assailed by terrifying thoughts: 'If I was thrown out of the house now, where would I go? To the hospital?'

That is why she was afraid of Jorge.

'He's dying to catch me out committing some gross misdemeanour, so that he'll have an excuse to get rid of me,' she told Tia Vitória, 'but I'm not going to give the cuckold that pleasure.'

And Luiza watched in amazement as, little by little, Juliana resumed her work, with apparent zeal; and yet there were still times when Juliana was too ill to manage; she was now and then seized by fits of dizziness that forced her to sit down on a chair, panting and clutching her heart. However, she always rallied. On one occasion, when she saw Luiza dusting the console tables in the drawing room, she even said angrily:

'I don't want you doing my job for me, madam! I can still manage, you know! I'm not in my grave yet!'

She would console herself then with tasty titbits. All day long she was sipping soup, nibbling croquettes, eating mashed potato. She had jelly and port wine in her room. On certain days, she even asked for a late-night bowl of chicken soup.

'I'm paying for this with my own body,' she would say to Joana, 'because I work like a black, you know! I'm killing myself!'

One day, however, when Jorge was feeling more than usually irritated by Juliana's wan figure and by the fact that she had failed to fill the ewer in the bedroom or provide a clean towel, he flew into a rage.

355

'I'm not going to put up with this incompetence any longer!' he shouted.

An anxious Luiza immediately came up with some excuse for Juliana.

Jorge bit his lip, bowed deeply and in a slightly unsteady voice, said:

'Oh, do forgive me! I was forgetting that the person of Juliana is sacred! I'll go and fetch some water myself!'

This time, it was Luiza's turn to get angry; if he was always going to be making sarcastic comments, then it would be best to dismiss the woman once and for all! Did he really imagine that she was so enamoured of Juliana? She only kept her on because she was a good maid. But if she was becoming the cause of bad moods and arguments, if he really hated her that much, then she should go! His constant irony was getting on her nerves.

Jorge said nothing

Luiza did not sleep that night, thinking that this simply could not go on. She had had enough! Putting up with the woman and with her tyrannical demands and having to listen to Jorge's endless jibes and allusions, no, it was too much. Enough was enough! He was starting to suspect, the bomb was about to explode! Right, then, she herself would light the touch paper! She would dismiss Juliana. And if Juliana showed Jorge the letters, that would be that! And if he put her in a convent or left her, fine! She would suffer and die! Anything was better than this ghastly, grotesque, banal, drip-by-drip martyrdom!

'What's wrong?' asked Jorge, half-asleep, sensing that she was awake.

'I can't sleep.'

'Poor thing! Count to one hundred and fifty backwards!' And he turned over and snuggled down under the blankets again.

The next day, Jorge had got up early. He had arranged to meet Alonso, the Spanish mine-owner, and to have dinner with him at the Hotel Gibraltar. He got dressed, went into the dining room – it was ten o'clock by then – and returned to announce to Luiza, with a low bow and weighing every word, that the table was not yet laid, that the tea cups from the night before had not been washed and that Dona Juliana, the illustrious Senhora Dona Juliana, had gone out for her walk!

'I asked her last night to go to the shoemaker's for me,' said Luiza, who was putting on her peignoir.

'Oh, forgive me!' broke in Jorge unctuously. 'I was forgetting yet again that we're dealing here with your lady and mistress, Juliana! Forgive me!'

Luiza immediately said:

'No, you're right. This really can't go on.'

She went straight up to the kitchen and said desperately:

'Why didn't you lay the table, Joana, since Juliana has gone out?'

But the girl had not heard Senhora Juliana go out! She had assumed she was downstairs in the drawing room. And now that the mistress had taken to doing everything herself . . .

When Joana brought the breakfast in shortly afterwards, Jorge came and sat down at the table, nervously fiddling with his moustache. He got up twice, smiling silently, to fetch a spoon, then the sugar bowl . . . Luiza saw his jaw muscles twitching; she was so distraught, she could barely eat; when she lifted the cup to her lips, it trembled in her hand; eyes downcast, she kept shooting furtive glances at Jorge, whose silence was a torment to her.

'You mentioned yesterday that you were dining out tonight . . .'

'Yes,' he said sharply, and added: 'Thank God!'

'You're in a good mood,' she muttered.

'As you see!'

Luiza turned pale and put down her knife and fork; she picked up the newspaper to disguise the tears filling her eyes, but the letters blurred before her and she could feel her heart pounding. Suddenly the doorbell rang. It was probably Juliana!

Jorge, who was about to get up, said at once:

'That must be the lady herself. I have a few words to say to her.'

And he remained standing by the table, slowly sharpening a toothpick with his knife.

Luiza too got unsteadily to her feet:

'I'll talk to her . . .'

Jorge grasped her arm and said calmly:

'No, let her come in. Let me enjoy myself!'

Luiza fell back in her chair, her face deathly pale.

Juliana's heels came clicking down the corridor. Jorge was still calmly sharpening his toothpick.

Luiza turned to him and said pleadingly, wringing her hands:

'Please don't say anything to her!'

He stared at her in amazement:

'Why ever not?'

At that moment, Juliana drew back the door curtain.

'What do you mean by going out without getting everything ready first?' said Luiza, rising to her feet.

Juliana, who had entered smiling, stood stock still in the doorway; despite her natural pallor, a faint wave of blood spread over her features.

'Don't ever let such a thing happen again, all right? Your duty in the morning is to be in the house.' But Juliana fixed her with a terrible look that silenced her. Luiza picked up the teapot with trembling hands. 'Put some more hot water in here.'

Juliana did not move.

'Didn't you hear?' roared Jorge. And he brought his fist down so hard on the table that the cups and plates jumped.

'Jorge!' cried Luiza, grabbing his arm.

But Juliana had run out of the room.

'I want her out of this house now!' exclaimed Jorge. 'Pay her whatever she's owed and get rid of her. I've had enough. I can't take another day of this. If I see her again, I'll tear her to pieces. It's my turn now!'

He stormed out to get his overcoat and, before going out, returned to the dining room:

'She's to leave today, do you hear! She's not to spend another hour in this house! I've put up with her for two weeks now and I've had enough. I want her out of this house!'

Luiza went into her room barely able to stand. She was lost! She was lost! A multitude of mad, immoderate ideas whirled about in her head like a pile of dead leaves whipped up by the wind: she wanted to run away and, at night, throw herself in the river; she regretted not having given in to Castro . . . She could suddenly imagine Jorge opening the letters that Juliana would hand to him and reading the words: 'My beloved Bazilio!' Then a debilitating wave of cowardice flooded her soul. She ran to Juliana's room. She would beg her to forgive her, beg her to stay and continue to torment her. And what about Jorge? She would tell him that Juliana had wept and knelt before her! She would lie, she would smother him with kisses. She was young and pretty and passionate; she would convince him!

Juliana was not in her room. Luiza went up to the kitchen; Juliana was sitting there, dumb with rage, her eyes flashing, her arms tightly folded. As soon as she saw Luiza, she leapt to her feet and shook her fist at her, shouting:

'The next time you speak to me like that, all hell will break loose!'

'Be quiet, you wicked woman!' yelled Luiza.

'Don't you tell me to be quiet, you whore!'

Joana ran over to her and slapped her so hard across the face that Juliana fell to her knees with a groan.

'For heaven's sake, woman!' Luiza screamed, hurling herself on Joana and grabbing her by both arms.

Juliana, too astonished to speak, fled.

'Joana, how could you? How awful!' Luiza was saying, clutching her hands to her head.

'I'll kill her!' the girl was saying through clenched teeth, her eyes blazing. 'I'll kill her!'

Luiza, her face white as chalk, was mechanically circling the kitchen table, saying over and over, trembling as she did:

'What have you done, woman? What have you done?'

Joana, still in the grip of rage, her face blotched with red, was clattering furiously about amongst the pans.

'If she says one word to me, one word, I'll kill her, the cow!'

Luiza went down to her room. Juliana ambushed her in the corridor, her false hair askew, the scarlet imprint of Joana's hand still on her furious face.

'Either that wretch leaves this house,' she bawled, 'or I'll go and sit myself down on those steps and as soon as your husband comes home, I'll show him those letters!'

'Show them to him, then, do what you like!' said Luiza walking straight past her, without even looking at her.

Despair and hatred had decided her. It was best to finish it once and for all!

She was filled then by a sense of painful relief at seeing an end to her long torment! It had been going on for months now. Thinking about what she had done and what she had suffered, the infamies in which she had become enmired and the humiliations she had endured, she felt sick of herself and disgusted with life. It seemed to her that she had been besmirched and spurned, that she had no pride and no pure feelings left, that everything about her, body and soul, was as begrimed as a rag trampled by the crowd into the mud. It was not worth fighting for such a miserable life. The convent would be a purification and death an even greater one. And where was he, the man who had disgraced her? In Paris, twirling his moustaches, making jokes, riding his horses, sleeping with other women! And she would die a stupid death here in Lisbon. And to think she had written to him asking him to save her and he had not even replied; he did not deem her worth even the price of a stamp! And the things he had said to her in that carriage, about how he would devote his life to her, how he would be happy just to be near her! The wretch! He probably already had his return ticket in his pocket! As long as she was the woman who blithely turned up each day, undid her bodice and showed him her lovely breasts, everything was fine. But as soon as she had a problem over which she wept and suffered . . . Oh, no, no, thank you! As long as you are a beautiful creature who gives me great pleasure, I'll give you anything you want, but as soon as you become a wounded animal in need of consolation or perhaps a few hundred *mil-réis*, then it's goodbye, I'm catching the next boat! How stupid life was! It was fortunate really that she was leaving it.

She went and leaned at the window. It was a lovely day of clear blue skies. The sun cast great splashes of pale gold on the white walls and on the streets, and there was a velvety softness about the air. Senhor Paula, in his carpet slippers, was warming himself in the sun at the door of the tobacconist's. Confronted by that sweet winter's day, her heart softened. Everyone was happy on that rosy morning, only she, poor thing, was suffering! And she stood watching, tears in her eyes, as if immersed in vague thoughts of the past. Suddenly she saw Juliana cross the street and go round the corner, then, shortly afterwards, return with a burly old man carrying a sack over his shoulder.

'She's leaving!' thought Luiza. 'She's having someone take her trunks away! And then what? She'll send the letters to Jorge or even hand them to him herself at the front door. Oh God!' She could almost see Jorge coming into her room, ashen-faced, the letters in his hand!

She was gripped by a kind of mad terror: she did not want to lose her husband, her Jorge, her love, her house, her man! A very female revulsion at the thought of widowhood took hold of her: going to rot in a convent when she was only twenty-five. No, she would not!

She went straight up to Juliana's room.

'Have you come to make sure I'm not stealing anything?' Juliana shouted angrily.

Underclothes were scattered about the bed and, on the floor stood pairs of boots wrapped in old newspapers.

'I've still got four chemises, two pairs of knickers, three pairs of stockings and six pairs of cuffs in the laundry. There's the list. And I want my money!'

'Listen, Juliana, don't go,' Luiza said, but her voice faltered, and the tears sprang into her eyes.

Juliana stood looking triumphantly down her nose at her, a patent leather boot in each hand.

'Give that wretch her marching orders, and I'll say nothing more!' And in a shrill voice, clapping together the soles of the boots, she added: 'Then it will be nice and peaceful again, just like it was before.'

Her eyes shone with an extraordinary happiness. She was having her revenge! She had made her mistress cry! She had driven out the other maid and would not now lose her comforts!

'Put the wretch out in the street!'

Luiza bowed her shoulders and went slowly up to the kitchen; the steps seemed to her immense, unending. She slumped down on a bench and, wiping her eyes, said:

'Come here, Joana, listen to me, you can't go on working here.'

The girl stared at her, horrified.

'Juliana didn't mean what she said. She's been crying, she's apologised. She's the oldest servant here. Your master is very fond of her . . .'

'You mean you're sending me away? You're actually sending me away?'

Luiza said again in a low, embarrassed voice:

'She didn't mean it, she's asked my forgiveness.'

'But I did it to defend you, madam!' exclaimed the girl, flinging her arms wide in a gesture of pained amazement.

Luiza began to feel indignant and, impatient to be done, she said:

'Look, Joana, let's not discuss it further. I'm the mistress of the house . . . I'll go and sort out what you're owed.'

'What kind of payment is that!' cried Joana in despair. Then she resolutely stamped her foot. 'We'll see what the master has to say about this! I'll tell him everything. I'll tell him exactly what happened! You're wrong, madam!'

Luiza stared at her stupidly. Now it was Joana! This girl stubbornly insisting on justice would be the new bringer of disaster. It was too much! A supernatural fear came upon her, as if her very conscience had taken fright, and, pressing the palms of her hands to her temples, she cried:

'Dear God, haven't I been punished enough!'

Then, as if she had suddenly taken leave of her senses, she grabbed Joana by the arms and, with her face very close to hers, said:

'Joana, for the love of God, go! Don't say anything! Just leave!' And losing all restraint, she went down on her knees to the cook, sobbing: 'By Christ's five wounds, Joana, dear Joana, please go! I'm begging you, Joana. For God's sake, go!'

Shocked, the girl broke into strident crying.

'Yes, I'll go, madam . . . dear madam, yes, I'll go!'

'Yes, Joana, yes! I'll give you something. You'll see . . . Don't cry . . . Wait . . .' She ran down to her room, removed her savings of two *libras* from the drawer and bounded back up the stairs, where she pressed the money into Joana's hand, saying quietly:

'Make up a bundle of your things, and I'll send on your trunk to you tomorrow.'

'Yes, madam,' sobbed the grief-stricken girl, her nose running. 'Yes, yes, dear madam!'

Luiza went back to her room where she fell face down on the chaise longue, sobbing convulsively, wanting to die, praying fearfully for God's pity!

But Juliana's harsh voice said brusquely from the door:

'So what's happening, then?'

'Joana is leaving. What more do you want?'

'I want her out now!' said Juliana imperiously. 'I can make dinner, at least for today.'

Luiza's anger dried her tears.

Juliana said:

'Now you listen to me!'

Her tone was so insulting that Luiza sat up as if wounded.

And Juliana stood over her, wagging her finger:

'From now on, you'd better treat me right, otherwise the cat is out of the bag.'

With that, she turned on her heels and click-clacked out of the room.

Luiza looked around her, as if a thunderbolt had entered the room; but everything was utterly still and as it should be; not a fold in the curtains had moved, and the two little porcelain shepherd boys on the dressing table were smiling their usual smug smile.

She threw off her peignoir, put on a dress without bothering to do up the bodice, put a loose winter jacket over the top, pinned a hat on her dishevelled hair and almost ran down the street, catching her feet in her skirts.

Senhor Paula leaped out into the middle of the road to watch her; seeing her stop outside Sebastião's door, he went in to the tobacconist's to say:

'Something's up at the Engineer's house!'

And he planted himself at the door, his eyes fixed on the open windows where the green cotton blinds hung in unmoving folds.

'Is Senhor Sebastião at home?' Luiza asked the freckled little girl who ran to open the door.

And she walked down the corridor.

'He's in the drawing room,' said the girl.

Luiza went up the stairs; she could hear the sound of a piano; she flung open the door, ran over to him, her hands pressed to her breast, and said in a faint, fearful voice:

'Sebastião, I wrote a letter to a man and Juliana stole it from me. I don't know what to do!'

He got slowly to his feet, looking shocked and very pale; he saw her tear-stained face, her hat all awry, the look of distress in her eyes.

'What?' he said. 'What did you say?'

'I wrote a letter to my cousin,' she said, her eyes fixed anxiously on him, 'the woman stole the letter from me. . . . I don't know what to do.'

She turned very white and her eyes closed.

Sebastião caught her and led her, half-fainting, over to the yellow damask sofa. And then he stood there, looking even whiter than she was, his hands in the pockets of his blue double-breasted jacket, not moving, too stunned to speak.

Suddenly he ran out of the room and returned with a glass of water which he sprinkled on her face. She opened her eyes, felt around her with her hands, stared at him in horror, then she hunched over the arm of the sofa, her face in her hands, and burst into hysterical crying.

Her hat had fallen off. Sebastião picked it up, gently dusted off the flowers and placed it carefully on top of the table; then he tiptoed across to her and bent over her.

'There, there!' he murmured. And his hands trembled like leaves as he touched her lightly on the arm.

He tried to get her to drink some water to calm her down, but she pushed the glass away with her hand, sat up slowly on the sofa, wiping her eyes and blowing her nose, still sobbing loudly.

'Forgive me, Sebastião, forgive me,' she said. Then she took a sip of water and sat, exhausted, her hands limp in her lap; and her tears continued to fall silently, ceaselessly, one by one.

Sebastião went and closed the door, then returning to her, he said gently:

'Now, tell me what happened.'

She raised her tearful face to him, a febrile light in her eyes; she looked at him for a moment, then hung her head in shame:

'It's awful, Sebastião, it's so shameful!' she muttered.

'Don't upset yourself so!'

He sat down next to her and said in a quiet, solemn voice:

'If there's anything I can do for you, anything at all, here I am.'

'Oh, Sebastião!' she cried in humble gratitude. 'Believe me, I have been well and truly punished. I have suffered so much, Sebastião!'

She sat for a moment, staring at the floor; then she gripped his arm hard, and the words flowed fast and abundant, like pent-up water gushing forth.

'She stole the letter from me, I don't know how, I suppose I wasn't careful enough. At first, she asked me for six hundred *mil réis*, then began the torment . . . I had to give her dresses, clothes, everything. She moved rooms, used my finest sheets, made herself mistress of the house. I'm the one who does all the housework! She threatens me every day. She's a monster. I've tried everything, kind words, kind gestures . . . But where can I get that amount of money? She could see that . . . Oh, I have suffered so much. People keep telling me I'm thinner, even you noticed . . . My life is an inferno. If Jorge ever found out! That wretch wanted to tell him everything today! And I work like a slave. First thing in the morning, I'm cleaning and sweeping. Sometimes I have to wash the breakfast cups. Please, Sebastião, have pity on me! I have no one else in the world to turn to!'

And she began weeping again, covering her face with her hands.

Sebastião said nothing, biting his lip; two tears rolled down his cheeks into his beard. Getting slowly to his feet, he said:

'But, my dear lady, why ever didn't you tell me about this earlier?'

'Oh, Sebastião, if only I had! There was one occasion when I was going to tell you, but I just couldn't bring myself to . . .'

'Well, you should have.'

'This morning, Jorge wanted to throw her out. He gets annoyed with her, he notices how badly she does the housework, but he doesn't suspect anything, Sebastião!' And she looked away, blushing scarlet. 'He tells me off sometimes because I seem so fond of her. But this morning, he got angry and told her to leave. As soon as he had gone, she burst into my room like a fury and insulted me . . .'

'Good heavens!' muttered Sebastião in amazement, putting his hand to his head.

'Believe it or not, Sebastião, I'm the one who empties out the chamber pots.'

'The wretch deserves to die!' he cried, stamping his foot.

He took a few slow, ponderous steps about the room, his hands in his pockets, his broad shoulders bent. He sat down again beside her and, shyly touching her arm, said very softly:

'We must get the letters back from her.'

'But how?'

Sebastião scratched his beard and head.

'There must be a way,' he said at last.

She grasped his hand:

'Oh, Sebastião, if only we could.'

'There must be a way.'

He sat for a moment pondering, and then in his grave voice, he said:

'I'll talk to her. It will have to be when she's alone in the house. You could go to the theatre tonight . . .'

He got up slowly and went to get the newspaper, spread it out on the table and studied the advertisements.

'You could go to the Teatro de São Carlos, which finishes quite late. They're doing *Faust* . . . You could go and see *Faust*.'

'We could go and see *Faust*,' Luiza repeated with a sigh.

And as they sat close together at one end of the sofa, Sebastião laid out a plan to her in whispered words which she eagerly devoured.

She must write to Dona Felicidade asking her to go with her to the theatre. Then she must send a note to Jorge, telling him that they would come and pick him up at the Hotel Gibraltar. And what about Joana? Joana had left the house. Good. So, at nine o'clock, Juliana would be alone.

'You see how it all works out,' he said, smiling.

It was true. But would Juliana give Sebastião the letters?

Sebastião again scratched his beard and head.

'She'll have to,' he said.

Luiza was looking at him almost tenderly; she seemed to see a lofty moral beauty in his honest face. Standing before him, she asked in a melancholy voice:

'And you'll do this for me, Sebastião, for me, when I've been such a bad woman . . .'

Sebastião blushed and replied with a shrug:

'There are no bad women, my dear lady, only bad men.'

Then he added:

'I'll reserve you a box, a good one right near the stage, eh?'

He smiled reassuringly. She put on her hat and pulled down her veil, still uttering the occasional heartfelt sob.

In the corridor they met Sebastião's old nursemaid, Tia Joana, her arms flung wide in welcome; she showered kisses on Luiza; what a miracle to see her there! And how pretty she was! The flower of the neighbourhood!

'All right, Tia Joana, that's enough!' said Sebastião, gently pushing her away.

There was no need for him to be so bossy! He had had her to himself for more than half an hour, now she wanted a little time with her too! He should get himself a nice wife like her! A decent young woman! A lily!

Luiza blushed with embarrassment.

And how was Senhor Jorge? What was he up to? She never saw hide nor hair of him nowadays. And how was Dona Felicidade?

'Now that's enough, Tia Joana!' said Sebastião impatiently.

'Don't be in such a hurry! Heavens, no one's going to eat the girl!'

Luiza smiled; then she suddenly remembered that she had no one to carry her messages to Dona Felicidade and to Jorge at the hotel.

Sebastião showed her into his study downstairs; if she wrote the notes, he would send them off; he chose the paper for her and even dipped the pen in the ink, more eager to help and more tender with her now that he knew of her unhappiness. Luiza wrote the note to Jorge, then, despite her anxieties, she remembered with horror a particular low-cut green dress favoured by Dona Felicidade and added a postscript on the note to her: 'I would suggest wearing black and nothing too elaborate. No decolletages and no bright colours.'

When she arrived home, she saw a porter coming out, carrying Joana's small bundle of belongings. Once in the corridor, she heard Joana's gruff voice on the kitchen stairs, addressing someone higher up in menacing tones:

'If I ever catch you again, I'll murder you, you wretch!'

'Oh, yes,' sneered Juliana from above. 'Get out in the street where you belong!'

Luiza listened, biting her lip. What had her house become? A common market? An inn?

'If ever I get my hands on you . . .' Joana was snarling as she came down the stairs.

'Get out, you filthy pig!' screamed Juliana.

Luiza called Joana over.

'Don't go looking for another job just yet, but come back here the day after tomorrow,' she said quietly.

Upstairs, Juliana was stridently, joyfully singing 'O beloved letter'.

Shortly afterwards, she came downstairs to announce tartly that 'dinner was on the table'.

Luiza did not respond. She waited until Juliana had gone back up to the kitchen, then ran into the dining room from where she fetched some bread, jam and a knife which she took into her room, and there she 'dined', on one corner of a small table.

At six o'clock, a carriage stopped outside the door. It must be Sebastião! She herself tiptoed to the front door and opened it. It was him, cheerful and red-faced, his hat in his hand; he had brought her the key to box number 18 at the theatre.

'And this . . .'

It was a bunch of red camellias, surrounded by double violets.

'Oh, Sebastião!' she murmured, touched and grateful.

'And have you got a carriage?'

'No.'

'I'll send one. Shall we say eight o'clock?'

And he went back down the stairs, happy to be of service. She followed him with eyes that grew wet with tears. She went to her bedroom window to watch him leave. 'What a wonderful man!' she was thinking. And she sniffed the violets, turning the bouquet round and round in her hands, taking pleasure in his protection and his kindness.

Someone rapped at the door.

'Aren't you having any supper?' asked Juliana impatiently.

'No.'

'Good, all the more for me!'

Dona Felicidade arrived shortly before eight o'clock. Luiza was relieved to see that she was wearing a high-necked black dress and her emerald brooch.

'And what, pray, is the reason for this profligate behaviour?' Dona Felicidade said jovially.

It was just a whim of hers! Jorge was dining out and she had suddenly felt very alone. And then she had had an irresistible urge to go to the theatre. They were to pick Jorge up at the Hotel Gibraltar.

'I had only just finished dinner when I got your note! I was quite taken aback, I can tell you, and I very nearly didn't come,' she said, sitting down, contentedly patting the folds of her dress. 'The thought of putting my corsets on after dinner . . . Fortunately, though, I had hardly eaten a thing!'

She asked what they were going to see. *Faust*! Oh, excellent. What side of the theatre was their box on? Number eighteen. What a shame, they wouldn't be able to see the royal family from there . . . Still, that night out at the theatre had come as a most unexpected surprise. Tightly corseted, eyes shining, she walked past the dressing table, shooting sideways glances at herself in the mirror, smoothing her hair and adjusting her bracelets.

A carriage stopped at the door.

'It's here!' she said, beaming.

Luiza, drawing on her gloves, her cloak already on, was looking around her, her heart beating fast; there was a febrile gleam in her eyes. Had she got everything? asked Dona Felicidade. The key to the box? A handkerchief?

'Oh, my bouquet!' cried Luiza.

Juliana was astonished when she saw Luiza all dressed up to go to the theatre. She silently lighted their way, then insolently slammed the front door shut.

'Shameless hussy!' she growled.

The carriage was already moving off when Dona Felicidade shouted and banged on the windows.

'Wait, stop! Oh, what a bore! I've forgotten my fan! I can't go without my fan! Coachman, stop!'

'It's getting late, my dear, I'll lend you mine. Here you are!' said Luiza impatiently.

All these agitations were playing havoc with Dona Felicidade's constrained digestion; luckily, as she herself said, she was at least able to bring up some wind. Yes, blessings upon God and the Virgin Mary, she was at least able to bring up a little wind!

The ride through the Chiado cheered her immensely. Dark, gesticulating knots of people stood silhouetted against the brightly lit doors of the Casa Havanesa; carriages drove past the Picadeiro with a flash of magnificent lanterns that lit up the white edges of the servants' jackets. Dona Felicidade, her rapt face gazing out of the window, was enjoying the winter air and the brilliant gaslight in the shopwindows; and it was with great satisfaction that she saw the Hotel Gibraltar doorkeeper in his scarlet breeches approach, cap in hand.

They asked for Jorge.

And in silence they scrutinised the elegant staircase, softly lit by the globe-shaped gaslamps. Dona Felicidade, agog to know what hotel life was like, spotted the ironing maid going in carrying a basket of laundry; then a lady, whom, she thought, looked slightly crazy, came down the stairs, dressed for a party, revealing feet shod in smooth, white satin; and she smiled to see the men brushing past their carriage and peering greedily in.

'They're dying to know who we are.'

Luiza said nothing, but clutched her bouquet. At last, Jorge appeared at the top of the stairs, deep in conversation with a very thin man, who wore his hat set at a jaunty angle, had his hands in the pockets of his narrow trousers and a huge cigar in one corner of his mouth. They paused, gesturing and talking softly. Finally, the man shook Jorge's hand, whispered something in his ear, creased up in silent laughter, clapped him on the shoulder, gravely forced another cigar on him, then, setting his hat at a still jauntier angle, went off to talk to the doorkeeper.

Jorge ran over to the carriage door, laughing:

'What extravagance! Theatre tickets, carriages ... I demand a divorce!'

He seemed to be in an excellent mood. He was only sorry that he was not properly dressed. He would sit at the back of the box. And in order not to crease the ladies' dresses, he climbed up beside the driver.

371

# XIII

It was gone eight o'clock when the carriage stopped outside the Teatro de São Carlos. A young lad with a hacking cough, his jacket fastened over his chest with a pin, ran to open the carriage door; and Dona Felicidade smiled contentedly at the sound of her silk train as it swished along the worn carpet in the corridor leading to the boxes.

The curtain was already up. On the dimly lit stage was the classic scene of the alchemist's cell; wrapped in a monastic robe sat Faust, a palsied old man with a superabundance of grizzled beard, singing of his disillusion with the sciences and, as he did so, placing on his heart a hand on which glittered a diamond ring. A vague smell of gas wafted through the theatre. Here and there people coughed and loudly cleared their throat. There were few people as yet. Most were just arriving.

In order to make themselves comfortable in the box, Dona Felicidade and Luiza were whispering and exchanging pleading glances and small indignant gestures of refusal.

'Oh, please, Dona Felicidade!'

'No, no, I'm fine where I am . . .'

'No, really, I can't allow you to sit there . . .'

In the end, Dona Felicidade sat at the front of the box, pushing out her chest. Luiza sat behind her, drawing on her gloves, while Jorge was trying to sort out the various coats and capes, and was infuriated because the same hat had already fallen onto the floor twice in succession.

'Have you got a foot stool, Dona Felicidade?'

'Yes, thank you, it's here somewhere.' And she felt around with her feet. 'What a shame we can't see the royal family!'

The subscribers' boxes were filling up with gleaming white shirtfronts and hideously tall coiffures bulked out with false topknots. Men were slowly taking their seats with weary nonchalance, carefully smoothing their hair. People were talking quietly to each other. There were restless murmurings amongst the young men in double-breasted jackets at the back of the auditorium; and at the entrance to the stalls, beneath the gallery, some pseudo-military splendour was provided by the lustrous braid on the uniforms of the municipal guards, the elaborate helmets of the police and the glinting hilts of sabres.

However, the orchestra brass was now blasting out harsh, metallic chords, suggestive of some supernatural horror; Faust was trembling like a bush in the breeze; there was the sudden clamour of tin sheets being shaken; the scarlet figure of Mephistopheles appeared at the back, stepping out with the air of a mountebank, eyebrows raised, a neat, insolent little beard, altogether *un bel cavalier*; and while he greeted the doctor in his powerful voice, the two red feathers on his hat waggled mockingly.

Luiza shifted her chair forwards, and, at this noise, heads below turned languidly to look; since she was clearly very pretty, various pairs of eyes examined her closely; embarrassed, she fixed her eyes gravely on the stage, where, behind wafting layers of veils, intended to give the impression of a vision, Marguerite appeared, dressed all in white and spinning flax; in the crude glare of the electric light, she looked white as plaster, and Dona Felicidade thought her as lovely as a saint!

The vision disappeared to the sound of quivering violins. And after singing an aria, Faust, who had remained motionless at the back of the stage, grappled for a moment with his monk's habit and his beard, and emerged as a plump young man, all dressed in lilac, his face heavily caked with powder, and primping his curly hair. The lights went up; the music grew jolly and expansive; Mephistopheles grabbed hold of Faust and eagerly dragged him across the stage. The curtain fell rapidly.

There was a slow rumble as the audience got to its feet. Dona Felicidade, slightly troubled by indigestion, was fanning herself. She and Luiza studied the families present and the costumes of various ladies, and, smiling, agreed that it was all 'terribly grand'.

The people in the boxes were talking soberly; here and

there, a jewel glittered, or the light lent a crow-black sheen to the dark heads of hair, which were adorned, perhaps, with a white camellia or the metal glint of a comb; the round lenses of opera glasses moved slowly back and forth, pricked with points of light.

In the stalls, men leaned back languidly on the now empty benches, eyeing the ladies; others stood in silence, stroking their gloves; ageing dilettanti with silk handkerchiefs were taking snuff and arguing; Dona Felicidade was particularly intrigued by two Spanish women in green, who sat stiffly in the balcony, their bordello bodies fixed in exaggeratedly chaste poses.

A skinny, dandified colleague of Jorge's came into their box; he seemed very excited about something and asked if they had heard the latest great scandal. No, they hadn't! And the man, gesturing animatedly with small hands sheathed in greenish gloves, told them that the wife of Palma, the member of parliament, had run away!

'Gone abroad you mean?'

'Oh, no!' And the man's voice gave a triumphant squeak. That was the best part! She had moved in with a Spaniard who lived opposite! Wasn't it divine? That aside, however, and his voice grew serious now, he thought the bass was really excellent!

Then having smiled and peered through his opera glasses, he fell silent, exhausted by his own gossip, occasionally patting Jorge's knee and now and then uttering a familiar 'Yes, indeed!' or a friendly 'So, what have you been up to?'

The interval bell was softly ringing. The man tiptoed out. And the curtain slowly rose to reveal a fair in full swing, lit by a harsh, white light. On the backcloth were the white walls of battlemented houses, perched on some wine-growing slope of the Rhine valley. On an inn sign, sitting astride a barrel, a lazy, potbellied King Cambrinus was roaring with laughter and raising a vast, German beer mug. And students, Jews, soldiers, and maidens in brightly coloured clothes moved about in automaton fashion to the steady beat of a festive tune.

The waltz developed languidly – a thread of a melody, in

gentle, swaying, fleeting spirals; Luiza followed the dancers' small feet, the muscular legs spinning around the stage; and the full, short skirts looked like an ever-quickening blur of revolving chambray discs.

'How lovely!' Luiza murmured, a look of pleasure on her face.

'Gorgeous,' agreed Dona Felicidade, rolling her eyes.

Luiza found certain delicate high notes on the piccolo particularly enchanting; and everything – her home, Juliana and her vile behaviour – seemed to recede into the depths of a long-forgotten night.

However, the jovial Devil came threading his way through the various groups, and then, with sweeping, rapacious gestures, he launched into the aria, 'The Golden Calf'. His forthright voice coolly affirmed the power of money; the music was full of the bright, tinkling sounds of someone frenziedly sifting through treasures; and the high, final notes were as short and sharp as triumphant hammerblows minting the divine gold!

Then Luiza noticed that Dona Felicidade seemed agitated; and following her dark, suddenly eager gaze, she spotted in the cheaper seats the polished pate of Councillor Acácio, who bowed and indicated with a generous wave of his open hand that he would come up and see them soon.

He did so as soon as the curtain went down and immediately congratulated them on choosing this particular night; it was one of the better operas and absolutely all the best people were there. He regretted having missed the first act, not that he cared much for the music, but he did appreciate its philosophical qualities. And taking Luiza's opera glasses from her, he went on to tell them who was who in the various boxes, he listed titles, identified heiresses, named members of parliament, pointed out the literati. Oh, he knew the theatre well! He had been a regular visitor for eighteen years!

Dona Felicidade, pink-cheeked, gazed at him admiringly. The Councillor only regretted that they could not see the royal box from there: the queen, as always, was looking adorable.

Really? What was she wearing?

She was in velvet. He wasn't sure whether purple or dark blue. He would find out and come back and tell her.

But when the curtain rose, he remained seated behind Luiza and immediately began explaining how that woman there (Siebel, picking flowers in Marguerite's garden), even though she was only playing a supporting role, earned five hundred *mil réis* a month . . .

'But despite such salaries, they nearly always die in poverty,' he said reprovingly. 'Well, it's the life of vice they lead, the late-night suppers, the orgies, the risky business ventures . . .'

The garden gate opened and Marguerite, dressed like a virgin, her hair in two long blonde plaits, walked slowly onto the stage, pulling the petals off a daisy as she did so. She was deep in thought, talking to herself, musing on her love: the sweet creature feels about her the heavy atmosphere and wishes that her mother might come back to her.

As Marguerite sang the melancholy ballad of the King of Thule, Luiza's eyes filled with melancholy; the melody evoked for her a pale country bathed in cold moonlight, beside a mournful sea, somewhere in the far north, a land of spiritual loves or of aristocratic sadnesses brooded over on a terrace, in a shady garden . . .

The Councillor, however, urged them to pay attention:

'This is it! Listen. This is the high point.'

The girl swayed as she knelt before the casket of jewels, her voice quavering; she clutched the necklace ecstatically to her; she put on the earrings with an exaggerated show of coquetry; and from her wide open mouth – to a murmur of bourgeois approval – came a series of shrill, crystalline trills.

The Councillor said discreetly:

'Oh, bravo! Bravo!'

He declared excitedly that this was the finest part of the opera, the one that really put the sopranos to the test.

Dona Felicidade was almost afraid that the singer might burst something in her throat. She was concerned too about the jewels. Were they false? Were they hers?

'It's to tempt her, isn't it?'

'It's a German play,' the Councillor told her in a low voice.

But Mephistopheles was luring the good Dame Martha away; Faust and Marguerite disappeared into the conspiring shadows of the aphrodisiac garden, and the Councillor remarked that, if truth be told, the whole of that act really was a touch lewd.

Dona Felicidade murmured, half-censorious, half-ecstatic:

'I bet you've had your fair share of such scenes, you rascal!'

The Councillor stared at her indignantly:

'Certainly not, madam! What, bring dishonour to the very bosom of a family!'

Luiza smiled and said 'Sh!' She was interested now. It had grown dark; a beam of electric light filled the garden with vague, bluish moonlight, beneath which the rounded shapes of trees stood out against an inky blackness; and Faust and Marguerite, faint with passion, their arms about each other, sang their duet in dying tones; a mournful music rose up from the orchestra, music of a delicate, modern sensuality, but tinged with an almost religious devotion; the tenor launched into his song with a languid sway of his hips, his hand pressed to his chest, his eyes clouded with tears; soaring away from the languorous bowing of the cellos, his song rose up to the stars:

> Beneath the pale moonlight
> Let me gaze upon your face . . .

Luiza's heart beat faster, for she had suddenly had a vision of herself sitting on the sofa in her drawing room, still breathless and sobbing after the act of adultery, and of Bazilio, cigar in mouth, distractedly picking out the tune of that aria on the piano. 'Beneath the pale moonlight, let me gaze upon your face . . .' All her misery flowed from that night. And suddenly, like long, muffling, funereal veils, memories of Juliana, the house and Sebastião came to darken her soul.

She looked at the clock. It was ten. What would be happening there now?

'Are you feeling unwell?' asked Jorge.

'A little.'

377

Marguerite, in a state of voluptuous languor, was leaning on her windowsill. Faust ran to her. They embraced. And amidst the Devil's guffaws and the sawing violins, the curtain fell, providing a modest ellipsis.

Dona Felicidade, face ablaze, asked for some water. Jorge hurried to her aid; would she like a cake, a sorbet perhaps? The excellent lady hesitated: she liked the very chic idea of eating a sorbet, but was constrained by her terror of getting the colic. She joined Luiza at the rear of the box and sat looking at the audience, feeling vaguely weary; there was a slow, low whispering; people yawned discreetly; and the cigarette smoke, wafting in from outside, created a barely perceptible mist that filled the room and drifted up to the chandelier, slightly dimming the lights. When Jorge left the box, the Councillor went with him; he was going upstairs to have a dish of jelly.

'That's my supper on the nights when I come to the theatre,' he said.

He returned shortly afterwards, dabbing his lips with a silk handkerchief, to rejoin Jorge, who was waiting on the landing near the entrance to the stalls, smoking a cigarette.

'Look at that, Councillor,' he said indignantly, indicating the wall, 'isn't it shocking!'

Someone had drawn huge obscene figures on the white-washed wall with the blackened butt of a cigar; and some other prudent person, a stickler for clarity, had written underneath, in a fine italic hand, the correct sexual terminology.

Disgusted, Jorge said:

'But ladies walk past here! They might see this and read what's written! It's the kind of thing one only gets in Portugal!'

The Councillor said:

'The authorities should definitely intervene . . .' Then he added cheerfully: 'But it was probably some young lads who managed to get hold of a cigar. It's a bit of fun really.' And he recalled smilingly: 'On one occasion, the Count de Vila Rica, who really is a most amusing fellow, most amusing, insisted on giving me a cigar butt so that I could do just such a draw-ing . . .' Lowering his voice, he said: 'I taught him a severe lesson, though. I took the cigar . . .'

'And smoked it?'

'No, I used it to write with.'

'What, an obscenity?'

The Councillor drew back and said sternly:

'You know my character, Jorge! Surely you don't imagine that I . . .' He calmed himself. 'No, no, I took the cigar and I wrote in a firm hand: VIRTUE IS ITS OWN REWARD!'

The interval bell was ringing and they returned to their box. Luiza, who was still feeling unwell, preferred not to sit near the front. And so the Councillor gravely took her place, next to Dona Felicidade. It was a moment of exquisite pleas-ure for that plump lady. They were there *together*, like bride and groom! Her abundant bosom rose and fell: she could see them leaving afterwards, arm in arm, getting into a small coupé, drawing up outside the marital home, walking across the bedroom carpet. Beads of sweat appeared on her temples, and seeing the Councillor smiling amiably at her, his bald head gleaming in the gaslight, she felt a profound sense of gratitude for the healer, who, at that very moment, in deepest Galicia, would be sticking pins into a heart of wax!

Then, suddenly, the Councillor clapped his hand to his head, picked up his hat and hurried out. They all exchanged worried looks. Dona Felicidade turned pale. Could he have been taken ill! Dear God! She was already mumbling a prayer.

But he returned at once and said in a triumphant voice:

'It's dark blue!'

They stared at him with wide, uncomprehending eyes.

'Her Majesty's dress! I promised to find out for you and I did!'

And he solemnly resumed his seat, saying to Luiza:

'You really shouldn't hide yourself away in a corner like that, Dona Luiza! At your age! In the flower of your youth, when one sees everything in life through rose-tinted spectacles!'

She smiled. She was feeling very uneasy now. She kept

glancing at the clock. She felt ill; her feet were icy cold and a slight fever was making her head feel heavy. Her thoughts were fixed on the house, on Juliana, on Sebastião, thoughts shot through with premonitions, hopes, fears ... And she watched, without understanding, as a crowd of soldiers dressed in parti-coloured uniforms and bearing obsolete weapons proceeded across the stage, then stopped, marching enthusiastically on the spot, their feet kicking up a faint cloud of dust from the unswept boards. A vigorous chorus of voices rang out: it was the proud, festive march of the German soldiers, celebrating the joy of their victorious forays throughout the lands of wine, their mercenaries' purses clinking with gold coins! And her eyes followed a burly, bearded fellow who, above the square hats of the crossbowmen, was monotonously waving a large square piece of cloth: the flag of the Holy Empire, black, red and gold!

Then a noise erupted from the rear stalls. Loud voices were arguing. 'Quiet, there! Quiet!' someone cried. Journalists sitting in the balcony stood on tiptoe on their straw seats. Four policeman and two municipal guards appeared at the rear door; and then, after a joke and some laughter, they led away a tottering, ashen-faced youth, the left side of his plush jacket all stained with vomit.

Silence fell once more: the backcloth was shaken slightly by the departing elbows of the festive soldiers and populace; and on the deserted stage, with, to the right, the swaying door of a cathedral and, to the left, the sad, low door of a bourgeois house, Valentin, wearing a long goatee, was standing near one side of the stage, passionately kissing a medal. But Luiza was not listening to him. She was thinking with aching heart: 'What will Sebastião be doing now?'

At nine o'clock, in a piercing northeast wind that made the gaslights flicker, Sebastião was making his slow way to the house of a police commissioner, a distant cousin of his, Vicente Azurara. An old servant woman, as wrinkled as a pippin, led him into the study, where the commissioner was nursing a bad cold: he found him with a large cape around his shoulders, his feet wrapped in a blanket, and sipping some hot grog while he read Paul de Kock's *L'Homme aux trois culottes*. As soon as Sebastião came in, he removed his spectacles from his hooked nose and, looking up at him with small, watery eyes, cried:

'I've had this damnable cold for three days now, and I can't seem to shake it off . . .' And he mumbled a few curses, drawing his thin, gnarled hand across his dark, gaunt face made fierce by a large, grizzled moustache.

Sebastião commiserated; he wasn't surprised, given the weather they'd been having! He recommended sulphur water and boiled milk.

'If the cold doesn't go away by tomorrow,' said the commissioner despondently, 'I'll try drinking half a bottle of gin. It'll be a case of kill or cure! Anyway, what's new?'

Sebastião coughed and said that he too had been ill, then, dragging his chair over to his cousin and patting his knee, he said:

'Vicente, if I were to ask you for a policeman to accompany me to a house, just to put the fear of God into someone, to make them give back something they stole, you'd give the order, wouldn't you?'

'What order?' Vicente asked slowly, his head down, his bloodshot eyes trained on Sebastião.

'To come with me and just be there. That's all. It's a bit of a strange case . . . Just to put the fear of God into them . . . You know I'd be useless at that. It's a matter of getting someone to return something they stole . . . without causing too much of a fuss . . .'

'What was it? Clothes? Money?'

The commissioner pensively combed his moustache with long, thin, nicotine-stained fingers.

Sebastião hesitated.

'Yes. Clothes, that kind of thing . . . I simply want to avoid any scandal. You understand . . .'

Vicente muttered gravely, and again fixed him with his eyes:

'You just want the policeman to be there.' He cleared his throat loudly. Then, frowning, he asked: 'It's nothing political, is it?'

'No!' replied Sebastião.

The commissioner tucked the blanket more tightly around his feet and rolled his eyes fiercely:

'And it doesn't involve anyone influential?'

'Of course not!'

'You just want a policeman to be there with you,' Vicente repeated thoughtfully. 'Yes, why not, you're a decent sort of chap. Hand me that file from on top of the chest of drawers.'

He took out a sheet of lined paper and studied it, positioning his spectacles on his nose, and pondered, with one hand clasping his head:

'What about Mendes . . . will he do?'

Sebastião, who did not know who Mendes was, said at once:

'Yes, whoever you like. It's purely for show.'

'Mendes it is then. He's a great big fellow. You can trust him, he used to be in the Municipal Guard.'

He asked Sebastião to hand him the inkstand and he slowly wrote out the order, re-read it twice, crossed the t's, held it to the glass of the oil lamp to dry, then solemnly folded it up:

'You'll find him in the second division!'

'Thank you, Vicente! You're doing me an enormous favour. Thank you. And keep warm, man. And don't forget, sulphur water from the pharmacist in Rua de São Roque, in half a cup of boiled milk. And thank you again. Is there anything I can do for you?'

'No. Just slip Mendes a tip. You can trust him, he used to be in the Municipal Guard, you know.'

And replacing his spectacles, he resumed his reading of *L'Homme aux trois culottes*.

Half an hour later, Sebastião, followed by the strapping figure of Mendes, who marched along in military fashion, arms slightly bent, was heading for Jorge's house. He had no definite plan. He assumed that Juliana, coming face to face, at that time of night, with a policeman and his sabre, would be terrified and, assailed by thoughts of the courtroom and prison and

382

exile to the coast of Africa, would hand over the letters at once, begging for mercy! And what then? He was thinking vaguely of paying her passage to Brazil or giving her five hundred *mil réis* to set herself up somewhere far away, in the provinces . . . He would see. The main thing was to frighten her!

When Juliana opened the door and saw the policeman coming up the stairs behind Sebastião, she did indeed turn pale and exclaim:

'Heavens! Whatever's wrong?'

She was wrapped in a black shawl, and in the shadow cast on the wall by the oil lamp she was holding, it was her monstrous head of false hair that seemed most prominent.

'Senhora Juliana, would you mind bringing a lamp into the drawing room?' Sebastião said calmly.

She looked at the policeman with a troubled, glittering eye.

'What's happened, sir? Heavens! The master and mistress are out. If I'd known, I wouldn't even have opened the door . . . Has something happened? What's all this nonsense about?'

'It's nothing,' said Sebastião, opening the drawing-room door, 'everything's fine.'

He himself struck a match to light one of the candles in the three-branched candlestick, conjuring out of the darkness glimmers of gold from the frames around the engravings, the pale painted face of Jorge's mother, the glancing surface of the mirror . . .

'Do sit down, Senhor Mendes!'

Mendes perched soberly on the edge of the chair, with his hand on his waist, the sabre hanging between his knees.

'This is the person,' said Sebastião, pointing to Juliana, who was standing, stunned, in the doorway.

She drew back, deathly pale.

'Is this some kind of prank, Senhor Sebastião?'

'No, not at all.'

He took the oil lamp from her and, touching her lightly on the arm, said:

'Let's go into the dining room.'

'But what is it? Is it something to do with me? This is ridiculous!'

Sebastião closed the door of the dining room, put the oil lamp down on the table, on which there were still a few crumbs of cheese on a plate and a little wine in a glass, took a few steps, all the while nervously clicking his fingers, then stopped suddenly in front of Juliana:

'Give me the letters you stole from your mistress.'

Juliana made as if to run to the window to call for help.

Sebastião seized her by the arm and forced her to sit down on a chair.

'There's no point calling for help, the police are already here. Now give me those letters or it's prison for you!'

Juliana had a sudden vision of a dark prison cell, a bowl of gruel, a mattress on the cold flagstones . . .

'But what have I done?' she stammered. 'W-what have I done?'

'You stole those letters. Now give them to me, hurry up.'

Juliana was sitting on the edge of the chair, desperately clasping and unclasping her hands, and muttering through clenched teeth:

'The cow! The cow!'

Sebastião, growing impatient, took hold of the doorhandle.

'Wait, you wretch!' she shouted, leaping to her feet. She fixed him with rancorous eyes, undid her bodice, plunged her hand into her bosom and pulled out a wallet. Then, stamping hard on the floor with her foot, she screamed:

'No, no, no!'

'Right, that's it, you'll be sleeping in a prison cell tonight.' He half-opened the door. 'Senhor Mendes!'

'Oh, take them, then!' she shouted, hurling the wallet at him. And shaking her fist, she added: 'And may you rot in hell, you scoundrel!'

Sebastião picked up the wallet. It contained three letters; one, very crumpled, was from Luiza; he read the first line: 'My beloved Bazilio', and, his face very pale, he immediately put all the letters away in the inside pocket of his jacket. Then he opened the door: Mendes' imposing bulk was there in the shadows.

'It's all sorted out, Senhor Mendes,' Sebastião said, his voice trembling slightly. 'I won't need to take up any more of your time.'

The man bowed silently, and when, on the landing, Sebastião slipped a one *libra* coin into his hand, Mendes again bowed respectfully and said in unctuous tones:

'If you ever require me again, sir, ask for number 64, Mendes, formerly of the Municipal Guard. Don't bother to see me out, sir. At your service, sir. My wife and children are most grateful. No, there's no need for thanks, sir. Just remember, number 64, Mendes, formerly of the Municipal Guard.'

Sebastião closed the door and went back into the dining room. Juliana was still sitting on the chair, a defeated figure; but as soon as she saw him, she sprang up.

'The strumpet went and told you everything, didn't she? You were the one who set this little trap. I suppose you've slept with her too, have you!'

Sebastião, white-faced, struggled to control himself.

'Go and get your hat, woman. Senhor Jorge dismissed you from your post. You can send for your trunks tomorrow.'

'I'll tell him everything!' she screamed. 'May the roof fall in on me if I don't tell him every little detail. Everything! The letters she received, where she went to meet the man. She lay with him right there in the drawing room, I found one of her hair combs there; it must have fallen out in the tussle. Even the cook heard them moaning and groaning!'

'Be quiet!' bawled Sebastião, bringing his fist down so hard on the table that he set the china on the sideboard trembling and the canaries fluttering. Then, white-lipped, his voice quavering, he said: 'The police have your name, you thief. You say one word, and you'll go straight to prison and be on the next boat to Africa! You didn't just steal the letters; you stole clothes, chemises, sheets, dresses . . .' He could see that Juliana was about to speak, to cry out. 'I know, I know,' he said loudly, 'she gave them to you, but only because you forced her to, because you threatened her. You took everything from her.

385

That's theft! That deserves transportation to Africa! And as for telling Senhor Jorge everything, go ahead. Go on. See if he believes you! He'll beat you black and blue, you thief!'

She was grinding her teeth. She was trapped! They had everything on their side – the police, the courthouse, the prison, Africa! She, on the other hand, had nothing!

All her loathing for 'the dumpling' exploded. She called her every obscene name under the sun. She invented infamies.

'She's worse than the prostitutes in the Bairro Alto! Whereas I,' she was shouting now, 'I'm a decent woman, and no man can boast of ever having touched my body. No scoundrel ever so much as saw the colour of my skin. But that slut . . .' She had thrown off her shawl and was desperately tugging at the neck of her dress. 'It was shameful what went on in this house! And after what I went through with that old witch of an aunt! And this is how they repay me! I've a good mind to go to the newspapers. I saw her myself with the dandy; she was all over him, like the bitch on heat she is!'

Sebastião was listening to her reluctantly, feeling a kind of painful curiosity in these details; he felt an intense desire to strangle her, and yet he devoured every word she said. When she stopped talking, her chest was heaving.

'Go on, put your hat on and get out of here!'

Juliana, by then half-crazed with rage, eyes bulging, went over to him and spat in his face!

Then, suddenly, her mouth gaped open, she bent backwards, clutching both hands to her heart, and collapsed, with a soft, crumpling sound, like a bundle of clothes.

Sebastião bent down and shook her; she was rigid, and a reddish foam appeared at the corners of her mouth.

He grabbed his hat, hurtled down the stairs and ran down to Rua da Patriarcal. An empty coupé was passing; he jumped in and told the driver to take him 'as fast as he could' to Julião's house; and he forced Julião, still in his slippers and with no shirt collar on, to come with him back to the house.

'It's Juliana, she's dead,' he stammered, deathly pale.

And on the way, amidst the rumble of wheels and the rattle of windows, he gave a garbled account of why he had gone to Luiza's house and how he had found Juliana in high dudgeon over her dismissal, and how she had been talking agitatedly and waving her arms about, when she had suddenly collapsed.

'It must have been her heart. It could have happened at any time,' said Julião, drawing on his cigar.

The carriage stopped. However, Sebastião, in his confusion, had locked the door as he left. The only person in was the dead woman! The coachman offered them his skeleton key. It worked.

'Don't you fancy a little ride down to Dafundo, gentlemen?' he said, putting the tip in his pocket.

But seeing them flinging open the door, he muttered scornfully, whipping his horses:

'Obviously not.'

They went in.

In the small courtyard, the silence in the house struck Sebastião as truly terrifying. He went fearfully up the stairs, which seemed endless; heart pounding, he was hoping that she might merely be sleeping after a simple fainting fit or already up and on her feet, pale, but breathing.

No. She was just as he had left her, stretched out on the rug, her arms flung wide, her fingers like claws. The convulsive movement of her legs had made her skirts ride up, revealing her bony shins, her pink-striped stockings and her carpet slippers; the oil lamp, which Sebastião had left on a chair nearby, shed a livid light on her head and rigid cheeks; her twisted mouth cast a shadow; and her horribly wide eyes, fixed by sudden death, were covered by a kind of mist, as if by a diaphanous spider's web. All around, everything seemed even more motionless than usual, filled by a deathly stillness. The silver gleamed dully on the sideboard; the cuckoo clock ticked uninterruptedly on.

Julião felt her pulses, then got up, brushing off his hands.

'Dead as a doornail,' he said. 'We'll have to get her out of here. Where's her room?'

Sebastião, looking very pale, pointed up the stairs.

Julião said:

'All right. You drag her, and I'll carry the lamp.' And seeing that Sebastião did not move, he asked, laughing: 'You're not afraid, are you?'

He said mockingly that it was just inert matter, like picking up a doll! Sebastião, with beads of sweat standing out on his temples, got hold of the corpse beneath the armpits and began, slowly, to drag it along. Julião went ahead, lighting the way; as a joke, he hummed the opening bars of the march from *Faust*. Sebastião was shocked and said in an unsteady voice:

'If you're not careful, I'll just drop everything and leave . . .'

'All right, all right, I'll respect your girlish nerves!' said Julião, bowing.

They continued on in silence. That scrawny body was like a lead weight. He was breathing hard. On the stairs, one of the corpse's slippers fell off and rolled down to the bottom. Then, with horror, Sebastião felt something bumping against his knees: it was the dead woman's false hair, hanging by a thread.

They lay her down on the bed; Julião, saying that they should keep up traditions, folded her arms over her chest and closed her eyes.

He stood looking at her for a moment:

'Ugly creature!' he murmured, placing a grubby towel over her face.

As he was leaving, he looked around at the room in wonderment.

'The useless wretch was better provided for than me.'

He closed the door and locked it.

'*Requiescat in pace*,' he said.

And in silence they went back down the stairs.

As they went into the drawing room, Sebastião, still very pale, put a hand on Julião's shoulder:

'So you think it was an aneurism?'

'Oh, yes. She fell into a fit of rage and quite simply exploded. It's a textbook case.'

'And if she hadn't got angry today . . .'

'It would have happened tomorrow. She was on her last legs. Leave the creature in peace. She's beginning to rot even as we speak, let's not bother her.'

Then, rubbing his hands together to warm them, he declared that he could do with 'a bite to eat'. In the cupboard he found a piece of cold veal and half a bottle of Colares wine. He sat down at the table and with his mouth full and holding the bottle high above his glass to pour the wine, he said:

'I suppose you've heard the news, Sebastião.'

'No, what news?'

'My rival got the job.'

Sebastião murmured:

'Oh, no, that's dreadful!'

'Oh, I could see it coming,' said Julião, making a careless gesture. 'I was going to kick up a fuss about it, but . . .' he giggled, 'they won me over! I've been given a post as a doctor! They tossed me a bone!'

'Really?' said Sebastião. 'Why, that's good news, man, congratulations. So what now?'

'I'll just have to gnaw the bone, I suppose.'

They had also promised him the first vacancy that occurred. And the post as a doctor wasn't bad. Things were definitely improving . . .

'But only very slightly. I'm still not out of the mire yet.'

After a silence, he said that he was tired of medicine. It was a dead end. He should have been a lawyer, a politician, an intriguer. That's what he was born for!

He got up and, taking long strides about the room, cigar in hand, stridently set out his ambitious plan: 'The country is ripe for some willing Machiavelli! The current lot are all old and ailing, afflicted by bladder conditions and ancient cases of syphilis! The whole thing is rotten inside and out! The old constitutional world is about to fall to pieces. They need men!'

And planting himself before Sebastião, he went on:

'This country, my friend, has, until now, got by with governments who have been living on their wits. Come the revolution, all that will be swept away, and the country will have to find people with principles. But are there any people with principles? Has anyone around here got any principles at all? No one: they might have debts, secret vices, false teeth, but they haven't got so much as half a principle between them. Consequently, if three jokers were to go to the trouble of concocting half a dozen serious, rational, modern, positive principles, the country would go down on its knees and beg them: Gentlemen, do me the great honour of saddling me up!' Now I should, by rights, be one of those jokers. That was what I was born for! And it infuriates me that while other idiots, more astute and more far-sighted, will be there at the top of the tree, shining in the sun, 'in the beautiful Portuguese sun', as the Spanish operettas put it, I will be prescribing poultices for devout old ladies or binding up the rupture of some decrepit High Court judge.'

Sebastião did not reply; his thoughts were with the woman lying dead upstairs.

'Stupid country, stupid life!' growled Julião.

At that moment, a carriage drove up the street and stopped at the door.

'The prince and princess have arrived!' said Julião. They went downstairs at once.

Jorge was helping Luiza out of the carriage when Sebastião flung open the door and announced bluntly:

'There's been an accident.'

'Not a fire?' shouted Jorge, turning around in great alarm.

'No, it's Juliana, she's died of an aneurism,' said Julião from the darkness of the doorway.

'Good God!' Jorge, greatly shaken, was feeling in his pocket for change to give to the coachman.

'Well, I'm not going in there!' exclaimed Dona Felicidade, appearing at the carriage door, her broad face framed in a white shawl.

'Nor me!' said Luiza, trembling.

'But where else can we go, my dear?' cried Jorge.

Sebastião suggested they stay at his house. There was always his mother's room; it would only be a matter of putting some sheets on the bed.

'Oh, yes, let's go there, Jorge. Please, it would be for the best!' said Luiza pleadingly.

Jorge was unsure. The street patrol were passing by further up the street and paused when they saw a group of people standing in the light from the carriage lantern. Much to his chagrin, Jorge was forced to agree.

'Bloody woman, fancy dying at this hour! The carriage will take you home, Dona Felicidade.'

'And me,' said Julião, 'I'm still in my slippers.'

Dona Felicidade then recalled, as a Christian, that there really should be someone to watch over the dead woman.

'Oh, for heaven's sake, Dona Felicidade,' exclaimed Julião, getting into the carriage and banging the door.

But Dona Felicidade insisted; it would show a lack of religion to do otherwise! At least put a couple of candles next to her and call a priest.

'Drive on, coachman!' bawled Julião impatiently.

The carriage turned around. And Dona Felicidade, leaning out of the window, with Julião tugging at her clothes, was still shouting:

'It's a mortal sin! It shows a lack of reverence! At least a couple of candles!'

The carriage set off at a trot.

Luiza was also beset by scruples, they really should send for someone.

But Jorge became angry. Who could they possibly call at that hour? It was all a lot of devout nonsense! She was dead and that was that! They would see that she was buried, but as to watching over the wretch! Should they perhaps organise a lying-in-state? Did Luiza want to watch over her?

'Jorge, please!' murmured Sebastião.

'No, really, it's too much! You're just trying to make matters even more complicated than they already are!'

Luiza lowered her head, and while Jorge, still cursing, stayed behind to lock up the house, she walked down the street, on Sebastião's arm.

'She had a fit of rage and died,' he said quietly.

Jorge continued to complain all the way down the street.

Why couldn't they sleep in their own house? It really was taking these womanish fancies too far!

Finally, Luiza said to him, almost in tears:

'Do you want to torment me still more and make me even more ill, Jorge?'

He said nothing, furiously chewing on his cigar. Sebastião, in order to calm Luiza, suggested sending his black servant, Tia Vicência, to watch over Juliana.

'Perhaps that would be best,' murmured Luiza.

They reached Sebastião's door. The rustle of Luiza's silk dress in his house at this late hour troubled him; his hand shook as he lit the candles in the drawing room. He went to wake Tia Vicência so that she could make them some tea; he himself hurriedly got the sheets out of the trunks, happy to play the host. When he came back into the drawing room, Luiza was alone and looking very pale, sitting at one end of the sofa.

'Where's Jorge?' he asked.

'He went to your study, Sebastião, to write to the priest about the funeral.' Then with shining eyes, she said in a low, frightened voice: 'Did you manage . . .'

Sebastião took Juliana's wallet containing the letters out of his pocket. She grasped it eagerly and, with a sudden movement, took his hand and kissed it.

Jorge came in just then, smiling.

'So, is the young lady feeling better now?'

'Oh, much better,' she said, with a sigh of relief.

They went to have some tea. Sebastião, blushing slightly, recounted to Jorge how he had gone to the house and how Juliana had told him of her dismissal, growing more and more worked up as she talked, until suddenly, just like that, she had dropped down dead.

He added:

'Poor woman!'

Luiza watched him telling these lies and gazed at him adoringly.

'But where was Joana?' asked Jorge.

Luiza, without batting an eyelid, replied:

'Oh, I forgot to tell you . . . She asked permission to go and see an aunt of hers who's very ill and who lives near Belas. She said she would be back tomorrow. Another drop of tea, Sebastião?'

They subsequently forgot about sending Vicência, and so no one watched over the dead woman.

# XIV

Luiza feverishly tossed and turned all night. In the morning, Jorge was alarmed by her rapid pulse and by the dry heat of her skin.

He himself had been too overwrought to sleep. The room, in which a fire had not been lit for a long time, had an uninhabited chill about it; there were patches of damp on the wall, near the ceiling; and in the fading glow from the night-light, the ancient, now curtainless bed with its turned wooden pillars and the old pier glass dating from the previous century, with its tarnished mirror, exuded a sad sense of dead companions. For some reason, finding himself there with his wife, in a strange bed, made him feel vaguely nostalgic; it seemed to him that his life had undergone a sudden shift, and from that night onwards, like a river that changes its course, his existence would begin to flow through very different landscapes. The northeast wind rattled the window frames and howled along the streets.

In the morning, Luiza could not get out of bed.

Julião, summoned in haste, reassured them both:

'It's just a nervous fever. You need rest, it's nothing serious. It was the shock of what happened last night I expect.'

'I dreamed about her all night,' said Luiza. 'I dreamed she had come back to life again . . . oh, it was awful!'

'Oh, you don't need to worry about that. The woman has been dealt with.'

'Sebastião is sorting out the whole dreadful business,' said Jorge. 'And I'll look in later.'

By then, the whole street knew about the demise of the 'Dried Prune'.

The woman who came to lay her out, a pockmarked matron with the bloodshot eyes of an inveterate brandy-drinker, was an acquaintance of Senhora Helena's. They stood in the sun for a moment at the door of the tobacconist's, chatting:

'I suppose you're very busy at the moment, Senhora Margarida.'

'Oh, yes,' replied the latter in her rather hoarse voice. 'There's always more work in winter. But it's mostly old people, who can't take the cold weather. Not a single pretty body to lay out.'

Senhora Margarida had artistic preferences. She liked a nice eighteen-year-old corpse, a young girl to wash and dress and make up. She spent little time over the older people. With young girls, though, she took immense pains; she arranged the folds of the shroud just so; she worried over which would be more chic, a flower or a ribbon; she worked with all the preening attention to detail of a dressmaker to the grave.

Senhora Helena told her all about Juliana, about the favours showered upon her by her employers, about her taste for elegance and the comforts of her carpeted room. Senhora Margarida declared herself 'flabbergasted'. And who would all that go to now, they wondered. The 'Dried Prune' had no relatives.

'It would be a real boon to my Antoninha!' said Senhora Margarida, ruefully drawing her shawl more tightly around her.

'How is she?'

'Oh, things just go from bad to worse, Senhora Helena. She's quite mad!' And she gave full vent to her sorrows. 'I mean fancy leaving that Brazilian who was so good to her. And who for? A wretch who takes all her money, gets her pregnant and beats her. But then, that's what girls are like nowadays. They just can't resist a handsome face. And he's certainly handsome! But, poor girl, the man's a drunkard! Anyway, Senhora Helena, I'd better go and lay the "beauty" out.' And, much disgruntled, she went into the house.

The priest had arrived too. He was in the drawing room with Sebastião, whom he knew from Almada, and was engaged in gruff talk about ploughing, grafting and irrigation, dabbing a rolled-up handerkerchief under his nose with a slow gesture of his hairy hand. All the windows were open to the gentle sun. The canaries were singing.

'And had the deceased been working here long?' the priest asked Jorge, who was pacing up and down the room, smoking.

'Almost a year.'

The priest slowly unfurled his handkerchief and shook it out before blowing his nose.

'Your wife must be most upset. But death, alas, is the one tax we all have to pay.'

And he blew his nose loudly.

Joana came tiptoeing in, wearing her shawl and headscarf. She had learned from the neighbours that Juliana had 'pegged it' and that her master and mistress were staying at Senhor Sebastião's house. She had just come from there. Luiza had called her into the bedroom. When Joana saw how ill her dear mistress looked, she sniffed and snivelled a great deal. Luiza told her that now 'everything was as it used to be' and that she could come back.

'But one thing, Joana, if Senhor Jorge asks, you've been in Belas with your aunt.'

The girl had immediately gone off to fetch her bundle of belongings and had now come to reinstall herself, rather alarmed at the idea of a dead body in the house.

Shortly afterwards, Senhor Paula knocked discreetly at the door.

He had come to offer his services during that difficult time. And rapidly doffing and donning his cap and shuffling his feet, he said in his catarrhal voice:

'Most terribly sorry, sir, to hear of the misfortune! But then we're all of us mortal.'

'Thank you, Senhor Paula, but we really don't need any help,' said Jorge. 'Thank you!'

And he brusquely closed the door.

He was impatient to rid himself of 'that tiresome business' as quickly as possible; and, annoyed by the slow hammering of the men upstairs putting the nails into the coffin, he summoned Joana:

'Tell those people to hurry up. We don't want to spend the rest of our lives here.'

Joana immediately went upstairs to report that the master was in a real state. She had already become firm friends with Senhora Margarida, who even went with her to the kitchen to have 'a little something'. Since the fire wasn't lit, she made do with some pieces of bread dipped in wine.

'Lovely grub,' she said, clicking her tongue.

But she was most put out with the deceased. She had never seen such an ugly creature. A body like a dried sardine! And casting an appreciative eye over Joana's luscious curves, she said: 'Now you, you look like you've got a very good body.' And she seemed to be measuring up Joana's robust figure for a shroud.

Joana, very shocked, said:

'Do you mind!'

The woman smiled; she had two teeth missing. She went on in mellifluous tones:

'A lot of very grand people have passed through my hands, my dear. Another drop of wine, if you please. It's from Cartaxo, isn't it? Nice velvety taste. Very nice indeed!'

To Jorge's great satisfaction, the men finally brought down the coffin at four o'clock. All the neighbours were at their doors. Senhor Paula even gave a mocking salute to the coffin, muttering:

'*Bon voyage!*'

As Jorge was leaving, he asked Joana:

'You're not afraid to be left here on your own?'

'No, sir. She won't be coming back!'

She was, in fact, afraid, but was planning to spend the night with Pedro, and her heart beat fast with joy at the thought of 'having the house to themselves' until morning and of being able to frolic amorously, just as the quality did, on the drawing-room divan.

Jorge and Sebastião returned to the latter's house, and Jorge went into the room where Luiza lay in bed, rubbing his hands and saying:

'Right, that's it. She's off to São João cemetery, suitably attired. *Per omnia sæcula sæculorum!*'

Tia Joana, who was sitting at Luiza's bedside, added:

'There but for fortune . . . Not that she was exactly a pleasant woman, of course, on the contrary.'

'She was a damned nuisance,' said Jorge. 'Let's hope she's boiling in Old Nick's cauldron at this very moment. Isn't that so, Tia Joana?'

'Jorge!' cried Luiza reprovingly. She felt they should at least say a few Our Fathers for her soul.

And at her death, that was all the Earth gave her, that woman setting off, drawn by two old nags, to the paupers' grave, that woman who, in life, had been Juliana Couceiro Tavira!

The following day, Luiza was feeling better; they even spoke, much to Tia Joana's chagrin, of going home. Sebastião said nothing, but secretly he almost wished the period of convalescence might keep her there for an indefinite number of weeks. She seemed so very grateful! She looked at him in a way that only he understood. And he was so happy to have her and Jorge there in his house! He discussed with Tia Vicência the menu for supper; he walked softly and respectfully, almost on tiptoe, along the corridors and through the drawing room, as if Luiza's presence sanctified the house; he filled the vases with camellias and violets; he smiled benignly to see Jorge, after supper, savouring and praising his oldest cognac; he felt something good warming him like a soft, quilted cloak; and it had already occurred to him that when she left, everything would seem much colder to him, as sad as a ruin!

Two days later, they did, indeed, return home.

Luiza was extremely pleased with the new maid Sebastião had found. She was a very neat, pale girl, with round, astonished eyes, and a most affectionate manner; her name was Mariana; and she ran to tell Joana that she simply adored their mistress, that she had the face of an angel! And she was so pretty!

That same day, Jorge despatched Juliana's two trunks to Tia Vitória.

When he went out later that afternoon, Luiza shut herself up in her room with Juliana's wallet and, drawing the curtains just in case, lit a candle and burned the letters. Her hands shook, and she watched, eyes swimming with tears, as her shame, her enslavement disappeared and dissolved into white smoke! She took a deep breath. At last. And it was all thanks to Sebastião, to dear Sebastião!

She walked into the drawing room, into the kitchen, all around the house; everything looked new to her, her life seemed full of sweetness; she opened all the windows; she picked out a few notes on the piano; out of superstition, she even tore up the music of 'Medjé' that Bazilio had given her; she talked a great deal with Mariana; and, savouring her convalescent's bowl of chicken soup, her face bright with happiness, she thought:

'How good everything will be from now on!'

When she heard Jorge's footsteps in the corridor on his return, she ran and flung her arms around his neck and rested her head on his shoulder.

'I'm so happy today. And Mariana is such a sweet girl!'

But that night, the fever returned. The next morning, Julião found that she was worse.

'It's intermittent fever,' he said gravely.

He was writing out a prescription when Dona Felicidade arrived in a state of high excitement. She was greatly surprised to find Luiza ill; bending over her, she whispered in her ear:

'I have something to tell you!'

As soon as Jorge and Julião had left, she sat down at the foot of the bed and unburdened herself, now in a low, confidential voice, now in a voice shrill with indignation.

She had been robbed, cynically robbed! That man she had sent to Tui, the great thief, had written to Gertrudes, her maid, saying that he had decided not to return to Lisbon, that the healer had moved to another town, that he wanted nothing more to do with the whole business, which he found distinctly odd, and that he was going to find work in Tui – and all this written in the fine hand of a public scribe, but in the most appalling Portuguese – and not a word about the money!

'What a scoundrel, eh? Eight *moedas*! If I weren't so ashamed, I would go straight to the police. From now on, I'm having no further truck with Galicians! That's why the Councillor didn't do as he was meant to! The woman never cast the spell.' For while she no longer believed in the honesty of Galicians, she had not lost her faith in the power of witches.

It wasn't the eight *moedas* she was angry about, it was all the trouble she had been put to! And who knew where the woman would be now! It was just maddening! What did Luiza make of it all?

Luiza shrugged; she was tucked up in bed, her cheeks scarlet, her eyelids drooping heavily; Dona Felicidade sighed and gave some vague advice about sweating it out; and since Luiza could offer her no consolation, she went off to the convent of the Incarnation to unburden herself to her friend, the widow Silveira.

In the early hours of the following morning, Luiza's condition worsened. The fever intensified. Jorge was so worried that he hurriedly got dressed and, at nine o'clock, went to fetch Julião. He was going rapidly down the stairs, still buttoning his overcoat, when he met the postman who was coming up, loudly clearing his throat.

'Any letters?' asked Jorge.

'One for the lady,' said the man. 'Yes, for Senhora Luiza.'

Jorge looked at the envelope; it bore Luiza's name and had been posted in France.

'Who the devil can this be from?' he thought, then stuffed it into his overcoat pocket and left.

Half an hour later, he returned with Julião in a cab.

Luiza was still drowsing in bed.

'We have to be careful. Let's see . . .' murmured Julião, slowly scratching his head, while Jorge looked anxiously on from the other side of the bed.

Julião wrote a prescription and stayed on for breakfast with Jorge. It was a cold, grey day. They were served by Mariana, bundled up in a jacket, her fingers red and swollen with chilblains. And Jorge felt himself grow sad, as if the mist hanging in the air were gradually condensing and filling his soul.

'What would cause such a fever?' he said gloomily. 'It's so

400

strange. She's been like this for the last six days, one minute she's feeling better, the next she's worse.

'These fevers can be brought on by all kinds of things,' replied Julião, calmly slicing up his toast. 'Sometimes it's a draught, sometimes it's an upsetting incident. I know of one curious example. A man called Alves was on the verge of bankruptcy and, for two months, the poor man lived in utter torment. Two weeks ago, by a stroke of good fortune – treacherous Dame Fortune does occasionally have these whims – he sorted out all his business affairs and found himself a free man again. Well, ever since then, he has been laid low with precisely the same kind of tortuous, complex fever, with all sorts of odd symptoms. Why? Because all that nervous excitement left him completely drained; the sudden happiness stirred up his blood too much. He could well die. Then, of course, comes the great bankruptcy into which we all eventually fall, with one implacable creditor demanding immediate payment . . . *per omnia sæcula!*'

He got up and lit a cigarette.

'Anyway, what she needs now is complete rest. Her mind must be kept wrapped in cotton wool. No talking, no chatter, and, if she's thirsty, a little lemonade. Anyway, I'll call in later.'

And he left, drawing on the black gloves he wore, now that he was a member of a medical practice.

Jorge went back into the bedroom; Luiza was still dozing. Mariana, sad-faced, was sitting nearby on a little low chair, gazing at Luiza with her large, rather frightened eyes.

'She's been very restless,' she murmured.

Jorge touched Luiza's hand, which was burning hot, and tucked the blankets more closely about her. He gently kissed her forehead and closed the shutters opposite the bed. Later, as he paced up and down in his study, Julião's words came back to him, about how such fevers can be brought on by some upsetting incident. He thought of that businessman, he remembered Luiza's recent, inexplicable state of exhaustion and weakness that had been worrying him so. What nonsense! What upsetting incident? She had seemed so cheerful when they were staying at Sebastião's house! Not even Juliana's death had shaken her! Besides, he did not much believe in such fevers. Julião had a very literary view of medicine. Jorge even wondered if it wouldn't be more sensible to summon old Dr Caminha.

Then, putting his hand in his pocket, his fingers came in contact with a letter; it was the one the postman had given him that morning for Luiza. He examined it again with curiosity; it was a cheap envelope, the kind provided to their customers by cafés and restaurants; he did not recognise the handwriting; it was a man's hand, and it came from France. He felt a sudden desire to open it, but he checked himself and threw it down on the desk, then slowly rolled himself a cigarette.

He went back into the bedroom. Luiza was still dozing; the sleeve of her peignoir was rolled back to reveal one slender arm covered in soft blonde down; her face glowed scarlet; her fine eyelids were closed and her long lashes rested heavily upon her cheeks; a ringlet of hair fell over her forehead, and in her feverish state she seemed to Jorge utterly adorable and immeasurably touching. For some reason it occurred to him that others might find her pretty too, others might desire her and, given the opportunity, might tell her so. Why would anyone write to her from France? Who would write to her?

He went back into the study, but the letter on the desk bothered him; he picked up a book, but impatiently threw it down again and resumed his pacing up and down, nervously fiddling with the linings of his trouser pockets.

Then he picked up the letter, and tried to make out the writing through the thin paper of the envelope; his fingers began irresistibly to tear open one corner of the envelope. No, it wasn't right! But the curiosity dominating his mind produced all kinds of persuasive, tempting arguments: She was ill and it might be something urgent; what if it were an inheritance? Besides, she had no secrets from him, certainly not in France! His scruples were mere childishness! He would tell her he had opened it by mistake. And what if the letter contained the secret that had caused the upset, the upsetting incident of Julião's theories? Then he should open it in order to help her back to health!

Almost without realising it, he found the letter open in his hand. He devoured it in one avid glance. But he could not quite take it in; the letters grew blurred; he went over to the window and read slowly:

My dear Luiza,

It would take too long to explain how it is that I only received your letter yesterday in Nice – I arrived back in Paris this morning – and, judging by the various postmarks, it seems to have followed me across the whole of Europe. Since it's over two and half months since you wrote it, I imagine that you will have sorted things out with the woman and no longer need the money. If you do, though, send me a telegram and the money will be with you in two days. I see from your letter that you do not believe my departure was due to matters of business. That is most unfair. My departure should not, as you put it, have destroyed all your illusions about love, because it was only when I left Lisbon that I realised how much I loved you, and, believe me, not a day goes by without my remembering our 'Paradise'. What delicious afternoons those were! Have you been back there since? Do you remember that lunch we had? I don't have time to write more now. I may well be back in Lisbon again soon. I hope to see you there, because, without you, Lisbon, for me, is a place of exile.

A long kiss from your ever-loving
Bazilio

Jorge slowly folded the letter into two, then into four, threw it down on his desk and said out loud:

'Well, well. How very nice!'

He mechanically filled his pipe with tobacco, his eyes vacant, his lips trembling; he took a few uncertain steps about the study. Then he hurled his pipe at the window, breaking one pane; he waved his hands about wildly, threw himself face down on the desk and burst into tears, rolling his head from side to side on his arms, biting the sleeves of his jacket and stamping his feet, utterly beside himself.

Then he sprang to his feet, picked up the letter and was about to go straight to Luiza's bedroom. However, the memory of Julião's words froze him: she had to be quiet, no chatter, no excitement! He placed the letter in a drawer and locked it, putting the key in his pocket. And standing there, trembling, his eyes shot with blood, he felt mad ideas flicker across his brain like lightning flashes in a storm – to kill her, leave the house, abandon her, beat her brains out.

Mariana knocked lightly on the door and told him that her mistress was asking for him.

A wave of blood rushed to his head; he stared at Mariana stupidly, blinking.

'I'll be right there,' he said in a hoarse voice.

As he went through the drawing room, past the oval mirror, he was horrified to see his blotched countenance, suddenly older. He went and wiped a wet towel over his face and smoothed his hair; when he went into the bedroom and when he saw her, with her great, wide eyes, bright with fever, he had to hold on to the bedstead, because he could feel the walls around him flapping like canvas in the wind.

He managed to smile:

'How are you?'

'Pretty bad,' she murmured weakly.

She beckoned him feebly to her side.

He sat down without looking at her.

'What's wrong?' she said, putting her face close to his. 'Don't upset yourself.' And she took the hand he had placed on the bed beside her.

Jorge brusquely withdrew his hand and sprang to his feet, his teeth clenched; he was filled by a violent anger; he was just leaving the room, afraid of himself, afraid he might commit some crime, when he heard Luiza's wounded voice:

'Jorge, whatever's wrong?'

He turned; he saw her half sitting up in bed, her wide eyes fixed on him, a worried look on her face; and two tears rolled silently down his cheeks.

He knelt before her and seized her hands, sobbing.

'What on earth is going on?' exclaimed Julião from the doorway.

Jorge, deathly pale, got slowly to his feet.

Julião led him into the drawing room and standing before him, arms sternly folded, said:

'Are you mad? You know perfectly well the state she's in and there you go weeping all over her.'

'I couldn't help it . . .'

'It's unbelievable. Here I am trying to bring her fever down, and there you are making matters worse. You're mad!'

His outrage was genuine enough. He was interested in Luiza as a patient. He very much wanted to cure her, and it pleased him to wield the authority of a person necessary to that house, where, previously, his visits had always had an edge of dependence; now, however, as he was leaving, he nonchalantly offered Jorge a cigar.

Jorge was heroic throughout the rest of that afternoon. He could not bear to spend much time in Luiza's bedroom, because despair was driving him in another direction; but he went in to see her frequently, he smiled at her and rearranged the covers with trembling hands; and when she was dozing, he would stand motionless, studying her, feature by feature, with a painful, prurient curiosity, as if hoping to find in her face traces of another man's kisses, hoping to hear her murmur in some feverish dream a name or a date; and he loved her even more since he had judged her to have been unfaithful, but with a different love, carnal and perverse. Then he would go and shut himself in his study and prowl up and down between its narrow walls like a caged beast. He re-read the letter again and again, and the same low, vile, gnawing curiosity tortured him without cease. What had it been like? Where was this 'Paradise'? Was there a bed there? What dress did she use to wear? What words did she say to him? What kisses did she give him?

He then re-read the letters she had sent to him in the Alentejo, trying to discover in her words some sign of coldness, the date of her betrayal! He hated her then, and ideas of murder flooded into his mind – he would strangle her, give her chloroform, make her drink laudanum! But then he would stand very still, leaning at the window, lost in dense thought, reviewing the past, the day of their wedding, certain walks he had taken with her, things she had said . . .

Sometimes he wondered if the letter was some kind of joke. Some enemy of his could have written it and had it sent on from France. Or perhaps Bazilio had *another* Luiza in Lisbon and had written his cousin's name on the envelope by mistake; and the momentary joy brought to him by these fantasies only made the reality seem even crueller. But what had really happened? If only he knew! He was sure he would feel calmer knowing the truth. He would tear that love from his heart as if it were a filthy parasite; as soon as she was better, he would take her to a convent and he would set sail for Africa or some equally distant place where he could die. But who would know? Juliana!

She knew! Of course! He understood everything now, Luiza's kindness to Juliana, the furniture, the room, the clothes! She was paying for her silence! She was her confidante! She was the messenger, she knew everything. And she was lying dead and silent in her grave, the wretch!

Sebastião, as he usually did, arrived in the late afternoon. There were no lights on as yet and, as soon as he came into the house, Jorge called him into his study and, without saying a word, lit a candle and took the letter out of the drawer.

'Read this.'

Sebastião was shocked by the expression on Jorge's face. He stared at the folded letter and trembled. As soon as he saw the signature, a death-like pallor spread over his face. It seemed to him that the ground was shaking so much he could barely stand. But he controlled himself and read the letter slowly before putting it down on the desk without a word.

Then Jorge said:

'Sebastião, this is like death to me. Sebastião, you know something. You came here. You know. Tell me the truth!'

Sebastião spread wide his arms and said:

'What can I tell you? I don't know anything.'

Jorge grabbed his hands and shook them, anxiously search-ing his eyes.

'Sebastião, for the sake of our friendship, for the sake of your mother's soul, for the sake of all the years we have spent together, Sebastião, tell me the truth!'

'I don't know anything. What could I possibly know?'

'You're lying!'

Sebastião said only:

'Sh, someone might hear us!'

There was a silence; Jorge was clutching his head in his hands and striding about the study with heavy steps that made the floor shake; then, planting himself in front of Sebastião, he said almost pleadingly:

'At least tell me what she did. Did she go out? Did someone come here to see her?'

Sebastião replied slowly, his eyes fixed on the candle flame:

'Her cousin came here sometimes, to begin with. When Dona Felicidade was ill, she went to see her . . . Then the cousin left . . . That's all I know.'

Jorge stood for a moment, staring abstractedly at Sebastião.

'But what did I do to her, Sebastião? What did I do to her? I adored her! What did I do to deserve this? I adored that woman!'

He burst into tears.

Sebastião remained standing by the desk, stunned and exhausted.

'Perhaps it was just a joke,' he murmured.

'What about what it says in the letter?' Jorge cried, spinning angrily round at him, brandishing the piece of paper. 'What about this "Paradise"!? The "delicious afternoons" they spent there! She's utterly shameless!'

'She's ill, Jorge,' Sebastião said simply.

Jorge did not reply. He walked up and down in silence for some time. Sebastião stayed where he was, his eyes fixed wear-ily on the candle flame. Jorge then put the letter back in the drawer and, picking up the candlestick, he said in a tone of gloomy, resigned lassitude:

'Would you like some tea, Sebastião?

And they never spoke of the letter again.

That night, Jorge slept deeply. The next day, his face was impassive and had a kind of ashen serenity.

From then on, he acted as Luiza's nurse.

After three days of uncertainty, it became clear that the illness was indeed intermittent fever; Luiza grew very weak, but Julião was unperturbed.

Jorge spent his days at her bedside. Dona Felicidade usually came in the mornings and would sit at the foot of the bed, not saying a word, her face grown suddenly older; the unexpected destruction of her hopes in the woman in Tui had shaken her like an old building from which a pillar has suddenly been removed – she was becoming a ruin; and she only cheered up when the Councillor looked in at around three o'clock to enquire after 'our lovely patient'. He always proffered a few grave words, which he uttered in a solemn voice, holding his hat in his hand, not wishing, out of modesty, to enter the bedroom.

'Good health is a gift that we only appreciate when we lose it.'

Or:

'It is only in sickness that we find out who our true friends are.'

And he would always close with:

'Jorge, dear fellow, the roses of good health will soon bloom once more in the cheeks of your virtuous wife!'

At night, Jorge would lie down, fully clothed, on a mattress on the floor; but he only managed to sleep for one or two hours at a time. The rest of the night, he spent trying to read; he would begin a novel, but never get beyond the first few lines; he would put the book down and, head in hands, would sit thinking; it was always the same thought: what had actually happened? Using logic and the few facts at his disposal, he had managed, more or less, to reconstruct events; he could see Bazilio arriving, coming to visit her, desiring her, sending her flowers, pursuing her, seeing her out and about, writing to her.

But then what? He had realised that the money must have been for Juliana. She obviously had some hold over them. Had she caught them in flagrante one day? Did she have letters of theirs? But in that painful reconstruction he found omissions and gaps, like dark holes into which his soul impatiently plunged. Then he would start remembering the months since his return from the Alentejo, and how loving she had been, how ardent her caresses. Why then had she deceived him?

One night, taking all the precautions of a thief, he rummaged through drawers, examined her clothes, even the folds of her underwear and boxes containing necklaces and lace collars; he found the sandalwood box, but it was empty; not even the dust from a dried flower! Sometimes, he would sit staring at and scrutinising the furniture in the bedroom and in the drawing room, as if he hoped to find in them some vestige of the adulterous act. Would they have sat there? Would he have knelt before her over there, on the carpet? The broad, comfortable divan in particular drove him to despair; he conceived for it a genuine hatred. He came to hate the house itself, as if the ceilings that had sheltered them, the floors that had supported them were conscious accomplices. But what tortured him most were the words 'Paradise' and 'delicious afternoons' . . .

Luiza was sleeping well again. After a week, the fevers disappeared. However, she was still very weak, so much so that when she got up for the first time, she fainted twice; she had to be dressed and then helped over to the chaise longue; and she could not be without Jorge for a moment, keeping him by her side like a demanding child! She seemed to receive life from his eyes and health from the touch of his hands. She had him read the newspaper to her in the morning and do his writing by her side. He obeyed, and her demands were like consoling caresses to his pain. She so obviously loved him!

Quite unwittingly, he experienced little clearings of happiness. He was surprised to find himself speaking tenderly to her, blithely laughing with her, as he used to. Luiza, lying on the chaise longue, happily leafed through ancient volumes of an illustrated encylopaedia which the Councillor had sent to her – 'wherein,' he had told her, 'you can, while amusing yourself with the illustrations, acquire a few useful notions of important historical events'; or else, with her head resting on the back of the chaise, she would savour the joy of getting better, of being free from the tyrannies of 'that woman' and from past bitternesses.

One of her pleasures was to see Mariana come in, with dinner set out on a cloth on a tray; her appetite had returned and she greatly enjoyed the glass of port wine that Julião had recommended; when Jorge was not there, she would have long conversations with Mariana, talking softly and animatedly while she ate spoonfuls of jelly.

Sometimes, she would lie, silently looking up at the ceiling, making plans. She would tell Jorge about them later; she would go to the country for two weeks to regain her strength; when she came back, she would start embroidering woollen covers for the chairs in the drawing room; because she wanted to live very quietly and do lots of things around the house; he wouldn't be going back to the Alentejo, would he, he wouldn't be leaving Lisbon again? Their life would thenceforth be one of continuous, easy sweetness.

Luiza sometimes found him very taciturn. What was wrong? He put it down to tiredness, to all those sleepless nights. If he was going to be ill, she would say, he should at least wait until she was stronger so that she could look after him and watch over him! But he wouldn't fall ill, would he? And she would have him come and sit next to her, and she would stroke his hair and gaze at him tenderly, for with her returning strength came the natural impulses of her loving nature. Jorge felt then that he adored her, and he was even more wretched!

Luiza kept other resolutions to herself. She would not see Leopoldina again and she would go to church. She had emerged from her illness possessed of a vaguely devout sentimentality. During the fevers, in nightmares that had left her with a hazy feeling of terror, she had sometimes found herself in a horrifying place where bodies, engulfed in scarlet flames, reached out their arms, where black shapes turned slowly on red-hot spits, and agonising cries rose up to a silent sky, and where tongues of flame from the fires would already be scorching her breast as she felt the cooling touch of something sweet and ineffable – the wings of a bright, serene angel, who took her in his arms; and she felt herself being lifted up and she rested her head against the divine breast, which filled her with a supernatural happiness; she could see the stars so close and hear the flutter of wings. That sensation had left her with a kind of nostalgic memory of heaven. And in her weak, convalescent state, she aspired to that heaven, hoping to gain entry to it by dint of regular attendance at mass and by repeated prayers to the Virgin.

One morning, she came into the drawing room and opened the piano for the first time; Jorge was standing at the window, staring down into the street, when she called to him, smiling:

'You know, I've hated that divan for ages,' she said. 'Could we get rid of it, do you think?'

Jorge felt his heart skip a beat; he could not reply immediately; then, at last, he managed to say:

'If you like.'

'Yes, let's get rid of it,' she said, and with that she left the drawing room, serenely dragging behind her the long train of her peignoir.

Jorge could not take his eyes off the divan. He even went and sat on it; he ran his hand over the striped upholstery and experienced a painful pleasure in knowing that *this had been the place*!

A kind of gloomy resignation had taken hold of him; when he heard her talking brightly of how much better she felt, speaking cheerfully of a tranquil future, he resolved to destroy the letter and to forget everything. She had doubtless repented, and she clearly loved him; what was the point, then, of coldbloodedly creating a perpetual unhappiness? But when he saw her lying languidly on the chaise longue or revealing the whiteness of her throat and neck as she got undressed, he thought how those arms had embraced another man, how that mouth had moaned with love in another's bed, and a wave of brute rage would flood through him and he had to leave the room in order not to strangle her!

In order to explain his moods and his silences, he began to complain of being unwell. And her solicitude towards him and the silent, anxious, questioning look in her eyes only made him even more unhappy – feeling loved when he knew now that he had been betrayed!

One Sunday, Julião finally gave permission for Luiza to go to bed later than usual and to hold open house to their friends. It was a joy to everyone to see her in the drawing room, still somewhat pale and weak, but, as the Councillor put it, restored to her domestic duties and to the pleasures of society!

Julião, who arrived at nine o'clock, thought she looked 'as good as new'. Then, opening wide his arms in the middle of the room, he exclaimed:

'And what do you think of the latest news? Ernesto's play is a triumph!'

So they had read in the newspapers. According to one article: 'the author, called up onto the stage, where he was greeted by an enthusiastic ovation, had received a magnificent crown of laurels'. Luiza declared her desire to go and see it at once.

'Later, Dona Luiza, later,' said the Councillor prudently. 'You should avoid all strong emotions at the moment. The tears that you would surely shed, for I know how soft-hearted you are, could provoke a relapse. Isn't that so, friend Julião?'

'It certainly is, Councillor, it certainly is. But I too would like to go. I want to see with my own eyes.'

But the sound of a carriage approaching at a brisk trot and stopping outside the door, interrupted him. The bell rang loudly.

'I bet you that's our playwright now!' he cried.

And almost immediately, the radiant figure of Ernestinho, in a tail coat, burst into the drawing room, and they all got noisily to their feet to embrace him: Many congratulations! Many congratulations! And the voice of the Councillor rising above the others was saying:

'Welcome to our much-celebrated author, welcome!'

412

Ernesto was breathless with joy. He had a fixed smile on his face; his nostrils were flared as if to breathe in compliments; his chest was puffed out with pride; and he kept moving his head from side to side as if it were second nature in him now to bestow grateful nods on the applauding multitudes.

'Here I am! Here I am!' he said.

He sat down, panting; and in amiable, hail-fellow-well-met fashion, he declared that the last dress rehearsals had not left him a single free moment to visit cousin Luiza. He had finally managed to get a moment to himself that night, but he had to be back at the theatre by ten o'clock; he had not even sent away his cab.

Then he gave a full account of his triumph. At first, he had had the most terrible nerves. Everyone got them, even old hands, even the most famous playwrights! But as soon as Campos had spoken the first monologue – and the way he had spoken it, they should have been there, it was simply sublime! – the audience broke into spontaneous applause. They had liked everything. In the end, there was the most tremendous uproar, with calls of 'Author! Author!' and standing ovations. He had had to be dragged onto the stage; he hadn't wanted to go at all, but they had forced him, Jesuína on one side and Maria Adelaide on the other! Madness! Savedra of *The Century* had told him: You're our Shakespeare, my friend! Bastos from *The Truth* had said: 'You're our Eugène Scribe!' There was a supper afterwards. And they had given him a crown of laurels.

'Does it fit you?' asked Julião.

'Perfectly. Well, it is perhaps on the large side.'

The Councillor said authoritatively:

'The great writers, the starving Tasso, our own Camões, are always depicted wearing their respective laurel wreaths.'

'That's what I would recommend you to do, Senhor Ernestinho,' said Julião, standing up and clapping him on the shoulder, 'have your portrait painted wearing a wreath.'

Everyone laughed.

Somewhat put out, Ernestinho unfurled his perfumed handkerchief and said:

'You will have your little joke, Senhor Zuzarte.'

'It's proof of your glory, my friend. When the victorious generals entered Rome in triumph, there was always a fool in the cortège!'

'Well, I don't know,' said Luiza, beaming, 'I think it's an honour for the family!'

Jorge agreed. He was pacing about the room, smoking; and he said that he was as pleased about the crown of laurels as if he himself had won the right to wear it.

Then Ernestinho turned to him:

'I decided to forgive her, cousin Jorge! I forgave the wife . . .'

'Like Christ . . .'

Yes, like Christ,' confirmed Ernestinho, pleased.

Dona Felicidade gave her approval:

'And quite right too! It's actually much more moral to do so!'

'Jorge was the one who wanted to have her killed,' said Ernestinho, giggling. 'Don't you remember, that night . . .'

'Yes, yes,' said Jorge, with a nervous laugh.

'Our Jorge,' said the Councillor solemnly, 'could not possibly maintain such extreme ideas. Doubtless long reflection and further experience of life . . .'

'Oh, I've changed, Councillor, I've changed,' broke in Jorge.

And he rushed off into his study.

Sebastião, concerned, followed slowly behind. The room was in darkness.

'Will those idiots never shut up? Will they never go?' Jorge said with quiet, barely contained anguish, gripping Sebastião's arm.

'It's all right!'

'Oh, Sebastião! Sebastião!' And his voice shook, on the verge of tears.

Then Luiza called from the drawing room:

'What are you two plotting in there in the dark?'

Sebastião immediately reappeared, saying:

'Oh, it's nothing. We were just standing around . . .' And

he added in a low voice: 'Jorge is tired. He's not feeling well, poor chap.'

When Jorge came back into the room, they noticed that he did indeed look strange.

'No, I'm not very well, a bit off-colour.'

'And the delicate Dona Luiza needs her rest,' said the Councillor, getting up.

Ernestinho, who could not stay any longer, immediately offered the Councillor and Julião 'his carriage, a caleche, if they were going to the Baixa.'

'What an honour,' exclaimed Julião, glancing at Acácio, 'to ride in the Great Man's carriage!'

And while Dona Felicidade was getting ready, the three of them went down the stairs.

Halfway down, Julião stopped and, folding his arms, said:

'Here I am flanked by representatives of the two greatest movements in Portugal since 1820. Literature,' and he bowed to Ernestinho, 'and Constitutionalism,' and he bowed to the Councillor.

The two men laughed, flattered.

'And what about you, Senhor Zuzarte?'

'Me?' And lowering his voice, he said: 'Up until a few days ago, I was a wild revolutionary. But now . . .'

'What?'

'Now, I am a friend of Order,' he cried jubilantly.

And pleased with themselves and with their country, they continued down the stairs in order to install themselves in the Great Man's carriage!

# XV

The next day, Jorge went to the Ministry for the first time in some weeks. He did not stay long. The street and the presence of both acquaintances and strangers, were a torment to him; it seemed to him that *everyone knew*; he saw malign intent in the most innocent looks, and an ironic squeeze of condolence in the sincerest handshakes; he suspected every carriage that passed of being the very carriage that had borne her to the rendezvous, and every house seemed to him to bear the odious façade of 'Paradise'. He returned home in a sombre, wretched mood, feeling that his life was ruined. And as he walked down the corridor, he heard Luiza singing the 'Mandolinata', just as she used to!

She was getting dressed.

'How are you?' he asked, placing his walking stick in one corner.

'I'm fine. I feel much better today. Still a little weak, but . . .'

Jorge took a few steps about the room, not saying a word.

'What about you?' she asked.

'Not too bad,' he said, but so disconsolately that Luiza, her hair still loose, put down her comb, went over to him and placed her hands fondly on his shoulders.

'What's wrong? I know there's something wrong. You've been behaving oddly for days now! You're not your usual self. Sometimes you've a look on your face like a condemned man's. What is it? Tell me.'

Her eyes sought his, but he looked uneasily away.

She put her arms about him. She insisted, she wanted him to tell 'his little wife' everything.

'Tell me. What's wrong?'

He looked at her for a long time, then, suddenly, with violent resolve, said:

'All right, I'll tell you. You're better now, so you can stand it . . . Luiza, I've been in hell these last two weeks. I can't bear it

416

any longer. You really are better, aren't you? All right, then, what is the meaning of this? Tell me the truth!'

And he held out Bazilio's letter.

'What's this?' she said, turning terribly pale. The folded piece of paper trembled in her hand.

She opened it slowly, saw Bazilio's handwriting and realised at a glance what it meant. She stared at Jorge for a moment, wild-eyed, reached out her arms, unable to speak, raised her hands to her head with the shocked gesture of someone who has been wounded, then, swaying on her feet, she uttered a hoarse cry, dropped to her knees and lay prostrate on the carpet.

Jorge cried out. The servants came running. They laid her on the bed. Jorge told Joana to call Sebastião, and then he stood, as if turned to stone, by her bed, looking at her, while Mariana fumbled with her mistress's corsets.

Sebastião came at once. Fortunately, they had some ether which they gave to her to smell; the moment she slowly opened her eyes, Jorge rushed to her side.

'Luiza, listen, speak to me! It will be all right. Just speak to me. Tell me, are you all right?

When she heard his voice, she fainted again. Her body was shaken by convulsive movements. Sebastião ran to fetch Julião.

Luiza seemed to be sleeping now, motionless, white as wax, her hands resting on the coverlet; and two slow tears were running down her cheeks.

A carriage stopped outside. Julião rushed breathlessly in.

'She became ill all of a sudden. You can see, Julião, she's really bad!' said Jorge.

They gave her more ether to inhale; she came round again. Julião spoke to her and took her pulse.

'No, no, no one!' she murmured, withdrawing her hand. She said again, impatiently this time: 'No, go away, I don't want . . .' Her tears redoubled. And as they were leaving the room so as not to antagonise her further, they heard her call out: 'Jorge!'

He knelt by the bed, talking to her, his lips close to her face:

'Are you all right? Look, we won't speak about such things ever again. It's over. Only, please, don't be ill. I love you, I swear I do . . . I don't care what happened before. I don't even want to know.'

And when she made to speak, he placed his hand over her mouth:

'No, no, I don't want to hear. I just want you to get well and not to suffer anymore. Tell me you're all right! You are, aren't you? Tomorrow we'll go to the country for a while, and forget all about it. It was just something that happened . . .'

In a faint voice she said only:

'Oh, Jorge! Jorge!'

'I know . . . But now you're going to be happy again . . . Where are you hurting?'

'Here,' she said, raising her hands to her head. 'It hurts me so!'

He got up to summon Julião, but she stopped him and drew him to her; devouring him with eyes that were once more bright with fever, she held up her face and lips to him. He gave her a long, meaning kiss, full of forgiveness.

'Oh, my poor head!' she cried.

Her temples were pounding, and her face was red, dry and burning hot.

She had often suffered from migraines in the past, Julião reassured them; until he returned, he recommended complete rest and the application of mustard compresses to her feet.

Assailed by presentiments and fears, Jorge remained by her bedside, silent, apart from the occasional sigh.

It was four o'clock by then; a fine, misty drizzle was falling; the bedroom was filled with a gloomy light.

'It's nothing serious,' Sebastião said.

Luiza was tossing and turning in bed, clutching her head in her hands, tortured by the growing pain and by a terrible thirst.

Mariana had just tiptoed in to tidy the room, slightly in awe of that house in which she had seen only misfortune and illness; but even the subtle sound of her footsteps was an agony to Luiza, like hammerblows on her skull.

418

Julião was soon back; he could tell by her appearance, as soon as he came into the room, that her condition was grave. He lit a match and held it close to her face; the light made her scream out as if a cold iron blade had pierced her head.

There was a metallic glint in her dilated eyes. She lay very still because even the slightest movement sent lacerating pains down her neck. Very occasionally, she would smile at Jorge with a look of serene, silent suffering.

Julião immediately had three pillows placed on the bed, to keep her head up. Outside, a damp twilight was falling. They tiptoed cautiously about; they even took the clock off the wall, to remove its monotonous tick-tock. She began to moan wearily and to turn over suddenly in bed, which caused her to cry out in agony; or else she would lie motionless, continually, anxiously sighing. They had wrapped her legs in a long compress now, but she could not feel it. Around nine o'clock, delirium set in; her tongue became hard and white, like a piece of dirty plaster.

Julião immediately applied cold compresses to her head, but the delirium only worsened.

Now her voice was a slurred murmur, a vague, drowsy whisper, in which the names of Leopoldina, Jorge and Bazilio came and went incessantly; she would writhe about and tear at her nightdress with her hands; and as her body arched, her eyes rolled back, like large silvery globes from which the pupils had vanished.

She grew quieter; she giggled gently, foolishly; she caressed the sheet, slowly, coaxingly, as if taking great pleasure in something; then she began to breathe anxiously, her face contorted in fear, she tried to hide herself in the pillows, in the mattress, fleeing terrifying figures; she would then clutch her head frantically, begging them to open it up for her, because it was full of stones, begging them to have pity on her, and tears streamed down her face. She could not feel the compresses; so they exposed her bare feet to the steam from boiling, mustard-filled water; a sour smell suffused the room. Jorge said all kinds of consoling, supplicatory words to her; he pleaded with her to be still, to recognise him; but suddenly she grew desperate, she demanded the letter, she cursed Juliana, or else she spoke words of love or listed sums of money . . . Jorge was afraid that her delirium would reveal everything to Julião and to the servants; beads of sweat stood out on his forehead, and when, for a moment, she imagined herself once more in 'Paradise' and, in her adulterous ecstasy, called out Bazilio's name, asked for champagne and uttered all manner of lewd remarks, Jorge, half-mad, fled the bedroom and went into the dark drawing room, where he flung himself down on the divan, sobbing, tearing at his own hair, and cursing God.

'Is she in danger?' Sebastião asked Julião.

'She is,' said Julião. 'If she could at least feel the compresses, but with these wretched brain fevers . . .'

They stopped talking when they saw Jorge come back into the room, his face blotchy, his hair dishevelled.

Julião took his arm and led him out of the room.

'Listen, Jorge, we're going to have to cut off her hair and shave her head.'

Jorge stared at him stupidly:

'Her hair?' Then grasping Julião's arms, he said: 'No, Julião, no. There must be something else you can do. I'm sure you know what you're doing, but not her hair. No, not that, for God's sake! She's not in any danger, so why do it?'

But that mass of hair was a real nuisance, it impeded the action of the water!

'If necessary, you can do it tomorrow. Tomorrow! Wait until then. . . . Please, Julião, please.'

Julião reluctantly agreed. He had them apply constant cold compresses, and since Mariana, shaking and clumsy, only succeeded in soaking the pillow, it was Sebastião who sat at the head of the bed all night, endlessly squeezing slow drops of cool water onto the compresses with a sponge; they put jugs of water out on the drawing-room balcony to keep the water icy cold. In the early hours, her delirium eased a little. But there was a wild look in her bloodshot eyes; her pupils were like two black dots.

Jorge was sitting at the foot of the bed, his head in his hands, looking at her; he vaguely remembered other nights when she had been ill, when she had had pneumonia and had recovered! She had emerged from that even prettier, with a slight pallor that gave her face a still sweeter expression! They would go to the countryside when she was convalescing; they would rent a cottage; he would catch the omnibus back from work and, in the soft evenings, he would see her from afar, in her light-coloured dress, standing on the road waiting for him . . . But then she gave a moan and he looked up, startled; and she did not look like the same woman; it was as if she were dissolving, disappearing in the feverish air that was filling the bedroom, in the morbid silence of the night, and in the smell of mustard. He would utter a sob and return to his immobile state.

Upstairs, Joana was praying. The candles were burning out with a long, thin flame.

Then a hazy brightness began to etch the shape of the window frames onto the transparent white drapes. It was growing light. Jorge got up and looked out onto the street. The rain had stopped; the street was drying off. The air was the colour of pale steel. Everything was sleeping; only a towel, left outside the Azevedos' window, flapped silently in the cold wind.

When Jorge went back into the bedroom, Luiza was speaking in a barely audible voice; she could almost feel the compresses, but the pain in her head was still there. She grew agitated again and, shortly afterwards, the delirium returned. Julião decided that they would have to shave her head.

Sebastião went to wake the barber in Rua da Escola, who came immediately, looking half-frozen, the collar of his jacket turned up, his teeth chattering; then with hands made soft by daily contact with greasy pomades, he slowly began removing his razors and scissors from a leather bag.

Jorge took refuge in the drawing room; it seemed to him that great mutilated chunks of his happiness were falling to the floor along with those lovely locks being scissored to destruction; and, head in hands, he remembered certain ways in which she had worn her hair, nights on which her hair had become tousled during the joys of passion, the different colours that her hair took on in the light . . . He went back into the room, drawn irresistibly; there was the sharp, metallic sound of the scissors; on the table, in a soap dish, was an old shaving brush and a lot of foam. He called softly to Sebastião:

'Tell him to hurry up! It's killing me! It's unbearable. Tell him to be quick!'

He went into the dining room and wandered about the house; the cold morning was growing brighter now; a wind had got up and was carrying off with it scraps of greyish cloud.

When he returned to the bedroom, the barber was putting away his razors with the same soft slowness; and picking up his hat, he tiptoed out, murmuring in a funereal tone:

'I do hope she gets better. God will make sure it's nothing serious.'

Her delirium did indeed cease within the hour, and Luiza fell into a restless sleep, broken only by faint moans, which, on her lips, sounded like the secret lament of defeated life.

Jorge said to Sebastião then that he wanted to call in Dr Caminha. He was the old doctor who had treated his mother and had cured Luiza of pneumonia in the second year of their marriage. Jorge retained a grateful admiration for that ancient reputation; and now his hopes again turned eagerly to him, longing for his presence as if for the appearance of a saint.

Julião agreed at once. He was even glad. Sebastião raced down the stairs to go to Dr Caminha's house.

Luiza, who had emerged for a moment from her torpor, heard them talking softly. Her feeble voice called out for Jorge:

'They've cut off my hair,' she murmured sadly.

'It's to make you better,' Jorge told her, almost as drained of life as she was. 'It will soon grow again. It will grow back stronger.'

She did not reply; two silent tears fell from the corners of her eyes.

That must have been her last sensation, for she lapsed thereafter into a comatose stillness, moaning occasionally with the same sad weariness, her head moving slowly and gently back and forth on the pillow; her skin grew paler, like a pane of glass behind which a light is gradually burning out; and she no longer noticed the noises from the street, as if they came from a long way away and were swathed in cotton wool.

At midday, Dona Felicidade appeared. She was horrified to see Luiza looking so ill; she had come to take her to the church of the Incarnation, perhaps to the shops! She immediately took off her hat and set to work; she had the room sorted out, the basins and old compresses removed and the bed tidied, 'because there is nothing worse for a patient than disorder in the bedroom'. And she very bravely attempted to cheer Jorge up.

A carriage stopped outside the house. It was Dr Caminha, at last! He entered, well muffled up in his green and black check scarf, complaining loudly of the cold, then, slowly removing his woollen gloves, which he placed neatly inside his hat, he walked in stately fashion into the bedroom, smoothing his grey locks which he now wore brushed close to his head.

Julião and he remained alone in the bedroom.

Next door, the others waited in silence, near Jorge, whose face was as pale as wax, his eyes as red as coals.

'We're going to try applying a mustard plaster to the back of her neck,' Julião told them.

Jorge was gazing with anxious eyes at Dr Caminha, who was calmly drawing on his woollen gloves again, saying:

'We'll see how that works. She's not at all well, but I've seen worse. I'll be back, my friend, I'll be back.'

The plaster proved useless. White and immobile, her face contorted, and the nerves in her face twitching as if afflicted by fleeting vibrations, she could not even feel it.

'She's lost,' Julião said softly to Sebastião.

Dona Felicidade looked terrified and immediately made mention of the sacraments.

'What ever for?' growled Julião impatiently.

Dona Felicidade declared that she, at least, had scruples, that it was a mortal sin; and calling Jorge over to the window, she said tremulously:

'Jorge, don't be alarmed, but shouldn't we be thinking about the sacraments . . .'

He murmured as if astonished:

'The sacraments!'

Julião broke in almost angrily:

'Look, forget all this nonsense about sacraments! What's the point. She can't hear, she can't understand, she can't feel. We should just apply another mustard plaster or cupping glasses perhaps, that's what she needs. Those are what I call sacraments!'

Shocked and shaken, Dona Felicidade began to cry. They were forgetting God and the only remedy lay now in God's hands, she was saying, loudly blowing her nose.

'What has God ever done for me!' exclaimed Jorge, emerging from his torpor. Then clapping his hands together as if in disgust at some injustice: 'I mean what did I ever do to deserve this? What did I do?'

Julião had ordered another mustard plaster. There was a frenzy of movement in the house now. Joana, her eyes red with crying, would enter bearing some soup that no one had asked for. Mariana was to be found in a corner of the house somewhere, sobbing. Dona Felicidade came and went, taking refuge in the drawing room to pray, making promises to the Virgin, and saying that they really should call in Dr Barbosa or Dr Barral.

Luiza meanwhile did not move; a deathly pallor gave her features a stiff, sunken look.

Julião, exhausted, asked for a glass of wine and a piece of bread. They remembered then that they had not eaten since the night before and so they all trooped into the dining room, where Joana, still bathed in tears, served them soup and eggs. But she couldn't find the spoons or the napkins; she mumbled a few prayers and apologised; Jorge, his face tense, his eyes puffy, sat staring at the table edge, making folds in the table cloth.

After a moment, he very slowly put down his spoon and went into the bedroom. Mariana was sitting at the foot of the bed; Jorge told her to go and serve the others; and as soon as she had left, he fell to his knees, took one of Luiza's hands in his and called to her softly, then more loudly:

'Listen to me. Listen, for God's sake, listen. Don't just lie there like this, try to get better. Don't leave me all alone in the world! I have no one else! Forgive me! Say that you do. At least make some sign that you do. Oh, dear God, she can't hear me!'

And he studied her anxiously. She did not move.

He then raised up his arms in a gesture of mad despair.

'You know I believe in you, God. Save her! Save her!' And he lifted up his soul to the heavens: 'Hear me, O God! Listen to me! Be kind!'

He looked around him, expecting a movement, a voice, a chance event, a miracle! But everything seemed to him even more immobile. Her livid cheeks grew more sunken; the scarf around her head had come loose, revealing her slightly yellow shaven head. Fearfully, hesitantly, he placed his hand on her head; she felt cold! He smothered a cry and ran out of the room, only to meet Dr Caminha, who was just coming in, slowly pulling off his gloves.

'Doctor, she's dead! Look! She can't talk, she's cold . . .'

'Now, now,' said the doctor. 'Remember, no noise!'

He took Luiza's pulse and felt it slipping away beneath his fingers, like the dwindling vibrations of a plucked string.

Julião came in immediately afterwards. And he agreed with Dr Caminha that the cupping glasses were useless.

'She can't feel them anymore,' said the doctor, brushing tobacco from his fingers.

'What if we gave her a glass of cognac?' Julião said suddenly. And seeing the look of horror on the doctor's face, he added: 'The symptoms of a coma do not necessarily mean that the brain is in disarray; it might just be inaction due to an exhausted nervous system. If death is inevitable, then we lose nothing; if it is just a depression of the nervous system, we might save her . . .'

Dr Caminha was shaking his head incredulously, open-mouthed.

'Theories!' he muttered.

'In English hospitals . . .' began Julião.

Dr Caminha shrugged scornfully.

'But if you had read. . . .,' insisted Julião.

'I read nothing now,' said Dr Caminha firmly. 'I have read too much. The books are the ones that are sick.' Then, bowing, he said ironically: 'But if my talented colleague wishes to try . . .'

'Bring me a glass of cognac or brandy!' Julião said from the door.

And Dr Caminha sat down comfortably in a chair to savour the sight of his 'talented colleague' failing.

They lifted Luiza up; Julião made her swallow the cognac; when they laid her down again, she remained in exactly the same state of comatose immobility; Dr Caminha took out his watch, checked the time and waited; there was an anxious silence; finally, the doctor got up, felt her pulse and noted the growing coldness in her extremities; and going silently over to pick up his hat, he began to put on his gloves again.

Jorge went with him to the door.

'Doctor . . .' he said, grabbing hold of his arm with unnecessary violence.

'We've done all we can,' said the old man with a shrug.

Jorge stood dumbly on the landing, watching him go down the stairs. The doctor's slow steps on the stairs fell upon his heart like a ghastly percussion. He leaned over the banister and called to him softly. The doctor stopped and looked up. Jorge reached out his hands to him in humble supplication:

'There's no more to be done, then?'

The doctor made a vague gesture, pointing heavenwards.

Jorge went back in, supporting himself against the walls as he did so. He went into the bedroom and fell on his knees at the foot of the bed, and there he stayed, his head in his hands, sobbing softly and continuously.

Luiza was dying: her lovely arms, the arms she used to stroke as she stood before the mirror, were now paralysed; her eyes, in which passion had ignited flames and which had once filled with tears out of sheer voluptuous pleasure, were growing dim as if beneath a light layer of very fine dust.

Dona Felicidade and Mariana had lit a small lamp beneath an engraving of Our Lady of Sorrows and were kneeling, praying.

The sad evening was coming on and seemed to bring with it a funereal silence.

The doorbell rang discreetly and, a few moments later, the figure of Councillor Acácio appeared. Dona Felicidade got up at once, and seeing her tears, the Councillor said gravely:

'I have come to do my duty and help you all through this difficult time.'

He explained that he had happened to meet good Dr Caminha, who had told him 'the fateful news'! Out of discretion, however, he did not wish to enter the bedroom. He sat down on a chair, mournfully placed one elbow on his knee and rested his head on his hand, then said quietly to Dona Felicidade:

'Continue with your prayers. God's designs are unfathomable.'

In the bedroom, Julião had been taking Luiza's pulse; he glanced at Sebastião and made the gesture of something flying away and disappearing. They went over to Jorge, who was kneeling, motionless, his face buried in the bedclothes.

'Jorge,' said Sebastião softly.

Jorge raised a disfigured, suddenly aged face, his hair falling into his eyes, which were encircled by dark shadows.

'Come along,' said Julião. And seeing the look of horror in his eyes, he added: 'No, no, she's not dead, she's in the same torpor as before. Come with me.'

Jorge got up, saying meekly:

'Yes, all right, I'll come. I'm all right. Thank you.'

And he left the bedroom.

The Councillor stood up and solemnly embraced him.

'Here I am, dear Jorge!'

'Thank you, Councillor, thank you.'

He took a few steps about the room; his eyes seemed to linger on a package that lay on the table; he went over and touched it; he undid the ends and saw Luiza's hair. He stood staring at it, picking it up and drawing it through his hands, and then, his lips trembling, he said:

'She took such pride in her hair, poor love!'

He went back into the bedroom. But Julião took his arm and tried to keep him away from the bed. He struggled half-heartedly and, seeing a candle burning on the bedside table, he pointed to it and said:

'Perhaps the light is troubling her . . .'

Moved, Julião replied:

'She can't see it now, Jorge!'

Jorge freed himself from Julião's grip and bent over her; he took her head in his hands, carefully, so as not to hurt her, and looked at her for a moment; then he placed a kiss on her cold lips, and another, and another, murmuring:

'Goodbye! Goodbye!'

Then he stood up, flung his arms wide and fell to the floor.

Everyone ran to help him. They carried him to the chaise longue.

And while Dona Felicidade, weeping bitterly, was closing Luiza's eyes, the Councillor, his hat still in his hand, was folding his arms, shaking his respectable pate and saying to Sebastião:

'A grievous loss to us all!'

# XVI

After Luiza's funeral, Jorge dismissed both servants and went to stay at Sebastião's house.

That night, at around nine o'clock, Councillor Acácio, well wrapped up, was walking down Rua do Moinho do Vento when he met Julião, who had just been to see a patient in Rua da Rosa. They walked along together, talking about Luiza, about the funeral and Jorge's evident distress.

'Poor fellow! He's really suffering!' said Julião feelingly.

'She was a model wife!' murmured the Councillor.

Indeed, he said, he had just come from good Sebastião's house, but he had not been able to see dear Jorge, who was in bed, sleeping deeply. He added:

'I read just recently that terrible blows such as this are always followed by prolonged sleep. Napoleon, for example, was just the same after Waterloo, after the great disaster of Waterloo!'

He paused a moment, then went on:

'Yes, indeed, I went to see our Sebastião . . . I went to show him . . .' He broke off and stood still: 'Because I felt it was my duty to write a tribute to the memory of that unhappy lady. It was my duty and I did not shirk it! And I'm glad to have met you just now, because I would like your considered and frank opinion.'

Julião coughed and asked:

'Is it a eulogy?'

'It is.'

And the Councillor, although he did not normally think it proper for a person in his position to enter public cafés, suggested to Julião that they might rest for a moment in the Tavares café, if there were not too many people, so that he could read him his 'composition'.

They peered in.

The only people there were two silent, behatted old men sitting at a table, their cups of coffee before them, and leaning

429

on walking sticks made of Indian cane. The waiter was dozing in the back. A harsh, intense light filled the narrow room.

'A propitious silence,' said the Councillor.

He bought Julião a coffee, then removing from his pocket a sheet of lined paper, he murmured: 'Unhappy lady!' He leaned towards Julião and read:

### EULOGY

#### TO THE MEMORY OF
#### SENHORA DONA LUIZA MENDONÇA DE BRITO CARVALHO

*Rose of love, rose so purple and fair,*
*Who, amongst the wallflowers, scattered your petals on the grave?*

'The words of the immortal Almeida Garrett!' And he went on in a slow, doleful voice:

'Another angel gone to heaven! Another flower, barely opened, torn from its tender stem by the whirlwind of death in all its inclement fury, and hurled into the darkness of the tomb . . .'

He glanced at Julião hoping to elicit his admiration, but seeing him bent over his cup, earnestly stirring his coffee, he went on in ever more funereal tones:

'Pause and regard the cold earth! There lies the chaste wife wrenched untimely from the caresses of her talented spouse. There, like a vessel caught in the waves that crash upon the shore, the virtuous lady foundered, she, whose playful nature charmed all those who had the honour of visiting her home! Why do you weep?'

'Coffee, António!' bawled the gruff voice of a heavily built fellow in a double-breasted overcoat, who sat down nearby, putting his walking stick on the table with a clatter, and pushing his hat back on his head.

The Councillor shot him a malevolent sideways glance. Then, lowering his voice, he went on:

'Weep not! For an angel belongs not here on Earth but in heaven!'

'Has Guedes been in yet?' asked the gruff voice.

From behind the bar, as he wiped the metal trays with a rag, the waiter said:

'No, not yet, Senhor Dom José!'

'There,' continued the Councillor, 'her spirit, flying free on snow-white wings, sings songs of praise to the Eternal One! Nor does she cease in her pleas to the Almighty to rain down graces and favours upon the head of her beloved husband, who, one day, never doubt it, will meet with her again in those celestial regions, homeland of all souls of great worth . . .' And to indicate that ascent into paradise, the Councillor's voice grew more mellifluous.

'Wasn't he in last night either?' insisted the man in the overcoat, leaning both elbows on the table and blowing out a large cloud of cigarette smoke.

'He came in very late, about two o'clock.'

In dumb despair, the Councillor rustled the sheet of paper. Behind the smoked lenses of his glasses his eyes flashed with the homicidal fury of an author interrupted. However, he proceeded:

'And you, O sensitive souls, shed your tears, but in shedding them, never forget that man must always bow to the decrees of Providence . . .'

Then interrupting himself, he said:

'I put that in so as to give strength to our poor Jorge!' He resumed his reading: '. . . of Providence. God has one more angel now, and her soul shines purely . . .'

'Was Guedes with 'is girl?' asked the man, tipping the ash from his cigar on the edge of the marble table.

The Councillor stopped, pale with rage.

'He must be a person of very low origins,' he snarled.

And from behind the bar, the waiter said in his shrill little voice:

'Oh, no, he's going with some Spanish piece from up the road now. A very thin woman, with curly hair, wears a red cape . . .'

'Ah, Lola!' said the other man with satisfaction. And he stretched voluptuously at the thought of Lola.

431

The Councillor was reading more quickly now.

'And what is life, after all? A swift passage over the earthly globe, and a vain dream from which we awake in the bosom of the Lord of Hosts, of which we are all unworthy vassals.'

And with that monarchical expression, the Councillor concluded.

'What do you think? Tell me frankly.'

Julião was sipping the last of his coffee; returning the cup carefully to its saucer, he licked his lips and said:

'Is it to be published?'

'Yes, in the *The Popular Voice*, with a black border.'

Julião nervously scratched his scurfy scalp, then, getting up, said:

'It's very good, Councillor, very good indeed!'

Acácio fumbled for change to give the waiter and asked:

'I feel it does credit both to her and to me!'

And they left in silence.

It was a very dark night; a cold northeast wind had got up; a few drops of rain had fallen. In the Praça do Loreto, Julião suddenly stopped and cried:

'Oh, I forgot! Have you heard the latest news, Councillor? Dona Felicidade has entered the convent of the Incarnation.'

'Really?'

'She told me so just now. I went to see her before visiting a patient of mine in Rua da Rosa. She had a bit of a fever. Nothing serious . . . It's just the emotion and the shock! And that's when she told me that she's entering the convent tomorrow.'

The Councillor said:

'I always knew that woman had retrograde ideas. The result of Jesuitical manoeuvrings, my friend!' And he added in the melancholy tones of the dissatisfied liberal: 'Reaction is raising its ugly head again!'

Julião took the Councillor's arm familiarly and said, smiling:

'What do you mean "reaction"!? It's all because of you, you ungrateful wretch!'

The Councillor looked confused:

'What are you insinuating, my noble friend?'

'You know perfectly well! I've no idea how the devil she did it, but she found out something very grave . . .'

'What? Believe me, I . . .'

'The same thing that I found out, you rascal! That the Councillor has two pillows on his bed, but only one head. She told me so herself!' And roaring with laughter, Julião strode off down Rua do Alecrim. The Councillor stood utterly still, his arms folded, as if he had been turned to stone.

'The poor woman! A fatal passion!' he muttered to himself at last. Then he smugly smoothed his moustaches.

Since he still had to write out a clean copy of the eulogy, he hurried home. He sat down with a blanket over his knees; soon, the responsibilities of the writer distracted him from the concerns of the man; and until eleven o'clock, in the silence of his *sanctum sanctorum*, his fine cursive, bureaucratic hand flowed nobly across a large sheet of fine paper. He had nearly finished when the door creaked open, and Adelaide, a thick shawl about her shoulders, came in to say in a hoarse, snuffly voice:

'Isn't it time we were off to bed?'

'I won't be long, Adelaide, my dear, I won't be long!'

He quietly re-read to himself what he had written. It seemed to him that the ending was not moving enough; he wanted to finish with a grieving exclamation, like a prolonged cry of pain! He thought hard, his elbows on the desk, his head resting on his splayed fingers. Adelaide came slowly over to him and stroked his bald head; and that sweet, amorous touch clearly made an idea leap out like a spark, for he quickly took up his pen and added: 'Weep! Weep! As for myself, grief o'erwhelms me!'

He rubbed his hands gleefully together. He repeated out loud in plangent tones:

'Weep! Weep! As for myself, grief o'erwhelms me!' And putting one concupiscent arm about Adelaide's waist, exclaimed:

'That's it, Adelaide, spot on!'

He got to his feet. He had completed his day. It had been both full and honourable: in the morning, he had noted with joy the news in the Court Gazette that there was no news to report about the royal family; he had done his duty as a friend, accompanying Luiza to the cemetery in a hired carriage; the rise in share prices ensured peace in his country; he had composed a remarkable piece of prose; and his Adelaide loved him! He doubtless took great pleasure in these certain happinesses, in such stark contrast to the sepulchral images evoked by his pen, for Adelaide heard him murmur:

'Life is an inestimable good!' Then he added like a good citizen: 'Especially in this era of great public prosperity!'

And he went into his bedroom with his head high, his chest out, his step firm, and holding aloft a candlestick.

His Adelaide followed him, yawning; her head cold had made her weary, as had the hour of love she had enjoyed in the afternoon with Arnaldo, the sweet, fair-haired shop assistant in the Loja da América.

At that moment, two men were getting out of a carriage at the door of the Hotel Central; one was wearing a check ulster, the other a long fur coat. Almost simultaneously, an omnibus stopped, piled high with luggage.

A German servant, talking quietly to the porter, recognised them at once, and taking off his bowler hat, cried:

'Senhor Bazilio! Viscount!'

Viscount Reinaldo, who was stamping his feet on the flagstones, muttered from inside his fur coat:

'Yes, here we are back in the pigsty!'

But what were they doing arriving at this late hour?

'What time do you expect us to arrive? According to the timetable perhaps? We are a mere twelve hours late! Why, in Portugal that's almost nothing!'

'Was there some accident?' asked the servant solicitously, following them up the stairs.

And Reinaldo, walking gingerly over the rough mats in the corridor, said:

'This whole country is one great accident! Everything was derailed. It is only by a miracle that we are here at all! What a pathetic place!' And he vented his spleen on the servant; he was in such a foul mood that he would have vented it on the cobbles in the street if necessary. 'For a year now, my one prayer has been: "Please, God, send another earthquake!" Every day I read the news to see if the earthquake has arrived . . . but no! A minister has fallen or a baron has risen. But no earthquake! The Almighty turns a deaf ear to my prayers. He protects this country. Well, all I can say is that they deserve each other!' And he smiled, vaguely grateful to a nation whose defects supplied him with so much material for his jibes.

But when the servant, in great trepidation, told him that the only rooms available were a salon and one bedroom with two beds, on the third floor, Reinaldo's anger knew no bounds.

'Do you mean we have to sleep in the same room? Do you think perhaps that Senhor Dom Bazilio here is my lover, you libertine! Is the place entirely full? But who the devil would want to come to Portugal? Foreigners? That's precisely what I find so horrifying!' He gave a bitter shrug of his shoulders. 'It's the climate, it's the climate that attracts them! That prodigious national lure – the climate! And a pestilential climate it is! There is nothing more vulgar than a good climate!'

And he continued to heap invective on his country, while the servant, with an unctuous smile on his lips, hurriedly placed on the table, plates, ham, some cold chicken and a bottle of Burgundy.

Reinaldo had come to sell off his last bit of land, and had accompanied Bazilio, who was here to complete 'that tedious rubber deal'. And he did nothing but mumble darkly from inside his fur coat:

'Here we are! Here are we again in the piggery!'

Bazilio did not reply. Ever since they had arrived at Santa Apolónia station, memories of 'Paradise', of Luiza's house, of last summer's romance, were beginning to come back to him and they had for him a piquant charm. He went over to the window where he leaned against the panes. A cold, pale moon was racing between large, leaden clouds; sometimes a great glittering mesh of light would fall upon the water, then everything would grow dark again; the vague shapes of masts stood

435

out against the diffuse blackness, as did the occasional coldly glimmering light from a ship.

'I wonder what she'll be doing now,' Bazilio was thinking. She would probably be going to bed. She did not even know he was there in a room in the Hotel Central.

He and the Viscount had supper.

Afterwards, Bazilio took the bottle of cognac over to his bedside table, and, with his face covered in powder, the ruffles of his nightshirt open over his chest, he stretched out, exhaling the smoke from his cigar and savouring a pleasant sense of lassitude.

'I know what you'll be doing tomorrow,' said Reinaldo. 'You'll be going straight round to see that cousin of yours!'

Bazilio smiled and his eyes drifted up to the ceiling; the memory of her particular beauties and her amorous temperament awoke in him a vague voluptuousness; he yawned.

'Well, damn it,' he said, 'she's a very pretty girl! She's worth a bit of trouble!' He drank another glass of cognac, and shortly afterwards, he was deep asleep. It was midnight.

At that hour, Jorge was waking up and, seated motionless in a chair, his body still shaken by weary sobs, he too was thinking about Luiza. Sebastião, in his room, was weeping softly. Julião was still at his medical practice, lying on a sofa reading a copy of the *Revue des deux mondes*. Leopoldina was dancing at a soirée held at Cunha's house. The others were all asleep. And the same cold wind sweeping along the clouds and stirring the gas in the streetlamps set the branches of the tree above Luiza's grave sadly rustling.

Two days later, in the morning, Bazilio was in the Rossio looking around for a decent coupé. Pintéus, spotting him from afar, drove straight over to him. 'Pintéus, at your service, sir!' He seemed delighted to see Senhor Dom Bazilio again. And Bazilio had only to say:

'To Rua da Patriarcal, Pintéus!'

'To the lady's house, you mean, sir? Right you are, sir.' And sitting very erect on his seat, he set off at a lick.

When the carriage stopped at Jorge's door, Senhor Paula

came out into the street, Senhora Helena of the tobacconist's shop emerged from behind the counter, the mathematics teacher's maid peered out of the window, and all of them, poised and waiting, watched with wide eyes.

Bazilio, feeling slightly nervous, rang the bell; he waited, discarded his cigar and rang the bell again, harder this time.

'The windows are all closed, sir,' said Pintéus.

Bazilio stepped out into the middle of the street; the green shutters were indeed closed; the house had a silent air about it.

Bazilio addressed Senhor Paula:

'Are the people who live here away?'

'They don't live there any more,' said Senhor Paula glumly, wiping his moustache with his hand.

Bazilio stared at him, surprised by the funereal tone of his voice.

'Where do they live then?'

Senhor Paula noisily cleared his throat, then fixed Bazilio with a desolate eye and said:

'Are you the relative?'

Bazilio said, smiling:

'Yes, I'm the relative.'

'So you haven't heard, then?'

'Heard what, man?'

Senhor Paula rubbed his chin and, shaking his head, announced:

'Well, I'm sorry to tell you this, but the lady is dead.'

'What lady?' asked Bazilio. And he turned very pale.

'The lady! Senhora Dona Luiza, the wife of Senhor Carvalho, the engineer. Senhor Jorge is staying at Senhor Sebastião's house, at the end of the street. If you want to call . . .'

'No!' said Bazilio with a rapid movement of his hand. His lips were trembling slightly. 'But what happened?'

'A fever. It carried her off in two days!'

Bazilio walked slowly to the carriage, his head bowed. He looked again at the house, then got into the carriage and slammed the door. Pintéus galloped back to the Baixa.

Senhor Paula went over to the tobacconist's shop.

'He didn't seem very upset! These noblemen, huh! Scum!' he muttered.

The tobacconist's wife said mournfully:

'I'm not even a relative, but I still say two Our Fathers for her soul every night . . .'

'So do I!' sighed the coal merchant's wife.

'And a fat lot of good that will do her!' snorted Senhor Paula, moving off.

He had been in a rather sour mood lately. Business was bad, and these deaths in the street had made him mistrustful of life. Every day he detested the priesthood more heartily and every night he read the copy of *The Nation* that Azevedo lent him, feasting vindictively on the devotional essays, which exasperated him and drove him further into atheism; his dissatisfaction with public life was inclining him more and more towards the Commune. According to him, everything was, as he put it, 'a load of old rubbish'.

It was doubtless under the influence of this feeling that, returning to the door of the tobacconist's, he said to his neighbours with a sombre air:

'Do you know what this is? Do you know what all this is?' He made a gesture that took in the whole universe, then looked at them irately and snarled out these words: 'It's all just a big pile of manure!'

As he was going down Rua do Alecrim, Bazilio saw Viscount Reinaldo standing at the door of a hotel. He ordered Pintéus to stop, and jumping out of the carriage, cried:

'Do you know what?'

'What?'

'My cousin has died.'

The Viscount murmured politely:

'Oh, poor thing!'

And they walked down the street, arm in arm, as far as the Aterro. It was a glorious day; a chill, subtle wind was blowing; in the light, luminous, sunfilled air, the houses, the branches of trees, the masts of sailing barges and ships stood out in stark outline; every sound could be heard clearly and brightly; the river glittered like blue metal; the steamboat to Cacilhas sent up coils of smoke that took on the colour of milk; and in the background, the hills created a bluish shadow in the dusty light, against which the houses gleamed whitely.

And the two men walked slowly along, talking about Luiza.

Viscount Reinaldo, out of politeness, expressed his regret that the poor lady had allowed herself to die at a time of such splendid weather!

'But then, I always found the affair absurd.'

Because, to be perfectly frank, what did she have to offer? He did not wish to speak ill 'of the poor lady now lying in that ghastly Prazeres cemetery', but the truth was that she was hardly a very chic mistress; she travelled in hired carriages; she wore woollen stockings; she had married a vulgar ministry hireling; she lived in a miserable little house; she had no decent friends to speak of; she probably played lotto and wore felt slippers around the house; she lacked both wit and elegance. Frankly, she was an encumbrance!

'But for the couple of months a year that I'm in Lisbon . . .,' muttered Bazilio, his head down.

'Yes, perhaps for that purpose, for reasons of hygiene!' sneered Reinaldo.

And they continued slowly on in silence. They laughed uproariously at a man struggling to control two black horses: Call that a phaeton! And the way the horses were harnessed . . . What a complete lack of style! It was the kind of thing that could only happen in Lisbon!

They turned round at the end of the Aterro, and Viscount Reinaldo, stroking his sideburns, said:

'So, you're without a woman, then.'

Bazilio gave a resigned smile. Then, after a silence, he scraped his walking stick noisily along the ground and said:

'Damned nuisance really! I could have brought Alphonsine with me!'

And they went into the Taverna Inglesa to have a glass of sherry.

*September 1876–September 1877*